DARK WATER

(writing as Jamal Mahjoub)
Navigation of a Rainmaker
Wings of Dust
In the Hour of Signs
The Carrier
Travelling with Djinns
The Drift Latitudes
Nubian Indigo

The Makana Investigations

The Golden Scales
Dogstar Rising
The Ghost Runner
The Burning Gates
City of Jackals

DARK WATER

PARKER BILAL

B L O O M S B U R Y

LONDON · OXFORD · NEW YORK · NEW DELHI · SYDNEY

Bloomsbury Publishing
An imprint of Bloomsbury Publishing Plc

50 Bedford Square
London
WC1B 3DP
UK

1385 Broadway
New York
NY 10018
USA

BLOOMSBURY and the Diana logo are trademarks of Bloomsbury Publishing Plc

First published in Great Britain 2017

© Jamal Mahjoub, 2017

Jamal Mahjoub has asserted his right under the Copyright, Designs and Patents Act,
1988, to be identified as Author of this work.

British Library Cataloguing-in-Publication Data
A catalogue record for this book is available from the British Library.

ISBN: TPB: 978-1-4088-6450-0
         ePub: 978-1-4088-6452-4

2 4 6 8 10 9 7 5 3 1

Typeset by Integra Software Services Pvt. Ltd.
Printed and bound in Great Britain by CPI Group (UK) Ltd, Croydon CR0 4YY

MIX
Paper from
responsible sources
FSC® C013604

To find out more about our authors and books visit www.bloomsbury.com.
Here you will find extracts, author interviews, details of forthcoming events and
the option to sign up for our newsletters.

I come and stand at every door
But no one hears my silent tread
I knock and yet remain unseen
For I am dead, for I am dead.

Nazim Hikmet

Prologue

Dark water rising. The spinning silver crescent of the moon. The earliest memory she has. The dream replayed itself time and again. She wakes spluttering and kicking, screaming for the mother she knows will never answer. It is the one thing that still frightens her. She has learned to deal with fear. This is what they taught her at the camp, drilled into her, year in and year out, ever since she was old enough to understand orders. But nothing ever came close to the fear that seized her in that dream.

Al-Muaskar. The Camp. That was all she knew for almost twelve years. She arrived at the age of three and she was fifteen when she left.

There was something about the dream that always stayed shrouded in mystery. It took her back to a time she could hardly recall in her waking hours; some part of her memory that was lost to her. It contained a force, an anger so powerful that it gave her special strength. A force that she would learn to harness, learn to make her own. The dreams were the only thing to connect her to who she had been, where she came from. Scary though they were – she would always wake up crying, waking everyone else in the dormitory – there was something about these dreams that was reassuring. She believed they returned for a reason. They were telling her who she was and where she came from.

Somewhere inside the scene that played itself over and over lay a key to how she had come to be here. She could not tell what it might be. In the dream she was falling in darkness. Falling from a great height. That was all. Then the darkness dissolved into water. It closed around her, sucked her in, pulled her down.

It was forbidden to talk about the past, to talk about anything outside of the camp itself. It was a place of dust and wind. Walls made of mud that kept the desert at bay. Beyond them there was nothing. Open ground. Not a tree in sight. Inside the compound life was hard. There were about two hundred children in all, who had come from all over. They had been picked up off the streets. Some had watched parents die in war. Some had been dumped on an orphanage doorstep, the offspring of sin. Others had run away from home. They were abused and abandoned, criminals and thieves. Where they came from did not matter. Once inside the camp that was where they belonged. Nothing else remained.

They were woken at dawn by a trumpet sound, an old elephant-tusk horn that blared out of the darkness for them to rise up, wash and say their prayers. Then followed an hour of callisthenics – jump and run, turn and stretch. The physical education teacher was a slim man with dark eyes as cold and black as stones. He had trained somewhere abroad and carried himself like a weapon, primed to explode. She once watched him drag a boy across the parade ground by his ear. Another time, when a boy answered back, he kicked him senseless.

They ate once a day. One simple meal of steamed sorghum, sometimes lentils you had to pick the grit out of. To go without food was to learn discipline. It was to show humility and thankfulness to Our Lord, the Almighty. They ate with their fingers, scraping their tin bowls clean. The food often left her sicker than not eating, but she forced herself to eat what she was given and be thankful for it, no matter how disgusting. She learned early on to keep her head down. Not to do so was to risk being dragged out and chained to the post in the middle of the yard. You were whipped with a leather switch, then left out in the burning sun. She had seen people die out there. The gnarled old pole told its own stories, its sides scarred and chipped, scratched with sharp pebbles and torn fingernails, daubed here and there with brown stains of dried blood. Flies buzzed around it, eager for more.

The afternoons were for skills training. Unarmed combat, karate, judo, how to use a knife, how to kill with your hands. They learned to climb ropes, to haul themselves over fences, crawl under barbed wire. They ran for hours at a time, down to the river where the air was cool and then back out into the burning desert heat. The girls were expected to be equal to the boys. No exceptions were made. Weapons training and target practice happened twice a week. They learned to strip and reassemble half a dozen small arms, from Kalashnikovs to M16s to handguns. They spent hours on the target range, shooting from a standing position, crouching, lying down, running. They learned about using cover, about concealment in open spaces.

They were taught that the greatest sacrifice was to give your life in jihad, for Allah. For four hours each day, two in the morning and two in the evening, they would learn the Quran by rote. Page by page, line by line, syllable by syllable – often without fully understanding what it was they were reciting. Understanding would come in the fullness of time their teacher, the sheikh, assured them. They would copy a passage onto their wooden tablets. They sat cross-legged in rows, reading the words aloud over and over, rocking back and forth, their voices rising into one complex chorus. The teacher passed among them. Whenever anyone faltered, or lost the rhythm, he would bring down the long, slender switch onto their heads or shoulders. As soon as they had learned one passage they would be ordered to wash the ink off carefully and start to copy out a new one.

Once she had asked the sheikh what it meant to dream about drowning. Drowning is a kind of hell, he told her sternly. To dream of drowning means that you have had impure thoughts, your weakness is making you stray from the path of virtue. She was nine years old at the time. If, however, you do not drown, he went on, it means you have corrected your mistakes, that your heart is pure and you are set on the path of righteousness.

'You survived for a reason, and that reason is to serve Allah.'

When she was thirteen she was told she had a special visitor, a very important man. He arrived one day in a big car with dark windows so you could not see inside. The sheikh stood in the sun waiting to greet him. The visitor didn't look all that special. He was dark and his face bore tribal scars, a cross on each cheek. A gold eye tooth glinted when he spoke. Everyone showed him respect, and she could see that they all feared him.

'Is this her?' he asked when she was brought forward. The sheikh nodded.

'She is one of our finest. Strong and fast. She shoots better than any of the boys. And she is clever, a quick learner.'

It surprised her that a man who had never shown any personal interest in her could sing her praises.

In the shade of the sheikh's office the man spoke.

'You know why I am here?'

'No, sir.'

'I have taken a special interest in your case. I have known you since you were born.'

She looked towards the sheikh, seeking permission to speak. He gave a slight nod.

'Did you know my parents?'

'I knew your father, many years ago.'

This was new. She had never met anyone who had known her parents. She wanted to ask more, but from the look on the sheikh's face she knew she was to remain silent. The visitor went on:

'Your time here is almost at an end. As you may know, the lucky ones are offered a place in the military academy, where their training continues. Everything depends on how well you do in the next couple of years.'

'I understand.'

'I shall be your sponsor. I will receive reports every week on your progress.' The man's voice was a low rasp. He moved about the room as if seeking shadows to hide in.

'When you are ready here you will go to live in his house,' said the sheikh. His nervousness vibrated in his voice.

'How do you like the idea of that?' the man asked, coming to a halt and turning to face her. His eyes were cold and unblinking, like those of an animal who sees only enemies around him, or food.

'What would I do in your house?'

'You would fetch and carry, clean and serve my family in any way you are asked.'

'I would be your servant? So you would pay me?'

'Your reward would be in learning humility.'

'Then, like a slave?'

She saw the beginnings of a smile on his face. There wasn't a lot of warmth in that smile.

'In time, even slaves have their reward,' he said.

She was curious to know who he was and how he had known her father, but she imagined, rightly, that that would come in the fullness of time. For now, all she had to do was be the best, and she knew she was good at that.

She still dreamed of falling into dark water, of drowning. In the darkness there was only one spot of light. As she struggled and called out to her mother, it floated ahead of her, drawing her in. Where was her father in her dreams? Why was he never there?

The light came from the glittering curve of the moon. A silver crescent that turned slowly on its axis. The chain it hung from was made of brass. It dangled from the rearview mirror. Where had it come from, she often wondered. A lucky charm? A family heirloom? A trinket that had caught her mother's eye one afternoon in the market? All she knew was that she would drown if she didn't reach the moon. She kicked against the water, reaching for the sliver of light. When she grasped it she held onto it so tightly that when they finally prised her hand open the moon's horns had drawn blood. It was the last thing she remembered, grabbing the moon and holding on. Then the darkness closed in.

When they pulled her from the water they thought she was dead. Then she coughed and spluttered, gasping for air, just as she still did now whenever she woke up from a dream.

Chapter One

Cairo April 2006

Makana was woken by the small brass bell on the lower deck that rang to announce a visitor. It took him a moment to remember where he was and to realise what had woken him. It seemed early for visitors.

He sat up and stretched. It was a clear day. The sun had that gentle spring warmth which held the vague promise of a rise in temperatures, an end to the winter rain, and to the cold that blew through the flimsy walls of the awama and cut deep into his bones. A promise that things would soon begin to warm up. The thin wooden walls of his houseboat were scant protection against extreme temperatures. In the winter you struggled to retain any warmth, and in the summer the hot air seared through the place like a blazing fire. Despite this, it felt as much like home as anywhere – so much so that he was having trouble these days reconciling the solitude he enjoyed here with the novelty of another person in his life. He would have had difficulty explaining exactly what his relationship was with the pathologist Jehan Siham. The situation still felt new and unfamiliar, and a part of him was resisting the prospect of change. Moments like this, waking up on the awama alone, helped him to centre himself.

In the distance the jangled chords of a million cars hooting at one another was settling into its familiar daily pattern. He rose to his feet, threw off the blanket and reached for the old brass coffee pot. He'd spent most of the night in the big chair, a habit of years. He almost never slept through the entire night without a break.

1

These days it seemed to be getting worse, as a growing restlessness tightened its grip on him. Work had been slow and sometimes he worried that he was losing his touch.

There was something else too, something he couldn't quite put his finger on. Something that left him tossing and turning, his mind running in circles, refusing to let him sleep. Instead he would sit on the upper deck and try to make out the stars that hovered beyond the glow of the city lights. Or he would read, one of the old Arab geographers he was so fond of, and travel with them on their journeys through the world, following old routes. Long, detailed descriptions of every road, each stone along the way, each tree, each village custom. He found it comforting to read their descriptions and it made him feel as if he too was on the move. Not sitting here in his favourite armchair, reading, but travelling through the world on an endless pilgrimage to nowhere. And he would stay like that, with the book in his lap, until his mind didn't realise he was gone.

He was not expecting anyone this morning, which meant that the bell could mean work. It might also mean a thousand other things, including unpaid bills or a salesman hauling a sackful of useless gadgets and household appliances that he had no need of. Work would be an improvement. It was over a month since he had had anything but mundane divorce cases, following unfaithful men to cheap hotels and nightclubs. Anything else would be a relief. Makana was in that half-awake, half-drowsy state of mind where everything was fluid and soft.

'I came straight up. I hope you don't mind.'

Makana looked round to see a man standing at the top of the stairs: tall, thin, and with the tanned complexion of a European who had spent long seasons in sunny climes. He was clad in a rumpled cream-coloured linen suit, elegantly tailored but also well worn. The suit of a man who liked comfort and had the resources to afford it, yet had apparently fallen on hard times. Either that or he was trying to appear not too concerned about his appearance. A man who had travelled a lot, one who could rise in one city and go to bed that night on the far side of the globe and still feel at home. While the jacket was wrinkled, the blue shirt underneath looked crisp and fresh. No tie. When the sunglasses came off they revealed creased lines around the eyes; a man who smiles a lot, or squints as he was in this case, at the light coming off the water. Without waiting for an invitation, or even a response, he moved across the room towards the open rear deck.

'I've always wondered who lives on these things. I suppose it must get damp and cold in winter, and hot in the summer.' The visitor gestured at the water. 'The river keeps it cool though, I would imagine.'

Makana realised he was still holding the coffee pot. He lifted it up in offering.

'Can I offer you coffee, Mr ... ?'

'Winslow. Marcus Winslow,' said the visitor by way of introduction, before turning away. He was clearly English. Makana estimated him to be in his fifties. He moved cautiously, like a man who needs constant awareness of his surroundings. Hands in his pockets, he seemed to be taking care not to touch anything.

By the window that served as a makeshift kitchen, Makana pumped the handle on the kerosene stove and struck a match, holding it forward until the blue flame came to life before turning it down low. Then he filled the small brass coffee pot with water and three spoons of coffee from the tin that he kept on a shelf. As he placed the pot on the stove he glanced out through the open window. Umm Ali's vegetable patch looked barren and untended. The steep path winding up the riverbank to the road was deserted. She was away, gone to visit her family in the delta, taking with her Aziza, her daughter. Their absence added a further touch of desolation to their home, a simple shack made of wooden pallets, crates and tin sheets hammered haphazardly together. At the top of the path Makana could make out the outline of a dark SUV, possibly a Range Rover, parked in the shade of the big eucalyptus tree whose branches curled down over the bank, like a hand. Marcus Winslow seemed to travel with no sign of any kind of protection, and yet Makana had the sense that his visitor was not a civilian.

'How can I help you?' he asked, turning back to his visitor.

'May I?' Winslow gestured at a chair and sat before Makana could reply. 'It's a very pleasant spot you have here. Basic, but very pleasant.'

'I take it you are here for a reason, and not simply to admire the view?'

With one eye on the coffee as it began to bubble, Makana shook a cigarette free from a crumpled pack of Cleopatras, keenly aware that Winslow was studying his every movement.

'Quite right. I have, as they say, a proposition for you.'

'I'm listening.'

'Your English is very good, by the way, where did you learn it?'

'My wife studied in England for a time. Many years ago. I accompanied her and took advantage of your public library service.'

'Alas, a thing of the past.'

'I'm sorry to hear that.' There was something absurdly British about the conversation.

'And where is she now, your wife?'

'She passed away.'

It was fifteen years since the car that held his wife and young daughter had gone over the side of a bridge. In his dream, he was always the one in the car drowning. Yet he hadn't been in the car with them. They drowned. He lived. It was a simple equation, but one he had never grown used to.

A moment's silence fell. Makana had the impression he didn't need to go into details; Winslow knew more than he was letting on.

'Let me come to the point, I represent Her Majesty's government.'

'Which part of her government would that be?'

'The part that doesn't like to announce itself.'

'Meaning the Secret Intelligence Services?'

'I'm what they call a consultant these days. It sounds less … threatening.' Marcus Winslow reached into his jacket to produce a packet of Benson & Hedges, along with a slim gold lighter with which he lit one. He blew the rich aroma into the air. Makana drew on his Cleopatra, feeling the acrid smoke bite at the back of his throat. Humility, the ancients believed, was the route to invincibility.

'They send for me when they have something of a delicate nature to deal with. Personal skills. These days very sadly lacking.'

'And that's why you've come to me?'

'Quite.' Marcus Winslow flashed a brief smile. Not cold, but not superior either. 'I'm told you are quite skilled at what you do.'

'That depends on who you've been talking to.'

'I understand you operate as a kind of private investigator.'

'Something like that.' Makana took a moment to study his cigarette. 'You don't have some kind of identification on you, by any chance?'

'Forgive me.'

Winslow produced a passport and a leather wallet from his pocket. He laid them on the table before getting to his feet and walking over to the railings. The passport carried a photograph that identified him as Marcus Richard Winslow. The wallet was embossed with a stamp that showed a lion and a unicorn. Inside, the same logo appeared on an inset medallion and the words *Semper Occultus* on a banner at the bottom. The card marked Secret Intelligence Services carried no picture, just a number. Makana set them down again. If they were fakes they were well done, but he couldn't count himself an expert. Everything about the man, from the cut of his clothes to his soft loafers, spoke of someone at home in unfamiliar settings. He wasn't trying to make an impression; this was the way he was.

'What I am going to tell you is confidential. I'm not asking you to sign anything silly at this stage because I believe we must build trust between us.'

'I'm listening.'

Makana shut off the flame, lifted the pot off the little stove and poured the dark coffee into two small white china cups. He set them on a brass tray alongside a green plastic sugar bowl.

'We have rather a delicate situation on our hands, and we need your help.'

'You have my full attention.'

Marcus Winslow sat down again and took a moment to taste the coffee. He smiled approvingly before setting the cup down carefully on the low table, picking up the passport and wallet in the same smooth movement. He tucked them away in his jacket as he spoke.

'Does the name Abu Hilal mean anything to you?'

'I'm afraid not.' Makana sipped his coffee and lit another cigarette. He had a feeling this was going to be a long story.

'I don't blame you. Men like him pop out of the woodwork at an alarming rate. Impossible to keep track of all of them. Still, this one is a little closer to home, a known associate of Daud Bolad, whom I believe you have had dealings with.'

Makana had come face to face with Bolad some eight years ago, while he was working on a missing-persons case, looking for a football player named Adil Romario. His inquiries had brought him in touch with Bolad, and he still recalled the moment he had first set eyes on the strange one-armed man, crouched over him in the basement of an abandoned building. Makana had always counted himself lucky to have got away from that encounter in one piece, and he knew that Bolad was the kind of person who never really went away, not fully, not until they were dead. There was always a chance they might surprise you one day, quite out of the blue.

'Abu Hilal was born Sayf al-Din Ahmed Khayr. A Jordanian small-time petty crook who progressed from burglary and car theft via armed robbery, with the occasional rape thrown in. A real charmer. He was too young to fight in Afghanistan but he did pop up briefly with the Arab Brigades in the Balkans in the 1990s, which is where he met Bolad. He came into his own of course after we invaded Iraq in 2003.' The Englishman gave a weary sigh. 'Our very own finishing school for terrorists.'

'He was part of the insurgency?'

'Abu Hilal, as he became known around then, had military experience. He knew how to run a low-key guerrilla force. He knew about IEDs and all the rest of it. He ran a tough ship and he was respected. The Americans put a price of ten million dollars on his head, which turned him into a star overnight. Nothing like a wanted sign to provide kudos.'

A grey heron landed gracefully on the railing of the balcony and surveyed the river.

'I take it nobody ever collected the reward?'

'The Americans came close, close enough to force him underground. He disappeared. People thought perhaps he was dead. Or maybe he'd retired or gone abroad. Instead, it turns out that Abu Hilal had morphed into a very dangerous animal indeed.' Winslow finished his coffee and set the little cup down. 'His wife and children were killed in a drone strike on his home. That made it personal. It wasn't about fighting to liberate Iraq from foreign invaders any more, it was about restoring Islam, about cleansing the world. He got religion, in a big way, started making speeches about the end of time, the Day of Judgement.'

It was Makana's turn to sigh. So far, so familiar. 'A monster of your own making.'

'It's become a speciality of ours, you might say.' Winslow's voice was heavy with irony. He looked like a man who had been fighting battles on so many fronts that he no longer remembered what the war was all about. Makana was intrigued. Winslow seemed to read his mind.

'You're wondering where you come into all of this.'

'Well, I admit I'm curious.'

'Understandably.' Winslow smiled. 'I shall try to get to the point, and I'm sure I don't have to remind you that all of this is confidential.'

'Of course.'

'Some months ago we picked up intel from one of our sources in Damascus that Abu Hilal was looking for a specialist.'

'What kind of specialist?'

'The kind that can make chemical nerve agents. Sarin gas to be precise.' Winslow lit another cigarette. He tapped the lighter against his knee. 'I don't have to tell you how dangerous a nerve agent would be in the hands of a man like Abu Hilal. This is our worst nightmare, or as close to it as we would want to get.'

'You said he was looking for a specialist.'

'Well, that's where the second part of this story begins.' Winslow paused for a moment to draw on his cigarette. He seemed to be studying Makana. 'Could I trouble you for another cup of coffee?'

'Certainly.'

Makana collected the cups and went over to the counter to start to prepare a fresh pot. Behind him, he heard Winslow get to his feet. Over his shoulder he watched him walk to the railing and look out across the river. The heron was long gone. Makana rinsed out the pot, refilled it and spooned in the coffee. He struck a match and set the pot on the flame. Winslow began talking again.

7

'Three days ago the British Consulate in Istanbul received a phone call from a man who claimed he had been abducted and brought to Turkey against his will. The man gave his name as Ayman Nizari.' Winslow exhaled, frowning at the deck. 'There was a chemical weapons expert by that name working for Saddam Hussein in the 1980s. You may have heard of the Anfal campaign.'

Makana had heard of al-Anfal, a genocidal plan to decimate the Kurdish population in northern Iraq in the closing stages of the Iraq–Iran war. The name came from a chapter in the Quran describing a decisive victory in early Muslim history. According to legend, angels intervened on the side of the Prophet's followers, ensuring their victory.

'You think this man is connected to Abu Hilal?'

'We believe that Abu Hilal was trying to recruit Nizari's services.'

'You have this man now?'

'No. The consulate's intelligence man is something of a dim light. He couldn't persuade Nizari to come in, or to give him much more information. All we know is that Nizari claims he was abducted in Spain, in Marbella to be exact, by what he believes was a Mossad team. We can't verify this. We can't go to the Israelis without revealing what we know. We want Nizari for ourselves. If they get him, he could disappear for ever, and that would put paid to our chances of getting hold of Abu Hilal.'

'Forgive me,' said Makana, 'but I was under the impression you were allies.'

Winslow sighed heavily. 'On paper, of course, we're all on the same side. In practice, we have our own agendas.'

The coffee was coming to the boil. Makana turned down the heat.

'I have a couple of questions.'

'By all means.'

'Assuming his story is correct, why would the Israelis take Nizari to Istanbul? And secondly, how did he manage to make a phone call?'

'The second question is easier to answer. According to Nizari there was a collision. The vehicle they were travelling in was struck and in the confusion he managed to get away. We're trying to confirm the details. As for why they took him to Istanbul, we can only speculate.'

Winslow came across the room to take the cup of coffee Makana was offering. He took a sip and set it down on the table before retrieving the briefcase he had brought with him. It was an old leather case, like the kind schoolteachers used to carry. He unclipped the brass fastening and pulled out a slim laptop that he set on the kitchen counter.

'We believe Nizari was planning to sell his skills to Abu Hilal. A meeting was set up on neutral ground, by an intermediary. From what little information Nizari gave us we were able to piece together his movements before his abduction. We found this.'

Winslow tapped the computer a few times and a fuzzy black and white image appeared on the screen. Another touch and the video began to play. The film had been shot from a high angle, a security camera close to the ceiling, Makana guessed.

'This is Marbella in Spain. The Cherry Beach club, frequented by Arab men and Eurotrash with money to burn who lounge around in the sun drinking champagne at a thousand euros a bottle to wash down the exorbitantly priced sushi.'

'Sounds like an unlikely place to find a terrorist with religious inclinations.'

'That's what made it so perfect.' Winslow sipped his coffee and set down the cup. 'Girls in bikinis dancing on tables, pouring bubbly over one another. You get the general idea.'

It wasn't exactly Makana's area of expertise.

The scene was the terrace of a restaurant on a sunny afternoon. There were a number of tables set around a low circular stage where two girls in what looked like the kind of feather headdresses that Indians wore in cowboy films, and not much else, were gyrating to the sound of what might have been considered music in some parts but to Makana sounded like a washing machine filled with assorted horseshoes.

Female waiting staff wearing a minimum of clothing tottered about on high heels between the tables. The clientele appeared to be made up of overweight Europeans, largely men, some young, many middle-aged, and all of them determined to make a spectacle of themselves. They whooped and cheered, grabbed at the waitresses as they went by and poured alcohol down their throats. To Makana it was as close to an image of hell as you would ever want to come. Winslow drew his attention to a corner table where three men sat, one with his back to the camera.

'The one on the right is our middleman, a Spaniard by the name of Miko Santamaria. He has his fat fingers in every pie you can think of – human trafficking, drugs, along with an impressive list of contacts in any branch of the mafia you care to name. Albanians, Kosovans, Bosnians . . .'

'Which one's the scientist?'

'The man on the left side.'

Makana leaned closer to study the grainy image. Ayman Nizari was a balding man of about sixty. He was quite overweight and had a greying moustache. The polo shirt he wore had large sweat stains under the arms. His puffy face wore the look of a small child who has been let loose in a toy store. He didn't know which way to look and he certainly didn't seem to notice that the waitress kept refilling his glass. Two of the dancers sashayed up and, climbing first onto a chair, stepped up onto the table. They were wearing tiny bikinis and the obligatory feather headdresses. As they began to dance the portly Spaniard encouraged them by clapping his hands and throwing his head back and laughing. The scientist's eyes blinked guiltily behind his glasses. He looked like a cat caught with a bird between its teeth.

'Who is the third man?' Makana indicated the man with his back to the camera.

'We don't know. He's the first one to leave. It's possible that he's another local fixer, a contact of Santamaria. It's also possible that he's connected to Abu Hilal.'

'The Israelis didn't grab him?'

'It's a loose end. Either he evaded them, or he was dismissed as unimportant. We simply don't know enough as yet.'

Winslow clicked the keyboard and the image jumped to a later time. The music was, incredibly, even louder now. The light had changed. It was evening. The Spaniard and the scientist were alone. The third man had gone. Miko Santamaria was leaning towards

10

the Iraqi, who was holding his head in his hands. Drunk or despairing, it wasn't clear which. A waitress was also leaning over him. She was different from the one who had been serving them earlier. She appeared to have fallen into the swimming pool. She was blonde and wore shorts and a wet T-shirt that was knotted to expose her navel. They watched the Iraqi reaching for his glass and managing to knock it over. The waitress was all smiles as she cleared up the mess. Ayman Nizari was helped to his feet. He had trouble walking. The waitress led him out of shot of the camera, his arm around her shoulders, her arm around his waist.

'And that's all we have. No records of Ayman Nizari on a commercial flight from Marbella to Istanbul. They must have used a false name. Probably they got him out by land or by sea. We simply don't know.'

'And the waitress?'

'Yes, we thought she looked interesting. Nadia Razvan. On paper a German national of Romanian origin, but her papers were false. She'd been working at the club for a couple of days. Nobody knew anything about her. Apparently this is not unusual; there's a rapid turnover of staff.' Winslow closed the laptop and slipped it back into the leather briefcase.

'What about your Spanish middleman?'

'Miko Santamaria claims he has no idea what happened. We had the local authorities pick him up for questioning, but he denies everything, claims that Nizari was a friend of a business associate who asked Miko to show him a good time.'

'Tell me again about Istanbul. Why did Nizari contact the consulate? What exactly did he want?'

'He says he wants to help us. He can lead us to Abu Hilal.'

'And in return?'

'In return, he would like sanctuary. He's afraid of the Israelis, scared they will kill him as soon as they get a chance. He wants protection, and for that he is willing to help us to lay a trap for Abu Hilal.'

'It sounds almost too perfect,' said Makana.

'Nizari is a wanted man. Saddam Hussein's murder of Kurdish civilians is a war crime. He could be prosecuted.'

'That didn't stop him trying to sell his talents to the highest bidder.'

Winslow shrugged. 'He's poor. He's spent the last twenty years living undercover. And there's another factor: his wife is ill. Cancer. That's the reason he risked travelling to Spain. She needs treatment. That would also be part of the deal.'

'It's a high price, wouldn't you say?'

'To catch one of the most dangerous terrorist masterminds out there?' Winslow shook his head. 'For that I would throw in the keys to Buckingham Palace.'

'So, just to be clear, right now you have no idea where he actually is.'

'We're pretty sure that he's still in Istanbul. We don't think he has any travel documents. He probably doesn't have much money. As far as we know he has no contacts there. We don't know who's holding him, or where he is staying.' Winslow leaned on the railing and tapped ash into the river. 'What we do know is that he's not going to turn himself in to anyone but you.'

'Me?' For the first time in the conversation Makana felt genuine surprise.

'You.'

Makana joined Winslow at the railings. A gust of wind from the river ruffled the Englishman's thinning hair.

'When things went bad for Saddam Hussein in 2003 our friend found himself *persona non grata*. He had nowhere to turn. Iran would have been an obvious choice, but since he had been responsible for the nerve agents that had made martyrs of so many of them in the Iran–Iraq war that option didn't hold much water. Instead he crossed the Red Sea and found refuge in your home country, Sudan. One of the only places in the world that would give him shelter. During his time in Khartoum our man found himself some new friends. One of them was an old friend of yours. A retired police superintendent.'

'Chief Haroun?' Winslow nodded. Makana said nothing. It was a name Makana hadn't heard spoken in years. In his early days as an investigator, it was Haroun's faith in Makana's abilities that eventually led to him being promoted to head the Criminal Investigations

Department. Haroun was a larger-than-life, unconventional man. He scared most people, but found some kind of bond with Makana. They had become friends, spending time together with their families. The chief's wife was a distant relation of Makana's wife, Muna, and so they were almost family. Looking back on that time was like recalling a lost empire.

Makana wondered if Winslow had put all of this together himself, or whether his inquiries had put him in touch with Sudanese intelligence. His thoughts led him back to one person in particular, Mek Nimr, the man who had once been his assistant, his colleague and in a way his rival, although it was not until the end came that Makana realised just how much the other man despised him. Everything was turned on its head after the regime change in 1989. In the purge that followed, many found themselves out of favour, and some, like Mek Nimr, were rewarded with new positions of power. The old CID was transformed into an intelligence department, more concerned with rooting out political dissidents than with criminals. Makana's old chief was offered long-overdue retirement and then stepped down, to live out his old age in peace, or so he believed.

'You left the country, went into exile, but he stayed behind.'

'He was an old man by then,' said Makana. 'In the end they got him too.'

'How so?' Winslow frowned.

'He was taken from his home. His body was found on a piece of wasteland on the outskirts of the city.'

'He was murdered? Did they ever find the killers?'

Makana shook his head. 'It was an execution. Someone was settling an old debt.' A large leafy branch floated by below, swept along swiftly by the current. It all seemed so long ago. Why would he never be free of the past?

'We're allies now,' said Winslow, choosing his words carefully. 'In the war on terror we need all the help we can get, and Sudan is keen to play ball, as the Americans say, at least on the official level. They want sanctions lifted. They want to be taken off the list of states sponsoring terrorism.'

'So, you're saying this man Nizari somehow heard of me through Haroun?'

'Something like that. Nizari is looking for somebody to trust, and yours is the first name that came to mind. Your old chief must have spoken highly of you.'

Makana swirled the dregs around in the bottom of his cup, wondering if there was anything written there that he ought to know. The connection to his old chief made it feel like this was a message from beyond the grave. In the beginning they had stayed in touch. Haroun would send word to Makana in Cairo from time to time, inquiring about his well-being, passing on news about mutual friends. Then, suddenly, he was gone. Makana knew of only one man who had reason to hurt their old chief: Mek Nimr. Makana glanced over at the Englishman.

'This is what you do?'

'This is what I do,' said Winslow. 'I sort out difficult problems.' The Englishman pushed his hands into his pockets. 'I know it sounds like an unusual situation. I would be suspicious myself. There are times when we need the help of a civilian, someone who is outside normal channels, someone like you. This is one of them.'

Makana thought about Ayman Nizari. He wasn't all that keen to help a man trained in the creation of deadly chemical weapons, but if it was a means of preventing others from putting his skills to work, then he knew it made sense.

'You're the only person he will hand himself over to. We can't do this without you.'

Nizari seemed an unlikely companion for his old chief to have had, but that didn't necessarily rule out the possibility of the Iraqi having heard enough about Makana to know he was trustworthy. It was an odd situation, and one that Makana wasn't entirely comfortable with.

'You're forgetting that I don't actually have a passport. I'm in a kind of official grey area. I can't travel.'

'That can be arranged,' said Winslow.

A glint of sunlight on metal drew Makana's gaze to a thick black plume of diesel exhaust cutting across the bridge. The city was working itself once more into its daily frenzy. He reached for his Cleopatras again.

'I need to think about this. What you are asking … well, the whole thing sounds a little out of my league.'

'I understand if you have reservations about working with us. We're not exactly popular in the region right now. I get that. Really, I do. I've been coming to this part of the world for a long time, and the invasion of Iraq went against everything I've learned. There are a lot of people who feel that way. We're not all bad.'

'I'm sure you're right,' said Makana. He still wasn't sure if he trusted Winslow.

'This is not the first time you've cooperated with the British security services.' Winslow went over to his briefcase and pulled out a folder. 'Seven years ago a Special Branch officer named Janet Hayden filed a report on a missing persons case. She praised you highly.'

Makana remembered Hayden, and the missing English girl, Alice Markham.

'You're the only person Nizari will accept.'

'I'm sure you could find a way around that.'

'You're right, I probably could. But we don't have much time.' Winslow produced an envelope which he handed to Makana. 'Why don't you think it over? This contains stills printed from the footage I showed you earlier. Naturally, Her Majesty's government will pay you for your time, and obviously you will be unable to reveal any of this to anyone.' Winslow made as if to leave. He stopped and turned back. He was wearing the same enigmatic smile Makana had grown familiar with in a short time.

'Oh, and one other thing that might interest you. Ayman Nizari says he has information about your daughter.' Winslow narrowed his eyes. 'He claims she is alive.'

Chapter Two

A water taxi ferried Makana across to Zamalek, where he walked to a quiet, secluded corner on a tree-lined street. Everywhere you looked there were images of football players and a bizarre logo, a football-kicking crocodile wearing a pharaonic crown. The city was still recovering from the euphoria of not only hosting the Africa Nations Cup, but also winning it. The tattered images that flapped on walls and advertising hoardings had already taken on the sad, faded appearance of past glory.

All of this Makana took in but barely registered. He felt numb. Winslow had no further information about Nizari's claim, which probably explained why he had not mentioned it earlier in the conversation – not until he thought he was not going to get Makana to cooperate. It sounded too far-fetched; Makana would have been suspicious if the Englishman had brought up the claim earlier.

Some years after he had arrived in Cairo, Makana had begun to hear rumours that his daughter Nasra might have survived the car accident. His wife Muna had been driving when she lost control of the car and it went over the side of the bridge they were trying to escape over. Both of them were lost. Makana had been thrown clear. He was given a choice that night, to run or to die. He had lost count of the nights when he had woken up wishing he had chosen to die.

He rapped twice on the roof of the old black and white Datsun as he went round to climb into the passenger seat. Springs squeaked in protest as Sindbad struggled awake.

'*Sabah al-foul, ya basha,*' the big man mumbled as he rubbed his round face vigorously with a fleshy hand.

'Good morning, Sindbad.'

Makana shifted his feet to accommodate some of the cardboard boxes and containers that were evidence of the other man's idea of passing the time. There were few activities more important to Sindbad than eating. Spending the night in his car on a stakeout was a perfect excuse to indulge himself.

'My wife put me on a diet.' The big man's eyebrows drooped in a mournful expression. 'She says people die of eating too much.'

'She may have a point,' Makana ventured, only too aware that commenting on anything said by Sindbad's wife was playing with fire.

'At home she only lets me eat salad. I'm not even allowed cheese. Imagine? Whoever heard of cheese being bad for you?'

Sindbad shook his head at the injustice of the world. Makana tried to steer him gently back to more pressing matters.

'How have things been here?'

'No movement.' Sindbad dug his hand into a bag of roasted nuts that rested on the zebra-striped furry dashboard cover before picking up his notepad. He held out a page of what looked like hieroglyphics scrawled by a drunken scribe. Makana handed it back and asked him to translate. Munir Abaza had not emerged since ten o'clock the previous night. The rest of the squiggles were apparently just that.

'He'll be out in a minute.' Sindbad nodded at the sleek black Mercedes parked in front of the building. 'They're getting his car ready.'

A doorman wearing a brown gellabiya was coating the car liberally with soapsuds. Makana looked at his watch. It was after nine. Unusual for a dedicated man like Abaza to be late for work. Even as this thought went through his head he saw a figure appear in the entrance to the building. Munir Abaza was in the same suit Makana had seen him wearing the previous evening, although he appeared to have changed his shirt and put on a different tie. He moved with the confidence of a man who owns the world, or enough of it not to worry too much. The door of the Datsun creaked in protest as Makana struggled to push it open.

'Perhaps it's time to have a word.'

Munir Abaza was already barking orders at the doorman who was rushing around with a rag trying to dry off the car. His irritation turned to resignation when he looked round and saw Makana approaching.

'You're not going to tell me this is a coincidence.'

'No,' said Makana. 'I'm not.'

'I thought not.' An expression of disgust crossed Abaza's face as he looked Makana up and down. 'Somehow I expected more from a man like you.'

Makana shrugged. 'We all have to eat.'

'Yes, but we should try and do it with dignity, don't you think?' Abaza folded his arms. 'So, which one of my partners hired you?'

'Both of them, actually.'

Munir Abaza swore under his breath. He ran one third of a successful legal practice, one of the biggest and most prestigious in the country. The firm's clients were construction magnates, multinational franchises, millionaire landowners, politicians, high-ranking military officers with business interests. In short, people with money and influence: the ruling class that ran the country. Abaza himself was rich and counted himself a personal friend of the president's eldest son, which was about as close as you could get to absolute power.

'They are greedy,' Abaza concluded.

'They seem to have doubts about your loyalty.'

'They think they can manage without me.'

'If it's any consolation, they wouldn't choose this path if they had anything more substantial.'

'Still, it's underhand. Not the kind of thing I would have expected from you.'

'What can I tell you? Business has been slow.'

Abaza rested his leather briefcase on a dry section of the roof of the Mercedes. It was a nice briefcase. Like everything about Abaza, it announced him as a man of wealth and taste. Reaching into his pocket, he produced a fresh packet of Dunhills and broke the cellophane wrapping with his thumbnail. He offered the pack and Makana took one. The two men leaned against the car smoking.

'So, what are you going to do?' Abaza asked eventually.

18

'They asked me to find your weak spot. I've done that.'

'They know about the girl?'

'Not yet, but I have to tell them,' Makana said. 'If I don't, they'll hire someone else who will find the same thing I did.'

Abaza blew smoke into the air. 'We are being considered for a huge contracting deal by the military. Once you get a contract with them you are set for life, but the faintest whiff of moral scandal will scare them off. They've been waiting for an opportunity to cut me out. Why have you come to me?'

With anyone else, Abaza would have asked him what his price was, but the two men had had dealings before, and he knew that wasn't going to work.

'They never mentioned the woman. I was told me it was strictly business,' said Makana. 'I don't like it when clients lie to me.'

'For a man who is short of work, you are certainly picky.'

'Like you said, we should at least try to retain our dignity.'

Munir Abaza smiled. Makana didn't owe the lawyer any favours, although Abaza had passed work Makana's way in the past. The first time was about a year ago. A family whose son had gone missing. Makana had found the boy, but too late to save his life. He had felt bad about asking the parents to pay, but Abaza had stepped in and paid Makana what was owed, with a generous bonus on top, out of compassion. Makana didn't feel a great deal of sympathy for lawyers in general, and certainly not for Abaza. On the other hand he felt less for the people who had hired him. Everything was relative.

'I was careless, I was hasty, but that's what love is all about, right?' Abaza dropped the half-smoked cigarette into the dust. 'I appreciate the warning.'

As Makana stepped back to allow Abaza to get into his car, a voice from above made both men turn to look up. The woman who was hanging over the balcony looked like a figure from a fairy tale. She was clad in a bed sheet, which slipped disarmingly off one shoulder as she blew Abaza a kiss. There was a cheer from a passing vendor carrying a mountain of brightly coloured plastic water jugs hanging from a pole.

Abaza climbed in behind the wheel. He preferred to drive himself, it seemed. The window slid down smoothly and silently. 'I am in your debt. I never forget a favour.'

19

'I can wait until sunset,' said Makana. 'But no longer than that.'

'It's okay,' Abaza smiled. 'That'll give me time to set a counter-move in motion. They want blood. I'm going to give it to them.'

As the car sped away, Makana wondered if he'd just made an error of judgement.

Marcus Winslow did not exist. At least on paper, or rather not exactly paper, but in the digital void that was cyberspace. Ubay was shaking his head, which was never a good sign. If he couldn't find anything then the chances were that nobody could.

The search was interrupted when Sami entered the room bearing a bag full of falafel sandwiches. For a time the three of them busied themselves with biting into the golden rissoles, still hot from the fryer. They were seated in a corner of the MIMCO offices – the Masry Info Media Collective. It was still early and the place was half empty. It tended to fill up later in the day and only really came to life late at night. The arrangement of desks and tables tended to change every few months, as did the faces behind the computer consoles. Sami Barakat was one of the founding members of the collective, along with his wife Rania, who was on the far side of the room, now heavily pregnant but showing no signs of letting up on her usual frenetic pace. Ubay, their resident hacker, internet genius and general geek, had spent over an hour trying to help Makana uncover something about his morning visitor. The lanky figure now sat back and rested his enormous feet on the desk as he munched another sandwich.

'My feeling,' he said between bites, 'is that he's been wiped clean. There's something too regular about the pattern.'

'Can you explain that a little more clearly?' Makana broke the seal on a new pack of Cleopatras and the fresh smell of tobacco hit his nostrils. It was the best part of the day. After that moment they grew more stale by the second. By midday it felt like you were smoking cardboard, but by then you didn't care too much.

'You know what Ubay is like,' said Sami. 'He lives in the Twilight Zone.'

'I don't even know what that is,' said Makana.

'You realise that smoking is a strategy by the industrialised world to exploit and eradicate the populations of less wealthy nations.'

'I know because you tell me almost every time you see me.' Makana gestured at the computer. 'Tell me something I don't know.'

'Okay,' said Ubay, sitting up and tapping a few keys. 'I found a few mentions of his participation in conferences here and there, either as an adviser or as a representative of the British Foreign Service. It seems he was attached to embassies in Baghdad, Tehran, Beirut, Tripoli and Damascus, but all in low-key positions. Assistant this and that. Most of that stops around three years ago.'

'When exactly?' Makana pressed. 'Can you be more specific?'

'Well' – Ubay squinted at the screen – 'I would say around 2003.'

'The time of the invasion of Iraq?'

'Yeah, maybe that fits.'

'Okay, what else?'

'I found another thread where he comes across as a professor, or some kind of Middle East consultant. He studied languages and Modern History at Cambridge University. I can't find out if he is married or has children, where he lives. He travels a lot, but even then, it's as if he pops up in places without warning.' Ubay's résumé was punctuated by pauses as he stopped to take another bite or reached for the can of Coca-Cola nearby, never taking his eyes off the screen in front of him.

'He's a spy,' nodded Sami confidently. 'What else could he be?'

'Did you find any pictures?'

Ubay clicked to another page which revealed half a dozen people named Marcus Winslow. None of them resembled the person Makana had met that morning.

'He's not here,' said Makana.

'What did I tell you?' said Sami. 'He's erased all images of himself. You know how hard it is to do that?'

'Either that, or he's not who he says he is,' said Makana.

'His virtual footprint is almost non-existent,' continued Ubay. 'Whoever he is, he's gone to a lot of trouble to clean it up.'

'His footprint?'

Ubay explained with the patience of a child telling a parent how the world worked: 'It's a trail left behind of what he has done

21

online. His purchases, his interests. Every time you log onto the net you leave a trace.'

'And you can't find anything?'

'Nothing that matches.'

'There's nothing to prove that he is or is not what he says he is.' Sami licked tahini sauce off his fingers where it had escaped from the sandwich. 'You said he showed you ID.'

'He did,' said Makana.

'But you know those things can be faked.' Sami cleared his throat and looked at the ceiling. 'The only people capable of pulling off something like that are the Israelis.'

Makana set his half-eaten sandwich on the desk, his appetite having suddenly vanished. He reached for his cigarettes, giving Ubay a warning look.

'How did he strike you?' Sami asked. 'I mean, what did your gut tell you?'

'That I probably wouldn't be able to tell a genuine British intelligence officer from a fake.'

'There's something else, isn't there?'

Makana glanced at him. Sami shrugged. 'Someone comes knocking at your door asking you to travel out of this country on a fake passport to retrieve some scientist who specialises in nerve agents, and you're tempted? This is not the cautious soul we all know and love.'

Makana blew smoke into the air, ignoring Ubay's theatrical efforts to waft it away.

'Nizari claims to know something about my daughter.' Neither of the others said anything. 'He thinks she might be alive.'

'How would he know something like that?' Sami asked.

'I have no idea. He spent some time in Khartoum. Claims to have known my old CID chief.'

'The one who was killed?'

Makana nodded. 'Executed and dumped in a rubbish tip.'

'You always suspected that it was some kind of revenge by someone inside the security forces, right?'

'He was an old man, a symbol of how the country used to be. He was killed to set an example.'

22

'Okay, I'm confused. How would this Iraqi chemist or whatever he is know anything about your daughter?' Ubay asked. 'I mean, he had no connection to you in the past, did he?'

Makana had been wondering the same thing. The only way Ayman Nizari could know anything about Nasra was if he had been in touch with somebody connected to Makana's past – some-one like his old chief. But it was difficult to imagine that Haroun would not have tried to contact Makana if he'd heard even the slightest rumour about his daughter being alive. So if Haroun hadn't known, then Nizari must have heard the story from someone else. Makana didn't like where his thoughts were leading him. Ubay leaned forward, resting his elbows on the table to tap the screen. He had another question.

'Whoever he is, you think this English guy is in touch with our Egyptian friends?'

It was a good question and one that Makana had already considered. He would have assumed that naturally British intelli-gence would have to inform their Egyptian counterparts about any operation they were undertaking in the country. That would seem logical. Then again, there was something about Marcus Winslow that struck him as anything but conventional.

'You need a safety net,' said Sami, returning to his snack. 'I mean, someone somewhere who knows what you are up to. Just in case, I mean.'

'I don't have one.'

Sami stopped eating. 'You're not seriously considering doing this, are you?'

'I wouldn't be here if I wasn't.'

Sami got to his feet and took Makana by the arm. 'Let's take a walk. You need to clear your head.' He waved across the room to Rania as he pointed Makana towards the door. Ubay handed him a large envelope.

'For what it's worth, this is what I found on Nizari.'

Makana thanked him and then followed Sami down the gloomy staircase to the street. The big, decaying art deco building stood on the corner of Bab al-Luq Square. Sunlight and the noise of traffic hit them as they stepped outside. Sami led the way down a muddy alleyway where a sewer had burst. The interior of the Horreya café was its usual sleepy self. Most of the white marble tables were deserted. Sami waggled two fingers at the man behind the bar as he led Makana to a corner and sat down with a sigh.

'You're old enough to be able to think this through for yourself, but I can see you're confused.'

'I'm not confused,' said Makana, looking around. The clientele was the usual mixed bag: taxi drivers at one table, a university lecturer at the next. 'I just want to be sure what I'm getting into.'

'Well, I'm here as your friend, telling you that you are making a mistake. How long have you lived in this country, fifteen years?'

'What is your point?'

'My point is that you've made a life for yourself here. Why risk throwing all of that away?'

'Who says I'm risking it?'

'If you go to Istanbul.' Sami paused as the waiter, a boy of about thirteen, set two bottles of Stella beer on the table, along with a couple of grimy glasses. Lowering his voice, Sami continued, 'You know that if you go, there is a chance you will not be allowed back into this country. You're a foreigner, you've had problems with the authorities. You have a history.'

'Everything carries a risk.' Makana considered whether it was wise, drinking beer in the middle of the day, then decided the question was superfluous and poured himself half a glass.

'I know what this is about,' said Sami. 'You've never given up the idea that your daughter was alive. All these years, at the back of your mind there was the possibility that she survived. But you looked into it. You called people. You made inquiries and nothing came up.'

'If there is the slightest chance that this man Nizari knows something, I have to go.'

'And what if it's a trap?' Sami asked.

Makana had considered the idea. 'I'm not that important.'

'There's something about this whole story that doesn't feel right.'

'I won't argue with that,' said Makana. 'The point is I won't find out by staying here.'

'Even if you're walking into a trap?'

Makana sighed and took a sip of his beer. He liked this place. Maybe he should spend more time sitting here and less time worrying about the world.

'What about Jehan?'

Makana raised his eyebrows. 'What about her?'

'Well, have you told her?'

'Not yet.' Makana drew a circle in the moisture that had drained off the bottle onto the table. He didn't need to be told that Jehan would not take it well.

'Do our friends in State Security know about all this?'

'I don't know.'

Sami rolled his eyes. 'Well, do you think that maybe it's an idea that you try to find out? If the British are up to something behind their backs, they won't be happy. That might leave you holding the baby. And believe me, you don't want that.'

Makana knew that Sami was right. He had enough experience to know how tough the Egyptians could make it for anyone, particularly a foreigner, who appeared to be working against the state.

'You do realise that this would mean you working for the same imperialist forces who are right now occupying Iraq and Afghanistan? That's going to make you a very unpopular man in some quarters.'

'I'll have to take that chance.' Makana got to his feet. 'I should be going.'

'Let me give you the number of a friend of mine. Kursad is a journalist. He can help you if you need something.' Sami shook his head. 'I don't know why I bother talking. No matter what advice I give you, you are still going to do whatever you want. At least, listen to what Jehan has to say.'

By the time Makana had reached the street his mobile was ringing. It was Marcus Winslow.

'I'm assuming that by now your curiosity will have overcome your reluctance …'

Chapter Three

Jehan Siham was where Makana expected to find her, where she always was: in the basement of the Department of Pathology at the University of Cairo. Her assistant, a young man named Hassan, greeted Makana with a nod.

'She's busy, but you can go through.'

As assistant director, Jehan pretty much ran things the way she wanted to. She was virtually running the entire department. The only thing that prevented her becoming full director was an old-fashioned board which demanded a more senior male figure. Her office adjoined the dissecting room where she spent most of her time, either teaching or working on cases the state sent her way. Makana pushed open the swing doors to find her in the process of removing the brain from a corpulent male body laid out on one of the steel dissecting tables. Her eyes flickered up, and over the mask he saw the query in her gaze.

'You shouldn't be in here,' she said. 'But when has that ever stopped you?'

She finished what she was doing and summoned Hassan to tidy up. Makana waited in her office while she washed up. The window that gave onto the dissecting room was partially blocked by shelves crammed with glass specimen jars containing various forms of life, some human and some, Makana guessed, not. There was a side to Jehan that he didn't feel he would ever understand.

'Why is it that we spend so much of our time in the company of the dead?' he asked as she came in.

'In my case it is in the cause of science,' she said, giving him a wary look as she sat down behind her desk. 'In your case, I'm not so sure.'

'I have to go away for a few days.'

'Away … ?'

'Out of the country.'

'I see.' Jehan picked up a brass letter opener whose handle was shaped like Anubis, the jackal god said to guard the Underworld. 'I thought you didn't have the papers to travel?'

'It's being arranged.'

'That sounds suspiciously easy,' she said slowly. 'Should I be worried?'

'I'm not sure.'

'Okay, now I am worried.'

'It's difficult to explain.'

'Try.'

'It's something from my past, something I thought I had put behind me.'

'Why don't you sit down.' Jehan gestured at the chair. 'You're making me nervous.'

Makana paused, resting his hands on the back of the chair. 'Somebody claims to have news about my daughter.'

Jehan sat back in her chair. 'What kind of news?'

'He claims she is alive.'

'That's amazing.' Jehan's eyes lit up for a moment. She pressed the point of the letter opener into the desktop. 'Do you believe him?'

'I don't know what to believe.' Makana resumed his pacing. She didn't try to stop him this time. 'If she's alive, after all this time …' He shook his head in disbelief.

'Who is this man?'

'I don't know him. He's on the run, in Istanbul. He wants me to come and get him.'

'That's crazy,' said Jehan. 'You're not going to do it, are you?'

'What choice do I have?'

'But it might be a trap. Your old enemies. The people who forced you to flee.'

'It doesn't matter,' said Makana, coming to a halt. His mind was now clear. 'None of that matters.'

'Doesn't it strike you as a little strange, that a man you've never heard of should turn up out of the blue with news of Nasra?'

'It all sounds a little strange,' agreed Makana. He had come to a halt again, leaning over the chair. Jehan got to her feet and came round to stand beside him. She rested a hand on his shoulder.

'You have no choice,' she said. 'You have to find out if there is any truth to it.' She was silent for a moment. 'Look, I'm not a psychiatrist, I just cut dead people up, but I can tell you that you need to resolve this. You need to come to terms with your past. You have to move on.' She leaned forward. 'If you don't do this thing now, you will spend the rest of your life wondering what might have been.'

Marcus Winslow was waiting for Makana at Maxim's river restaurant. He was clearly known to all the staff who fussed around the table. A bottle of Jordanian arak stood on the table in front of him, along with bowls of snacks and an ice bucket. He stood up as Makana approached, the now familiar smile already in place, ushering him into a chair and shooing the waiters away.

'I used to come here as a student, years ago, when I was learning Arabic. We would sit here like sultans gazing at the Nile. I loved it.' He turned to stare out of the window. 'I thought I would spend my life here, get married, lose myself in the whole strange wonder of it all. And now look at me.' Winslow threw his hands up and grinned. He looked younger, his face lit by the memory of his youthful dreams. Makana was wary. He suspected that all of this was for show: the kind Englishman who loves and respects this country. Generous, too. Staff bowed and smiled as they went by. Winslow lowered his voice and his tone became more sober.

'We can't stay here too long,' he said, as he poured a hefty measure of the clear liquor into Makana's glass. He gave the slightest nod over his shoulder. At a table over by the window two unlikely-looking patrons sat doing a bad job of pretending to look out of the window. 'The local watchdogs. I don't think they are here for me, but we don't want them snooping around.'

Makana glanced casually round the room. The men were unmistakably Egyptian security. Hard to say which service, but they were clearly taking an interest. He turned back to the Englishman.

'Does this mean that you are not here in an official capacity?'

'Well …' Winslow rocked his head from side to side. 'That's a moot question. Generally, it's a good idea not to get more people involved than is necessary. That's pure pragmatism. The fewer people who catch wind of this, the less risk there is of a leak.' Winslow set the bottle down and added a couple of lumps of ice to his glass. 'We're in an unusual situation, and I don't mind telling you that there are quite a few people on my side of the table who are adamantly opposed to the idea of bringing in – no offence – a complete stranger. We don't like to think we need to rely on outsiders.

'We used to be better at this sort of thing, I admit that. The fact is that we have a history of intelligence failures when it comes to the Middle East. I don't need to tell you that. The reason is simple. Old-fashioned prejudice. We never feel we can ever fully trust anyone other than ourselves. Now we put our faith in IT experts who worship at the temple of al-Khwarizmi.'

'Sorry?' Makana frowned.

'They reduce everything to algorithms.' Winslow sipped the milky liquid from his glass. A waiter placed plates of pickled turnip and olives, hummus and tahini on the table between them.

'I took the liberty of ordering. I hope you don't mind. I assume you have no objection to lamb?'

'None at all.' Makana raised his glass and used the opportunity to take another glance at the two men sitting in the corner. One of them was using a mobile phone. Someone somewhere was no doubt busy trying to identify the Englishman's guest.

'I realise that what we are asking is a little unusual. You have no connection to us, or to Ayman Nizari, but your part in all of this is crucial, believe me.'

'Tell me about Nizari's time in Sudan.'

Winslow sipped his drink before answering. 'You probably know this better than I do, but in the 1990s Khartoum was teeming with every radical organisation you cared to name. All of them passed through. The government had an agenda: they wanted to revitalise Islam in the Middle East, to push it though Africa as a revolutionary force. Mad as hatters, but you have to admire their nerve. They gave Nizari a home.' Winslow tilted his head back. 'Ayman Nizari is a very dangerous asset. In the wrong hands he could do a lot of damage. We can't risk losing him.'

'And yet he seems willing to come in.'

'In large part due to his wife's condition. As far as we can ascertain she needs expensive treatment, and we can offer that.' Winslow seemed to read the look on Makana's face. 'You're uncomfortable with this.'

'I'm trying to understand what's going on.'

'What specifically are you concerned about?'

'I'm not really sure. You said Nizari claimed to have information about my daughter.'

'That's what he told us. The details are vague.'

'How would he have come across something like that?'

Winslow held up his hands in a gesture of defeat. 'I can't tell you. I assume from one of the people he met during his time in Khartoum, perhaps even your old chief, Haroun.'

Makana shook his head. 'Haroun would have come to me himself.'

'Look, I don't know what to say. Maybe Nizari heard something. Maybe he's making it up, trying to sweeten the deal. All I know is that we have an opportunity on our hands. Ayman Nizari is a very useful asset.'

'You mean in terms of catching this Abu Hilal character.'

'Him or a hundred others like him.' Winslow placed his hands on the table. 'The world has moved on, Mr Makana, and maybe that's partly our fault, but there's little rhyme or reason these days. New splinter cells break out all the time. The invasion of Iraq left a vacuum in its wake, ideologically and economically. We've only just begun to see the fallout from that. Men like Abu Hilal have no specific aim, but when they start talking about the Day of Judgement, or bringing on the apocalypse, there are people crazy enough to listen. My job is to stop them, to prevent the next massive attack before we get the pictures on our screens of bodies being pulled out of the wreckage. Imagine what a nerve agent like that could do in Europe. It takes twelve hours to drive from Istanbul to Vienna. They could be in Berlin or Paris in two days. That's not a remote threat, that's real. Will you help us?'

Makana studied the Englishman. 'I can't help wondering just how much you're not telling me.'

'Well, what can I say?' Winslow sat back in his chair. 'That's the nature of the beast, it's what we do. We lie, we deceive. It's not personal. You have to remember there is a purpose here, larger than you or I. To get there, all the pieces have to fall into place.' He refilled their glasses. 'Look, Makana, I like you. There's a certain frankness about you that is refreshing. Most people I work with have learned to talk the talk. They sound as though they know what they are doing, but they lack experience in life, something that you seem to have in spades.'

'Why would he mention my daughter?'

'Is that what's making you uncomfortable?'

'It makes it personal,' Makana said. 'That makes me wary.'

'I told you because I wanted to be honest with you. Maybe it was an error of judgement. I thought you could handle it.' The ice tongs hung in mid-air. 'So you won't do it?'

'I'll do it,' said Makana. 'Because I can't *not* do it. But I don't like it.'

'I understand.' Winslow finished with the ice and raised his glass in a toast. 'I wish I could explain it, but I can't, just as I can't promise this isn't just something Nizari is making up. Don't get your hopes up.'

'Don't worry, I've been dealing with this for a long time.'

'The good thing is,' smiled Winslow, 'that in this case you are on the side of the angels.'

'I'd like to believe that makes a difference.'

'Naturally we will pay you for your time, and we'll make all the necessary arrangements. Ever been to Istanbul?'

'You're forgetting that I can't leave this country. I don't have a valid passport and nobody is likely to provide one right now. Neither my government nor this one. I have a history, you might say.'

'I'm aware of your situation,' said Winslow. 'Since arriving here from Khartoum you have remained in a kind of limbo. It's not a problem. A passport will be issued by Her Majesty's government.'

'A British passport?' Makana raised his eyebrows.

'Effective at once, but for a limited time. You'll hand it back when the job is over. Much as I'd like to help you, there is a limit to the miracles I can perform.' Winslow lit a cigarette and leaned over the table. 'You arrive in Istanbul, make contact with Nizari and deliver him to the extraction point. Someone else will take care of things from there.'

'How do I find him?'

'You don't. Nizari has specified a time and place. All you have to do is be there and he will find you.'

'So you're in touch with him?'

'Not exactly.' Winslow sighed. 'He communicates with our people at the consulate when he chooses.'

'So the only way to reach him is through this meeting place.'

'It's not that complicated, not for a man like yourself. I'm confident of that. On the chair next to you is an envelope that contains ten thousand US dollars and some photographs. That's for your transport out. Study the pictures but don't take them with you.'

'Who's in them?'

'Our man, Ayman Nizari, and the waitress from the club in Marbella.'

'You think I might bump into her?'

'If the Israelis are still around it's best to be aware what form they might come in.'

Three waiters arrived bearing platters of lamp chops and skewers of kebab and grilled vegetables, more salad, bread and dips. Makana felt tired just looking at it. He swirled the ice around his glass.

'Do you have a family?'

If the question caught Marcus Winslow off balance, he recovered smoothly.

'You know what I do in my spare moments, Mr Makana? I sit in a dark room and play the saxophone. I imagine I am Ornette Coleman, or Sonny Rollins, and for a time, in that darkness, I shine. It's the closest I shall ever come to understanding religion. We all have something. Maybe for you it's redemption, the thought of finding your daughter again. I can't really speculate. The point is that we're not going to become friends. Not now, not ever. We're going to do a job together as professionals and then we shall go our separate ways. It's who we are. It's what we do. Here's to noble causes.' Winslow raised his glass. 'Now, please, we should try to make it look as if we're enjoying a meal together.'

Makana wasn't hungry. He chewed a lump of pickled turnip thoughtfully.

'Why don't you tell me about your daughter. She died in an accident, didn't she?'

'Somebody tampered with my car.'

'You know this for a fact?' Winslow stopped heaping food onto his plate.

'It's never been proven, but I know there were people who meant me harm. They thought I would try to escape the city in that car.'

Winslow reached into the basket for a piece of warm bread. 'Tell me who you are worried about.'

'Who says I'm worried?'

The Englishman looked him in the eye. 'You believe that Nizari's message about your daughter was not from him, but from someone else.'

Makana lit a cigarette. Whatever appetite he might have had was now well and truly gone.

'A man named Mek Nimr. We worked together for a number of years. I was an investigator with the Criminal Investigation Department, he was a uniformed sergeant.'

'So you knew him well, you were close?'

'We had a different way of looking at things. We tolerated each other.'

'You distrusted him.'

Makana considered the idea. 'Some men have something in them. A poison, like a rabid dog that has been infected but has yet to show signs of illness. You sense it within a few minutes of meeting them. You can't say exactly what it is but you know that one day it will come out.'

Winslow took a long drink before setting his glass down. 'You think this man has some kind of personal vendetta against you.'

It was always hard to explain what had happened, because Mek Nimr had never protested or given any indication of discontent. Makana knew that over the years of working together, Mek Nimr had built up a powerful hatred for him. Envy. Ambition. Who could say what it really was? Perhaps it was the influence of the alcohol, or the possibility that Nasra might still be alive, but Makana found himself telling Winslow about the past in a way that he hadn't done in years. It was as if all the unresolved questions in his life suddenly demanded further scrutiny. He was talking because he wanted to understand something he had never fully been able to comprehend.

'We met at the police academy. His scores placed him at the bottom of the class. I was chosen as officer material. He wasn't.' Mek Nimr never lacked the desire to prove himself, to rise above all those around him. 'I don't think he ever got over that. He thought it was favouritism. He worked hard, did all the work, and he just could not understand why that didn't make him officer material.'

'What do you think he was lacking?'

'Empathy. On the surface he was the most conventional man you could hope to meet. He followed regulations to the letter but he had trouble understanding people. He saw the world his way and he despised anyone who didn't see things as he did.'

Mek Nimr's moment had come with the power shift in 1989. Priorities changed after the coup. Suddenly, being an investigator no longer meant solving cases, or bringing people to justice, it was about conformity. Makana found himself isolated and under suspicion for the very qualities that had singled him out early on.

'There was a restructuring. Chief Haroun was replaced by a military officer close to the new junta, and Mek Nimr got the promotion he was after. It was his hour. He ran a special unit of the People's Defence Forces, which was a kind of informal militia to do the government's dirty work – running down dissidents, students, trade unionists. They made them disappear.'

'Was he involved in your being banished from the country?'

'Banished?' Makana echoed the word as he stubbed out his cigarette. It made him sound like a bygone chapter in history. Maybe he was. 'There was a cover-up, in a murder case. A number of young women were being preyed on by the militias. Someone high up was involved. He was looking for a reason to get rid of me. I was arrested.'

'Under what charge?'

'In those days they didn't bother much with such formalities. This was outside the law. I was held in what they used to call a ghost house. An unofficial prison. There are no records.'

'I know what a ghost house is,' said Winslow quietly.

'There was no purpose to it. It was simply to intimidate, to scare, to wipe out all possible opposition.'

'I had the impression you weren't political.'

'That didn't matter. I was simply not one of them.' He could have been a communist, a traitor, an apostate. He was whatever they wanted him to be.

'Sooner or later they would have killed me. It was a little awkward because I was a senior investigator, so they released me and gave me the opportunity to flee. I think that's where they planned to get rid of me. Somewhere out in the desert where nobody would ever find me.'

Suddenly thirsty, Makana paused to take a drink. The arak was heady and sweet.

'You crashed while making your escape. Your wife and child were in the car.'

Makana nodded. 'They didn't make it. I did.'

'And you think that this man, Mek Nimr, is somehow connected to Nizari mentioning your daughter?'

'I don't believe in coincidences.'

'I understand.' Winslow chewed for a time, then dabbed his mouth with his napkin. 'It's a complicated situation. Sudan is on a list of states that support terrorism, but 9/11 was a game changer. They are keen to prove they're on the side of the good. Nobody wants to feel the wrath of the United States. And besides, just take a look around you.' Winslow nodded in the direction of their State Security chaperones. 'It's a good cover for going after your political opponents. Anyone who doesn't agree with you is a terrorist. Welcome to the age of paranoia. The war on terror is the best thing that ever happened for Mubarak and his men. We've never had a problem doing a deal with the devil. Khartoum came in with plenty of useful intel.'

'How am I supposed to get Nizari out?'

'That happens with the help of a man named Nadir Sulayman, a local entrepreneur, former heavy metal rock musician, would you believe, and radical journalist. He ran a number of cultural journals on alternative lifestyles, transcendental meditation, legalising marijuana – that sort of thing – before going straight. Maybe he just grew up. He went into business and now runs a number of small, mostly legal enterprises – import/export. He's been helpful in the past and he has a lot of contacts, particularly across the border in Bulgaria, which is important.'

'Why Bulgaria?'

'It's too risky to fly you straight out, so you will be driven to Sofia to catch a plane. It's a short drive – a few hours. The advantage you have is that you're a cleanskin. Nobody knows you, nobody will be looking for you.' Winslow tapped his fingers on the table, then flashed a smile. 'You'll be in and out of there before you know it.' He helped himself to more kebab. The bread basket was whisked away and replaced by another filled with loaves warm from the oven.

'Remember that Nizari wants to come in. He's not an unwilling passenger. All you have to do is make contact and bring him to the location. Nadir will take care of the rest.' Makana sipped his drink as Winslow continued. 'Pay him half before and half on arrival. That's the deal. We can't risk you travelling with a larger sum. There will be more waiting for you in your hotel room safe for expenses. Your fee will be paid separately, after completion of the job.'

Over Winslow's shoulder Makana saw the two men in the corner whispering. They looked agitated, which wasn't a good sign.

Winslow placed a business card for something called the Green Crescent Travel Bureau on Kasr al-Nil Street on the table. 'The place actually exists, but you can't reach them on that number. You call me every day at six p.m. on the dot. If I'm not there, someone else will take the call. Use a landline, never a mobile. Try not to use the same one twice.' Makana tucked the card into his pocket. 'The last digits of the number will open the safe in your hotel room where you will find the extra cash and a weapon. Please do not use this unless absolutely necessary. The most important thing is the daily rendezvous at one o'clock at a place called the Iskander Grillroom. That's where Nizari will try to contact you. There will be a map in your room with the location marked on it.

36

'All that remains is for me to wish you good luck.' Winslow raised his glass. 'Now, please eat some of this delicious food. You're making me look like a glutton.'

Makana looked at the platter and hesitated. There was something about the skewers of meat that put him in mind of a sacrificial lamb.

Chapter Four

The early hours found Makana leaning on a balcony staring out across a six-lane road at the tranquil vista of the Nile. Palm trees and greenery flourished, leaves stirring gently in the shadows like a reminder of some primordial innocence that had long been lost.

Talk of Mek Nimr had stirred up old memories and emotions that he thought he had put behind him. Makana felt as though he had lived for centuries with the images of that night's events on the bridge burned into his mind's eye. He had thought he was coming to terms with the death of Muna and Nasra. Now he realised he would never be at peace until he put Mek Nimr out of his life for ever.

Makana jumped as two arms came around his sides and he felt a soft warmth press against his back. He knew that underneath her robe Jehan was wearing nothing. She rested her head against his shoulder.

'I don't know how you do it,' she said. 'I'm a wreck if I don't get a full night's sleep.'

He let her rest there against him, finding comfort as always in her presence. This too, this new beginning that he thought he had begun with Jehan in his life, was now brought into doubt.

She moved alongside him, pulling the robe tighter and plucking the cigarette from his fingers.

'Are you sure you've really thought this through?'

'I wish I could say I had,' said Makana. 'But I'm not sure I'm thinking clearly.' He gazed out over the dark river. 'I feel like I'm being pulled back down.'

'Perhaps that's not so strange.' She twisted him round to study his face in the half-light. 'You've never come to terms with their being gone. Maybe some part of you didn't want to believe it. They have always been there, in some kind of twilight existence, on the edge of your life. Most of the time you keep them out of the way, but they are never fully gone. And now they're back.' She stroked the side of his face. 'You have to let go, for your own sake. You can't carry them with you for your entire life.'

'I don't know,' he said, and tightened his grip on the railing. 'I can't seem to let go of them. What if it's true? What if this man Nizari does know something about Nasra?'

'Then you will find her and you will have to learn what that means. It's not going to be easy. Whatever happens, you must live your own life.'

Makana had lost count of the number of times he'd tried to tell himself the same thing.

'There wasn't anything you could do,' Jehan went on. 'You can't torture yourself with guilt for something that was beyond your ability to change.'

'Maybe that's the problem.'

'You feel guilty for leaving them behind' – she corrected herself. 'You feel guilty for living.' She handed back his cigarette and folded her arms across her chest. 'I don't like the idea of you going away like this, on the spur of the moment.'

'There's no other way.' Makana took her hand in his. 'I thought you said I should go.'

'That doesn't mean I like the idea. You don't know if you can trust this Englishman, or what Nizari is up to. You've never been to Istanbul in your life.'

'It's a city. I've lived here for long enough to understand how they work.'

'Not all cities are the same. They don't even speak Arabic there.'

Makana smiled. 'I'll manage.'

'I'm sure you will. You always do.' She returned her head to his shoulder. 'But I'm going to miss you and I'm going to worry about you.' Straightening up, she looked him in the eye. 'Go, but just remember that I'm here. If it doesn't work out for some reason, if this story isn't true, if this man is lying, you have something to come back to.'

Makana looked at her. 'I've never been very good at this kind of thing.'

She covered his mouth with her hand. 'We agreed, no promises and no apologies, remember?'

'I just want you to know that I appreciate this, everything, having you in my life.'

'Just promise me you'll be careful.'

'I'm always careful.'

'Well, more so than usual.' Jehan squeezed his arm before turning to go back inside. 'Aren't you coming back to bed?'

'In a moment.'

He listened to her moving around the room for a time before climbing into bed. After a time there was silence. He was willing to bet that she wasn't asleep yet, but she would be soon. He switched on a low lamp, sat down in the living room and opened the envelope Ubay had given him. He had put together a fair amount of background information on Ayman Nizari.

Born in 1947 in Kufa, Nizari had studied in Baghdad and later in Paris. When he returned to Iraq with a PhD he started out as a researcher at the university but soon transferred to the military. In the mid-1980s he was part of Project 922, the Iraqi nerve-gas programme. They concentrated on developing mustard gas and a nerve agent, tabun, which was later abandoned in favour of sarin. This was during the Iran–Iraq war and chemical weapons were dropped on the waves of Iranian troops who launched themselves at the Iraqi lines, intent on martyrdom.

There was a document on the effects of mustard gas, which had claimed some fifty thousand victims, but that number could double if you counted long-term effects. The symptoms made hard reading: blistering of the skin and mucus membranes, causing respiratory problems and blindness. The long-term effects included cancer.

Sarin was a nerve agent that produced muscle convulsions and was generally lethal. There was evidence that the use of these gases had been sanctioned by the US Defense Department. The Americans had not only known what the Iraqis were planning, but provided a wealth of intelligence to help them track Iranian troop movements. After the war Ayman continued work on VX gas, an organophosphorus nerve agent. More deadly but also more unstable, VX had proved difficult to produce in sufficient purity.

By Makana's watch it was almost five in the morning. How long had he slept that night? He wasn't sure, but he knew there was little point in trying to sleep more. It would be light soon. He paused on his way out to look into the bedroom. Jehan was sleeping soundly. He ought to wake her and say goodbye, but instead he moved as quietly as he could towards the door.

It was a modern building, but the staircase was hot and stuffy. Coming out into the open felt like a release. Makana drew in a lungful of cool night air. In the early hours, when the traffic had slowed to a trickle and a breeze swept the city clean, the air felt clearer. Despite his feelings for Jehan, he felt uncomfortable in her world. Something told him he would never shake off his sense of guilt. He had spent too long alone, perhaps, to ever feel really at ease in a relationship. Sharing his life with another person, no matter how clever, beautiful or caring, was not something he was sure he was capable of any more.

A solitary taxi cab trundled by, its driver half asleep. He could barely sit upright behind the wheel, let alone register a man standing by the side of the road, yet he managed to pull over without hitting anything. As Makana stepped off the kerb, a set of powerful headlights came on, dazzling him. He turned to see a dark SUV gliding towards him, and recognised it as the Range Rover that had been parked under the eucalyptus tree by his awama the previous morning. The rear door opened as it drew level with him and Marcus Winslow beckoned him inside. They took off before the door was fully closed. There were two men in the front who said nothing.

'You were waiting for me?'

'I'm afraid that the situation has changed.'

Winslow looked as though he'd had even less sleep than Makana, which was impressive considering the amount of alcohol he had put away the previous evening.

'A couple of hours ago we intercepted a message out of Istanbul, sent to Tel Aviv. It confirms our fears that the Israelis are involved.'

'They know Nizari is in Istanbul?'

'They're looking for him.' Passing streetlights painted Winslow's face with pulses of orange. 'We also picked up the word Hammurabi, their codename for Abu Hilal.'

'Isn't this going to complicate matters?'

'Not necessarily. It means you have to be quick. In and out. Find Nizari and get him to the extraction point. There's no need to panic just yet.'

Makana watched the city floating by, smooth and silent as silk. It was almost deserted at this hour. Through the windows of the car the dark, empty streets, the metal shutters on windows and shop-fronts made it look derelict. A pang of nostalgia ran through him, for a life he feared might be coming to an end. He'd always had mixed feelings about Cairo: it wasn't a place you could love uncon-ditionally in his view. Still, it had become home, and this wasn't the last memory of it that he wanted to take with him.

'There's a flight to Istanbul leaving in just over an hour.' In the gloom of the interior Winslow held his watch up to catch the strobe of a streetlight. 'I thought we would have more time, to lay the groundwork, to prepare you. That's not the case, so you're going to have to rely on your instincts. We've put together a suitcase for you with some clothes. We had to guess your size but hopefully some of them will fit. Your cover story is that you are in Istanbul to buy used agricultural machinery for resale in Egypt.'

'I know nothing about agricultural machinery.'

'Well, it's not as if you're going to sit an exam. There are some brochures in the bag just in case, and a file with invoices and addresses of suppliers. It all checks out, but you might like to spend a moment familiarising yourself with some of the terminology – grain threshers and so forth. There are a couple of guidebooks and maps in there for good measure. A room has been reserved for you at the Pera Palas hotel. It's one we've used before. If you need to change money, do it in small amounts. Try not to draw attention to yourself, but I don't have to tell you that, do I?'

'How do I explain the British passport?'

'You lived for a time in London. Your wife was from there. She passed away. Now you live in Cairo. Stick as close to the truth as possible, but spare the details.'

The airport was already looming into sight. They were coming off El-Orouba Street. In the distance a wide stretch of open ground was bathed in the orange glow of sodium lighting. The Range Rover slowed and pulled in to the side of the road. Makana glanced back to where a small blue Fiat had been tailing them. It too was drawing to a halt.

'We don't want to announce our connection, so you will be arriving in a regular car.' Winslow removed his glasses and wiped a hand over his face. 'You won't be alone. People will be with you all the time. You won't see them, hopefully, but they'll be there. If anything out of the ordinary happens, you let us know – if you are contacted, or if something goes wrong. I need to know immediately. I can't stress that enough. These things can play out very quickly.' Winslow sat back. 'Any questions?'

'What happens if I don't find him?'

'You'll find him and you'll bring him back. I have complete faith in you.' Winslow smiled, the harsh glare of the lights giving his features a strained, almost macabre edge. 'Don't look so worried, you'll be back here in three days.'

'If everything goes smoothly, you mean.'

'Look on the bright side. This could earn you not only a substantial fee, but also the gratitude of Her Majesty's government.'

'Who could ask for more?'

The air outside was cool, and Makana found the smell of dust strangely reassuring after the interior of the car. To the east the sky was beginning to lighten. The Range Rover pulled smoothly away, its dark windows hiding its passengers. The blue car puttered slowly up to him. Makana got into the front seat beside the driver, who didn't speak. They drove on in silence, passing the ticket barrier and up the ramp to the Departures Hall. The driver got out and opened the boot, took out a slightly battered and rather cheap suitcase and handed it to Makana. Then he got into his car and drove away.

Chapter Five

A t that hour the Departures Hall was a garish grey zone through which travellers stumbled in a haze of suppressed panic and weary resignation. People struggled to push trolleys piled high with monstrous volumes of luggage. Lines of passengers waited their turn at the counters, some patiently, others less so. Makana circled the hall in a random fashion, changing direction as if unsure where to go, hoping this erratic behaviour would reveal anyone who might be following him. Nobody struck him as taking an obvious interest, and so he moved on.

At the security check he handed over his new British passport to the woman in the booth, half expecting it to be met with a laugh. The woman glanced from document to face and back again as if trying to work out which one did not fit. Finally, she summoned her superior, a short, ugly man in an even uglier suit. He leaned over her to examine the document briefly before, with barely a glance at Makana, turning and walking away.

'Is there a problem?' Makana asked.

'Wait,' said the woman curtly, shooing him away with a flick of her fingers. He stepped aside to let the next people through – a couple with a small, bawling child. Over the heads of the other waiting passengers he watched the ugly man disappear into a room on the far side of the hall. It would be a shame, Makana thought, if the whole scheme were to fall at the first hurdle. Having said that, he knew the risk he was running. 'Are you sure you've thought this through?' Jehan had asked him. It was a little late to be thinking about that now. If the passport was rejected he would be lucky to avoid winding up in prison, at the very least. He had the feeling that Marcus Winslow would vanish into the woodwork the moment things turned awkward with Egyptian security, leaving him alone to face the consequences.

A glance at his watch told him that time was running out. If the delay lasted much longer he would miss his plane and that would be the end of it. Asking for more information would provoke them. All he could do was be patient, and wait.

He had just about resigned himself to his fate when a barrel-bellied man in a uniform stepped out of the room and yelled his name.

'Through there.' Makana was ushered into a corridor that led deeper into the building. 'Keep going,' said the voice behind him. Still trailing his suitcase, he walked on until he reached an open door on his left.

'Put your bag on the table, open it up and stand back.'

It was a small, bare room, furnished with only a table against the wall. Doing as he was told, Makana stepped away from the bag. The scruffy officer rummaged through the contents, although with no great conviction. It was possible they were just planning to delay him long enough for his flight to depart. Looking for an explanation was often pointless; sometimes someone simply took a dislike to you and made it their day's decision to make life awkward for you. Makana folded his arms and waited. It took less time than he had expected. A door on the other side of the room opened and another person stepped into the room.

'Lieutenant Sharqi.'

'Major.' Sharqi tapped the eagle on one of his epaulettes.

'Forgive me,' said Makana. 'You've moved up in the world.'

Sharqi snapped his fingers and the immigration officer disappeared from the room without a word.

'Just when I thought that I'd managed to forget your existence, your name comes up again. How am I to explain that, Makana?'

'Maybe it doesn't need explaining.'

'You don't believe in coincidence any more than I do,' said Sharqi. 'Yet here we are.'

'I'm curious. How did you manage to get promoted and demoted to airport security at the same time?'

'I'm not with airport security.' Sharqi turned the passport over in his hands. 'I'm still with military intelligence and counterterrorism. They have to run queries by me.'

'Is there something wrong with the passport?'

'No, nothing. It's perfect. But you know how it is. Sometimes it's just the way you look. A man like you carrying a new British passport.' Sharqi shrugged as though the conclusion was obvious. 'Imagine my surprise to find myself looking at a familiar face with a new name …' He squinted at the page. 'Mustafa Amin, agricultural services? You're selling tractors these days?'

'A man has to make a living.'

'You disappoint me. After all the years we've known each other I would expect you to be a little more honest.'

Makana had first encountered Sharqi some seven years ago, and since then their paths had crossed a number of times. Sharqi was a military man who had started out with the crack Special Forces Unit 777. Over the years, Makana had watched him rise steadily up the ladder of promotion. One thing was for certain: this was no coincidence. If Sharqi was here, it meant he knew something about Makana's mission.

'You know that I'm about to miss my flight?'

'Don't worry about your flight. It leaves when I say so.' Sharqi wagged the passport in the air. 'Do you want to tell me what this is all about?'

'I have a feeling you already know.'

'What are you going to do in Istanbul?' Sharqi picked up the guidebook from Makana's suitcase and idly flipped through it. 'You may think this places you out of my reach, but it doesn't.'

'If you were going to detain me, you would have done so already.'

'We don't have to be enemies. We can help one another.'

'You mean by me telling you what I know?'

'Why not?' Sharqi smiled, revealing a perfect set of even, white teeth. 'You might need my help one day. There are places in this country that not even the British can touch'

'I can't help you, Sharqi, even if I wanted to.'

'You and I have never really seen eye to eye, have we, Makana?' Sharqi glanced at his watch. Perhaps there was a limit to the degree

46

of control he could exercise over air traffic, or perhaps he wasn't that keen on antagonising the British.

'You're out of your depth, Sharqi.' Makana reached for the passport and the other man's hand drew back. Makana sighed. 'If you detain me, or make me miss my flight, you will have to answer for that, and we both know the British will not be happy.'

'I don't work for the British.'

'You're fishing, Sharqi. If I could tell you any more I would have done so by now. You know that.'

'I could still refuse to let you get on that plane.' Despite the passing of the years and his rise in rank, Sharqi still resembled a kid on the school volleyball team.

'We both know you're not going to do that. You can't prove this passport wasn't issued by the British government. Think of your chances of promotion. You have responsibilities now that you're a married man.' Makana nodded at the ring on Sharqi's finger.

Sharqi relented, handing back the passport. 'Just remember …' He leaned close. 'The British have a habit of forgetting who their friends are when they no longer need them. One day you'll be back here with no one to protect you.'

'I'll deal with that when it comes along.'

By the time Makana reached the plane they were ready to close the doors. He struggled to stow his bag and find his seat, aware of the glares he was receiving. When he greeted the ample lady in the seat next to him, he received a practised scowl in return.

It was a long time since Makana had travelled by plane, although things seemed more or less the same as he remembered, a few minor changes aside. His companion gave a cry of horror when he produced his cigarettes and lighter. He put them away quietly.

They were served with a parody of a meal: plastic food on plastic trays thrown at them in rapid succession proved to hold spongy bread rolls covered in cling film and some type of dish that contained meat of no recognisable type along with a heap of soggy rice. Makana decided to steer clear of it. A walk down the length of the plane towards the bathroom gave him a chance to study his fellow passengers. Somewhere among that crowd of faces he suspected were operatives working for Marcus Winslow, possibly with a couple of Egyptian security people thrown in for good measure. Nobody stood out, and he returned to his seat none the wiser, smiling at the large lady, who threw him the same wary look.

Chapter Six

Istanbul Day One

The guidebook Winslow had provided told Makana that Turkey stood on a zone of highly unstable ground: interlocking tectonic plates that left the substrata looking like a jigsaw puzzle. From the air, Istanbul resembled Cairo, if God had picked up the map and crushed it into a ball with his fist. Where Cairo had the Nile running through it like a guideline of clarity, Istanbul was as fractured on the surface as the underlying crust was further down. The Bosporus Strait divided the city into two halves, the Asian and the European, and linked the Black Sea to the north with the Sea of Marmara.

For centuries this spot had marked the centre of the known world. Empires were founded here by the Romans and Byzantines, and stretched far across the globe. The Ottomans succeeded them. When the elegant skyline of the old quarters came into view, the slim minarets and majestic domes were reminders that once this had been the centre of the Caliphate that ruled much of Central Asia as well as the entire Middle East, including Egypt and Sudan. This city had stood since the seventh century BCE. Before the Chinese were ferrying silk through here, there had been jade and precious stones carried by Scythians and Persians. Alexander the Great passed through on his conquest of the East.

None of this was evident from the all too familiar mid-morning traffic chaos on the ride into town. Makana's first impression was a jumble of hills and tightly packed buildings. Concrete lanes had been driven through to help the flow, and these too were familiar.

They drove a little faster here perhaps, and the cars were generally in better condition, but otherwise he felt strangely at home in the grey morning light.

His arrival had gone smoothly. He received no more than a cursory glance from the woman behind the glass screen when he handed over his passport for a tourist visa. That moment stirred Makana with an odd sense of freedom. Unable to travel for so many years, all at once this document, false though it might be, allowed him to move, away from Cairo, from his past. He felt privileged. The thought that there was nothing to prevent him skipping off with both money and passport brought a smile to his face. How long would he have before they caught him? The passport would run out before long, and the money too. But people had made their way in the world with less.

'First time Istanbul?'

Makana became aware that the driver was trying to catch his eye in the mirror as he made conversation, or rather tried to drum up extra work for himself. 'You want Sultan Ahmet Mosque? Blue Mosque? You Muslim?' The neck craned to see him. Was he? In principle yes, since the son of a Muslim is automatically a Muslim. Makana was never quite at ease with that question. Most people were not forward enough to ask; they simply assumed, and he was happy to let them draw their own conclusions.

'For you, I make special price, yes?'

'I'm not going to have much time for sightseeing.'

When they arrived at the hotel the driver leapt out and ordered someone to come and take the bag, giving Makana a chance to study him. At the airport he had simply picked out the most honest face he could see. Now this man handed him a card.

'Koçak, at your service.'

Makana tucked the card away and repeated his words about his limited time, noting that the taxi driver continued to smile and nod regardless, which suggested that he might not have fully understood.

Once through the doors of the hotel, Makana found the striated walls and stained-glass cupolas of the magnificent marbled interior somewhat intimidating. He was the canary in a gilded cage, waiting for a cat to show up. The man behind the reception desk was so short he barely topped the high marble counter. What he lacked in stature he made up for in enthusiasm.

'Welcome, welcome sir, Amin! *Merhaba*. I am Haluk, at your service.'

It was a little disconcerting, but Makana played along. He filled out the forms, answered the questions about his intentions. No, it was his first time in the city and he had heard many good things about the Pera Palas hotel. Yes, he hoped to acquaint himself with some of the city's sights and no, he didn't need a guide.

'We are offering you one of our most popular rooms,' said Haluk triumphantly, as he handed over the key.

A bellboy led the way and Makana followed his suitcase around a corner past a long slab of marble with the names of some of the more illustrious visitors who had stayed here carved in gold lettering: Kemal Atatürk, Grace Kelly and Ernest Hemingway among them. It made it feel less like a hotel and more like a mausoleum.

An ancient elevator with its own operator awaited. The iron gate was squeezed open, doors rattled shut and the operating handle swung into place. They rose shuddering through the building. The room was reassuringly drab after the excesses of the lobby, and Makana tipped the bellboy with some of the money he had changed at the airport. He opened the double doors and stepped out onto the balcony to smoke a cigarette only to be hit by a blast of traffic from a highway that ran just below. So far, so familiar.

A brief survey revealed an electronic safe in the wardrobe. Usually they were left open so that the guest could set their own four-digit code. In this case it was locked. Makana keyed in the last four digits of the telephone number Winslow had given him and it gave a satisfied whirr as it unlocked itself. Inside was an envelope containing five thousand dollars and a small nylon case that held a 9mm pistol: a Turkish-made Yavuz that looked like a local variant of the Browning automatic. There was a spare ammunition clip. He checked that it was clean and the mechanism working smoothly before he replaced it in the safe. Makana had been a good shot back in his days in the police, but as a rule he disliked guns. They created more problems than they solved and he hoped he wouldn't have need of the weapon. Was Winslow preparing for the worst, or had he understated the level of danger Makana was facing?

He found a couple of envelopes in a folder on the dresser, along with more stationery and a room-service menu. He divided all the money into three parts and locked two envelopes inside the safe. After that he lay down on the bed and stared at the ceiling. The hotel was, he realised now, one of the biggest and best-known in Istanbul. Atatürk himself, father of the nation, had stayed here, as well as all those foreign celebrities, writers and actors. It wasn't the kind of place you would stay if you wanted to keep a low profile.

Makana closed his eyes and tried, unsuccessfully, to catch up on the sleep he'd missed the night before. Whenever he was about to slip away he found his eyes opening. A glass cabinet on the wall housed a couple of shelves laden with dog-eared paperbacks. Over it hung a large photograph of a middle-aged English woman. No matter where he stood in the room she was staring at him. Abandoning all hope of rest, Makana got to his feet and lit a cigarette before wandering over to investigate. The cabinet was locked with a cheap padlock and there was no key in sight. Under other circumstances he might have been curious as to who this woman was. As things stood she served only to remind him that he was here in the service of the British government – not something he felt comfortable about.

He decided to unpack the bag Winslow had prepared for him and discovered a new set of clothes. Cotton shirts, trousers, a light grey suit. All Egyptian-made. All very nice. After emptying the bag of its contents he ran his fingers around the lining, looking for anything that shouldn't be there. Satisfied the bag was clean, he hung the suit up in the wardrobe and studied it for a moment. Perhaps this was the start of a new life.

After that he called the number for Nadir Sulayman's office and spoke to an assistant of some kind who arranged for him to meet Mr Sulayman that evening after office hours. Taking the street map Winslow had placed in his bag, Makana decided to avoid the rickety lift and instead took the staircase to the lobby, where he circled looking for anything that seemed out of place. He sat in the Orient Bar and ordered coffee. A crowd of elderly Japanese women tottered in twos and threes past his table wearing transparent plastic ponchos and sun visors. They smiled at him and bowed as they went by.

When he'd finished his coffee Makana left the hotel. It was early afternoon. He spent the next hour or so exploring the immediate vicinity, and walked a couple of blocks either way, to orient himself. He located the Iskander Grillroom on the main avenue of Istiklal Street and started towards it.

Although the city was alien to him, Makana could already sense enough that was familiar for him to feel at ease. He didn't understand the language but there were words that he recognised, in speech, in the names along the street. He even saw a shop selling *dendourma*, which took him back to childhood memories of the ice-cream man who used to cycle around his neighbourhood. The Ottomans had left their traces in many places far from here. In that sense being here was like calling in on some distant, forgotten relative.

The Iskander Grillroom was a simple, unremarkable restaurant. He had already passed half a dozen almost identical places. The façade was brightly lit, with the name emblazoned in cheap lettering painted on red glass. The interior was gloomy, lending the place a desolate air. The tiled floor and steel counter gave it a dated look. The bar ran along the right-hand side of the room and a glass-fronted display cabinet offered refrigerated shelves of prepared dishes. Behind this a young man shaved thin slices of meat from a rotating column of lamb using an electric knife. The buzz of the knife competed with the hissing of steam from the coffee machine and a radio that emitted bursts of song broken by excited talk.

Makana chose a table close to the wall, about halfway back, and sat facing the street. The waiter was a surly man with hollow cheeks peppered in black stubble. He dragged himself away from the paper he was reading and wandered over. Makana pointed to the gyrating meat, and the man grunted something that sounded like a question.

'*Çay*,' replied Makana, having learned that the Turkish word for tea was, unsurprisingly, the same word as in Arabic. Satisfied, the waiter retreated, calling out the order.

People came and went. There was nothing remarkable about the place, but it was clearly popular. A steady stream of visitors came and went. Young men in leather jackets ordered sandwiches, more smartly dressed people in suits stopped by for a snack, clutching bags of takeaway food as they left. Along the window a couple of solitary old men lingered over coffee as they watched the street go by.

Along the wall to Makana's right hung a row of black and white photographs of the city back in the Fifties. From reading the guide-book on the plane he recognised the Hagia Sophia, Topkapi Palace, and the six minarets that provided the Blue Mosque with its distinct silhouette. The stark monochrome images restored some of the dignity the present seemed to have lost.

Makana drank his tea and dug his way through the heap of sliced kebab. As he ate, with the slow deliberation of a man who has nowhere to go, he realised how hungry he was. The food was not bad, familiar and yet slightly different from what he was used to. The waiter had settled himself back on his bar stool, where he sat smoking and flicking through a magazine, lifting his eyes only to follow a pretty woman walking by.

As he ate, Makana went back over the reason he was here. Ayman Nizari. This place represented the weakest link in the plan. Sitting here day after day would make him a target, and there was no guarantee that Nizari would actually show.

He inspected the rest of the clientele. In the far corner a man in his sixties chewed on a toothpick and stared at the street. His face showed what looked like three days of stubble. He was clearly a regular. From time to time he made a loud comment. It wasn't clear who these were addressed to, but they were generally ignored. The waiter carried on with his work. The man behind the counter occasionally replied but most of the time pretended to be busy with something.

Two tables away sat a young woman reading a book. She made a point of not looking at the old man, who was clearly seeking an audience. The waiter came by once in a while but was respectful of her space. All the way over on the other side of the room sat a couple of tourists. They were consulting a guidebook and asked the waiter for advice. A French flag on the girl's rucksack suggested where they came from. None of them looked promising.

By the clock above the bar it was one o'clock, the time for the arranged rendezvous. Makana ordered more tea. The whole idea was flawed. It wouldn't take long for anyone running surveillance to figure out what was going on. They would have two or three days at the most; after that the whole operation would be at risk.

He drank his tea. Nobody showed. The restaurant emptied and then filled again – shoppers pausing to sit for a while eating pastries, families with children clamouring for ice cream and Coca-Cola. The old man in the corner departed, casting him a wary glance as he went. Makana understood why: he was the incongruous element. It was plain he was waiting for something or someone.

An hour after the rendezvous, Makana decided he needed to leave. He left the café and circled the block, pausing to look in shop windows and doubling back until he was sure he wasn't being followed. It was always possible that Nizari was keeping his distance, watching from some vantage point. He was again reminded how little he knew about the Iraqi.

As he made his way down through the town, Makana reflected on the fact that he was in a strange city, doing a job for someone he wasn't sure he trusted, looking for a man he didn't know. That made him wonder about Nizari. How was he surviving in Istanbul? Did he have friends here? Money? A place to stay? There were too many un-answered questions, too many loose ends. Makana had been hoping for a quick resolution. Now he had the sense that wouldn't happen.

In one of the sidestreets near the Galata Tower he found what he was looking for: the Sultana Harem Hotel was a simple estab-lishment with a modest two stars to its name. The narrow entrance presented a squeaky aluminium door and a narrow set of stairs leading up to a reception area on the first floor that was just about big enough to turn a suitcase around in. Behind the desk sat a young man with earplugs fixed and his eyes set on the flashing colours of a computer screen. He looked surprised, as if he had no idea where he was or what he was doing here.

'Do you have a room?' asked Makana in English.

'Room?' echoed the man cautiously. He got to his feet and leaned over to yell something through the doorway behind him. He waited for a time and then, muttering to himself, he sat back down.

'You want room?'

'That's right.'

'One room. How many peoples? How many nights?'

'One people,' said Makana, mirroring the other man's English in an attempt to ease communication. 'Three nights, maybe more. I can pay in advance. Cash.'

The sight of the money seemed to resolve whatever doubts the receptionist had. The young man was not concerned that his new guest did not have a bag, nor did he bother to record his details. He barely glanced at the card Makana filled in before tossing it to one side. He seemed to be sitting in for someone. A key was handed over and Makana climbed a narrow, twisting staircase that had recently been painted a drab shade of green with purple stripes. On the third floor he wrestled with the lock before edging into a narrow room the size of his bathroom at the Pera Palas. He tested the bed cautiously. A television mumbled in a neighbouring room. As for the view, it was possible to glimpse a little patch of blue sky above the gap before the next-door building. It was noisy and cramped and somewhat run-down, but it would serve his purposes.

He looked at his watch: time to go. Another advantage of the hotel was that it was possible to take the stairs all the way down to the street without passing the reception desk. He glanced through the open doorway and saw the young man, now busy chatting on the telephone. He didn't look round as Makana slipped by. At the foot of the narrow staircase Makana pulled open the aluminium door and stepped out into the busy street. Again he took the precaution of walking a round-about route, doubling back on himself several times. None of these manoeuvres revealed anyone who appeared to be following him.

It was strange, the idea that he could be under surveillance – a reversal of his usual situation. As he turned through the cramped locality Makana began to get a sense of the city closing in on him. The steep, narrow streets rose and fell, dark grey buildings loomed on either side. Cats pooled together in doorways, waving their tails softly as they watched him go by.

Back at the Pera Palas, Makana spent the next couple of hours listening to the sound of the traffic droning by down below. He used the telephone in his room to call Sami's journalist friend, Kursad.

'I'm trying to find someone who was involved recently in a traffic accident.'

'Can you be more specific?'

'Not really,' said Makana. He gave him the dates for when Ayman Nizari would have arrived in Istanbul. 'This accident would have involved a couple of vehicles at least, and there may have been something unusual about it. I'm afraid I can't tell you what.'

Kursad laughed. 'Sami said working with you would be interesting.'

After that Makana went back over the scene in the Iskander Grillroom. He tried to recall the faces of the people he had seen in there. The old man sitting in the window. The people who came and went. The noisy ones, the quiet ones, the tourists, passers-by. Nothing had attracted his attention, but maybe he hadn't been looking properly. He tried to think of anything that might have spooked Nizari from approaching. Nothing stood out, but he filed away the faces in his memory.

The old hotel hummed around him. He could hear the lift rising, stopping and then descending again. Like slow steady breathing. How much danger was he in, he wondered. Marcus Winslow had been cautious, but the chance of Mossad involvement did put a certain slant on things. He checked that the money was still in the safe, then removed the Yavuz, unloaded it and took it to pieces to make sure it was clean and in good working order. He took his time. The exercise brought back memories of when he was a cadet, of his days as an inspector, when he had an office of his own and reported to Chief Haroun. Makana was not given to nostalgia, but the action of dismantling and reassembling the Yavuz had a thera-peutic effect. By the time he was finished he felt calmer. It wasn't much, he reflected, as he returned the gun to the safe, but he felt as if he had actually achieved something.

By six o'clock the sky had grown dense and overcast. It felt as though it was about to rain. Makana circled the lobby, which was crowded with retired Americans wearing baseball caps and che-quered trousers. They studied him with the wary look of those who expect to find a terrorist behind every unfamiliar face.

On his walk earlier he had noted the location of three call shops, all within ten minutes of the hotel. The nearest, the Mukarrameh, had a view of Mecca daubed on the front window. The interior was divided by plywood partitions and a counter that could have been built by a one-armed gorilla. The man who lurked behind this was pale enough to be Slavic. He had a broad red beard that came halfway down his shirt. He wasn't big on conversation, wordlessly indicating a row of booths in the back. Makana dialled the number on the card Marcus Winslow had given him and it was answered on the third ring.

'Everything all right?'

'Nothing to complain about so far. I had a look at the place. I'll be there tomorrow.'

Through the little porthole in the door Makana watched the counter. Redbeard was talking to a young man wearing sunglasses.

'Remember, you must make contact with Nizari as soon as possible. If we're lucky, he'll be as keen to leave as you are. Take in the sights, whatever, just make sure you are at the rendezvous on time every day.'

On the wall, just in front of his nose, was a sticker bearing a printed page from a Quran. Surat al-Qamar: The Moon.

'Did you notice anything out of the ordinary?' asked Winslow.

'Everything is out of the ordinary. I'm in a city I don't know, travelling under another name.'

'I see what you mean.'

'Is there anything else I should know?'

There was a pause, not long and not short, but it was there. 'All you need to do is focus on doing exactly what I told you. Everything else will take care of itself. When are you planning to meet Nadir Sulayman?'

'As soon as this call is over.'

'Then I won't keep you.'

The line went dead. Makana sat for a moment with the receiver in his hand. Then he hung up and stepped out of the booth. The man with the sunglasses had vanished. A noisy group of teenagers were gathered round a computer in one corner doing something immoral, or so it appeared from the look on Redbeard's face. He handed Makana his change without even looking at him.

Chapter Seven

O utside, night had fallen and the air was damp with a light driz-
zle. Makana turned up the collar of his jacket against a chill
wind that blew in from the sea. With the sun gone, the temperature
was dropping. Persians, Spartans, Byzantines, Romans, the city's
history was a parade of kings, emperors, conquerors and pretend-
ers; this was the grand prize. Constantine, Tamerlane, Suleyman
the Magnificent, Alp Arslan. All of them tried, only some of them
succeeded, The weight of history clung here the way damp clung to
the stone walls. It had the romance of a seaport, a place of departures and arrivals, of loves lost and battles won, of distant palaces
and forgotten kingdoms. For centuries this had been the centre of
the known world. Leave here in any direction, and you were sailing
into darkness.

Nadir Sulayman's office was on the third floor of a ramshackle
building close to the Çukurcuma baths. The entrance was in a
covered alleyway. A worn staircase, the steps rounded by time, led
up to an open gallery that ran around the building's inner court. He
felt as if he was entering a medieval fortress. Cables and old washing lines looped across from one side to the other. Canned applause
from a television echoed through the space overhead. On the far
side of the gallery a heavy wooden door set in a stone archway
displayed a brass plaque: Sulayman Enterprise Company. Over
the door a naked yellow bulb glowed faintly. When he pressed the
doorbell a hatch slid open to reveal a face framed by the square-cut
metal grille. Before he had time to explain who he was the hatch
slid closed again and a moment later the door opened to reveal
a thin-lipped woman dressed in a housecoat. Clearly in a hurry,

she sped away from him, speaking over her shoulder as she went. Makana took it as an invitation to follow her.

Once inside, he found himself in a long corridor. The woman disappeared down a hallway to the right. There was nobody else in sight. The reception area had a stone floor and battered walls on which hung a couple of canvases of nude figures that might have been human or animal. Perhaps a mix of the two. Not so much a display of talent as of confusion. On the left-hand side another arched door led deeper into the building. It was slightly ajar. Makana knocked and pushed.

The way was barred by heavy drapes. Fighting his way through these he found himself in a large, cluttered room, its high ceiling browned with age, stained with dirt and nicotine. The corner windows offered a welcome surprise: a panoramic view of the skyline descending towards the Golden Horn, and beyond that, across the water, to Seraglio Point and Topkapi Palace. The open vista stood in stark contrast to the cluttered room. Here it was hardly possible to move for the cardboard boxes stacked waist-high. Some of these contained books or stacks of files, others sprouted styrofoam pellets, heaps of magazines and newspapers, even pairs of jeans. The office seemed to function as a showroom, depot, archive and general living quarters.

The eye at the centre of this storm sat with his back to Makana. He was reclining in a large leather chair in the midst of the chaos, a telephone in one hand and a bottle of beer in the other. His feet, shod with a pair of unlaced basketball boots, rested on the window-sill alongside a row of half-finished cups of tea and boxes that had once held takeaway meals.

'Yes?' the man asked as he swung round.

'We had an appointment.' Makana tapped his watch. 'I came from Cairo.'

Nadir Sulayman could only be described as scruffy-looking. Around fifty years old, he dressed like a man twenty years younger. His hair was long and his eyebrows thick and dark, almost joining in the middle. The grey streaks in his hair betrayed his age, as did the expanding waistline, a comfortable paunch that jutted from his denim jacket when he stood up to shake Makana's hand.

'Forgive me,' he said, wagging the telephone in the air before dropping it onto the table. 'My mind was distracted. Some people can't get over the sound of their own voice.' He gestured for Makana to sit before rushing round the desk to clear the chair he had just offered him. An armful of clothing wrapped in plastic was unceremoniously dumped onto the mountain of objects that partially concealed a sofa.

'Please,' he gestured again. Makana sat, inadvertently dislodging a stack of travel brochures as he did so. The other man ignored them.

'Tell me,' said Sulayman, going back behind his desk and picking up a pack of Marlboros. 'Everything is okay? No problems?'

'No problems.'

'Good. Good.' Nadir Sulayman lit a cigarette, dropped the lighter on the table and rubbed a hand over his face as if to clear his mind. He sank back down into the big chair and glanced left and right, as if expecting another question to appear before him. 'This is good. We want everything to proceed smoothly.' He nodded to himself and then looked up. 'Did you make contact with your passenger?'

'No luck, I'm afraid. It might take a couple of days.'

Sulayman held up both palms. 'All of that is your business. I don't want to know anything. When you are ready you call me and we go to work, okay?'

'Okay.' Makana took another look around the room. Whatever else it might have said about Nadir Sulayman, it didn't proclaim his skills of organisation. 'What exactly is your plan?'

'No problem. I tell you but …' Nadir Sulayman sat back. 'Before we go into details, do you have something for me … ?'

Makana produced an envelope containing five thousand dollars. Sulayman took a moment to thumb through the contents.

'What is this?'

'I was told you would receive half now and half later.'

'Yes, but this is not enough.' He tossed the envelope back onto the desk. 'Not enough. I have people who are waiting to be paid. Additional costs. A job like this is complicated. You can't take chances.'

'I'm sure we can reach an agreement.'

'I hope so, because otherwise I can do nothing.' Nadir Sulayman tapped ash into a heavy cut-glass bowl out of which a winged sprite rose up. 'I only work with the best. In this business they don't wait around. Either you produce the money or they are gone.'

'I can check with Cairo.'

'You call Winslow. I told him the price would be higher.'

'The main thing is that everything is in place. Once I have our passenger we'll have to move fast.'

'You don't have to worry. Everything will be taken care of.'

Sulayman waved smoke aside as he rummaged through the clutter on the table until a map of the city surfaced. Spreading it out, he pinpointed a spot with a stubby finger, sprinkling a halo of cigarette ash around it. 'Ortaköy Mosque. The van will be waiting there for you. Blue van. No windows. Two drivers. Nobody else. The van is not there, you see another car, anything at all, and you walk away. You go somewhere else. Not back to hotel. Somewhere new. You give me a call.'

From his desk Sulayman produced a small mobile phone which he handed over. 'Only one number on it. Not registered. You call me if you have problems. I do the same.' He leaned back and studied Makana for a moment.

'You're not what I expected. I don't know who you are or what you are transporting. It's better I don't know.' He got to his feet again and held out his hand. 'I'm sorry about the misunderstanding, but people don't realise the risk I am running here. If things go wrong I am the one who is caught with his trousers down. You understand?'

'I think so.'

The two men shook hands.

'The rest of the money. Tomorrow, please, or else my hands are tied.'

As he left the building Makana wondered what it was that was making Sulayman so nervous. Perhaps he was always like that, or perhaps it was just Makana's own imagination running rings around itself.

It wasn't that late and yet the street felt oddly quiet. The rain had stopped and the sky appeared to have cleared. He even thought he could see a couple of stars out over the dark water, above the glow of the city. He breathed in the night air and began what was becoming routine, walking in a seemingly aimless fashion, moving up and down the streets, changing direction until he felt sure that no one was behind him. The walk cleared his head, but it also reminded him that he hadn't eaten for hours. He was just off the main pedestrian street when he came across a small restaurant tucked into the corner of a tiny square.

The interior was deserted but for the staff. A woman knelt behind a low table patiently rolling out rolls of dough into flat sheets. She looked up as he came in but said nothing. Makana chose a table close to the door. There was no menu, no plastic-coated sheets with pictures on them. It was almost as if you had stepped into somebody's living room. A bearded man emerged from a doorway in the back and came over to speak to him. Makana signalled that he didn't understand, so the man repeated what he had said in Turkish interspersed with a few words in English, all the time pointing to the low grill that sat in an open fireplace at the far end of the room. A cook was stoking the coals using tongs and a set of leather bellows that looked as though they had been borrowed from a museum. The bearded man growled something and the cook held up several long steel skewers with elaborate brass handles. Makana nodded and they took that for an answer.

While he waited they brought him tea. The bearded man lost interest in him and went back to sit cross-legged on the floor totting up numbers in a battered school exercise book to which a broken biro was attached by the use of string and Sellotape. The woman rolling out the dough got to her feet slowly and moved across the room as if sleepwalking towards a round clay oven. She stretched a sheet of dough onto a large glove and then reached in through the circular mouth to slap them on the inside of the bulbous oven. The flickering flames bathed her face in a warm glow.

Makana was happy to be ignored. He had been in Istanbul for only a few hours, and yet he had the feeling that he had walked into something much deeper than he had expected. If he was in such a hurry to leave here, Ayman Nizari should have been at the meeting place today as agreed. Did that mean something had happened to him? Had the Mossad caught up, or someone else?

If they had not, then Nizari was somehow managing to stay alive and out of sight. How? Where was he sleeping? Who was feeding him? Nizari didn't want to end up in the hands of the Israelis, and that was understandable. His past record made him a dangerous asset, even without the association with Abu Hilal. What had happened in Marbella had clearly scared him – also understandable. He'd scrapped his dreams of cashing in on his skills and decided to trade in what he knew about a dangerous terrorist in exchange for asylum in Britain and medical treatment for his wife. Whichever way you looked at it, Ayman Nizari was playing a dangerous game.

Through the window he saw a few stray people hurrying by across the square. None of them paid attention to the restaurant. They looked as if they were making their way home. A boy carrying a bundle of newspapers leaned through the doorway and shouted something. The old man replied without looking up and the boy took himself off. There seemed to be no real rush, which was fine, had he not been starving. The cook was wagging a fan made of straw at the coals. He seemed to be taking his time. The smell of roasting meat stoked Makana's hunger.

Nizari would have known that hinting he had information about Nasra would make it impossible for Makana not to come to Istanbul. So the question was, did he really know something, or had he just picked up information somewhere that he decided to use in his hour of need? Chief Haroun was one of the straightest people Makana had ever known. He asked for loyalty and disliked intrigue. He had a strong sense of right and wrong. It was hard to reconcile that kind of a man with someone who developed chemical weapons for a living. What kind of relationship could have existed between the two men? It was always possible that Haroun had known nothing of Nizari's past, that while he was living in Khartoum he had another story to tell, one that gave nothing away about his profession, but that was asking a lot. Had Nizari and Haroun been close? What had happened to Nizari during his years in Khartoum?

The woman appeared at the table, breaking into his train of thoughts as she set down a basket of bread fresh from the oven. Makana thanked her. She held his gaze for a moment too long before turning away. He ignored it, having accepted that here he was something of an unknown quantity. His clothes, his accent, the colour of his skin, all painted him as an outsider.

When the kofta arrived, it was as good as his instincts had told him it would be. When he came to leave he found the woman blocking his way. Close up he could see she was older than he had thought, in her late forties or early fifties. She began to speak. The bearded man came over but the woman shook off his efforts to lead her away. Speaking urgently, she seemed to be repeating the same words over and over.

'What is it? What is she saying?'

The man pried her hand loose from Makana's arm and tugged at her, trying to lead her away.

'Crazy woman.'

Makana reached out to stop her.

'Wait. What is it? What are you trying to tell me?'

The woman turned to face him. He searched her eyes for some sense of meaning. Something was upsetting her. Then, to his surprise she smiled at him. She stretched out a hand to take his.

'She is here.'

'Who?' asked Makana. 'Who is here?'

But the man had had enough. He was yelling by now. Shoving her ahead of him.

'Wait a moment. Let her speak,' said Makana, but it was too late. With a final, mournful glance, the woman turned and made for the back of the restaurant, disappearing through a doorway on the right.

'*Majnun*,' said the man, tapping the side of his head to make his meaning clear. It was unnecessary. The word was the same in Arabic.

'Is she going to be all right?' he asked. The man nodded, impatient to get him out of the door and away from there, a mixture of impatience and embarrassment.

Makana had once known a woman, a neighbour of his grandmother's, years ago, who claimed to have the gift of seeing things. She saw the dead and could commune with departed relatives. All of that was strictly speaking *haram*, but like so many things it came from another place, older, more deeply rooted in the African beliefs that had existed long before Islam arrived. People don't just shake such things off. They hide them, put them aside until there is a need for them. As a child it had been somewhat alarming, but what surprised Makana was that his feelings right now were not so much different from then.

What had she meant? He knew what he wanted to believe she meant: that she was referring to his daughter, Nasra. But the fact was she could have been talking about anything, or anyone. She might be so far out in her own little orbit that she was not connected to anything in this world.

Back on Istiklal Street men stood idly around in the shadows, calling out offers of illicit pleasure: contraband cigarettes, hashish, willing women. It was late now and groups of men had replaced the families that had been strolling through earlier. Drunken tourists were making a nuisance of themselves. Makana cut through the crowd, remembering a shortcut to his hotel he had discovered that afternoon. He was almost there when it happened.

At first he thought it was an accident. The three figures in dark clothes turned into the shortcut through the alleyway. He moved to step aside to let them by. They brushed past him, a little too close, a little roughly, but still, not enough for him to take offence. If it had ended there. Only it didn't. Instead of moving on they fenced him in, pressing him against the wall. His shoulders were forced back as one of them tried to grab his arm. Makana managed to slip his right arm free and swung his elbow, feeling it connect with someone's jaw. There was a satisfying cry of pain, but his triumph was short-lived. The third one stepped up in front of him. He had the hard face of a man who had seen the inside of a prison. The youngest was in his twenties. The others were older. A smell of alcohol and some kind of machine oil came off the man to his right, the one nursing his jaw.

All further thoughts were suspended as the man in front of him hit him low down in the gut. He felt the air fly out of him and doubled up, receiving another blow to the side of the head. Not from a fist, but a hard, solid object that sent him reeling. They

66

let him slide down, out of their hands, no longer a threat, and he landed up on the cold, damp ground that smelled of cats. He felt their hands running expertly over him, reaching into his jacket, and he remembered with regret that he had his passport on him. Through the ringing in his head he heard a shout. Then came the sound of feet running away, and they were gone. Makana tried to sit up. A man wearing a kitchen apron had stepped out from a doorway, about to light a cigarette. He threw this aside as he was joined by another, and both of them spoke to him as they helped him to his feet, Turkish first and then in English.

'You okay? Good? Police?'

Makana insisted that he was fine. He was not keen on involving the police at this stage. He assured them he would be all right and thanked them for their kindness. Leaving them muttering about what the world had come to, he walked on, a little unsteadily. His wallet had also been taken, but he still had the phone Nadir Sulayman had given him.

The Pera Palas was closer than he had thought. It took him less than ten minutes to get back. Haluk, the receptionist, raised his eyes when he saw the state he was in.

'Mr Amin, you have accident?'

'I'm afraid so. Nothing too serious.'

'Oh, but it looks terrible! The head. I call doctor for you?' The little man was beside himself.

'I don't think that's necessary. But perhaps you have something so I can clean myself up?'

'But of course.'

Haluk produced a large first-aid kit for Makana to take up to the room with him. Already they were receiving more than enough attention from other hotel guests in the lobby and reception. The prospect of climbing the stairs was beyond him, but then he had to endure the stares of a young couple in the lift. He nodded a civil greeting that was completely ignored. They were dressed up in evening clothes, as if they had spent the night on the town. Beside them, he felt like a caveman who had wandered in from the wilderness.

Chapter Eight

Istanbul Day Two

M akana took a long warm shower before cleaning up the cuts on his forehead and the scrapes on his hands and knees. The damage wasn't too bad, although the trousers he had on were ruined. He opened up the safe to check that everything was still there, and weighed the Yavuz in his hand before replacing it, grateful that he hadn't been carrying it. It could have ended much worse for him.

After closing the safe he collapsed, exhausted, onto the bed and fell at once into a deep sleep. He woke a few hours later feeling better, although the slightest movement told him his body had stiffened up. He could feel the soreness in his ribs and arms as well as a dull ache in his head. He got up and swallowed a couple of aspirins and then stepped out onto the balcony to smoke a cigarette.

In his mind he ran over the attack again. Was there anything to indicate it had been more than a simple mugging? He didn't exactly look like a wealthy tourist, but he was off the beaten track. Perhaps he had presented too tempting a target?

As Makana looked down over the city, he realised how completely he was working in the dark. He had to assume that everything could be connected. Nadir Sulayman, who ought to have been an ally, struck him as the kind who would trade off any partnership against a better offer. The mercenary kind. Come to that, Makana wasn't even sure how far he could trust Winslow. Even if he was being entirely truthful with Makana, there was always the fact that, no matter which way you looked at it, he was an Englishman. Winslow had his own interests at heart, and what he understood of the world would not always chime with how things really were. Winslow was an outsider. They both were. Trusting him was one thing, relying on his judgement was something else again. Makana ground his cigarette butt under his heel. He had a bad feeling it was all about to unravel, right before his eyes.

The airy dining room where they served breakfast still had a touch of faded nineteenth-century luxury about it. It wasn't hard to imagine starched Englishwomen and their travelling companions drinking tea while deciding which sights to visit that day. There was something dated about the staff too, in their threadbare uniforms. The food however – yoghurt and fresh figs, dried fruit, scrambled eggs – was good, and Makana ate more than his fair share. In the broad light of day the previous night's events seemed hard to believe, had it not been for the aches and pains in his body.

But although the violence lingered, his mind kept returning to the earlier incident at the restaurant with the woman who'd wanted to speak to him. The loss of his passport should have been more of a concern, yet it was that brief episode that stuck in his mind. Was she deranged, or had she really seen something? And if so, what exactly?

When he emerged from the dining room the little receptionist bounded up.

'Mr Amin Bey, how are you feeling this day, after your terrible ordeal last night?'

'Much better Haluk, thank you.' At some stage Makana would have to inform him about the loss of his passport, but it might be wise to speak to Winslow first.

'I am so happy to hear. Amin Bey, you have a visitor waiting for you.' He shook his head. 'This city is plagued by outsiders coming here to seek their fortune by any means. Scoundrels!'

He hurried away, leaving Makana to find his way back to the front lobby, where he was surprised to find Koçak, the taxi driver from the previous day, waiting for him. He jumped to his feet as Makana appeared.

'*Merhaba*, I hope you good sleeping.' A broad grin split his bristly face.

'Did we have an appointment?'

'Most definitely, *effendim*.' Koçak beamed. 'I promise to show you best sights in Istanbul.'

Makana was pretty sure that he had not made an agreement to go sightseeing. On the other hand, perhaps it made sense to at least look like a dutiful tourist.

'I only have a couple of hours free.'

'No problem, *effendim*.'

It was a sunny day and Koçak was eager to convince his passenger that he had made the right decision.

'You are wise man,' he said, wagging his head as he watched Makana in the mirror. 'Everybody hurry hurry, but Istanbul has been here thousands of years.' He chuckled at his own wisdom. 'I take you Sultanahmet and Hagia Sophia. For a good Muslim is best. Topkapi Palace tomorrow, maybe?'

'Maybe,' conceded Makana. If all went according to plan, he hoped to be on his way across the border by then.

At the Hagia Sophia, Koçak re-enacted the actions of Mehmet the Conqueror, when the city first fell before him. Kneeling on the ground, the taxi driver took a handful of dust and threw it over his head, much to the amusement of other onlookers.

'He is wearing turban on his head, yes? He want to show, I am good man, honest man, so he kneel before this great building. He gives thanks to God for his victory.'

'An act of humility,' said Makana, helping the man to his feet. There was something endearing about the hard-working driver.

Crowds milled around the entrance of the famous Sultan Ahmet Mosque. Dazed tourists trailed behind weary guides trying their best to sound excited about a story they had already told a thousand and one times. Makana threaded his way through and up the front steps. Removing his shoes, he placed them on one of the low wooden shelves that flanked the entrance before stepping over the threshold. The interior of the mosque was dominated by impressive vaulted arches that surrounded the central dome. A band of golden letters spelled out phrases from the holy book. The massive pillars were decked with the coloured tiles that gave the building its nickname, the Blue Mosque. A low-hanging halo of lights floated in the dark air as if suspended by a mystic force.

70

Makana experienced the odd and inexplicable comfort he often felt in such places. He was not an observant man, but he had been brought up as a Muslim. Although familiar with Islamic tradition, he felt more connected to the long history of dissenters, to men like Al-Hallaj, who was hanged in Baghdad in the tenth century and then cut into quarters for good measure. Makana had a suspicion, which came back to him whenever he entered such places, that in another age he too would have been declared an apostate.

He paused, glancing over his shoulder, and ran a swift eye over the other people moving around the mosque. It was a habit now, but after last night he felt he should be even more vigilant. Only one figure stood out – a solitary woman. In itself it seemed unusual to see a lone female visitor in a place like this. There was something about her that did not quite fit. She didn't look local, but if she was a tourist then it seemed unlikely for her to be alone. He searched for signs of a family somewhere at a distance, a husband or group of friends, but found nobody as far as he could see. He examined her again. She was dressed from head to toe in black, her head covered by a black scarf. She had her back to him and Makana moved cautiously, circling around to try and catch a glimpse of her face.

As if she sensed his attention the woman began moving towards the exit on the far side. Some impulse made Makana follow. A crowd blocked his way. He pushed his way through and finally reached the wide doors that led to the inner yard. By the time he reached them she was already halfway across, moving swiftly away from him.

The marble was cool beneath his feet. He walked quickly, aware that she was raising her pace towards an exit on the far side. By the time he reached it there was no sign of her. Just a black headscarf lying on the steps, abandoned in haste. He picked it up. It told him nothing. It was as if she had vanished into thin air.

Koçak was waiting by the car when Makana came out. Tossing his cigarette aside, he straightened up.

'*Merhaba*,' he beamed. 'Most beautiful mosque in world, yes?'

'Sure,' said Makana, accepting the offer of a cigarette. It was his first taste of local tobacco, and it wasn't bad. He made a note of the brand, Samsun, and decided it was a decent alternative to his usual Cleopatras, which were fast running out. The two of them smoked in silence, Koçak seeming to guess that he had something on his mind. Makana tried to make sense of what had just happened. Had the woman been watching him in the mosque, or had she simply panicked when he came after her? It could all have been a product of his imagination, after his experience last night. The scarf was the kind that could be picked up from a box by the door for female visitors. It could easily have been dropped by a careless tourist. There were enough of them about. Coincidence, then, or something more? Either way, he was no longer in the mood for sightseeing. He looked at his watch. It was still early. Koçak interpreted the gesture as eagerness.

'Maybe you want see Basilica water cistern, very famous, built by Romans.'

'How about some *çay*?'

Koçak's face lit up. 'Tea? But of course. Please.' He opened the taxi door and Makana climbed in. The faces of the people in the square gave way to those on the streets leading away from the tourist attractions. Makana watched them all, not knowing really what he was looking for, or who. They drank tea by a railing overlooking the Golden Horn.

'*Effendim*. You are very worry man. Always thinking, thinking!' Koçak threw up his arms. 'Allah! Life is not for thinking, but for life itself.'

'You may have a point,' agreed Makana.

'What is problem?' Koçak twisted his hand in the air as if trying to depict a strange creature that defied description.

'I came here to do a job, and now I'm not sure if I know what I'm doing.'

'Ah, I understand. Nothing is more worry than work.' Koçak shook his head, trying to look stern, but failed and broke into another smile.

On the drive back up to the hotel he caught Makana's eye in the mirror.

'You have family, *effendim*? Wifes, childrens?'

'A long time ago. One wife, one daughter.'

'Only one?' Koçak's face lit up. 'There is your problem. You must have more children. A man needs children.'

Makana was reminded of Sindbad. Was there some law of the universe whereby ancient sages were reborn as taxi drivers? He decided to remain silent. He tipped Koçak well and consented to another attempt at seeing the city's sights the following morning. If anyone was watching him it would give him the appearance of a tourist with time to kill. And if all went well he would already be on his way out of here.

Chapter Nine

The mood at the Iskander Grillroom had not improved overnight. Nor had the décor, which somehow looked even more
gloomy.

The waiter had the same dour look on his face. He hadn't shaved,
although his stubble didn't seem to have grown either, which was
something of a mystery. Makana chose a table against the wall
where he had a clear view of the door and the street through the
window. Deciding that words were not the currency in this place, he
pointed at one of the photographs above the counter. The waiter
spun on his heels, calling out the order as he went. He appeared
to remember Makana, as he brought him tea without being asked.
After that he returned to his stool at the bar where a cigarette
smouldered and a newspaper was folded over to the page that he
now resumed reading.

As before, the place was almost empty. Makana studied all of the
customers in turn. He saw nothing too alarming in the couple holding hands over by the wall. An intellectual type wearing a tweed
jacket and thick-rimmed glasses was using a pencil to underline
passages in the book he was reading. Elsewhere, two young men in
leather jackets looked like pickpockets taking a break. Nobody bore
any resemblance to the images he had seen of Ayman Nizari.

The food, when it arrived, was a disappointment – a heap of
döner kebab meat and bread swimming in tomato sauce. Makana
ate a couple of bites before pushing it aside. At the table next to him
a grey-haired man gazed so mournfully at the plate that Makana
was tempted to offer it to him, but didn't want to cause offence.
Instead, he sipped his tea and smoked another cigarette. A tall

European man entered and settled himself at a table in the corner before producing a guidebook from his rucksack and ordering a beer.

A crumpled local English-language newspaper had been left behind on the next table, and Makana spent some time reading through it with one eye on the door. The front page was dominated by stories about a new shopping mall, recently inaugurated by a government minister. Museum visits had broken new records this year, ran another item, alongside pictures of tourists, waving and smiling. A visiting trade delegation from China was in town, hoping to improve links between the two countries. Bored-looking men wearing headphones sat in a vast hall. Nobody looked too happy, but maybe that was the nature of delegations.

The bad news was buried halfway through the paper: a grainy photograph of an object being lifted out of the sea on a crane proved to be the body of a young woman. It had been spotted by a passenger on one of the ferries that shuttled between the European and Asian sides of the city. The woman was believed to be the latest victim in a series of murders that was currently 'mystifying' police. The journalist claimed that the whole city was living in fear, obsessed with the idea that a madman was on the loose. Nobody would sleep peacefully until the killer was caught.

Makana shoved the paper aside and resisted looking at his watch. As time went by the clientele slowly changed. A middle-aged couple entered, clearly Turkish, the woman berating her husband as he stared at the illuminated menu like a man seeking salvation. The woman snapped orders at the waiter as the husband arranged the shopping bags around a table.

Other tables were now occupied by solitary men, the odd couple. Still nobody who looked like Ayman Nizari. The tall European in the corner was marking things in his guidebook and drinking another beer. A young man entered and sat by the window. A red tram clanged its bell as it went by outside, sparks spitting from the overhead cables.

Like yesterday, there was a stream of people from nearby offices who came in, ordered and left with styrofoam packages in plastic bags. Was Nizari out there somewhere trying to make up his mind whether to trust him, or had something happened to prevent him making the rendezvous? Was one of these people a friend of his, a collaborator, a colleague, someone he trusted? Nobody seemed to be paying too much attention to Makana. Nizari could already be dead. If Mossad had caught up with him he could be bound for Tel Aviv, or some black-ops site that could never be traced. A man with his specialist skills could draw interest from some very shady quarters. Not for the first time Makana found himself wishing he was back in Cairo, where life, whatever you might say about it, was at least simpler.

A hand tapped him on the shoulder.

'*Pardon, bakar misiniz?*'

'I don't speak Turkish,' replied Makana in English, turning as he spoke. 'I'm sorry.'

The speaker was the large European man who had been sitting two tables away drinking his beer. Now, instead of returning to his place, he sat down right behind Makana. He held up the book he was holding – not a guidebook after all, but an introduction to the Turkish language.

'I must admit, it's quite intimidating trying out a new language, but perhaps I should stop inflicting pain on people.' The man chuckled at his own joke. Tossing the book onto the table in front of him, he asked, 'Here on holiday?'

'Business.' Makana twisted round in his chair to get a proper look. Scandinavian or German, he decided.

'What a coincidence.' The man beamed broadly while signalling to the waiter for another beer. 'I am also here on business. I come here every couple of months, but I can't even say thank you. I decided that enough was enough. I had to make an effort. And you?'

He was a big man, tall, with broad shoulders and a head like a watermelon. Lank brown hair that was pushed clumsily away from his pale face. He was chewing a mint. The table he had abandoned was strewn with wrappers. Clearly, he was in the mood for conversation.

'First time.' There seemed no point in lying. He would quickly be found out if he tried to pretend he knew the city.

'Henk Sneefliet.' The man held out a large hand which Makana was obliged to take. 'From the Netherlands.'

76

'Mustafa Amin, from Cairo.'

'Ah, then you are practically a neighbour.' The man again chuckled at his own remark. The waiter appeared with a fresh bottle of beer and a crooked smile on his face that made him look like a Picasso. The smile broadened when the European waved the change away. Clearly, Makana must learn to tip better.

'I'm sorry to inconvenience you,' said the Dutchman. 'Are you waiting for someone?'

'No, not at all.' Makana lit a cigarette and threw a casual glance towards the door. Over an hour had passed since the agreed rendezvous time. The chances of Nizari showing now were minimal, yet there was every chance that he, or someone else, was watching Makana.

The Dutchman might be just what he appeared, a lonely businessman in a foreign city, striking up a casual conversation, but there was too much at stake to make such assumptions. There was always the chance that this was some kind of test, in which case it made sense to play along and stick to his alibi.

'And what brings you to this fair city?'

'Machinery. I'm here to buy agricultural machinery.'

'New or used?'

'Used, mostly.'

The question suggested that the other man had some grasp of the subject. Agricultural machinery was not something most people had much knowledge of. That, at least, must have been the thinking on Winslow's part.

'What the industrialised world casts off, the developing world gives new life to.' The Dutchman again seemed pleased with his own take on the state of things. 'It tells us so much about the world we live in, don't you think?'

'There's a market in almost everything, if the price is right. Clothes, cars, medical instruments.' Makana tried to summon the waiter, who solemnly ignored him. The Dutchman nodded understandingly.

'We pride ourselves on recycling our waste, plastic, paper, glass. Really, it's about easing our own conscience. But in Africa, yes, that is where true recycling takes place.'

Makana got to his feet, gathering up his cigarettes and lighter.

'I'm sorry, I really have to be going.'

'Of course, of course.' The Dutchman was all smiles. 'No need to apologise.'

'Nice to meet you.'

'Same here, same here.'

The two men shook hands. Makana nodded at the book that lay on the table.

'Good luck with learning the language.'

'Ha ha, thank you. Perhaps I am deluding myself into thinking that I can manage to learn a language at my age, but we have to try, don't we?' There was a shrewd, observant look in the other man's eye.

'I suppose that's what it's all about,' smiled Makana.

He walked slowly back towards the hotel, pausing to look in shop windows, but not making a big effort to shake anyone off his tail. Bored businessman killing time in a foreign city. He thought he was beginning to get the hang of it.

Chapter Ten

Makana had the sense that something waited here, in this city, that connected to him in a way that he couldn't put his finger on, something dark and unforgiving.

It felt good to be secure in his hotel room, listening to the hum of distant traffic. When he closed his eyes it would revive the same image, the black veil drifting to the ground on the steps of the Blue Mosque. The blurred figure of the woman who had been wearing it floated before him, like a ray of light passing through the falling dusk.

As the sun began to sink into the hills to the west, he washed his face and put on his shoes and jacket. The lobby was quiet for once. He circled the hotel, first in one direction and then spinning on his heels without warning to reverse his steps. Nothing unusual jumped out at him – no face, no hint of warning. He drank hot, bitter coffee at a street stall that sold roasted corn on the cob. When he was quite satisfied that no one was following him, he took a shortcut he had discovered earlier that brought him to the entrance of an alleyway facing the Mukarrameh call shop and internet café. Redbeard was still there behind the counter; if he remembered Makana he gave no sign of it. He chose the same booth as last time. Closing the door, he clamped the receiver on his shoulder and reached into his pocket to light a cigarette while dialling the number he'd memorised.

Marcus Winslow was not happy to hear any of his news.

'Do you think it is connected?'

'From where I'm standing everything seems connected,' said Makana.

'It could just be a random attack.'

'It's possible.' Makana heard Winslow talking to someone else in the room with him. Then his voice came back. 'Look, this could mean your cover is blown. Have there been any indications that anyone is onto you?'

'I've been careful, but of course it's possible,' said Makana.

'It's important you stick to the routine. Behave as normally as possible.'

'How sure are you that Nizari is still here?'

'Of course he's there.' Winslow sounded impatient.

'Well, he doesn't seem pressed to come forward.'

'He may just be being cautious. That's why you have to be patient.'

'How long?' asked Makana. 'I mean, how many more days before we have to conclude he's not coming?'

'A day, maybe two. He's cautious, afraid. Give him time to trust you, to find his way.'

Winslow made it sound like they were fishing for some rare creature. Through the little porthole in the door, Makana could watch the front of the shop. He studied the glowing tip of his cigarette.

'We're sure there's no other way of contacting him?' It was a question Makana suspected Winslow already knew the answer to, but he asked it all the same.

'If there was, you can assume I would have used it by now.' Winslow sighed. 'Look, I know this is not easy, but we're close, very close.'

'Well, if you're happy to pay me just to stay here and wait, then I have no problems with that.'

'Two more days, that's as far as we'll let this thing run. As for the passport, I'll get onto finding you a replacement as soon as I put the phone down.'

'How far do you trust Nadir Sulayman?'

'As much as I trust any businessman.'

'He wasn't happy when I showed him the money,' said Makana. 'He wants more.'

'I'll talk to him. In the meantime, you have some extra money at the hotel. Give him a couple more thousand and we'll see if that quietens him down.'

Makana considered telling Winslow about the woman at the mosque, but he wasn't sure how to begin. He was no longer sure if he was imagining things. Maybe he was getting paranoid.

'Everything else is all right?'

'A man tried to strike up a conversation with me today, at the rendezvous point.'

Winslow's tone sharpened. 'What kind of man?'

Makana took a long drag on his cigarette. One of the young men sitting behind a computer looked over his screen at him. Makana thought he recognised him from the last time he had been in. He turned his back and carried on talking.

'A businessman. Northern European. Dutch.'

'What did he want?'

'Idle conversation, or that was how it appeared.'

'Did he give a name?'

'Henk Sneefliet.'

'I'll look into it. In the meantime, you must take no chances. If you ever see him again you must assume it's not a coincidence.'

That much Makana had managed to work out by himself. The young man by the computer was now eating a packet of roasted melon seeds, spitting the husks onto the floor at his feet while staring at the screen in front of him.

'I was thinking about Nizari,' said Makana, turning his attention back to the call. 'Just how would a scientist survive in a foreign city without money or papers?'

'He's a resourceful man.'

'What I mean is, does he have friends here? People who know him? Someone he could go to for help?'

'Not so far as we know.'

There was a rap on the door of the booth and the door was heaved open by Redbeard. You didn't need to speak Turkish to understand that he was unhappy about Makana smoking. Lifting a hand in apology, Makana dropped the cigarette to the floor and ground it out with his shoe, kicking it into the corner to join the handful of butts that were piled there. The man moved on, muttering to himself loudly about the state of the world. The melon-seed man was again staring sullenly at him from across the room.

Makana wondered at the wisdom of using the same place twice in succession. He needed a new set of skills; he was used to being the hunter, not the quarry.

'Call me again tomorrow. I need to know how things are going. And I'll arrange a temporary replacement for your passport to be issued by the British Consulate for collection tomorrow.' Winslow was silent for a moment. 'When you get there, you may find that there is some interest in yourself and your reason for being in Istanbul. They might even ask about me. Better to say nothing. It's more secure that way. We can't risk any kind of leak. Do you understand?'

'I think so,' said Makana.

'It's nothing to worry about. They won't press you.'

Hanging up the telephone, Makana fought the urge to light another cigarette while he thought for a moment and then dialled another Cairo number. Sami was at his desk in the Masry Info Media Collective.

'Ah, our roving investigator! How is life in Turkey? I hear the women are extraordinary, but don't let Rania know I said so.'

'I need your help on something.' Makana explained to Sami what he needed.

'I'll get Ubay onto it straight away. How do I get in contact with you?'

'You don't. I'll have to call you back.'

'Okay, then give us a day. This time tomorrow?' Sami paused. 'Oh, and Rania says be careful. Whatever it is you are doing out there.'

'Tell her I'm always careful. I'll be back before you know it.'

'Tomorrow, then.'

'Tomorrow.'

Makana hesitated, still holding the receiver. He felt like calling Jehan, if only to comfort her, but he knew it wasn't wise. Best to have as few threads as possible leading out from him. Contacting anyone was potentially putting them at risk. He still had no solid idea of how big this thing was. Redbeard's scowl did not alter when Makana told him to keep the change. Some people were determined not to have a nice day.

At the entrance to Nadir Sulayman's building Makana paused to survey the street. If someone was following him they were doing so very discreetly. The stairs were dark and had a fetid smell about them. He emerged onto the upper gallery to find it gloomy and deserted. Across the elevated walkway he glimpsed the yellow light over the doorway. This time when he rang the bell a buzzer let him in. Makana made his way across the entrance hall and through the heavy drapes to find that Sulayman was not in his office. That left him surveying the chaos until the sound of a toilet flushing came from somewhere to his right. A door opened and Nadir Sulayman appeared.

'Please, don't wait to be invited. Have a seat.'

'There seems to have been some misunderstanding about the money,' Makana began, but Sulayman held up a hand. Marcus Winslow must have got through to him quickly.

'Please, do not apologise. The mistake is mine.' Compared with the last time they'd met he seemed preoccupied, as if the money was the least of his worries. He sank down into the big leather chair behind the desk and started rummaging for his cigarettes, while talking in a distracted fashion.

'How do you like Istanbul? It's great, isn't it? Did you find a good place to eat? You must try the fish, much better than Cairo, I can assure you. I was there a few years ago, and frankly, I was disappointed.' As he talked Sulayman lit a Marlboro with a slim black lighter and blew a plume of smoke into the air before setting lighter and cigarettes firmly in the centre of the desk in front of him, no doubt in a bid to keep them handy amidst all the paperwork.

'Actually, you know what? Where are my manners? I take you myself, to one of the best fish restaurants in town.'

'Is that a good idea, for us to be seen together?'

'It's perfect,' Sulayman grinned. 'Confirms that you're here for business. I deal in everything, including agriculture machinery. You want an old tractor, I get you one, and besides' – he threw up a hand dismissively – 'we go late. Nobody sees us. Afterwards, I take you to a nice place where we have a few drinks, maybe even we are lucky to meet some girls, eh? What do you say?' He frowned. 'You're not a Muslim, are you?' he asked, dismissing his question straight away. 'Of course, you are. We all are, right? I mean, you're not a good Muslim, right? Ha ha ha.'

'I'd be happy to join you,' said Makana.

'Excellent! Then that's settled. Why don't we say we meet here, tomorrow night? Nine thirty. Is a good time, no, not so early. We have a little raki and we talk while they prepare the fish. I promise you will never forget it.' Sulayman looked at his watch. 'Unfortunately, I have a prior arrangement, otherwise ...' He held his hands up in apology as he got to his feet to walk Makana to the door.

A light rain accompanied Makana back to his hotel. The air felt warm and muggy. It was hard to make sense of his contact's change of heart. Could a simple phone call from Winslow have been enough? he wondered. There was something about Sulayman's chatty theatricality that had sounded forced. Had Winslow offered him a lot more money, or was there some other explanation?

In the hotel lobby he picked up an English-language newspaper from a rack. Under the headline 'Living with Fear' he found another article on the recent spate of murders. Police sources, one paper declared, had confirmed unofficially that they believed the perpetrator to be a foreigner, though no explanation was given as to why this should be so.

There was an envelope waiting at reception. It contained a couple of newspaper clippings and a note from Sami's journalist friend, Kursad: 'Perhaps this is what you are looking for?'

The article was in Turkish, but Kursad had included a brief summary of the story. There had been an accident involving an ambulance and an overnight bus. A woman in the ambulance was killed. She had not been identified, but she didn't work for the ambulance service. The ambulance had been stolen from outside a hospital. There was evidence that others had been in the vehicle at the time of the crash but they had fled the scene.

The photographs showed a mangled ambulance lying on its side, the driver's cab badly crushed. Inset was a photograph of the dead woman. Makana recognised Nadia Razvan, the waitress from Marbella who had taken such an interest in Ayman Nizari.

On the balcony of his room he smoked a cigarette, listening to the distant wail of sirens and cars honking their endless protest.

He now knew how Nizari had managed to get free of his Israeli handlers. Tomorrow, if he was lucky, everything would be resolved. Nizari would appear at the Iskander Grillroom, and the consulate would provide him with a new travel document. As he prepared for bed, he wondered if he might be accused of being overly optimistic.

Chapter Eleven

Istanbul Day Three

Koçak was waiting patiently for Makana again the next morning, studying the elaborate marble ceiling of the lobby with a dreamy look. He jumped to his feet when Makana appeared.

'*Effendim*, today Topkapi, yes?'

Makana had a couple of hours to kill before the next potential rendezvous with Ayman Nizari at the Iskander, but while it made sense to act out the routine of a visitor with too much time on his hands, the prospect of traipsing round the old palace surrounded by picture-snapping tourists did not appeal to him.

'Let's just drive around a bit.'

'Drive?' Koçak's face darkened momentarily as if this posed a terrible challenge, before his expression lifted. 'Okay. No problem.'

As he drove, Koçak offered his views on everything from the Pope to the qualities of his favourite football team Beşiktaş, versus their rivals Galatasaray and Fenerbahçe. Makana let him talk. He smoked and watched the buildings go by, wondering idly if he was perhaps missing an opportunity to explore the city, one that might not come again any time soon. Perhaps if he did not have so many other things on his mind.

He tilted the wing mirror so as to watch the cars behind them. Was this just from habit? He couldn't shake off the idea that he was being followed, yet he could not really say by whom. He assumed that Winslow would have people somewhere, shadowing him, but they were either very good, or they didn't exist – he wasn't sure which ought to worry him more. Then there was Nizari, his friends or handlers, along with Abu Hilal, the Mossad and other parties with an interest in the scientist. The woman at the Blue Mosque. The clumsy European at the restaurant. And then the mugging. All in all it didn't add up to much more than a cloud of unease – nothing he could really put his finger on. Yet he couldn't dismiss the feeling that his every move was leading him deeper into a dangerous place. All he could hope was to have enough time to take action when matters finally revealed themselves.

At a stall overlooking the Marmara Sea they stopped for *çay* and *kokoreçi* – a sandwich of lamb intestines. The entrails were wound into long sausages that turned slowly on a spit, dripping fat. He suspected this was something of a test on Koçak's part, but Makana had eaten worse. The sandwich was tasty, if a little greasy. Koçak had other things on his mind. He stabbed a finger at the front page of a newspaper pinned to the side of the stall. It showed an artist's sketch that looked like it was based on a photofit.

'*Karakoncolos.*'

'What is that?'

Koçak pulled an ugly face. 'Very bad thing. Killing people.'

'Is this the murders that have been happening, the body they pulled out of the sea yesterday?'

'Crazy person.'

'Is it a man or a woman, do they know?'

Looking at the photofit picture it was hard to tell. Either the artist lacked talent or the witnesses they had were too vague.

'Is *karakoncolos*,' shrugged Koçak. 'Monster. Man, woman, no matter. If you see it, you are dead.'

'Right.' The killer had been transformed into a figure of myth. Whoever was committing these murders, they were certainly scaring people. Makana decided to change the subject. He pointed into the distance.

'What are those?'

'Prince Islands. Ottomans send bad people there.'

Makana recalled reading in the guidebook Winslow had slipped into his bag that Leon Trotsky had once been exiled on such an island near Istanbul. Perhaps this was it.

'You like to visit bazaar?' Koçak had cheered up.

'Bazaar?' The idea conjured up images of the Khan al-Khalili back in Cairo: crowded with tourists and enterprising Egyptians trying to seduce them with a smattering of phrases in English, French, German, Spanish, even Japanese.

'Is very beautiful.'

'I'm sure.' Makana must have sounded less than enthusiastic, because Koçak only renewed his efforts to convince him.

'Please, *effendim*, you must see. Best bazaar in whole world.'

Makana surrendered. He had nothing better to do, after all. A glance at his watch told him there was still time until the rendezvous.

'Fine, let's visit the bazaar.'

'Excellent choice, sir. You will not regret. You can buy gifts for lady wife.'

The interior of the domed bazaar had been recently refurbished by the looks of things. It was bright and bustling. Crowds eddied by, bumping into one another, pausing to chat to friends and acquaintances, stopping to examine items of interest. There were tourists buying souvenirs, housewives dragging laden shopping trolleys and reluctant children behind them. The air was thick with the smell of spices, scented soaps and tanned leather. Makana wandered past bright mounds of chillis, aniseed, cloves and cumin, stacks of porcelain, chatty salesmen calling out their wares.

He found himself staring at a wall of mirrors of all sizes and shapes. They hung suspended in the air and stirred gently, swinging from side to side in the breeze that blew through the arched tunnels. One particular crescent-shaped mirror drew his attention. It was made of brass inscribed with curved shapes and squiggles. It reminded him of one that he'd had long ago: a trinket that hung from the rearview mirror of his car, something he hadn't thought about in years. As he stretched out a hand towards it, a breeze sweeping through the arcades caused the mirror to swivel out of reach. In that instant he saw something that caused his heart to skip a beat.

A glimpse, no more, but it was enough. In disbelief, he spun round, searching for the face he thought he had just seen. Swerving fast through a party of tourists, he burst into an open space and came to an abrupt halt. He saw the chequered boards that he had glimpsed in the reflection; chessboards and backgammon sets decorated with mother-of-pearl inlay. The doorway was empty now. He peered inside, jostling a startled shopkeeper. Nothing. There was no sign of the person he was convinced he had just seen; someone he hadn't seen in over fifteen years, though not a day had passed in all those years when he had not thought of her.

Making his way back through the crowds, Makana stumbled into shoulders, backs, people walking behind him, against him. He forced them aside, clearing a path, ignoring their protests, chasing every shadow, until he was out in the sunlight and Koçak was waving to him.

'Everything all right, *effendim*?'

Makana ignored him, trying to catch a glimpse of the impossible. The square was full of moving people. Pigeons swept through in waves, distracting the eye. All he wanted was something to confirm, to tell him that he wasn't crazy, that he hadn't just imagined it. And yet, how could it be otherwise? His mind told him he could not have seen Muna, that she had died all those years ago.

His heart refused to believe that it wasn't possible. He felt it with such conviction. It was Muna. Alive and well, and not a day older. Could his mind be playing tricks – a combination of not sleeping properly and of being in an unfamiliar city? That sounded rational, but it collided with that other part of his mind: the one that told him he knew what he had seen. The only other possible conclusion was that he must be losing his mind.

Shaken and deeply confused, Makana asked Koçak to drop him off so that he could walk up through Beyoğlu. He had time and he needed to clear his head before he reached the rendezvous. The taxi, the traffic, the city, all of it seemed to be closing in on him. He walked slowly, rehearsing in his mind exactly what he had seen. He had to have been mistaken. Whatever it was, whoever he had seen, there had to be a rational explanation. Muna was dead. So who or what had he seen? A woman just like her, or some sort of projection on his part? He'd never really believed in ghosts, but on the other hand he'd never quite dismissed their possibility. He'd grown up in a world in which prayer was real and divine intervention a possibility, and although his rational mind refused to submit to such nonsense, there was still a part of him, he realised now, somewhere deep inside him, which had not entirely abandoned the idea.

Chapter Twelve

The Iskander Grillroom was more or less unchanged from his previous visits. The surly waiter stood by the counter, picking his teeth with a matchstick. He paid no attention to Makana – a sign perhaps that he was fast becoming a regular. What more could one ask for than indifference? He sat at the same table against the wall, facing the door, and ordered lamb this time. With one eye on the street he flicked idly through a discarded newspaper. The world had problems of its own. The American invasion three years ago had brought Iraq to the verge of civil war. Sectarian conflict had erupted following the bombing of the al-Askari mosque in the town of Samarra. Thousands had died in a matter of days and now the violence was spreading.

Still no sign of his contact. People wandered by, going about their lives. Young ones laughing, others looking lost. A child crying while being hauled along by a woman who stopped from time to time to shout at the boy, which only made him cry all the harder. A man with a scruffy beard stepped in through the door and looked around the room before calling something to the waiter and settling himself in the opposite corner. Makana watched him for a time, wondering if he could be a messenger of some kind, but the man paid him no attention. The air was cold and damp and it looked as though it might rain. A tram rumbled by, rattling the glass in the windows.

There were no more pictures of victims being hauled from the water in today's paper. Surely that was a good thing. He wondered how much of the language he might understand if he could read the alphabet. He put down the paper as his food arrived. Stuffed vine-leaves and roasted lamb. The lamb fell off the bone when he put his fork to it. The vine-leaves were stuffed with aromatic rice. He lost himself for a time in eating. When he had finished he called for coffee to wash it down, which turned out to be strong and bore no relation to the watery substance they served in the hotel.

Other than that, there was nothing. Nobody approached him. There was no sign of Ayman Nizari. No sign of the tall Dutchman either. Makana drank another cup of coffee and gestured for the bill. If Nizari was refusing to show himself there had to be a reason. He still had time to visit the British Consulate before they closed. If Winslow had done as he promised there would be a new passport waiting for him. Makana realised he was itching to leave. Ayman Nizari and Abu Hilal and all the rest of them would just have to make their own luck.

He was counting out his money when a boy of about eleven appeared in front of him.

'Postcards? You like?' Makana waved him away as he started to get to his feet, but the boy was persistent. Without waiting to be asked he spread ten of them out on the table in quick succession, with the slick confidence of a seasoned card sharp. The waiter was already on his way over. The boy held Makana's gaze for a long moment before gathering up his cards in time to be bundled out of the door. Glancing back down at the table Makana realised that one card remained. He looked up but the boy was gone, out through the door and away down the street. Makana studied the card. It showed a wall of pretty blue faience tiles; the interior of a mosque, he guessed. When he turned it over he read: Rüstem Pasha mosque – 16th Century.

In the centre of the card were the numbers 18.00. Nothing more.

The woman at the British Consulate said her name was Fateema Brown. Makana wondered how you got a name like that. An English husband, perhaps? The building was one of a row of stately mansions, testament to the five centuries when this city was the capital of the Ottoman empire. It was a grey, rather formidable-looking building with high square windows and serrated corners. Security was severe, as expected from a place that had been the target of a bombing less than three years ago.

Makana had anticipated complications gaining access to the interior, but his fears proved ungrounded. A man with a clipboard found his name on a list, a button was pressed and an electric door buzzed open. He stepped into a short corridor and waited as the door behind him was locked and the one in front of him opened.

Fateema Brown was waiting for him in the reception area, a small, nervous woman in her thirties wearing a navy-blue hijab. Makana wondered how many veiled women the British employed. Perhaps it was symbolic, an indication of how tolerant and liberal-minded they were. Since he was, in a way, working for the British government himself, perhaps he too ought to be a little more open-minded.

What struck him about Fateema Brown was how uncomfortable she was. She gestured stiffly for him to enter a small office. The room was bare but for a simple table and four chairs. On one wall was a framed photograph of their queen. Naturally. Opposite this was a poster for British Airways that displayed a picture of a waterfall and green rolling hills with Visit Britain written in flowing letters along the bottom. Fateema Brown stood by the window, silhouetted against the skyline.

'This is an unusual situation,' she said as she came to the table.

'Unusual in what sense?' Makana asked.

She made no immediate attempt to answer the question. Gesturing for him to be seated, she produced a key that was attached to her waist by a chain and turned to the flat metal box that rested on the table.

'I understand you are in Istanbul on business?'

'Agricultural machinery.'

'I understand you were robbed two nights ago,' she said, as she unlocked the box.

'That is correct.'

'Did you file a report with the police?'

'No,' said Makana. 'I wasn't sure that was necessary.'

'It's always recommended. In fact, it is usually a requirement.' She rested her hand on the box, as if unsure whether to proceed or not.

'Usually?'

Fateema Brown nodded. 'When you asked me what I meant by unusual, this is what I meant. Your application for a temporary replacement document went through the system in twelve hours. That has to be something of a record.'

'Surely that's a good thing.'

Her look suggested that she knew there was something else going on. Makana reached for his cigarettes and lighter.

'You can't smoke in here,' she said curtly, as she lifted a brown envelope from the box. Inside was a folded document. 'Did you bring a passport photograph with you?'

'I hadn't thought of that.'

'It's not a problem. There's a machine at the end of the hallway. Just go out of this door and turn left.' She held out some coins. 'You'll need these.'

Makana followed her instructions and found the little photobooth as promised. He pressed all the right buttons and then, while he was waiting for the machine to process the pictures, a voice behind him spoke his name. He turned to find a tall man of around forty. He wore a blue short-sleeved shirt and had rumpled sandy hair that needed cutting.

'Do you have a moment?' The man gestured towards an open doorway just to the right. Makana hesitated. The machine whirred and the photographs dropped into the delivery tray.

'I need to hand these over.'

'I'll take care of that,' said the man. Taking the strip of photographs he indicated the door again. Makana walked through to find himself in a large room. The wallpaper was green with a pattern of gold pinstripes down it. On the fireplace a large carriage clock ticked away beneath a painting of a naval battle. The canvas was a rage of darkness and flame, burning sails and exploding ships on blue-black water. The only furniture in the room was a table with two chairs that stood between the high windows.

'Please, take a seat,' the man said. He sat opposite Makana and placed the photographs carefully on the table in front of him.

'My name is Marty Shaw. I understand you are here to collect an emergency passport. I wonder if you could just spare a moment to talk about what you are doing here in Istanbul.'

'I thought I had already explained that.'

'Agricultural machinery.' A smile crossed Shaw's face. 'Yes, I know all about that. I should perhaps explain. I know about your connection to Marcus Winslow.'

'You know?' Makana sat back in his chair. 'Then you can ask him.'

'Believe me, I'd like to, but unfortunately Mr Winslow has taken it upon himself to act independently.' Shaw was watching Makana's face for his reaction. 'He's running this show on his own.'

'I'm not sure I follow,' said Makana.

'It's very simple. Just tell me everything you can about this operation.'

'Why don't you just ask Winslow?'

'Look, I understand your reluctance.' Shaw smiled again. 'I can assure you that you're not jeopardising anything by talking to me. After all, we're on the same side.'

'With all due respect, Mr Shaw, I don't know you.'

Shaw shook his head. 'No, you don't know Marcus Winslow.'

'How do I know I can trust you?'

'How do you know you can trust Winslow?'

It was a good question and the answer was obvious. He didn't know. All Winslow had in his favour was the fact that he was the one who'd started all of this. Makana remained silent. Shaw held out a hand in a gesture of reconciliation.

'Look, I understand that it's not easy. All of this is new to you.'

'All I need is a day, maybe two, and then my work here is done.'

'What if I can't do that?' Shaw paused and changed tack. 'What happens if things don't go the way Winslow told you they would?'

'You seem to be saying that I can't trust Winslow,' said Makana. 'At the same time you're asking me to trust you. That doesn't make a lot of sense.'

'You're right, it doesn't,' agreed Shaw, 'and there's a limit to how much I can tell you. But let me ask you this. You look like a smart man. Have you had no doubts about Winslow yourself, about this whole mission?'

'I don't really understand what is going on here. Winslow arranged the replacement passport for me. That means he has some kind of authority here.' Makana got to his feet. 'You need to get in touch with him and make sure that you're all on the same side.'

'Winslow is on a personal mission. He's out on a limb,' said Shaw. He rested his hand on the door handle and held out a card. 'If you find yourself in need of a friend, you can call that number, day or night.'

Once clear of the building, his replacement travel document safely in his pocket, Makana found a phone box and called Koçak, asking him to meet later by the Galata Bridge. He could have found the Rüstem Pasha mosque by himself, but it might be useful to have a reliable car on hand. He turned the postcard over in his hand as he waited for the taxi to arrive. If it came from Ayman Nizari it confirmed that he was being extra-cautious. No name, no message, just a time and a place. A public space, somewhere he could feel safe.

He made his way back to the Sultana Harem Hotel, stopping along the way to buy a few things. This time the reception desk was occupied by an overweight woman who spoke no English. Makana laid his key on the counter alongside the required cash. He leaned over to indicate the calendar that covered the desk blotter.

'I need the room for two more nights.'

She appeared to get the message, nodding and speaking, regardless of the fact that he clearly did not understand what she was saying. Patiently, she counted the money three times before writing him out a receipt.

Now Makana could go up to his room. Although considerably smaller than the room at the Pera Palas, it would be enough for Nizari to rest in if they needed to stay out of sight for a few hours. Using the heavy-duty tape he had bought along the way, he fixed an envelope with five thousand dollars in it to the bottom of the bedside cabinet.

There was a knock at the door and Makana opened it to find the same young man who had been on the reception desk the first time he had been here. He was holding a vacuum cleaner.

'No, it's all right. The room is fine.' As an afterthought he reached into his pocket for some banknotes and counted a couple out. The boy looked at the money for a moment and then grinned, snatched the notes up and disappeared down the hall, dragging the vacuum cleaner behind him. The look on his face suggested that he suspected Makana was up to no good and the bribe was to make him look the other way. It didn't make much difference what he thought the money was for, so long as he thought Makana was good for more of it at some stage. He looked at his watch. Koçak would be waiting for him.

The historic heart of Istanbul lies on a peninsula that is separated from the rest of the city by the estuary known as the Golden Horn. It resembles a horn, twisted and bent, that has been driven into the land by the gods for the sole purpose of separating one side from the other.

The Rüstem Pasha mosque stood in what had once been the city's Latin quarter, occupied at various times by Venetians, Amalfians, Genoese and Pisans, and later home to a small Jewish community. None of this was in evidence today. The mosque was relatively modest compared with other, more illustrious temples in the vicinity, but its beauty lay in the delicate intricacy of its design, and the distinctive blue Iznik tiles that decorated the walls. Having left Koçak with instructions to wait for him and to be ready to leave quickly, Makana made his way in through the entrance gate. A narrow set of stairs brought him up to a long colonnade that ran along the side of the main building. A stall offered embroidered purses and postcards like the one Makana had in his jacket pocket.

It was almost time for sunset prayers, and a handful of men had already gathered. Leaving his shoes by the door, Makana entered the main part of the mosque. The interior was cool and airy. Light reached it through a series of elegant red and white striped arches that divided the main part of the interior from a couple of smaller recesses. The walls were dominated by more of the same intricately patterned blue tiles.

Makana's watch told him it was almost six. He stood to one side and watched the men filing in through the entrance. They came in twos and threes, some alone. None looked familiar, but he studied the faces, looking for one he might have seen before, in the street, at the hotel, or at the Iskander Grillroom. He drew a blank. Each man chose a spot on which to stand and pray. The carpet was patterned with rows of doorways, representing the mihrab, the niche in the wall they faced, which indicated the direction of Mecca. Makana had edged along down one side, moving slowly, taking his time to study the faces once more. A few turned to observe him and he withdrew to the back of the room.

It was past six now, and there was no sign of Nizari. As he stood by the entrance watching the men at prayer, Makana was surprised to realise that he found something like spiritual comfort in their murmurs. He assumed this was related to the disorientation brought on by being in a foreign place, an unfamiliar city. As so frequently over these days, the sense of dislocation led him back to the event that dominated his life: the deaths of his wife and daughter.

While his new superiors were only interested in hounding him, Makana had thought he could manage. It was when they turned their persecution on his wife that he knew they had no option but to flee. Mek Nimr would stop at nothing to wipe out both his rival and his family. They drove out of the city at night, just before the curfew. Muna was driving. When they reached the top of the incline, a blinding row of lights came on ahead of them. Through the dazzle she saw soldiers lined up waiting, and in panic put her foot down. Had she hoped for some lucky way through? In any case it didn't matter. Makana felt something give beneath the car. In the heat of the moment he thought it was one of the worn tyres bursting. Now he was no longer so sure. He wondered if Mek Nimr had done something to the car, to make sure they didn't escape him. In any event, the old Volkswagen veered to one side and bounced up the kerb to hit the railings, hard enough to bend and dislodge them.

By some quirk of fate, the offside door sprang open, and the same jolt threw Makana clear. The memory stayed vivid. Everything seemed to stop. He was watching the weight of the car slowly bow the railings over, tipping it into the river. He sprawled helpless. The sound of the car hitting the unseen water still echoed in his mind: a giant door slammed shut. He tried to throw himself in after them, but was pinioned.

The last image Makana had of his daughter was of a three-year-old child pressing her fingers to the window of the car as it tilted slowly past the tipping point before falling into the darkness below. The image had engraved itself for ever, the details as sharp and clear as they had been nearly fifteen years ago. How many times had he replayed the scenes leading up to that moment, trying to work out what he might have missed, if there'd been any way to avoid them being taken from him.

Makana's train of thought was brought to a halt by a man jostling deliberately past him. He turned to look, and noticed for the first time that there was a staircase in the right-hand recess. The prayers were ending and people were making their way out again as Makana eased his way across the interior to the far side of the mosque.

White marble stairs led down into the shadows. With a casual glance around in case of watchers, Makana descended into the gloom to find himself in a dark passage. When his eyes adjusted he could make out enough to follow it, one hand on the wall. It brought him to a storage room of some kind. It was damp and warm here. Makana came to a halt.

Ahead lay only darkness. Behind him he could still see the light filtering down the staircase from above. A sound made him turn back towards the dark.

'Hello?'

He started to step forward and then stopped abruptly when a powerful torch beam came on, blinding him. The light was broken by vertical striations that he realised were the bars of a heavy iron grille that sealed off an arch. A voice spoke in Arabic.

'Step closer. I want to be sure.'

With one hand held up against the glare, Makana could make out a large stooping figure.

'Ayman Nizari?'

'Are you Makana?'

'Maybe you could lower the light a little bit.'

There was a moment's hesitation and then the light went out completely.

'Don't come any closer.'

'I'm here because you asked me to come,' Makana said slowly. 'You don't have anything to fear from me.'

'You came alone?'

'That's what you wanted, isn't it?' The other man's breathing came in quick, nervous stabs, and Makana felt the need to reassure him.

'It's not safe for me,' said Nizari.

'That's why I'm here,' said Makana. 'To take you somewhere safe.'

'They tried to kill me.'

'I know, in Spain.'

'They want to take me in. Who knows what they would have done to me if they had succeeded.'

'Well, luckily they didn't.' Makana placed a hand on the iron gate and gently pulled and then pushed. It didn't budge. It must be locked or bolted.

'How do I know you're who you say you are?'

'You sent for me, remember? The boy who brought me the message, has he been watching the café? Is that why you didn't show up?'

'It's not safe.' Nizari's voice dropped, and for a moment Makana wondered if he was speaking to someone else. '*They* are watching.'

'Who are they? Who is watching?' In the darkness, Makana had the sense that he was trying to catch a sprite, something not flesh at all, that might vanish at any moment.

'How do I know you are who you say you are?' Nizari repeated.

'You asked for me to come from Cairo, remember? I don't even know why you asked for me, but here I am.'

The light clicked on again, momentarily blinding Makana before the beam was aimed at the ground. In the diffuse glow he saw the glint of spectacles. Nizari's face was puffy, the flesh sagging with age and sprinkled with grey stubble. He wore a tracksuit and new trainers and might have been a football coach gone to seed. A rim of scruffy bristles crowned his head. The dishevelled appearance might express his being on the run and in fear of his life, but there was something in his eyes that didn't fit. He gripped the bars tightly, the torch beam wavering like a nervous halo.

'Tell me the name of Chief Haroun's wife.'

'I'm here to help you.'

'Just answer the question!' Ayman Nizari's voice cracked in a strangled squeak.

With every exchange Makana felt his concern growing. Nizari looked like a man out of his depth. Not surprising, perhaps, considering what he had been through recently.

'He used to joke that he could never marry a woman unless she had the same name as his mother. He did exactly that. His wife always joked that he thought he was married to his mother.' Makana fell silent. Nizari was already waving him to stop.

'You've come alone?'

'That's what you wanted, isn't it?'

'Why do you keep answering questions with more questions?'

'I'm alone.'

'Okay, okay.' Nizari swung the torch beam into the far corners of the cellar, as if looking for something. He rubbed a hand nervously over his face. 'I want money.'

'That wasn't part of the deal.'

'I'm not interested in what was,' snapped Nizari. 'Consider it a token of faith. Two million dollars. Either that or I go elsewhere.'

'Where?'

'What?'

'Where will you go?'

'Never mind that, just tell them!' Nizari's state of panic was rising. He stepped backwards, dissolving into the shadows. Makana's hand tightened on the iron bars.

'Wait. How do I find you again?'

'If they agree to the money, you go back to the restaurant. The same time. If they don't agree, don't bother coming.'

'Wait a moment. Can't we discuss this?'

But Nizari was already gone. Makana shook the grille, scrabbling around for a bolt or some kind of a latch. Even as he did so, he could see the torch beam dwindling and then, as if turning a corner, it blinked out.

Chapter Thirteen

'How did he seem to you?' Winslow asked.

Makana sighed. He had decided to let Koçak go and walk back instead. He had crossed the wide square, passing by the old stone walls of the bazaar. The space had been hectic with people hurrying to get home at the end of their day. Buses, cars and yellow *dolmuş* transit vans hooted frantically as they jockeyed past one another.

His mind absorbed, Makana passed blindly through the turmoil, feeling like a revenant. On the bridge over the Golden Horn he found himself passing countless amateur fishermen. He took up an empty spot and leaned on the railing, smoking a cigarette as he pondered the situation. A huge red flag snapped its white crescent in the breeze. Dozens of fishing lines hung like fine hairs into the water, while their owners viewed the sun with fading hope, worshippers watching the departure of a deity unwilling to grant their wishes. The mobile phone Nadir Sulayman had given him buzzed to announce a message: Tanpinar restaurant. Nevizade Sokak. 9 p.m.

A passing vendor had caught his attention, singing out as he pushed a cart loaded with fresh-baked simit rings. Eating one, Makana had walked thoughtfully up through the steep, winding streets and crumbling buildings of Beyoğlu. The decaying façades still had a touch of nobility. Here was a city of legend, of conquests and intrigues. An imperial city. It lived and breathed the sea. To his right the channel of the Bosporus cut north through the gap between the European continent and the Asian. A man could lose himself in this city without even noticing.

'I think he's disturbed,' Makana said finally.

'You think he's lost his mind?'

'I think we have a big problem on our hands.'

With a telephone card bought from a tobacconist's along with a fresh supply of Samsun cigarettes, Makana had found this windy corner where a solitary yellow phone booth, scarred and abandoned, was perched. It stood like a relic from another age, a time capsule all but forgotten. The door creaked open with difficulty. He was unsure it would even work, so that the dialling tone, when it came, sounded like something of a miracle.

'And what's all this about money?'

'I think he's testing us,' said Makana. 'Or else he's stalling, playing for time.'

'Why would he do that?'

'I don't know,' was the only valid answer. On his walk Makana had thought back time and again over his encounter with the renegade chemist, how to account for his change of heart. He was still in the dark about how Nizari might be surviving. Where was he staying? A hotel? A private apartment? Was he sleeping rough? Whatever his situation, it had him scared and agitated, yet instead of being desperate to leave he seemed to want to delay his departure. Perhaps his nerves accounted for it. Someone had tried to abduct him, after all. That would transform a man's outlook.

'You have to play him along,' said Winslow. 'Whatever happens, he has to believe that we are willing to do whatever he wants to bring him in.'

'Are you really going to give him that amount of money?'

'We'll cross that bridge when we come to it. For now, go to the meeting place and reassure him that he'll get whatever he needs. Did he mention Abu Hilal?'

'No.'

'Maybe that's a good thing, maybe not. Anything else to report?'

Makana wanted to talk about his meeting with Marty Shaw, but something deterred him. He wasn't sure what it was, but until he understood more about where Winslow stood, he felt inclined not to show all his cards.

When Winslow had rung off, Makana once again keyed in the card digits followed by the number in Cairo. It took nine rings before Sami answered.

'I'm sorry, things are a little crazy right now.'

'What's happened?'

'Didn't you see the news? There was a bomb in Dahab. Reports of thirty people killed and more injured.'

Makana knew Dahab by reputation. It was a laid-back village on the Sinai Peninsula, popular with a certain kind of tourist, the kind that just wanted to smoke a joint and sit on the beach to watch the sunset.

'The government is trying to tie this to Al Qaeda. People are saying the security services dropped the ball, too busy chasing journalists and political opposition.'

'Sounds like you've got your hands full.'

'Well, I've been up all night chasing this. Ubay went over there.' Sami sighed. 'Seems he has lots of long-haired friends in Dahab. Anyway, how are you getting on?'

'Hard to say. I met our mystery friend.'

'Ah, finally. So that's it, right, you'll be coming home?'

Makana suppressed a laugh at the word. He wasn't sure what home even meant any more, but in a way it was true. Where else did he have, after all?

'I have a feeling this is not going to be all that straightforward. He seems a little confused.'

'You'll find a way. You always do.'

'You sound like you have more confidence than I do at this point.' Makana was happy to hear Sami's voice. It was a relief to be speaking to someone he could trust.

'You're too pessimistic. How many times do I have to tell you? Lighten up.'

'How's Rania?'

'Fine, putting on weight like there's no tomorrow. Seriously, she's fine, healthy and growing. Everything as it should be.'

'I'm glad to hear it. Tell her I said hello.'

'I will. Okay, this is what Ubay turned up before he left.' Makana could hear the clicks from Sami's keyboard. 'Ayman Nizari, you wanted to know about contacts in Turkey. We had to go back quite far. It seems that at a certain point he became *persona non grata* in the academic world. No one would touch him, which is not surprising, given what he was up to.'

103

'That would coincide with …' Makana studied a man who had rounded the corner then abruptly stopped, before turning around and going back the way he came. Too obvious, he decided, if he was tailing him.

'Well, it would fit with Halabja. Nineteen eighty-eight. A Kurdish village that Saddam Hussein gassed. Five thousand civilians were killed: men, women and children. Maybe you remember, it caused a sensation in the world press.'

Makana didn't need reminding. He could recall the horrific images. If Nizari had been working on Saddam's biological weapons programme at the time, he would certainly have been involved. It made him wonder again exactly what kind of a person he was trying to help.

'And after that he disappears?'

'Well, almost,' Sami replied. The rest of the sentence was lost in the buzz and crackle of the line. '… a paper together. Published in an academic journal in St Petersburg of all places.'

'I didn't get the first part. You're saying he wrote a paper with a Turkish colleague?'

'Her name is Hatice Aksoy, she's a professor at Istanbul university.'

Makana had the sense that he'd just been handed the missing part of the puzzle. This was how Nizari was managing to stay out of sight here: a colleague, one of the few he had left, perhaps. Someone he had collaborated with. His second thought was that if Ubay had managed to find this former colleague, then someone else could do the same, including the Mossad. And no doubt they had better resources than Makana did, which meant that it was only a matter of time before they found the connection to Professor Aksoy, if they hadn't already.

'Okay, what about the other name I gave you?'

'Oh, yes. Sneefliet. Ubay found a nineteenth-century commun-ist activist by the same name, oh and a Metro station in Amsterdam.'

'That could be mere coincidence, couldn't it?'

'I thought you didn't believe in coincidence.'

'I'm not sure what I believe in any more,' said Makana.

'When do you think you'll be back?'

'Right now it looks as though my time here is running out faster than expected.'

'The way you say that doesn't sound encouraging,' said Sami before they said their goodbyes.

Makana ate in a nondescript place where the neon lighting was so bright it made his eyes ache. The service was brisk and indifferent, the clientele mostly young men, stepping inside for a quick snack eaten on their feet, before resuming their journey. He sat close to the wall at a table scratched and scarred by previous customers. A football match was playing on a set above the counter. Two men drinking beer seemed to be the only ones watching it. From time to time they would comment, or grow more animated, leaving at last in a flurry of curses before the final whistle was blown. Makana pushed his plate aside and nursed a cup of tea.

Something about this city disconcerted him. Not for the first time, he had the sense that he was overlooking some key perspective, that fate had something very special in store for him here, and he needed to be ready. The odds had been stacked against him from the start, and the meeting with Nizari that afternoon had not gone to plan. Far from it. His mind kept harking back to the meeting with Marty Shaw at the British Consulate. What had he been hinting at? It seemed entirely possible that Winslow was setting him up in some way, but how and to what end?

Makana was beginning to feel like a goat tethered to a stake, waiting for a lion to appear. Right now the best hope he had was that Nadir Sulayman would hold up his end of the bargain and arrange their transport out of the country. One thing he knew: delightful though it was, Makana had no intention of staying in this city for a moment longer than was necessary.

At the Pera Palas he showered in the marble bathroom. The opulence of it made him uncomfortable and he longed to be back home on the awama. After he had dressed he smoked a cigarette. Strictly speaking, smoking in the room was forbidden, but he kept the windows open and used a saucer as an ashtray, which he then deposited on the little balcony before locking his room. In the lobby he spoke to the beaming man behind the reception desk.

'Do you have a telephone directory? I'm looking for an old friend of mine and we lost touch over the years.'

'But of course, Amin Bey. You have only to ask,' Haluk smiled. 'Might I enquire, what is the name of your friend?'

'Hatice Aksoy. She's a lecturer at the university.'

'No problem, Amin Bey. Your wish is our command.' The diminutive figure bowed his head. All he needed was bells on his toes to complete the image of a court jester. He disappeared from sight, resurfacing with a tower of directories which he dumped on the counter. As he began to leaf intently through them, he continued to bark orders over his shoulder to his staff without even turning his head.

'Aksoy is her married name or maiden name?' Haluk's eyes bounced upwards with interest.

'I don't know,' said Makana, which was the truth. Haluk's face clouded with confusion. Makana smiled at him. Of course he had no idea. The question raised a whole list of further queries: if she was married, would she adopt her husband's name or stick with her own? She was a chemist of some kind, a scientist. Not sentimental. Makana suspected it made no difference as far as the listings in the phone book were concerned, but he didn't blame the man for his curiosity. An occupational hazard, one might imagine. Twenty minutes later, however, the diminutive receptionist had to concede defeat.

'A thousand apologies, Amin Bey, but I fear I cannot fulfil your request.'

'Never mind, Haluk, it was a nice try.' It would have surprised Makana if they had found the professor so quickly.

Nevizade Sokak, on the other hand, proved easy to find. It was closer than he'd thought, although locating the right restaurant proved slightly more difficult, since the street was lined with tables on both sides. It was crowded too, with tourists hungry for their evening meal. Before he was even halfway along, Makana was cursing Nadir Sulayman for not choosing a quieter spot. No doubt he was trying to be a good host and show his guest the kinds of places that visitors tended to love, having not realised that this was the exact opposite of what Makana would like.

Ignoring the pleas of waiters waving menus in his face, Makana made his way slowly along, reading off the names of the restaurants as he went. The Tanpinar was a small place towards the end of the narrow street. No more than four tables set outside and perhaps twice that many inside. In contrast to most of the others around it, the Tanpinar seemed to take a nonchalant approach to the matter of attracting clients. No one stood out on the pavement trying to drum up business. Inside, the décor was simple and somewhat dated. The walls displayed medieval sketches of the city and old maps. The tables were covered with simple white cloths. The fact that it was deserted might mean that it was popular with locals rather than with tourists, who tended to eat later in the evening.

There was no sign of Sulayman, so Makana chose one of the tables outside and sat with his back to the window. They brought him a bowl of pistachios and a small bottle of raki. He poured himself a glass and added water, watching the clear liquid turn cloudy. By his watch he was five minutes early. He sipped the aniseed-flavoured drink and wondered whether he would ever be able to acquire a taste for it. As people wandered by he studied their faces, looking for anything familiar that might have lodged in his subconscious over the past few days. Nothing stood out. He thought about Ayman Nizari: how he seemed to have been able to observe him over several days without him noticing.

While he waited he thought about Winslow. In his mind a question mark still hung over the Englishman. Makana had the sense of having been launched into this with a faulty map, and no compass to speak of. What purpose that might serve, he could not say. He wondered whether he could trust Marty Shaw.

He looked at his watch again. Sulayman was now ten minutes late. He wondered if punctuality was a Turkish quality. Against his better judgement he poured himself another glass of raki. He needed to be able to rely on Sulayman to get them out of the city and across the border with little or no notice. Turning up late for dinner was not encouraging.

'Hey stranger!'

It took Makana a moment to respond, unable to imagine that such a greeting might be addressed to him. He felt his heart sink as the red-faced man stepped forward.

'Remember me?'

107

It was the Dutchman who had introduced himself at the Iskander Grillroom.

'What a coincidence!' the newcomer said, beaming like a schoolboy who had won a prize, which seemed to confirm Makana's worst fears. But it was too late to avoid him. Henk Sneefliet was already settling himself, uninvited, into the chair opposite.

'Small town,' smiled Makana.

'I see you're getting acquainted with local customs.' He picked up the bottle of raki and grinned, revealing two uneven rows of yellow teeth. 'I'm not fond of the stuff myself. I prefer beer.' The man's blue eyes widened as he signalled to the approaching waiter.

There was something about this forwardness that rankled. It was a boldness born not of familiarity but of arrogance.

'Actually, I was just about to leave,' said Makana, looking at his watch. So unsubtle an encounter worried him. Snowfleet, or whatever his real name was, must have known that Makana would be suspicious, yet at the risk of blowing his cover he had come forward. Suddenly, Makana had concerns about Nadir Sulayman. Maybe there was a reason he'd been delayed. Makana handed some money to the waiter and gathered up his cigarettes from the table.

'What a shame,' said the man. 'I was hoping we could get to know one another a little better.'

'I'm afraid I have an appointment.'

'Oh, I understand. It's always difficult, mixing business with pleasure.'

'Some other time perhaps.'

'Yes, some other time.' The Dutchman went through his pockets until he found a business card. From another pocket he produced a pen. 'Taxim Palace Hotel. You can give me a call.'

Makana took the card. Henk Sneefliet, Engineer. There were contact numbers, email accounts and an address in The Hague.

'Thank you. I'll do that.'

They both seemed aware that they were playing a part, and that the next time they met the setting might not be so civil, but for the moment neither of them was prepared to let on.

Leaving Sneefliet behind, Makana reached for the mobile Nadir Sulayman had given him. He needed to warn him off and arrange a new meeting place. The call went straight through to a recorded voice speaking in Turkish. Makana cut the line.

He walked in a wide circle, first one way and then the other, taking more time and being more cautious than usual, varying speed and direction until he was fairly sure he was not being followed. After twenty minutes Nadir Sulayman had still not called back. Now Makana knew something was wrong. The Dutchman had known something, he was sure of it. He took another sharp turn and headed for Nadir Sulayman's office.

Makana walked quickly now. It was getting late and the streets were flooded with evening revellers veering like shoals of fish from one distraction to the next. Tourists and locals brushed past one another as if passing through two versions of the same city. Drunken Germans sang football songs and screamed at one another. Families pulled small children out of their path. Somewhere a siren was wailing, elsewhere there was laughter. Young men and women, all determined to have a good time. Through open doors music drew people into the bars. Red and green neon strips seared the night like streaks of lightning cut through from beyond the stars.

The lighting around the office building seemed fainter than the evening before as Makana climbed slowly to the first floor and made his way round the open gallery. The light over the heavy door was dark. Soft shards of broken glass crunched underfoot as he drew near. In the alleyway just below a loud group of people went by, and he paused, waiting for their laughter to fade. A radio was talking somewhere high up in the building and a woman was calling her child. When he pressed the doorbell he could hear it buzzing within. It sounded clearer than the previous day. Nobody came. A cat brushed past his legs and pushed itself against the door, which moved. He was already regretting the raki he had drunk at the restaurant, although the truth was that his mind was as cold and clear as it ever was. Reaching out a hand, he watched the door yawn open before him.

Walking into a darkened apartment had never struck him as an inspired idea, but Makana saw no other choice. His instincts told him to proceed no further. Better to turn around, head back to his hotel, wait and see what Winslow suggested. But that wasn't going to help anyone, least of all him. Right now, Nadir Sulayman was his only way out of this city.

He stepped inside and stood for a moment, shutting out the muffled sounds of neighbours and people in the street, and music from above. The cat mewed at his feet. It looked up at him as if to ask him what he thought he was doing before it slipped between his legs and disappeared into the night. Makana sighed. He didn't need any more bad omens.

The corridor to his right was dimly lit. Across the darkened vestibule he could make out the door to Sulayman's office, a shard of light just showing. He trod slowly across the open space, not knowing what to expect. With the back of his hand he pushed open the office door and peered around.

At first sight nothing jarred. The room was the same chaotic mess, though maybe more so. Nothing moved save a blue tumbling planet earth bouncing slowly across the window pane. The computer screen stood on the desk with its back to him. The reflection of the planet rebounded from corner to corner like a portal into another universe.

As Makana stepped carefully into the centre of the room, his foot caught a mound of paper. There were files and newspapers scattered all over the floor. Someone had been looking for something. He registered a tap running somewhere, and recalled Sulayman emerging from a bathroom on the right.

Later he would wonder why he had not taken a moment to consider that sound a little more carefully. Instead, his attention centred on what lay behind the desk. The big chair had been tipped over and Nadir Sulayman lay on the floor on his back. The light from the computer screen played over him in soft waves. It took a moment for Makana to realise that the blue plug sticking out of his mouth was his swollen tongue, thick enough to choke him. Something certainly had. His eyes were open. They had the wide, glazed look of someone who had caught a glimpse of eternity.

Makana inched his way around the body. There were sheets of paper scattered around and over it, and splashes of blood. Sulayman's neck seemed to have swollen into two thick rolls. When he leaned closer Makana could make out a thin white band of hard nylon. A plastic cable tie less than half a centimetre thick was so deeply embedded in the flesh that it was almost completely concealed.

The blood came from a wound to the side of the head. There was a scrap of flesh and hair on the sharp corner of the desk which suggested that Sulayman had struggled and hit his head as he went over. There was bruising on his face, one eye was swollen and there were cuts on his left cheek and ear. Two of his fingers looked broken.

As he knelt beside the body, a distinctive buzzing sound drew Makana to lean over and glimpse a green light pulsing. He reached under the desk to fish out the mobile phone, whose screen showed a sealed envelope. When he tapped it the message was simple, and in English: 'In the midnight hour – Blue Ozan?' The sender's name rang a bell. Kara Deniz. He tried to recall where he'd seen it before, and memorised her number before erasing the message and re-placing the phone where he'd found it.

Something caused him to glance up. A sense that the air in the room had shifted in some subtle way. He knew straight away what it was. The running tap he'd heard when he came in was no longer running. His eyes flicked up to the window as a shadow crossed it, fluid and light as silk. An instant's more time, and he might have unbent from the floor It didn't come. When the blow struck him he was still rising, and then he wasn't any longer. The room tilted onto its side, and now he was hugging the floor as if it were a wall.

Chapter Fourteen

H e opened his eyes to find Genghis Khan staring down at him. The long, drooping beard was more than convincing, but Makana was confused. He had always had the impression that the Mongols dressed in furs and animal skins, while this one appeared to be wearing some kind of a uniform. There were shadows moving around the edge of his vision, which seemed to have narrowed. He tried to move, which made his head hurt and caused a commotion around him. The Mongol emperor was yelling at him.

'I'm sorry, I don't understand.'

He was helpless to fend off the hands that searched through his clothes until they came up with his wallet and his new temporary passport.

'English?'

Not so much a question as a statement of disbelief.

They hauled him to his feet, his head feeling like a block of ice balanced on a sharp spike. It should have fallen off, but somehow it didn't. His hands were wrenched behind his back and he felt the metallic crunch of handcuffs clamping tightly around his wrists. Genghis Khan appeared in front of him again and did some more yelling, then two men escorted him from the apartment.

Makana managed to count twenty officers of various ranks before he lost track. His head felt giddy and his hearing was fuzzy. Murder was clearly a major attraction in Istanbul, and no one seemed too concerned with preserving the crime scene. He could imagine something similar happening in Cairo, although the Turks seemed a little better prepared, perhaps even a little more modern. Certainly they were better equipped than their Egyptian counterparts. Paramedics in fluorescent jackets raced past him. Heavy boots rushed into the apartment and out again.

The two officers guarding him stood close by, as if half expecting him to make a run for it, though it was plain he could barely keep his feet. Eventually even this became too much, and he slid down onto the ground, not much caring about the stench of cat piss that rose up to meet him. He felt slightly nauseous and wondered if he was going to throw up. Most of all he felt riled at the time being wasted. He had been reduced to a spectator, not to mention a spectacle. The crowd tramping in and out of the apartment paused to examine him the way you might a caged bear. His two guards stood there proudly, grinning like hunters displaying their catch.

Sitting out of the way on the ground allowed Makana space in which to gather his thoughts. Nadir Sulayman's broken fingers displayed lacerations and cuts, and jagged nails, all of which suggested he had struggled. The killer had slipped the noose over his head and pulled it tight before stepping out of the way to watch him flail. Sulayman must have thrashed about trying to get the noose off, tipping the chair over, tearing his fingertips and ripping off his nails in the fight to breathe. It seemed a dreadful way to end one's life.

He was hauled to his feet. There seemed to be a tension in the air and a sense of order had entered the proceedings. It didn't take long to work out the cause of this change. A man clad in civilian clothes had appeared at the top of the stairs and was making his way around the gallery towards them. From the way his two guards responded, Makana knew the newcomer was a policeman, most likely a senior officer. Cigarettes were hurriedly stubbed out and uniforms straightened.

The new arrival carried himself with the caution of a man who has learned the hard way the perils of rushing in. He was in his mid-forties, but youthful-looking, with a scruffy beard and unruly hair that seemed to speak defiance of regulation. His eyes were baggy and bloodshot, indicating a continual lack of sleep. At the same time they alerted him to everything around him. When he spoke he did so softly but still commanded general attention. The men on either side of Makana took in every syllable.

113

Genghis Khan was back in a hurry, holding up a plastic bag containing Makana's personal effects. The officer glanced at this before turning away. He ran an eye over Makana and then he was gone, disappearing inside the apartment with the same lack of ceremony that had marked his approach. Shouting broke out from within almost at once, and the men who had crowded eagerly inside now began to emerge steadily, pooling around the doorway to kick their heels sullenly as they awaited orders. There was a round of mutual recriminations as they appeared to blame one another for their predicament.

By now a few onlookers had emerged from the neighbouring apartments, lining the railings of the gallery above them. One woman called out a comment that triggered a round of laughter. This too was familiar territory for Makana. More faces appeared at windows and leaning over balconies. The policemen strutted round like players on a stage. The smiles vanished when the detective emerged. Suddenly everyone seemed to find new purpose, and orders were issued and swiftly obeyed.

When he saw order prevailing, the detective turned his attention to Makana. He held up his identity card.

'Inspector Serkan, Department of Homicide.' He spoke in English and held up Makana's temporary British passport. 'How is your head?'

'I'll live.'

'Okay. So ...' He gestured over his shoulder. 'What happened here?'

'I had an appointment with Mr Sulayman.'

'You are friends?'

'We only just met. He was arranging some things for me.'

'What kind of things?' Serkan's eyes searched Makana's.

'Business things.'

'You don't speak Turkish.'

'No. I'm visiting. From Cairo.'

'What is this?' Serkan held up Makana's replacement passport.

'I was robbed. The consulate gave me that.'

'Well, I'm sorry to hear that Mr ... Amin?' The detective flapped the document in his hand as if trying to dry it. 'We will have to check with the British consulate naturally. These temporary passports are easier to fake than the real thing.'

'They will confirm what I have just told you.'

'You say you are here from Cairo?' Serkan sounded sceptical. 'That is where you live, in Egypt, with your British passport?'

'It makes travel much easier.'

'I'm sure.' On second thoughts, perhaps it was more disapproval than doubt in the detective's tone. 'And do you travel a lot, Mr Amin?'

'Yes. Am I under arrest?'

'Good question.' Inspector Serkan seemed amused, but didn't answer. He carried on scribbling notes. Then he looked Makana up and down while tapping his pen absently against the back of the notebook. 'He was dead when you found him?'

'Yes.'

Serkan pointed at Makana's head. 'But someone was still there. The killer?'

'Possibly.'

'You're not sure?' Serkan seemed intrigued.

'I didn't witness the murder. I saw someone reflected in the window, then I was knocked out.'

'Okay, so tell me. From the beginning. You arrive at what time?'

'Around nine forty-five.'

'And how do you get inside?'

'The door was open.'

'Okay.' Inspector Serkan tapped the nib of his pen against his notebook. 'Then you find Mr Sulayman. Then what do you do?'

'I checked to see if he was still alive. I could find no sign of life.'

Serkan frowned. 'You are a doctor? No? No medical training of any kind?'

'You didn't need medical training to know that he was dead.'

Inspector Serkan held up a hand and turned to speak briefly to Genghis Khan, who leapt into action clearing the onlookers away. The inspector turned back to Makana. 'My apologies. You were saying?'

'I said that it was clear he was dead.'

'Of course. Of course.' Serkan studied Makana for a moment. 'Perhaps you can go back to the beginning. You had an appointment with Mr Sulayman?'

'Yes, but not here, we were due to have dinner together. When he didn't appear and didn't return my calls, I came to see if he was here.'

'Where did you have dinner?'

'I didn't have dinner. When he didn't show up I decided to come here.'

'Yes, of course.' Inspector Serkan nodded. 'Continue. Where were you to meet?'

'The Tanpinar restaurant in Nevizade Sokak, at nine o'clock.'

The questions came in an odd, apparently random order, clearly designed to disorient the subject. Makana was familiar with the tactic. It was a way of getting people to lose patience, to become confused, to tie themselves in knots with lies. How he answered was at least as important as what he said. What he said, what he left out, all of it was being carefully recorded. The notebook was a prop. Inspector Serkan waved it about, jotted a few things down, apparently at random, suggesting that he wasn't paying too much attention. It gave the impression that either he was a very poor detective or, as Makana rather suspected, a very good one.

Serkan spoke without looking up. 'When Mr Sulayman did not appear, how long did you wait?'

'I don't know. Half an hour, perhaps.'

'And then what?'

'Well, I tried to call him, and when I got no reply, I decided to walk over here and take a look.'

'There was no guarantee that Mr Sulayman would be here.'

'No,' said Makana. 'It was the only thing I could think of.'

'You were perhaps concerned for Mr Sulayman's safety?'

'Why would I be concerned about his safety?'

Serkan shrugged. 'I was asking the question.'

'No, I just thought he might be working late.' Makana met Serkan's gaze steadily, until the detective looked back down at his notes.

'Was there anyone at the restaurant who could confirm your story?'

'The waiter would remember me, I suppose.' As he spoke Makana thought back to the encounter with the Dutchman. Had his purpose been to try and delay him in some way, to keep him at the restaurant? He held up his hands. 'Do I really need to keep these on?'

'I don't think that is necessary.' Serkan waved to an officer to remove the handcuffs. 'My apologies, but we have to, how you say, tie up all the loose ends?' He consulted his notes, flipping pages back and forth. Makana waited.

'So, you arrive here and find Mr Sulayman lying on the floor. You discover he is dead. Did you touch his phone?'

'At that moment, I wasn't actually too concerned about his phone.'

'Perhaps you want to call for the police?'

'I had my own phone.'

'Of course, but you didn't use it.' Serkan raised an eyebrow.

'I didn't have time.'

'Yes, of course. This person who is hitting you.'

'I'm not making this up.'

'My apologies.' Serkan gave a slightly theatrical bow. 'It was not my intention. My English, you understand.' Makana was convinced there was nothing wrong with the detective's English.

'I didn't kill him.'

'Please, Mr Amin. Nobody is accusing you, but you see my situation.' The detective circled a finger in the air. 'Nobody else saw this mysterious person.'

'That doesn't mean she doesn't exist.'

'She?' Serkan's finger stopped moving. 'You think the killer was a woman?'

Makana had spoken impulsively. He hadn't looked into the thought before this moment, but he realised that was what he believed. It had only been a fleeting glimpse, and yet something in the way the person moved had belonged to a woman.

'I saw something. Someone.'

'You were at the scene of the crime. That makes you …'

'A witness. Not a suspect.'

'Let us say, a person of interest.' Serkan looked as if he had something else on his mind, but whatever he might have been about to say was cut short by the return of the sergeant, whose look suggested that Makana was still more of a suspect than a witness, at least in his eyes. The two officers fell into conversation, ignoring Makana, before Inspector Serkan addressed him again.

'You are Egyptian?'

'I'm originally from Sudan.'

'But you live in Egypt, in Cairo?' Makana nodded. 'And you are here on business, you say. What kind of business?'

'Agricultural machinery.'

'That's why you came to visit Mr Sulayman this evening, to discuss tractors?'

'We were to have dinner together, as I told you.'

'Of course you did. Forgive me.' Serkan translated for the benefit of the other detective, who gave a tut of impatience as though he didn't believe a word of it. With an eye trained on Makana he grumbled a series of his own questions, which Serkan translated into English.

'Sergeant Berat asks, was the body cold? Did you touch anything?'

'No, of course not.' Makana waited while his answer was relayed. Now he had the attention of both of them. The bulky sergeant began mumbling again, but Serkan silenced him with a raised hand.

'Sergeant Berat raises the same question I put to you earlier. Most people when encountering a man in this condition would be, shall we say, alarmed. They might try to revive him. You did nothing of the kind. On the contrary, you touched nothing.'

'I could see he was dead. I realised there was nothing to be done.'

'It is almost as if you have experience of these matters.' Inspector Serkan smiled again, in his enigmatic fashion.

'How difficult can it be?' Both men were staring at him in a curious way. Makana wondered if he was overselling himself or not giving them enough. 'He had clearly choked to death. His eyes were wide open and he was not breathing. You didn't need a medical degree to see that he was dead.'

Sergeant Berat sniffed and rubbed the tip of his nose with his thumb. He seemed to bear some kind of a grudge against the world, as if he felt he was constantly being slighted. In that sense, although physically he resembled Genghis Khan, Sergeant Berat put Makana in mind of his old partner, Mek Nimr.

The sergeant had one more question.

'Tell us about the person you claim knocked you out.'

'As I said earlier, I only caught a glimpse of them.' Makana looked Sergeant Berat in the eye as he spoke.

'Sergeant Berat wonders if you have something to hide.'

Makana almost laughed. 'Please, Inspector, this has been a long evening and I am very tired. My head hurts and this whole experience has been quite a shock.'

'Of course. You should be examined by the paramedics before you go. I understand you are eager to return to your hotel, and we shall return you there as soon as possible.'

'If there's nothing more you need from me, then yes, I would like that.'

'A car will be arranged. We will need to take a full statement from you, for our report. A formality, nothing more.' Inspector Serkan gave the order. Sergeant Berat muttered something before moving off, and Serkan apologised. 'He's a good man, especially in a dangerous situation. Brave, if a little old-fashioned. He likes things to stay as they are. You understand?'

'I think so.'

'For him the problem here is that he finds it hard to believe that a woman could be capable of such a murder.'

'I'm surprised,' said Makana. 'I would have thought that experience would have taught him that anyone, man or woman, is capable of taking a life, under the right circumstances.'

A slow smile appeared on the inspector's face. 'The way you answer, one might almost believe you were the detective and I the suspect.'

'I assure you …'

'Please.' Serkan held up a hand. 'It's quite all right.'

'I may have been mistaken.'

'Your answer was instinctive. It came from here.' The inspector touched a finger to his heart. 'You must repeat exactly what you have told me in your statement.' He waved a hand in the air and two uniformed men came forward to escort Makana to the ambulance parked by the building entrance. In the bright glare of the interior a paramedic examined Makana's head and cleaned some blood from the bruise on the back of his head. He was just finishing up when Serkan reappeared.

'I shall take you to the station myself.'

Waving back the uniformed men, the detective led the way down the road to where a battered white Fiat was parked on the pavement. As he struggled to unlock the door he explained. 'My father used to sell carpets in the bazaar. I used to sit in the back and watch him make deals with all kinds of shady characters. I convinced myself they were all criminals. That's when I decided to become a detective.'

'And your father?'

'He died penniless. He was not good with money. He liked to spend more than he had. When he bought this car he was so proud. One day this will be yours, he said. I thought he was joking, but here I am twenty years later, still driving the same car.'

At police headquarters on Tarlabaşi Boulevard they sat in a drab room, ringing with furious telephones that went unanswered as Makana repeated his story. The No-Smoking signs on the wall were masked by a cloud of grey smoke. Overflowing ashtrays adorned every desk. Before he could even reach for his own cigarettes, the inspector had offered him one of his – a Turkish brand he hadn't seen before. Makana nodded gratefully. Across the room he saw the woman in the raincoat who had opened the door for him on his first visit to Nadir Sulayman's office. She was waiting to be interviewed. Above her a small portable television rested on a shelf. On the screen were images of the ongoing war in Iraq. A reporter wearing a flak jacket and a helmet spoke into a microphone, behind her the blackened skeleton of a car bomb. The world and its problems went on.

Makana's own statement was transcribed by a woman in her fifties with dyed black hair pinned tightly back. She wore cotton gloves and tinted glasses. Between them sat an interpreter, an unshaven man who kept yawning and calling for cups of coffee between sentences. The transcriber said nothing. She didn't look once at Makana. The screen was covered with words he could not read, and the finished statement might have said anything – a fairy tale, a full confession, he simply had no way of knowing. Inspector Serkan had disappeared for a while, but when he returned he perched on the edge of the desk.

'Your hotel confirms that there is someone of your name staying there. How long have you held a British passport?'

'Oh, some years now.'

'You used to live there?'

'For a time, yes. My wife was English.'

'You are no longer married?'

'She died.'

'I'm sorry to hear that.'

'It was a long time ago,' Makana said. He was tired. 'Does it make a difference?'

'No, this is mere curiosity. Background. The British are generous with their blessings, wouldn't you say? It makes travel easier for you …'

Again Makana sensed something in the detective's tone.

'You don't approve?'

Inspector Serkan gave a shrug. 'Who am I to judge? I believe a man should be proud of his origins.'

'Having a British passport doesn't change who I am. It's a practical arrangement.'

'Yes, so you said. The British Consulate is closed now, but we shall check with them in the morning to confirm the validity of this document.'

'You're welcome to. I'm sure they will remember me.'

'You have no objections?'

'Not at all.' Makana resisted the temptation to ask if he might leave. Serkan seemed to enjoy toying with him, making him wait, so he would wait.

'Tell me, Mr Amin, can you think of anyone who might have a motive to kill Mr Sulayman?'

'I barely met the man. I'm sorry I can't be of more help. I imagine he had enemies.'

'Enemies?'

'He was a businessman,' said Makana. 'He must have had rivals.'

'Rivals perhaps, but enemies is another matter, wouldn't you say?'

'Could it have been political?'

'Perhaps. Nothing in Turkey is political,' Serkan shrugged. 'And everything is political.'

'I get the feeling that what you are really asking,' said Makana slowly, 'is whether Nadir Sulayman's death is in some way related to my business here.'

Serkan gave a little bow. 'I could not have put it better myself.'

'Are you worried I might be in danger?'

'It is a concern,' Serkan said. 'I am trying to protect you, Amin Bey.'

'Well, I appreciate your concern, but I can't see that anyone would be that interested in used agricultural machinery.'

Having finished his work, the interpreter got to his feet and wandered off, still yawning. The typist remained where she was, watching the two men from behind her dark glasses. She sat perfectly still, as if gripped by the unfolding drama.

'You are right.' The detective looked thoughtful. 'It seems an unlikely explanation, but naturally we shall pursue this line. It would be irresponsible not to do so. We must go through his papers, find out where he was getting the machinery from. Perhaps there is a link to organised crime.'

'Nadir Sulayman didn't strike me as the kind of man who would have dealings with the underworld.'

'This is your first visit to Istanbul, Mr Amin. Sometimes things are not as clean as the tourist brochures lead one to believe.'

Makana wanted to help Serkan. Most of all he wanted to know who had killed Nadir Sulayman. He considered telling him about the Dutchman staying at the Taxim Palace Hotel, but he had no evidence of a connection and so nothing to offer. He also knew that to do that would be to compromise his mission to recover Ayman Nizari.

'The woman you saw …'

'Like I said, I might have been wrong. The light was poor, it was a reflection in a window at night, which is never clear at the best of times.'

'So, now you're not sure?' Sergeant Berat was waving from across the room. The inspector clicked his tongue impatiently. 'If he had his way, you'd spend the night in an interrogation room. Luckily for you we differ in our methods.'

'That's reassuring to hear.'

'There's a car to take you to your hotel. I would like to talk to you again, however, if you have no objections?'

'I'm happy to help in any way.'

'Excellent, and Mr Amin Bey, please do not leave Istanbul without informing me.'

Sergeant Berat was waiting by the door, that sullen look of distrust engraved on his face. They made quite a team, the mild-mannered inspector and the bullish Genghis Khan. Serkan shook Makana's hand.

'Rest assured, we will find the person who killed Nadir Sulayman. Here in Istanbul we take murder very seriously.'

Chapter Fifteen

So did Makana. He had taken murder seriously for a very long time. There was, however, a nagging feeling at the back of his mind that he didn't want Inspector Serkan to succeed in finding the person responsible for Nadir Sulayman's murder; at least, not before he himself did.

When Inspector Serkan had asked if he had recognised the woman he had seen in Sulayman's office, he had lied, and only partly because he wasn't sure. There'd been no more than moments between catching a glimpse of a blurred figure in the window pane and being hit on the head. What he had seen, or what he had thought he had seen, was impossible to explain, even to himself. It tied into the rising sense of confusion that had been building in him since his arrival in this city. He couldn't possibly explain what he thought he had seen without sounding as if he was losing his mind. And here lay his dilemma.

The figure he had glimpsed in Nadir's apartment was the same woman he had seen in the bazaar, the one he had mistaken for Muna. It was possible his mind was playing tricks on him. For a man who'd spent most of his career confronting death, it was perhaps odd that he had never been able to come to terms with the loss of his wife and daughter. Maybe it was the way they had been taken from him, torn from his sight so abruptly, without warning. There was nothing strange in grieving for your dearest loved ones, but this grief had entailed a fatal charge, a sense of being condemned by destiny to relive their final moments over and over again.

Makana didn't believe in many things, and he certainly didn't believe in the spirits of the dead walking the earth as large as life.

So what did that leave? Coincidence? Here too his imagination did not stretch far. Something had sparked in his memory, something he had never been able to shake off. The only other explanation was the one he had the most trouble allowing himself to even contemplate.

When rumours had first surfaced that his daughter might have survived the accident, Makana had refused to believe them. He suspected this was part of a campaign to wound him by old enemies. At the same time, naturally, he began to make inquiries. Nothing conclusive ever came up, but the stories refused to go away. According to some, Nasra had been paralysed in the fall and was in full-time care in hospital. Others said she had been adopted by a high-ranking official in the government. Friends warned him that it was all a trap: his enemies were trying to lure him home.

For fifteen years Muna and Nasra had lived inside him. The two most precious things in his life, his wife and daughter, had been taken from him. They were always with him. Not ghosts, but presences. Stored safely within, like love, like the inevitability of death. Until that vision in the market, when he'd caught sight of something that he knew he could not possibly explain. An instinct, a feeling. A conviction.

Since that moment he had been busy trying to convince himself that he had imagined it, that first time, that his mind was playing tricks. Except that he had seen her again, as he crouched over Nadir Sulayman's body. And that led him to another question he could barely bring himself to address. One that went above and beyond the matter of who she was. Could she have killed Sulayman? It felt as though he was unravelling from within.

At the hotel he found that the lift was occupied by a woman not quite as young as she wished to appear. She was wearing a tight black dress upon which golden dragons writhed with her every move. She watched him in the little mirror on the rear wall as she fixed her lipstick.

'Oh,' she said. 'Are you the one?'

She had an unusual accent. She was Turkish, and yet her English had the uneven tone of one who has spent time in the company of foreigners.

'I'm not the lift operator.'

'But I have been waiting,' she pouted. It was an expression she had clearly been practising.

'Let me try.' Makana imagined Jehan shaking her head in disbelief. 'Which floor?'

'Four,' she said, somewhat breathlessly, and a little too close to his ear for comfort. Makana forced himself to ignore the cloying scent of her perfume and focused instead on the mechanics of the situation. He swung the handle round, and quite miraculously the delicate iron cage began to move. He slumped back against the wall, too exhausted to contemplate what it would have been like to have to walk up. When they reached the fourth floor he swung the handle to the stationary position and pulled open the gate.

'I can always be easily found,' she purred. 'Just ask on reception for Aysun.'

'I'll try to remember that.'

Makana's thoughts were elsewhere. He listened to the sound of her footsteps receding along the corridor, wondering who was waiting for her, then he swung the handle and rose one more floor. After stepping out of the lift, he followed the carpeted hallway through the building to his room.

Out on the balcony he lit a cigarette and tried to devise his next move. He was running out of options, and waiting around was poor strategy. He needed some kind of leverage. After a time, he went back into the room to retrieve the card Marty Shaw had given him and used the hotel phone to make the call.

'I was hoping to hear from you,' Shaw said.

'We should meet.'

'Sure.' He could almost hear the Englishman smiling. 'Just say where and when.'

After that he tried to settle down, but his mind was restless. Sleep would not come. The room felt claustrophobic. He pulled an armchair from the corner of the room and set it by the open doors to the balcony and sat there smoking, watching the stars slip across the darkened skyline as the city below fell quiet. Electric lights glittered like highly charged insects. There was something about this city that seemed to want to expel him, or failing that, to swallow him whole.

Nadir Sulayman's death made things urgent. He had to bring Nizari in quickly. How he would get him out was another matter. He hoped Winslow would have an alternative plan. There was a faint chance this murder had nothing to do with him, that Sulayman had other problems – even, as the inspector had suggested, some link to organised crime.

At some point Makana must have fallen asleep, because he lurched awake with a start from a dream in which Nadir Sulayman's dead body had been crushing him, bearing down on him with all his weight. Makana had kept on rolling from side to side to get out from under him, but no matter how he tried he could not shift him. The rotten stench of the man was suffocating. The engorged face and blue, swollen neck were vivid.

He was cold. The room was filled with shadows. He sensed there was something there, something that floated in the dark-ness before him, just out of reach. It was drawing steadily closer, not seen so much as felt, a figure at once familiar and strange. A woman dressed from head to toe in black. He knew who she was. He reached for his wallet and fished out the creased snapshot that he carried everywhere with him. The years had taken their toll. It was a cracked, dog-eared thing, the lighting was off and the colours showed the faded wash of time. Still, it was the most precious object he possessed: the image of Muna holding their baby daughter. He set the picture upright on the bedside table next to him.

Guilt endured as much as longing. He had survived after all, and they had not. A dark haven in his mind that wished he had surren-dered to his emotions and taken his own life. There were times he had considered it, times when he had convinced himself that it would have been the honourable thing to do. The sequence of events played out over and over like a film on continuous loop. If only he had done this, or that. If only he had not chosen that route to escape by. If only he had been driving, rather than Muna. If only he hadn't been prevented from throwing himself into the river after them …

It was almost midnight. His head throbbed and he would give anything for a good night's sleep, but it seemed that must wait. He opened the envelope with the newspaper clippings Sami's friend Kursad had left him and looked at the name of the journalist who had written the article on the traffic incident involving Nadia Razvan. Kara Deniz. This was where he'd seen the name before.

Chapter Sixteen

Istanbul Day Four

The Blue Ozan was a dark and smoky place after midnight. The music had an oriental feel to it, with soft hands sweeping across drums that sounded as if they were being played underwater. Reedy horns twisted in the background. The song sounded vaguely familiar, like a Turkish version of an old jazz standard, and it took Makana a moment to place it.

It was hard to see in here, but maybe that was the idea. Low blue and red lights provided barely enough illumination to navigate the furniture. Thin neon strips behind the bar lit up rows of coloured bottles. People were sprawled on couches and bowl-shaped armchairs set around coffee tables bearing glass lamps in which coloured wax shapes rose and fell, giving the place a dated feel. The clientele, however, appeared to be mostly young. Dressed in jeans and crumpled jackets. Intellectuals. On the walls were black and white images of distinguished-looking men and women whom Makana took for poets and writers. It was that kind of a place. A drunken man in a corduroy jacket was wandering from table to table, spilling his beer as he tried to interest people in buying a pamphlet. Makana shook his head, which invited a long lecture of which he understood not a word. When he finally moved on, Makana tried to pick out Kara Deniz. No face suggested itself, so he dialled the number he had memorised from Nadir Sulayman's phone. A small woman in her thirties, sitting alone by the window, produced a mobile from her leather jacket. She was still staring at the screen when Makana sat down in the stool next to hers. She glanced over at him.

'In the midnight hour,' he said in English, taking the stool next to her.

'I'm sorry?' Kara Deniz wore her dark hair cut short, which emphasised the economical lines of her face.

'Is that some kind of code you shared? A song you both liked.'

She glanced at him briefly then. 'You're wasting your time,' she said dismissively. 'You're not my type.'

'I'm not talking about me. You sent the message to Nadir Sulayman.'

She was in the process of lighting a cigarette, but blew out the match before it burnt her finger.

'Who are you?'

'You sent Nadir a message that you would be here.'

She glanced around as if to look for help, then started to get to her feet. Makana put out a hand.

'Please,' he said. 'Just hear me out.'

'Why? Tell me why I should listen.'

'Because Nadir meant something to you, and I intend to find out who killed him.' He gestured at the stool she had vacated. 'Please. I'm not here to hurt you.'

Kara Deniz dumped her shoulder bag back down on the table and slid onto the high stool. The news of Nadir's death didn't seem to surprise her.

'How did you hear that he's dead?'

She bowed her head. 'I got a call from a contact in the police.' She looked up at him. 'How did you know him?'

'Nadir was arranging something for me.'

'What kind of something?'

'Transport.'

She stared at him. 'Did you kill him?'

'I had no reason to.'

'So you say.'

'I got there just after it happened.'

'Why should I believe you?' Her eyes searched his.

'Because I have no reason to lie to you. I came here because I need your help.'

She seemed unconvinced. She took a sip from her bottle of beer and picked at the label with her nail.

'Is that how you found me, the message I left for him?'

'In the midnight hour. It was on his phone.'

'It was our own little joke, a code. It meant nothing.'

'But you came here all the same, knowing he was dead.'

'Did you ever lose someone close to you?' she asked. She looked away again. 'Nadir and I always said that if something happened to one of us, the other one would come here and get good and drunk.' She took a long drink. 'I just didn't count on you being here as well.'

'Do you have any idea who might have wanted him dead?'

The music had changed to some kind of rock ballad. It wasn't a good change.

'Look, you sound like a cop. I have no idea who you are, and I don't know what you want, but if you don't leave me alone I'm going to start screaming.'

Makana produced the newspaper clipping Kursad had sent him and put it on the table.

'You wrote this.'

Kara Deniz picked up the clipping and held it up to the light for a second before placing it back on the table. 'It's a story I filed about an accident.' There was a defiant look in her eyes. 'What's your interest in this?'

'Tell me about this accident.'

'It's all in the article. There's not much more to tell. In the early hours of the morning, an ambulance was in a collision with a bus that had just come in from Anatolia. It happens all the time. The drivers fall asleep at the wheel.'

'Why were you interested in the case?'

'Why? Because it was a bit of a mystery. The ambulance had been stolen some hours earlier. An unidentified woman died and there were reports of two others fleeing the scene.' Kara Deniz shrugged and reached for her beer. 'End of story.'

'You never followed it up?'

'There was nothing to follow up.'

'The identity of the woman, the people who fled the scene. Weren't you interested?'

'What has this got to do with Nadir's death?' Kara Deniz frowned at him.

131

'I'm trying to find someone. I believe he was being taken somewhere in that ambulance. After the accident he managed to escape. Was there any description of the people who survived?'

'Nothing that was any use to anyone.'

'There must have been something to go on. Why didn't you follow it up?'

'I'm a reporter,' she laughed. 'Not a detective.' She grew serious. 'What do you want from me?'

'Nadir was helping me,' Makana said. 'I'd like to know who killed him and why, but I don't know this town. You're the only person I know who knew him.'

'I thought the police were supposed to do that kind of thing.'

'I don't know how things work here, but where I come from the police don't have a reputation for being helpful.' Makana glanced around, but nobody was paying them any attention.

'Where would that be?'

'Cairo.'

She fished through her bag for cigarettes. 'Why should I trust you?'

'Because he was your friend.' Makana studied her face. It was a hard face and would not be described as pretty, but she had a striking gaze. She looked at him as if she was weighing every word, but she was hesitating, and that was in his favour. He watched her light her cigarette.

'You're right about the police; they are useless. They'll do nothing, especially for Nadir.'

'He wasn't popular with the authorities?'

She blew smoke over his head. 'He was mixed up in politics. A long time ago. They never forget that kind of thing.' She swung round to signal to the bartender, who waved back. She swivelled back to Makana.

'So, if this is about trust why can't you tell me what Nadir was helping you with?'

'Transport. He was helping a friend out of the country.'

'A friend without papers? You mean, smuggling him into Europe?'

'Something like that.'

She looked him up and down. 'You don't look like a smuggler.'

'What do I look like?'

'Like a cop.'

Makana smiled. 'I take it you don't much like the police.'

'What's to like?' The waitress arrived with what looked like whisky and ice. Kara Deniz drank down half of it in one swallow and wiped her mouth with the back of her hand. She slid off her stool, wrestling the bag back onto her shoulder. 'I have to go.'

'You haven't finished your drink.'

She reached for the glass and drained it. 'Happy?'

'If you decide to help me, you have my number.'

'Don't count on it.'

She moved swiftly towards the door, her slim hips twitching left and right as she edged her way through the crowd, pausing to drop some money onto the waitress's tray. Through the window Makana watched her walk down the street. Every opportunity he had seemed to be slipping out of his grasp.

He emerged from the bar to be greeted by the angry chatter of a helicopter overhead. It was joined by another, and the two circled like clumsy insects. Others along the street had noticed the activity too. There were raised heads and a few comments. Curious, Makana followed the crowd that gravitated down a long, winding street towards the waterfront. It brought him out onto a busy road where on the other side a jumble of vehicles was bathed in the blue and red stutter of flashing lights from emergency vehicles.

Looking north Makana could see the arc of lights over the Bosporus on the high bridge that tethered the edge of Europe to the Asian continent. A horn blast caused him to step aside as an ambulance nosed its way into the confusion. Beyond the vehicles and the restless crowd, more lights could be seen out on the water. Powerful searchlight beams played back and forth over the same section of dark water. A couple of police cruisers bobbed around a large rusty vessel. Garbled orders over a megaphone were drowned out by the clanking of chains and the high whirr of a winch. A fishing net was being hauled up into the air.

In the harsh, fragmented light, the water dripped off in sheets like diamonds pouring into the sea. A groan of dismay went up from the crowd as the object trapped within the nylon netting grew clearer. The fish had not had time to do their work, but something had bitten a chunk from the side of the body. Perhaps the propeller of one of the countless ferries that shuttled across here every day, or one of the huge ships that ploughed regularly up and down this strait. It was starting to rain now. There was some kind of technical problem with the winch, and the teardrop-shaped net swayed back and forth with its gruesome cargo trapped in the beams of light.

Turning away, Makana caught sight of a familiar figure. The tall Dutchman. Wearing a long coat that was already slick and shiny with rain, he was standing off to one side, talking to somebody Makana could not see. He moved to try and get a better view, but people kept getting in the way. When his line of sight finally cleared he saw the lanky figure walking away, alone in the distance with his hands in his pockets.

Chapter Seventeen

W hen he woke up and disentangled himself from the damp
sheets, feeling more tired than when he'd closed his eyes,
Makana took a long shower. He felt mildly better by the time he
dressed and left the hotel.

The call shop he had used before was closed, so he went back to
the phone box on the corner. It was occupied by a woman dressed
in dirty trousers and an unravelling jumper. She was surrounded
by half-a-dozen plastic carrier bags of various shapes and colours.
Turnips and carrots stuck cheerfully up out of one. She eyed
Makana warily, holding the receiver at a distance from her ear.
Someone was shouting down the line from somewhere. By the time
she had finished her call a small arc of cigarette butts littered the
ground around her feet.

Makana smoked another cigarette before the phone booth was
finally free. First he dialled Marcus Winslow's number in Cairo.
After three rings there was a beep. He left a message:

'Our travel agent is no longer able to offer us his services. We
need an alternative plan.'

Makana hung up and then tried Sami, whose phone was answered by Rania.

'He's in the Sinai doing some background on this Dahab bombing. How are you doing?'

'It's getting complicated.' Makana gazed into the distance. Cairo
suddenly felt a long way away. They talked for a few minutes and
then he rang off, promising to call back. He dialled Jehan at home,
half hoping she wouldn't answer. When she did he was taken aback.

'You're home.'

'Today's Friday, or have you already forgotten? We don't work on Fridays. I was getting ready to take my nephews to the zoo. Heaven knows why, I hate the place, and it's always full of the noisiest people.' He had fallen silent. 'Are you all right?' he heard her ask.

'I'm fine.'

'You sound worried.'

'I'm not sure this is going the way it was planned,' said Makana slowly.

'Are you talking about your work, or us?'

'I thought I was talking about work.'

'You left without saying goodbye.'

'I know, I'm sorry.'

There was another long pause. He could hear her scrabbling about for cigarettes, followed by the rasp of the lighter. She exhaled.

'How much longer do you think it will take?'

'It's hard to say.' He turned to look out at the view again.

'I'm worried about you,' she said, her voice slow and measured. 'I have the feeling you're in a lot of danger.'

He tried to strike a brighter note. 'I've been doing some sightseeing while I'm here.'

'That's nice. I was there, you know, years ago, when my husband was still alive. It's such a romantic city.' There was another pause. 'You're not worried about coming home?'

'Me? No, why should I be worried about that?'

'I don't know. You just sound … so far away.'

'It's not a very good connection,' he said.

'I don't mean that,' she shot back.

'Look, I can't explain what it is,' he began. 'It's as if there's something here, some part of me …' He was halfway through the sentence when he realised he didn't know what he was talking about.

'Come home soon, please. I miss you.'

'As soon as I can, I promise.'

He heard her start to say something but then the line cut out. Jinn at play, or something more? More likely the card had simply run out of credit. As he made his way back to the hotel he wondered at the wisdom of calling. All he'd achieved was to worry her more. He would have to wait until the assigned time to call Winslow again.

As he came through the door of the hotel, Haluk, the diminutive receptionist, skipped towards him and bowed. What with the high marble walls, the crystal chandeliers and the gilt-framed doors, Makana felt as if he had just wandered into the court of the Sultan.

'Your honourable guest has arrived, Mr Amin.'

'My guest?'

'I took the liberty of showing him into the dining room, where you will be most comfortable.'

The man appeared to somehow have got it into his head that Makana was a visiting dignitary of some kind. With great ceremony he led the way into the vast dining room. The breakfast crowd had already departed, desperate to get out and see the sights in case they had disappeared from the face of the earth overnight.

Inspector Serkan was sitting on the far side of the room gazing out of the high windows. He was still wearing his coat, a rather threadbare camel-coloured cashmere. In the morning light he looked older than he had the night before, as if the hours had rubbed out the last vestiges of innocence from his face.

'Good morning, Mr Amin Bey.'

There was something quaint and respectful about the way he got to his feet. By his side Makana heard Haluk sigh with contentment, as if in longing for some lost age of chivalry. There was something rather old-fashioned about the Turkish detective. It confirmed Makana's first impression, that the inspector, despite his humble appearance and manners, was a shrewd and rather cautious man.

'I took the liberty of ordering coffee. I hope you don't mind.'

'Not at all.' Makana glanced over his shoulder. The receptionist was already issuing orders on his way out of the room. There was honour in entertaining a police inspector, or perhaps he was just being prudent.

'You certainly believe in travelling in style, Mr Amin. I must salute you.' Serkan gestured at their surroundings and smiled, as though everything about Makana amused him. 'This hotel has played a part in the history of this city. Once upon a time the elite of Europe would travel to Istanbul and stay in these fine rooms.' He waved, as magnanimous as a modern-day Kublai Khan. 'And now you are here.'

'I don't think I quite fit that category.'

'Times change,' said the detective philosophically. 'What matters is how they change us.'

A waiter appeared, to start energetically sweeping up bread-crumbs with a brush and a little silver tray. Serkan waved him away and asked him where the coffee was. That much Makana could follow. The waiter nodded over his shoulder as if to some blank spot from which coffee would magically emerge. Serkan waited from him to move out of earshot before he continued speaking.

'I must confess that I am here because of my wife.'

'Your wife?'

The inspector shrugged. 'I am a poor sleeper. When there is something on my mind I wake up in the night, I wander the house, I smoke in the kitchen. Naturally, all of this disturbs her rest, so she tells me, and she always tells me the same thing, as though I forget that she has told me a thousand times before. She tells me to find out what it is that is bothering me and to go straight to the source and address it. So here I am.' Serkan held out his hands as if to underline the fact.

'I am the cause of your sleeplessness?'

'Does that surprise you?'

'I've been accused of worse.'

A pause ensued as the waiter arrived, rattling cups. He set them down before proceeding to fill them from a pot. The coffee looked thin and unpromising.

'Have you given any more thought to the death of Mr Nadir Sulayman?'

'Why would my opinion be of any value?'

Inspector Serkan sipped his coffee and pulled a face. 'American tourists are causing untold damage to our coffee-drinking habits.' He snapped his fingers and the worried waiter came over. Serkan addressed him sharply and he hurried away. Another example of the way the inspector wielded authority: quiet but effective.

'I may be wrong, Amin Bey, but I believe you have some under-standing of murder.'

138

'I trade in agricultural machinery.'

'Yes, so you said.' A faint smile played on the inspector's lips.

'You think I'm lying.'

'Lying is a strong term.' The inspector frowned as the waiter returned to remove the pot and cups. 'Sergeant Berat would no doubt prefer me to put it more strongly.'

'He thinks I am lying.'

'He is my subordinate.' Inspector Serkan tilted his head, 'but I must listen to what he says.'

'If you take a look at Mr Sulayman's business records, you will find they confirm my claim.'

'That is what Sergeant Berat is doing as we speak.'

Makana sat back. Serkan's eyes were those of a cat patiently observing a particularly tricky bird.

'I thought that you had concerns about Nadir Sulayman's business dealings?'

'I do.'

'Yet you come to me because you're not sleeping.'

Serkan gave a shrug. 'I am a light sleeper. If something does not sit right with me, then I am disturbed.' The detective sighed. 'No doubt it will lead me to an early grave, as my wife tells me.'

'I'm not sure what I can do to put your mind at rest.'

'Well, perhaps you could begin by telling me why you did not report the assault in which your passport was stolen.'

'It seemed an unnecessary bother.'

'Most people when violently attacked in a foreign city and relieved of their passport would automatically go to the police. Yet you did not.'

'As I say, I had a lot of things to do. It happened late at night. The British Consulate provided me with a replacement. I thought it best to move on.'

'Apart from the passport, did they take anything else?'

'A little money, not much.'

The coffee arrived, this time already poured into the little cups. It was worth the wait just for the aroma. Serkan nodded approvingly.

'Did you get a look at your attackers?'

'No, and that was part of the problem. I didn't think I had much to offer the police.'

'How would you describe them?'

'Young men who had probably had a little too much to drink.' Makana stirred sugar into his coffee. 'Sometimes they get carried away.'

'Nevertheless, you could have been seriously hurt, or worse. Some of these ruffians carry knives.'

'I don't think they wanted to hurt me.'

'They could easily have done so.'

'But they didn't.' Makana watched the inspector and waited for his next move.

'Well, you're a lucky man, Mr Amin. Not only did the attack do no harm to yourself, but the British consulate also made an exception. Normally a police report is needed for a replacement document to be issued. In your case they waived that rule. Is that not a curious fact?'

'I'm not sure. Is it?'

'I find it strange that a man such as yourself, well travelled, experienced in the ways of the world, should avoid such formalities.'

Makana had been trying to put off lighting a cigarette, worried that it might make him look nervous, but it was a losing battle. He offered the packet to Serkan, who politely declined, producing his own from his coat pocket instead. There were no waiters in sight and no ashtrays, so Makana retrieved a saucer left on the next table. In such a grand room it felt like an act of vandalism.

'I would like to put your mind at rest, Inspector, but I'm afraid I can't really explain. At the time I wanted to just get back to my hotel, and the next morning there seemed little point.'

'Let us leave that matter for the moment.' Serkan squinted at the ash on the tip of his cigarette. He snapped his fingers again and the waiter returned, bearing an ashtray. 'Can you tell me, please, what is your opinion of Mr Sulayman's death?'

'Like I said, I'm really not sure my opinion would be of much use to you.'

'You were the first person at the scene of the crime, apart from the killer. You might have noticed something that escaped our attention.' The inspector cleared his throat. 'Some of our officers have more enthusiasm than sense.'

'You mean they trampled over the crime scene?'

'We are a long way from perfect. Perhaps it is not so different where you come from.'

'Police procedure? I wouldn't know.'

'Of course not. Still, I would like to hear your impressions.' Serkan gestured for Makana to continue.

'It struck me as a nasty way to die.' Slipping a noose over someone's head and watching them choke to death wasn't just taking a life, it was about watching someone die. To kill that way suggested a degree of cold-blooded sadism.

'Yes, I see,' Serkan mused. 'Not the fight. You know, perhaps, that most murders are like that.'

'How would I know something like that?'

The Turkish detective smiled. He drew slowly on his cigarette as he watched Makana. 'Some people dream for years of killing their husband or wife, or lover. They never bring themselves to commit the act until one day it just happens. Almost by itself. They have no explanation of why they chose that moment.'

'This was different.'

'Yes, I think we can agree on that. The killer watched him struggle. That takes a certain kind of character.' Inspector Serkan stubbed out his cigarette. 'Have you ever killed a man?' he asked, his eyes flicking up to meet Makana's.

'There isn't much call for that in my line of work.'

'Perhaps in some previous job.' Serkan studied the tablecloth. 'Military service, the security services?' The inspector shrugged as if it were a casual inquiry.

'Are you asking me if I work for Egyptian intelligence?'

'Do you?'

'No.' Makana finished his cigarette and pushed his coffee cup aside. 'I can assure you that I have no connection with them.'

'My apologies, Amin Bey, I was just … speculating.'

'I'm sure.' Makana felt as if he were in a complex chess game against a very able adversary.

'You have perhaps heard that Istanbul has recently suffered a series of murders.'

'I read something about that the other day.'

'You are well informed.'

'You're asking yourself if this could be related?'

Inspector Serkan moved his coffee cup away to lean his elbows on the table. 'The interesting thing is that the murder weapon is the same. I don't know what the name for it is. American forces use the plastic loops instead of handcuffs in Iraq and Afghanistan. More economical, I suppose. We are trying to trace the manufacturer of the one used, but it's almost impossible. You find them everywhere in the market.'

'You think there is some kind of political angle?'

'It's possible. Many people feel we should be more vocal in our rejection of US policies, particularly with regard to Kurdistan.'

'The other victims were killed the same way?'

'Yes. Three of them so far, four if we include Mr Sulayman.'

'The *karakoncolos*.'

Serkan dismissed the name with a cluck of his tongue. 'People like to believe in fairy tales.'

'So that's all there is to it?'

'It's easier to believe that a monster is loose than that it might be a simple person, perhaps even someone you know.'

'There must be a lot of pressure on you to solve the case.'

'As you can imagine. Politicians, the business community. Powerful men, let us say. Such news can damage a city's reputation.'

'The tourists will stay away.'

'Exactly.' Inspector Serkan toyed with his lighter, a tarnished silver device that looked like a family heirloom. 'On the other hand I have people like Sergeant Berat who are so eager to please that they would pin the murder on the first likely suspect who comes along.'

'Meaning me?' Makana queried.

'We are speaking in strict confidence, you understand?'

'I think so.'

'I don't believe you killed Mr Sulayman. I also do not believe that he was murdered by the same person as the other three victims. All

142

of those murders took place in public places. Everything suggests the victims were chosen at random. They were alone late at night. A drunken girl passed out on a bench. A blind man who sold lottery tickets. A taxi driver asleep in his car.' Inspector Serkan took a deep breath. 'It suggests the killer wanders the streets seeking opportunity. We are possibly looking for someone mentally unstable. The city is full of lost souls. Our killer is one of them.'

'And there's nothing to connect them with Nadir Sulayman.'

'Not at all.'

'The killer might have changed their method.'

'It's possible, but in my experience unlikely. There is also evidence of torture, broken fingers, lacerations. Not simply defensive wounds. We are awaiting the report from the autopsy, but what I've seen so far suggests that the killer wanted information from Nadir Sulayman.'

Makana had drawn the same conclusion himself, but didn't say so. 'Could the person who killed Nadir Sulayman have tried to make it look as though the serial killer was responsible?'

'In a clumsy fashion.' Serkan nodded his agreement. 'It suggests a profound lack of faith in the abilities of the investigators.'

'I wouldn't take it personally. Perhaps it was simply intended to put you off the scent for a while.'

'Interesting theory.' The inspector's eyebrow rose again. 'Maybe you missed your calling, Amin Bey. You might have made a good detective.'

'I was just stating what you had made obvious. Wasn't that what you were implying?'

Makana reached for his coffee. It was cold now, but he sipped it anyway. Serkan seemed to sense that the conversation was over.

'For a man who deals in agricultural machinery, you take death remarkably calmly. Most people would have been shaken after what you saw last night, but not you.' Inspector Serkan rose to his feet. 'I don't believe you killed Nadir Sulayman, but I do believe you know more than you are telling me. Are you aware that withholding information is an offence?'

'I told you everything I know about what I saw.'

'Exactly.' Inspector Serkan tapped his lighter on the table. 'I have been frank with you, perhaps more so than I should have been. What you know might hold the key to this case. It might save other lives. In any case, you can rest assured that I intend to find out exactly what is going on here. I repeat what I said last night: do not attempt to leave Istanbul without informing me. Good day.'

Makana watched him cross the room and disappear through the doorway past the waiters. He was in no doubt that Serkan was a resourceful man. It would only be a matter of time before he started to take a real interest in Makana's affairs, and then he might find himself in trouble. Everything seemed to be conspiring to push him out of this city as fast as possible. Yet he knew he couldn't leave, not yet.

Chapter Eighteen

Restless after his encounter with Serkan, Makana decided to try Winslow again. He bought another pack of cigarettes and a fresh phone card, but was beaten to the phone booth by an old man carrying a sack on his shoulder, bound, he noted, with one of those plastic loops. As Serkan said, everyone had them. The sack writhed suspiciously as he set it down against the wall. The hind legs of a rabbit protruded into the air, He glanced warily at Makana as he gave the loop a good tug to make sure it was tight before lighting a cigarette and addressing himself to the matter of the telephone. Makana turned away and gazed out over the crowded hillside and narrow streets on the other side of the valley. Behind him the man was shouting into the receiver as if trying to reach a number on the moon. When he finally conceded the booth it smelt strongly of sheep. This time Marcus Winslow answered on the first ring.

'I was beginning to worry.'

'Things took a bad turn last night. Nadir Sulayman is dead.'

'Yes, so I gathered.' Winslow sounded weary. 'It was on the news reports.'

'I was there.'

'You saw it happen?'

'No, but I must have disturbed whoever it was. I was knocked out.'

'Do you have any idea who did it?'

Makana stared out of the booth, towards the sea.

'No. The police seem to be in the dark.'

'Forget about the police, they're not going to be any help to us.'

'Sulayman was tortured. Someone wanted to find out what he knows.'

'Okay, we can work around this,' said Winslow.

'How? He was our way out of here.'

'Don't worry about that!' Winslow snapped. He took a moment to compose himself. 'Your main priority remains Nizari. You have to get to him fast. Bring him in. Leave the rest to me.'

'Aren't you forgetting something?' Makana dug out his cigarettes. 'Whoever killed him knew what Sulayman was up to.'

'We don't even know his death is related to our operation.'

'We can't take the gamble it's not.'

'So what are you saying?'

'That there's a leak somewhere. Nobody followed me, I'm sure of it. So someone knew of Sulayman's involvement. They took him out to put a dent in our operation. Without Sulayman we're stuck. We can't move Nizari.' Makana clamped the receiver to his shoulder as he lit the cigarette. 'Oh, and by the way, there's a police inspector taking an interest in me.'

'Are you a suspect?'

'He's working Sulayman's case and he thinks I'm hiding something.'

'Look, I could try to pull a few strings, but that might make it worse. Turkey is unpredictable. The best advice I can give you is to stay away from the police.'

'I intend to. But I'd still like to hear what your alternative plan is for getting us out of here.'

'Forget that. You just focus on getting hold of our friend.' Winslow sounded impatient.

Through the grimy perspex Makana noticed that the grim-faced woman with the collection of bags had turned up again. He had thought her old and frail, now he saw she was younger, still in her thirties. Her face had been disfigured somehow, as if it had been pressed against a hot iron. She set down her bags and stood at a distance, rocking back and forth, glaring at him.

'What about Nizari's money?'

'You must stall him. I don't have clearance yet, but the main thing is to assure him he will get whatever he asks for. We can deal with the fallout later.'

146

'Two million dollars is a lot of money,' said Makana. The woman was still outside the booth watching him. Her face was weather-beaten and ingrained with dirt, her hair wild and cut unevenly.

'The money is not an issue. If that's what he's asking for, then you have to convince him that he will get it.'

Makana could hear Winslow turning away to talk to someone else. It wasn't the first time, but now it made him think, reminding him that beyond the solitary figure of the Englishman there lay an entire world of which Makana knew nothing.

'You must carry on as before,' Winslow said when he came back on the line. 'Follow the routine, just as he ordered. Go to the rendez-vous, make contact and bring him in.'

'What do I tell him?'

'Tell him what he wants to hear. If he's after money, a new iden-tity, relocation, whatever. Just get him ready for when I give the word. I'll have something for you within twenty-four hours. In the meantime, keep your head down. Nadir was a very cautious man, he wouldn't have left anything lying around, so the police won't find any connection that leads back to us.'

The woman was rocking back and forth, fiddling with her carrier bags, talking to herself.

'It could have been an old girlfriend, or some kind of business rivalry.' Winslow was clutching at straws. Makana wondered if he was still in Cairo. 'Do whatever you have to to bring Nizari in. Stall him, promise him the earth, just until we have our hands on him.'

'And what do I do with him once I've got him?'

'You'll need to be prepared to sit tight for a couple of days.'

'I already have a place in mind,' said Makana.

'Good. Just sit on him till we can get you out.' Winslow's breezy con-fidence had returned. 'Twenty-four hours, maybe less. I'll get it sorted.'

Makana hung up. When he stepped out of the booth he held the door for the woman. She ignored him, scowling and turning her back.

Koçak was in the hotel lobby reading a newspaper and drink-ing coffee, chatting with the waitress from the café. The sight of Makana brought him to his feet.

'Amin Bey! Ready to see greatest palace in world?'

Makana found himself joining the crowds trailing through the brass-plated imperial gates of the Topkapi Palace. Families chattered excitedly as they made their way through the grounds where gazelles once roamed freely. They followed pathways past fountains and lawns, lush flower beds and gardens, tall cypresses and pines, Judas trees and lilacs. They consulted guidebooks and waved cameras as if they had just discovered a treasure long lost to humanity.

Makana passed through them, turning to follow a sign that led off to the right and to the museum now housed in the former barracks. Stone lions guarded the entrance. Inside he found himself walking past the sarcophagi of Byzantine emperors and Persian satraps, statues of ancient gods.

In another room glass cases displayed daggers, heavy sabres and rifles long enough to take out the enemy's eye without firing a shot.

'Nasty-looking piece of equipment, eh?'

The man standing alongside Makana wore a crumpled pink cotton shirt, navy-blue slacks and a cheap straw trilby, the perfect tourist.

'I'm not an expert,' said Makana. They were almost alone. A couple of middle-aged Americans strolled by like contented pandas, cameras nestling on bulging midriffs.

'Nobody ever is.' Marty Shaw glanced over his shoulder. 'I'm glad you called me.'

'The other day you hinted that you knew why I was here,' said Makana. 'I need to know if I can count on your help.'

'Well, that depends.'

'On what?'

Shaw turned to face Makana. 'On how far you are willing to co-operate.'

'You understand my position?'

'You're here on Winslow's orders. That much we know. As for the rest, we're in the dark.'

'Winslow seems to think there is a leak at the consulate.'

'Winslow is paranoid. He's gone rogue.'

'What does that mean?'

148

'He's flying solo.' Shaw sighed. 'It means that we're no longer sure we can control him.'

'But he's still on your side?' Makana stared at the Englishman. There was something of the outlaw about him, the scruffy clothes and the cheap hat. In place of Winslow's sophistication, Shaw offered the rough charm of the working class.

'In theory, yes. Look, we don't want this to get out of hand. Winslow has a reputation. He's been in the service for a long time.'

'You can't just turn against him,' said Makana.

'This is strictly confidential. I need to know what you know.' Shaw fell silent as a couple went by. 'Does Winslow know you're here?'

'No.' Makana shook his head. 'I told you, he thinks there's a leak.'

Marty Shaw let out a gentle laugh. 'That sounds about right.' He looked at Makana. 'If he was anyone else he would have been thrown out on his backside. He's trying to prove himself. Don't ask me why. Maybe it's all about getting old. I don't know.'

Makana thought back to the conversation he'd had with Winslow, and the voices in the background. He wondered who Winslow's new friends might be.

Marty Shaw led the way to the next cabinet. A row of golden warriors on horses rushing down from the steppes of Central Asia. Makana waited a moment and then followed. Shaw spoke to the glass.

'Winslow's trying to prove something by bringing in Abu Hilal single-handedly – well, with your help. He thinks he has a way of getting to him.'

'Tell me about the Israelis.'

Shaw feigned surprise. 'What makes you think they're involved?'

'How do you expect me to trust you if you treat me like an idiot?' Makana asked. 'Are you working with them? Does the Mossad have a team here in Istanbul?'

'Even if I knew, what makes you think I would tell you?' Shaw looked bemused. 'Tell me who you are again.'

'I'm wasting my time.' Makana shook his head. 'I'm sorry, this was a mistake.' He made to turn away and Shaw grabbed his arm.

'Wait. You can't just walk away.'

'I'm not some native informant. Either you talk to me, or I cannot help you.'

'All right.' Shaw held his hands up in defence. 'Okay, there has been chatter. It's possible the Mossad have a team here.'

'Are you in contact with them?'

'No.' Shaw shook his head. 'Okay, your turn.'

'A man named Nadir Sulayman was murdered last night. Does the name mean anything to you?'

'Small-time entrepreneur. He handles contraband and some people smuggling.'

'He was supposed to get us out of here,' said Makana.

'Nice plan. Well done, Marcus.' Shaw frowned. 'Who's us?'

'Ayman Nizari, an Iraqi specialist.'

'What kind of specialist?'

'The kind who worked for Saddam Hussein in his chemical-warfare programme.' Both men fell silent as a small and noisy crocodile of people filed in through the entrance, led by a woman wagging a Korean flag over her head. Makana resumed his story.

'Nizari wants to come in. Winslow has promised him sanctuary and medical care for his wife.'

'And Winslow thinks this guy can lead him to Abu Hilal?'

'That doesn't matter,' said Makana. 'The question is, if I bring Nizari to you, can you get both of us out of the country safely?'

'You can bring Nizari in?' Shaw asked.

'I'm trying.' Makana glanced at his watch.

'You bring him to me and I'll find out what can be done.' Shaw watched the room behind him in the reflection in the glass. 'I can't make any promises, but I'll do the best I can.'

Pushing his hands into his pockets, Shaw sauntered away. Makana stared into the cabinet in front of him. A malachite tortoise presented by the Sultan to his wife. The details weren't enlightening, though he wondered at the significance of a tortoise.

As he made his way back towards the waiting taxi, the phone Nadir Sulayman had given him buzzed with an incoming call. It was Kara Deniz.

150

'Have you changed your mind about helping me?' Makana asked.

'Perhaps.' There was a pause. 'I care about who killed him.'

'How well did you know him?'

'Not over the phone,' she said. 'It's not safe. We should meet.'

'Where?' asked Makana.

Chapter Nineteen

In the hands of a moderately skilled artist, the interior of the Iskander Grillroom might have modelled for a still life of human despair. In one corner, a woman in a red coat sat weeping into her handkerchief. A grizzled drunk swirled his tongue around a set of toothless gums, nursing a beer, waiting impatiently for nightfall, or the next bottle, or perhaps a visit from his guardian angel. In the middle of the room, two men drew Makana's attention, one twice the size of the other. The bigger one was shaven-headed and had a lumpy face that showed evidence of a bad case of acne. The other was small and scruffy, with thin, unkempt hair that was combed over his rounded head. Both were dressed in cheap sports clothes and both wore neatly trimmed beards that framed their chins but left their faces clear.

All of this Makana observed from his vantage point, sitting at the steel counter of a tiny hole-in-the-wall café across the narrow sidestreet. Through the open doorway he watched the boy from the previous day, making his way from table to table outside the restaurant with his little cardboard tray of postcards, lighters and assorted knickknacks. Two men in leather jackets wanted to buy chewing gum and cigarettes, haggling over the price. The boy was impatient, dismissing their offers with a toss of his head. He didn't seem to realise they were just having a little fun teasing him. The men looked as if they might be some branch of Turkish security, or plainclothes police, clumsy enough to be surveillance officers trying too hard to blend in. Makana tried to memorise their faces.

The boy vanished inside and Makana watched him moving round between the tables, making two circuits before the waiter sent him packing, lodging himself in the doorway to block his entry. The boy cupped his hands to the window to take another look at the interior. This was enough for the waiter to chase him off, and the boy took himself out of range to stand on the corner picking at his sheet of cardboard before turning and trudging back down the hilly streets past the Galata Tower, unaware that Makana was close behind.

Tailing a boy no more than eleven years old brought its own disadvantages. His lack of height meant that he could disappear in a crowd in an instant, which was what happened as they skirted past the tower. The boy vanished, a pebble swallowed by a wave of shuffling humanity. In the distance the soft chant of a muezzin zigzagged up towards the heavens. Makana slipped through the crowds, seeking a better view. The boy resurfaced on the corner of an adjacent sidestreet. A few metres further down he could be glimpsed climbing uneven steps into a narrow entrance. Makana slowed his pace. The boy appeared to be speaking to someone just out of sight. As Makana edged along, staying as far back as possible, the shambling figure of Ayman Nizari emerged from the shadows. Nizari was wearing an oversized jacket hung lopsidedly over a tracksuit. He was unshaven and looked even more unkempt than when Makana had seen him at the Rüstem Pasha mosque.

The boy was talking, and Nizari listened for a time before waving him away with a handful of crumpled notes, which the boy licked his thumb and carefully counted. The boy was clearly unhappy with the terms of their agreement, but Nizari shook him off with a gesture of impatience. He remained in the doorway long enough to watch the boy wandering slowly away, then turned to go back inside.

Makana moved in to take a closer look. It was a café, a small, dark place with a scruffy look about it. As he watched, Nizari emerged again, but this time he was on the move. He vanished through an archway and out into a yard. There were tables and chairs spread out and young couples sitting in the sun smoking and drinking coffee. Tourists in sunglasses sipped wine and ate lunch. The clink of cutlery and glasses accompanied Makana as he passed through. Descending some steps, past a zither player who provided a jumpy soundtrack, brought him to a quiet street that curved down towards the silver glint of the sea below.

Ayman Nizari walked with the nervous, clumsy gait of a man too preoccupied to care much about his surroundings. He paused to buy cigarettes from a vendor on a corner, impatiently tearing off the cellophane wrapper and dropping it in his wake as he lit one.

Makana's explorations in his first days here were now paying off. It was easy to become disorientated in the threaded weave of streets, but he found he had developed a certain understanding of the city's layout. A steep alleyway spilled them out onto the broad quayside. Ahead of them, he realised, lay the waterfront and the ferry station. The air was rich with a raw mix of fish and diesel oil. The smell of frying came from a nearby snack bar, while the high-pitched cawing of seagulls clashed with the low moan of ferryboat horns.

Nizari was slowing down, as if he were nearing his goal. He began to look around him, over his shoulder. Perhaps it was the open space that made him more cautious. People milled about, weaving through the gridlocked vehicles. Clumps of tourists huddled here and there, as if suddenly intimidated to find themselves out on the edge of the European continent. A brisk wind blew in off a choppy sea, and Makana hung back, not wanting to risk the man turning and seeing him. He would be easier to spot in this open space. He skirted the walls, moving past a row of run-down shops and restaurants, conscious also of the risk of others waiting and watching.

Seeing Nizari disappearing into the shadows of the ferry terminus, Makana increased his speed, suddenly conscious that he might lose his quarry. He was almost at the terminus building when somebody stepped into his path.

'Going somewhere, Mr Amin?'

Inspector Serkan had the smug look of a child who has trapped a butterfly in his hands. Over the inspector's shoulder Makana watched Ayman Nizari dissolve into the milling crowd and vanish from sight.

'I feel I should have made myself clearer at our last meeting. I would prefer it for you to stay on this side of Istanbul.' Serkan cast a wary glance to his left, as if implying that once you set foot in Asia, anything might happen.

'I wasn't planning to leave just yet.'

'That's good.' The inspector shrugged his shoulders in an offhand gesture. 'People are sometimes not even aware what they are planning until it is too late.'

'I thought I wasn't a suspect, Inspector.'

'Clearly that's true, but as you know, or perhaps you don't' – the detective beamed at his own humour – 'everyone is a suspect. It has to be so. It's nothing personal, you understand, but I have been in this line of work for many years, and in that time I have learned that even the most trustworthy person is capable of deception.'

'I had no reason to kill Nadir Sulayman.' Makana resisted the temptation to look back in the direction of the ferry terminal.

'Perhaps, but you must be able to see that I would be guilty of negligence if I did not regard you as a possible suspect, since you were on the scene.'

'Doesn't that put me in the category of valuable witness, rather than prime suspect?'

Inspector Serkan smiled. 'I prefer to consider everyone a potential suspect.'

'I think I understand.'

'Do you?' The inspector's eyes probed him for further elaboration.

'Better than you think,' said Makana.

Inspector Serkan chewed the answer over like a cautious man prepared to find a bone in a mouthful of fish.

'In that case, let me ask you another question.' The inspector's eyes looked back towards the ferry station. 'What exactly are you doing here?'

'The guidebook said it was an essential part of the city's character,' Makana improvised, allowing his gaze to follow the inspector's towards the terminal. A ferry was pulling out of the terminal, water foaming around the stern. He could make out the name Heybeliada on the destination board outside the ferry station.

'Let me buy you a coffee.' Without giving Makana the option of turning him down, the inspector led the way along the quay to a space where knee-high plastic tables and stools were ranged in a disorderly sprawl. Gulls hoping for scraps perched at a vigilant distance. The stall was nothing but a flimsy cart run by two energetic men who greeted the inspector with toothless smiles. People sat eating freshly fried fish off paper trays. Inspector Serkan chose a spot close to the water's edge and slid a photograph across the table.

'What is this?'

Inspector Serkan gave a snort of laughter.

'Her name is Kara Deniz, and please don't insult my intelligence by pretending you don't know her.'

Makana looked up from the picture. 'You're having me followed?' He was annoyed, mostly with himself, having been convinced that he had succeeded in losing any possible tail.

'I would be negligent in my duties if I was not watching you.' Serkan tapped the photograph. 'In her spare time she writes for political journals, the more radical kind. She has a history of political agitation and support for terrorist organisations.'

'You mean the Kurds?'

'You are well informed.' Inspector Serkan folded his arms. 'So, I am curious. Why should a man who comes here to buy agricultural machinery be associating with a known political radical?'

'Perhaps I simply like her company.'

'I suppose in a certain light she might be considered an attractive woman, but …' A busy waiter hurried by and the inspector ordered without losing his thread. 'She is hardly the kind of woman I would associate with you, Amin Bey.'

'Perhaps you don't know me that well.'

'Perhaps.' Serkan shrugged. 'I am a simple detective. Every once in a while I catch someone who has done a bad thing, and that makes me feel better about myself, but the truth is that most of the time we just follow the routine.' The inspector glanced back out at the water as a ferry sounded its throaty wail. 'Then I come across a man like yourself and I wonder.' Serkan nodded at the photograph of Kara Deniz. 'Her parents were activists. Her mother died in prison and her father went into exile for the same reason. The little girl grew up hating the state. She has made a career out of it. What would a person like you want with someone like that?'

'She knew Nadir Sulayman.'

'Sulayman introduced you to her?'

'You could say that.'

'Let me be frank, Amin Bey, I feel that you are not being entirely honest with me.'

'I have nothing to hide.'

'Perhaps, but no reason to trust me, either, I suspect.'

'As I explained, I had no reason to kill Nadir Sulayman. He was helping me, remember?'

'Yes, with your ... agricultural machinery.'

If Makana had been hoping his flimsy alibi would convince, the Turkish detective's tone suggested that it was already a leaky vessel. Serkan leaned forward.

'I believe you are innocent of this murder. I also think you are in some trouble, but I cannot help you if you do not confide in me.' He sat back to light a cigarette as the coffee arrived. The sight of the steaming dark liquid seemed to lift the inspector's mood. 'Here we are at the meeting place of two continents,' he smiled. 'It's a cliché, but it's what makes Istanbul special. It also makes us vulnerable. We have the Russians to the east, Europe to the west and Muslim fanatics to the south.'

Neither of them spoke for a time, the silence between them contrasting with the noise around them. Seagulls darted through the thick gouts of black diesel exhaust. Ferries arrived and departed in a flurry of churning wakes and grinding engines, while around them were the sounds of people chatting or calling to one another, the occasional burst of laughter. People living their lives, worrying about everyday matters. Under other circumstances Makana could imagine that he might enjoy the inspector's company, but as things stood he knew that every question was a potential trap waiting for him.

'I heard there was another murder last night. Your *karakoncolos* killer.'

Inspector Serkan gazed out at the water. 'To be frank with you, Amin Bey, we are nowhere near catching this killer. There's nothing to go on. No link between the victims, personal or professional. Nothing.'

'You have no suspects? No profile?'

'No eyewitnesses, no DNA matches. There appears to be no sexual motive. It is not about robbery. It is simply about killing.'

'A serial killer?'

'The killer is clearly psychotic.' The inspector shook his head solemnly. 'The murders take place in remote, unlit parts of town. Even using our traffic cameras, we have been unable to identify a vehicle connected to the murders.'

'The killer changes cars?'

'Perhaps. Or they move on foot. Either way, it's as if the killer can just melt into the city walls.' Inspector Serkan allowed himself a long sip of coffee and smacked his lips. 'Funny, isn't it? Anyone listening to us might imagine we were colleagues discussing a case.'

'Simple curiosity,' said Makana, downplaying his interest.

Serkan wagged his head in a manner that suggested he wasn't entirely convinced. 'When we spoke yesterday, I tried to impress upon you the delicacy of my position,' he continued. 'This complicates my investigation into Nadir Sulayman's murder.'

'They want you to solve the *karakoncolos* killings first.'

'It's high-profile. All the media are crazy about it. Every time a new victim turns up the Minister for Tourism appears for a photo-opportunity, and then I start getting calls demanding results.'

'So the Sulayman case is put aside.'

'For the moment, until we catch the culprit.' Serkan studied his fingernails. 'There is also interest from our intelligence services, the MIT.'

'Really? How so?'

'They think Sulayman was involved in something much bigger.'

'I thought you were working on the idea that one of his underworld contacts had done it?'

'That was a line of investigation,' confirmed Serkan.

'But not any longer?'

'The Milli Istihbarat Teskilati will never share what they have, but we have to assume they have information connected to Sulayman.'

'Why are you telling me this?'

'I'm giving you a chance. If MIT come after you, they won't be as understanding as I am.'

Makana nodded. 'I appreciate that. And if I could help you, believe me, I would.'

'There are a number of things that interest me about you, Amin Bey,' Serkan said, getting to his feet. 'Your knowledge of police procedure. Your habits. Even here, now. You claim to be taking in the sights, but you were walking quickly, in a determined fashion, but also cautiously, like a man who was following someone, say.' He stood over Makana. 'I don't know who you are working for, or what you're after, but I suspect you are involved in something far more serious than buying agricultural machinery. It's a dangerous game you are playing, Mr Amin, especially if you are a stranger in this city. You should be careful. Everybody needs friends at some time.'

Makana watched the inspector walk away. Then he turned to look out at the sea. The ferryboat to Heybeliada was long gone.

The coffee was on the house. The toothless men laughed when he tried to pay. He wandered along the waterfront, reduced now to his alibi, taking in the sights. The choppy water looked deep and troubled. Beneath its surface lay the sunken evidence of countless wars and conflicts. The Marmara Sea had, after all, been the centre of the world for centuries. The rise of the West had shrunk it to a miniature of its former self, an exotic ghost, a sentinel on the borderline forever signalling the decline of the East.

Now Makana saw in the delicate shapes of the minarets, the horned crescents, the complex architecture of domes and spires, a sad longing for the past, for the old world that was unknown except through books and buildings. With the bid for glory went the urge to make the world a better place, in contrast to the resignation that seemed to dominate the present. This city seemed to be teeming with ghosts, and some of those, he knew, were his alone.

Chapter Twenty

In the old Egyptian Spice Bazaar, scarlet heaps of chilli powder, golden turmeric and dusty cumin lent a weary exoticism to the scene. It was easy to imagine traders from the fifteenth century strolling these same aisles. The air was rich with smells and sights. Aniseed, cloves, dried tomatoes, figs like dried ears, pistachios like mounds of seashells. The light and sound threatened to overwhelm Makana. He was looking for a single wisp in a field full of corn. Around him shopkeepers called out prices, offered cut slices of halva, green and yellow cubes of lokoum dusted with powdered sugar. He arrived at the hanging mirrors and watched them spin and rotate, reflected images bobbing back and forth. Today, none of them had the magical power to waft him back in time.

Was this what he had been secretly hoping for – to meet the ghost of his long-dead wife? There was a name for such delusions. What surprised him was how he had managed to avoid this madness for so many years. For so long he had worked on consigning her to the watery grave into which he had seen her fall. All of that for what? To find himself now confronted by her spirit, walking freely without a care in the world through a crowded bazaar in a city he had never dreamed of visiting?

The way Makana had seen it, the true mystery of his life was why any woman as beautiful and intelligent as Muna would ever marry someone like him. Maybe this explained why their marriage had always had the slightly unreal quality of a dream about it. He could never quite believe it was really happening. In the last few days he had found himself going back to that era in a way that he had not done in a long time. Perhaps it was the strangeness of this city. The sense of being adrift in the world once again. Rootless. Formless. In the narrow streets, amongst the grey, haunted buildings, the wandering cats. All seemed to present a kind of menace that was less physical danger than a threat to his soul.

Makana had grown better, or so he had thought, over time, at living with the guilt, the sense of failure. But now it was as if all the intervening years had been swept away, as if the past was reaching out to pull him back in.

Why had Ayman Nizari asked for him? Was it that he was truly the only person he trusted to bring him in, or was it something more?

Who had he glimpsed for a brief second that afternoon in the bazaar, gliding across the mirrored surface, disappearing into the crowd even as he turned? And then the second time across a crowded mosque: a young woman dressed all in black, trousers and a long jacket with flared sleeves, a scarf draped loosely over her head to cover her hair. And finally, in the reflection in Nadir Sulayman's window. A trick of the light? A lie of the mind? Madness would have come as a relief.

For once in his life, the alternative to losing his mind seemed even more terrifying. Logic told him it was impossible for it to have been Muna. The woman he saw had been too young. Yet he still couldn't bring himself to believe that it might have been his daughter. How could Nasra be alive? How could she have been alive for so long, all these years that he had mourned her? Why appear here? Why now? There were too many questions. It was too painful. Easier to believe that he was losing his mind.

Kara Deniz was waiting as agreed in a small café that was no more than a couple of low tables in a dark corner of the bazaar. She fitted in perfectly. The image of anarchic disillusion. With nicotine-stained fingers she shook a pack of Marlboros.

'Were you followed?'

'No,' he said. 'I'm pretty sure I wasn't.'

'I'm not sure this is a good idea,' she said, lighting a fresh cigarette from the butt of the one she was smoking.

'What are you worried about?'

'Well, Nadir is dead, so that's a good place to start.'

'Tell me about him.'

She studied him through the smoke. 'Nadir used to be a journalist. I mean, a real tough son of a bitch. He broke all kinds of stories on corruption and government failures. He wasn't scared of anyone. So they went after him. Eventually, they got something to stick. They threw him in prison and beat him. Badly. If police brutality was an Olympic sport we would win gold medals every time. When he came out he wasn't the same. They broke his spirit.' She spoke as if talking was a race, whoever finished first would win. Clearly it was a story she had told many times, but the bitterness still shone through.

'You admired his writing.'

'To my generation he was a legend.'

'You didn't feel that he had sold out?'

A brisk shake of the head, smoke spewing from her nostrils. 'What right do I have to judge him? Prison does things to a person.' It was a statement that invited a whole raft of new questions.

'That's when he went into business?'

'I'm done with politics, he said. Everyone laughed. What do you know about business, we asked. What's to know, he said. The key to success is understanding people, he would say. We're all the same. Ask yourself what you want and how much you are willing to pay.'

It sounded like the solution to all problems, thought Makana. Perhaps he should ask himself what he really wanted, maybe then he would understand why he had come here.

'Motivation is the same, whether it's about journalism or making money,' Kara laughed. 'He lost a lot of friends, but Nadir could be very persuasive. People liked him.'

'I get the feeling he didn't entirely lose contact with his old world.'

'You're right. He made a point of helping his old friends. He knew everyone and still had the best contacts in the city. Prison brought him a new circle of contacts, if you see what I mean.'

'You mean in the underworld? Organised crime?'

She was smoking as though it was about to be banned. For once Makana couldn't keep up. She stared at him.

'You're asking for my help and here I am spilling my guts out to you, yet I still get the impression you don't trust me.'

'What makes you say that?'

162

'Okay, why don't you tell me what your interest in that ambulance is?'

Makana looked at her for a moment. 'I believe a man I am trying to find was in that accident. I think he managed to escape from the people who were holding him.'

'And where is he now?'

'I'm not sure.'

'And why is he so important?' she asked.

Why was Ayman Nizari important? Because of his lethal skills? Because of the interest people like Abu Hilal took in him? Or because he was the only way Makana was ever going to get out of this city?

'He's a dangerous man, and he has important connections.'

'This is what Nadir was helping you with?'

'Yes,' said Makana. 'He was going to help us to get out of Istanbul.'

Kara Deniz nodded. A waiter appeared, dressed like an Ottoman lackey, in a turban and waistcoat over a silk shirt and balloon trousers. Kara ordered a beer. Makana opted for coffee. The waiter bowed and disappeared without a word.

'I think he might have been killed because of what he was doing for me.'

'You feel responsible?' She gave a light laugh. 'Really?'

'Is that so strange?'

'Strange, maybe not, but old-fashioned. In a good way,' she added. Her beer arrived and she took a quick slug. 'And with Nadir gone you need someone else to get you out of here.'

Makana nodded and took a sip of his coffee.

'Interesting.' She rolled her cigarette between thumb and index finger. 'So that leaves you with a problem.'

'You could say that.'

'Let's just say you need me more than I need you.' She squinted at him over the bottle. 'You don't know anyone here. You need friends.'

'Do you have any ideas?'

'Perhaps you should speak to Nadir's business partner, Nikos Godunov.'

'That doesn't sound Turkish to me.'

'Half-Greek, half-Russian: Nikos is a world citizen.' He sounded like a character from a novel. It might have been the alias of an international criminal. 'He's a car dealer. He and Nadir were partners.'

'He has cars?'

'He has everything. Any kind of transport you need, Boris can find it.'

'Boris?'

'It's a nickname. Everyone calls him that.'

'Do you think he will speak to me?'

Kara Deniz lifted a shoulder. 'You have money, don't you?'

'I appreciate your help.'

'It's not for you,' she said. 'Nadir mentored me. He was kind to me over the years, and he wouldn't be impressed if I just walked away from his death.'

'Who do you think killed him?'

'What I think doesn't count.' She drained the rest of her beer and got to her feet. She paused, fists thrust into the pockets of her leather jacket. 'You don't trust me. I understand, but maybe if I help you you'll tell me everything you know. Face it,' she grinned, 'you need me. In this part of the world you don't get far without friends.'

She was the second person to tell him that, and Makana couldn't argue. He hadn't been sure about trusting her, but then again who did he trust?

Chapter Twenty-one

The sun was setting over the sea and the sky was peppered with gulls. Makana stood for a moment watching the light turn red, listening to the muezzin calling the faithful to prayer. It was a rare moment of tranquillity. It reminded him of another age, another time in his life, when words like happiness and contentment didn't sound alien. He didn't understand how someone could hate so much that he could dedicate himself to destroying another man's life, ruining his family. Yet Makana needed no reminding that such hatred existed in the world. He had never really given up trying to understand evil, even though he knew he never would, not fully, not ever.

At the root of all of this was the unknown entity that was Abu Hilal. Everything came back to this man. Ayman Nizari was just a cog in the machine. They all were. But the heart of it was occupied by a man prepared to condemn thousands of innocent people to an unspeakable death. To such a man, the means justified the ends. Whereas Nizari was a technician. He mixed the potions up and handed them over. It wasn't necessarily evil, what he did. It took a certain kind of ignorance, a blindness, a lack of conscience, but that was all.

As he strolled down across the open square towards the road, Makana became aware that he was being followed. He wasn't sure who was following, where they were, or how many, but he knew someone was there. He turned left and glanced back up towards the bazaar and the mosque. The minarets were silhouetted against the fading light like twin pillars, as thin and white as bone; a fragile skeleton holding up the sky. He saw him then, about fifty metres away. As soon as Makana's eyes passed over him, the man dropped his face, as if studying the ground. If there had been any doubt, this gave it away.

Crossing the street, Makana increased his pace, heading upwards between two rows of buildings. He wasn't sure where he was going, but he knew there was a taxi stand outside the bazaar. If he could double back he could catch one there.

As he walked he realised that he had seen the man before. Shaven-headed, with a pockmarked face. He had been inside the Iskander Grillroom that afternoon, together with another man. Who were they? He heard the angry whine of the van before he registered what it was. Then it was beside him.

'Inside,' said the voice behind him.

The shaven-headed man was clutching a newspaper and wearing sunglasses despite the fact that the sun was no longer touching this section of the street. He jerked the newspaper aside to show that it concealed a gun. By the look of him he was jumpy enough to use it. As he climbed inside, Makana caught a glimpse of the man behind the wheel; it was the second man from the Iskander.

There was nowhere to sit inside the van except on the floor. Makana sat with his back to the panelling behind the driver's cab. The man slid the door shut and crouched down before him, tossing aside the newspaper. The van was already moving again.

'Your hands,' he gestured with the gun. He spoke in Arabic, in an accent that Makana could not recognise. Makana held out his hands and from his pocket the man produced a thick white plastic zip tie fashioned in a loop. He slipped the band over Makana's wrists and pulled it tight enough to make him wince. At least it was his wrists and not his neck. Cause for optimism perhaps. Also his hands were tied in front of him rather than behind.

Satisfied that Makana was secure, the man sat back. He removed his dark glasses and rubbed a hand over his shaven skull. He resembled a cross between a champion wrestler and the village idiot. Both options offered their own possibilities.

There were no windows in the sides of the van. Makana tried to work out which direction they were going in from the turns they made and the sounds he could hear. They had returned to the square, he was pretty sure of that. The noise of the traffic, even the cooing of pigeons. A newspaper vendor who had been standing by the taxi rank. The cobblestones under the wheels. Then, with a screech, they turned again and began to accelerate. He tried to pay attention to the noise of the engine and the echo of the streets they drove through. He heard vehicles hooting, drivers protesting, police whistles. They lurched into a busy thoroughfare and began to move more quickly along a fast road. They exited onto a slip road that twisted round on itself and began to slow. Then they were moving uphill, and Makana guessed they were in the narrow streets of Eyüp. More horns, the sound of voices, people brushing against the sides of the car, speaking as they went. The creaking wheel of a pushcart, stallholders calling out offers, music and smells, too. The roasting of meat, the spicy *kokoreçi* he had tried with Koçak. By now the car was moving at walking pace.

It took another fifteen minutes before they slowed to a halt. The shaven-headed man leaned forward.

'Don't try anything,' he warned, tapping Makana's shoulder with the barrel of the automatic. He pressed the newspaper into Makana's hands so that it covered the plastic tie, then slid open the side door.

It was now almost dark outside. They were parked in a narrow sidestreet lined with low, rundown houses. A row of streetlamps came on at that moment like a string of pearls leading down through the gap between the houses. There were no street signs, nothing to indicate exactly where they were. When they reached the corner Makana looked back through the gap between the houses and tried to fix the angle in his mind. Across the Golden Horn to the high-rise buildings in Taksim and down to the sea, shimmering in all its dark glory, the running lights of ships threading the void like constellations in an uncharted universe. They crossed the street with the man leading Makana by the arm. Producing a key from his jacket, he unlocked a battered door. The hallway was dark and smelt of woodsmoke. Three steps led up and a second key brought them into a courtyard. Ahead of them was a long room with a simple veranda. With a word to his colleague to remain outside, the shaven-headed man led him in through another door to their left.

Inside it was quiet. The room was big and long, dark save for a faint glow that filtered through windows covered with sheets of newspaper. Other than that it was bare of furniture except for a scarred table and three rickety chairs. One corner was taken up with what looked like abandoned junk: heaps of yellow newspaper tied with string, a television set with a cracked screen, a fruit crate filled with used tins of paint.

'Sit,' said the man. Makana sat down on one of the creaky chairs, a window onto the street to his right, to his left the door they had just come through. That was it. There was a long silence. The man remained by the door. From his pocket he produced a switchblade that he snapped open before using the tip to clean under his nails. Then he came forwards, flipping the knife in his hands. Makana held up his wrists.

'Perhaps you could remove these.'

The man's face remained impassive. He stared at Makana but said nothing. Instead he stabbed the knife into the scarred tabletop and then grabbed hold of the back of Makana's chair and dragged it over to the wall behind him, tipping it over until it was balanced on the two rear legs, the other two left suspended in midair. Off balance, Makana couldn't move without risking falling on his side.

'Where did you learn your Arabic?'

'Where?' The shaven-headed man frowned as if he hadn't expected the question. 'Where else? Your home. *Al Khartoum.*' He chuckled. 'What a shithole. No wonder you left.'

'You were there? When?'

'Where? When? So many questions.'

'What were you doing there?'

'What I was doing?' The man leaned closer. Now Makana could see the bristles that sprouted from the shaven head were silvery grey. 'I was fighting. Jihad.'

'You must have been very young.'

'No choice,' he said dismissively. 'I grow up in Bosnia. When war is over I go Chechnya, but is bad. Russians are crazy. So, we go to Africa.'

A poor man's holy war. Travelling the globe in search of a battle to win. Makana cast his mind back to the 1990s. Bosnian jihadis

168

had travelled to Sudan to fight on the side of the god-fearing, turning civil war into holy war.

'Were you in the South?'

'South shithole, more than Khartoum.'

Makana wondered what kind of war zone the young jihadi had had in mind. Somewhere with a beach terrace perhaps? A poolside residence with room service thrown in? There was something about his accent that was odd. At first, Makana had thought it was the product of having picked the language up on his travels. Mixing with Arab jihadis from all over the place, he might have picked up different accents that way. Now, however, Makana was beginning to question that assumption. He suspected that the Bosnian's mannerisms, and his accent, were more carefully constructed than they appeared.

'So you know Khartoum well?' Makana asked.

'Why? You miss it? I told you, is a shithole. You couldn't pay me to go back.'

'Where were you staying?'

'Hey!' The Bosnian grabbed Makana's lapels and pulled him up and then threw him back against the wall, knocking the air out of his lungs and banging his head. 'I ask the questions, okay?'

'Okay,' Makana gasped, his head ringing. 'Have it your way.'

The shaven-headed man reached back to the table and freed the blade from the wood. He ran his thumb over the tip.

'Where is Nizari?'

'Who?'

This time he punched Makana in the throat. It was hard enough to make him choke, soft enough not to kill him. Whoever he was, he knew his business.

'We try again. Where is Ayman Nizari?'

Makana coughed and tried to heave air into his lungs. 'I don't know who that is,' he managed.

For that he received a backhanded slap across the mouth. He tasted blood.

'Who are you?'

'You know who I am,' Makana said.

'No.' The Bosnian shook his head before repeating his question. '*Who* are you?' Makana watched the tip of the blade as it came closer. 'Are you Abu Hilal?'

'What?' The question came as a surprise.

'You will tell me. Or you will stay here until you tell me.'

The tip of the knife dug into Makana's left shoulder. He felt the threads of his jacket parting and the first prick of the blade into his skin. The Bosnian leaned on it, digging the knife in deeper. Makana felt a burning pain. He tried to shift away but that only seemed to increase the pain. He didn't have much leverage and he was off balance.

Desperately, he lifted his right leg and kicked hard at the Bosnian's left knee. The blow glanced off but spun Makana further to one side, the chair swivelling on one leg beneath him. The Bosnian stumbled back as Makana crashed down, hitting the floor with his right shoulder. The Bosnian cursed and rubbed his knee before advancing towards him. The look on his face suggested he was determined to do some damage.

Makana wriggled away, backwards across the floor. The Bosnian followed, still rubbing his knee and waving the knife. He seemed to be enjoying himself. The blade flashed forward. Makana felt it snag in his trousers and heard the cloth rip. He kicked out blindly and his foot was caught in a firm grip. Jerking free, he twisted over onto his stomach, scrabbling for a purchase. His outstretched hand caught the wooden crate and it slid towards him as he was yanked backwards. There was something farcical about the situation. He grabbed at the crate again and felt the brittle side crack under pressure. It tipped on its side spilling out its contents. The smell of paint hit him and his hand touched something wet. He realised he was holding the handle of an old-fashioned oil lamp. Without thinking he swung it behind him and heard the Bosnian's scream of agony. He staggered backwards desperately rubbing his eyes, which were now filled with kerosene. Makana caught a glimpse of his bloody face before the man turned, crashed into the door and then threw himself out of it. Grabbing the knife the Bosnian had dropped, Makana stabbed it into the floorboard and sawed his hands free.

There was only one way out of the room, and that brought him into the courtyard. There was no sign of either of the men. The double door into the long room to his left was open. A light was on, and he could hear a commotion within. Through the papered-over windows he could see figures moving around. Makana ducked out into the alleyway next to the house. If he went to his right he would bump into the van and driver. He turned left.

His head was ringing and he felt blood running down his arm. At the next corner he turned right. Many of the houses here were made of wood. Some were unoccupied and dark. He heard more voices behind him, men shouting, only it wasn't in Arabic. He dived in through a broken door that brought him into a cobbled court-yard. It looked like the kind of place in which they might once have kept horses or cattle. He went straight across and into what looked like a barn on the other side.

He was in total darkness, but he could make out a crack of light which turned out to be a boarded-up window. The wood was rotten and the planks came away in his hands with little effort. Squeezing through the gap he saw more lights ahead of him and cars moving at high speed. He crossed a patch of waste ground and then climbed over a concrete barrier to find himself on a slip road. A taxi was coming towards him. Makana stepped into the road and raised both arms.

Haluk spied him as he came through the door of the hotel and rushed around the counter, intercepting him as he wearily climbed the steps past the huge plaque of famous names.

'Mr Amin Bey, how wonderful to see you! I was hoping to have a word.' The diminutive receptionist was an anxious stork hopping from step to step. He fell silent as he surveyed Makana and noted with some distress the state of his clothes, which were dirty and torn, with a streak of paint down one sleeve of his jacket.

'Another attack, Amin Bey! I can't tell you how sorry I am on behalf of the city.' Haluk shuffled alongside him, wringing his hands.

'It looks worse than it is,' Makana managed. Even as he spoke he realised that the look on the receptionist's face told him this wasn't particularly reassuring.

'It is urgent that I speak to you on a matter of great importance.'

'Can't it wait?'

'My most sincere apologies, but no, I'm afraid not.' Haluk blinked earnestly as he tried to step in front of Makana to block his path.

'What seems to be the problem?'

'As you know, we pride ourselves on our discretion. Our guests can sleep peacefully knowing that their confidences are safe with us.' Haluk mimed zipping his mouth shut. Makana pulled up.

'What exactly are you talking about?'

'Of course, we fully understand that our guests might desire companionship. And considering the honourable nature of your good self, I would be most happy under the circumstances to make an exception, but we cannot allow women, of, shall we say, questionable reputation to be alone in the room of a guest. It is unwise.'

'I still do not follow.'

'It concerns the young lady.'

Makana recalled the woman who had shared the lift with him the previous evening, but something told him this was not who Haluk was referring to.

'Aysun?'

Haluk glanced up and down the hallway. 'Not Aysun.'

'Another woman?'

'I'm afraid I asked her to leave.'

'You did?'

'Yes, unfortunately she refused to heed my request.'

'Where is she now?'

'She insisted on going up to your room to wait for you. Forgive me, Amin Bey, but we have our reputation to think of.'

'Of course you do.' Makana thanked him and was about to turn away when a thought occurred to him. 'This woman, can you describe her?'

'Describe?' Haluk seemed confused for a second, but a good receptionist clearly took everything in their stride. He drew himself up, slipped a finger between his collar and neck as if he felt too warm. 'Young. Tall. Dark and very beautiful.'

'Dark? You mean she had dark hair?'

'No, sorry, I mean dark like you. The skin?' He smiled and then bowed apologetically and beat a swift retreat.

The lift operator was asleep, sitting on his fold-down stool, his head leaning on the lever. Makana decided to leave him to it and turned to climb the stairs. Everyone deserved whatever rest they could get in this world. He regretted his decision almost at once, feeling the pain all over his body.

Outside his door he paused, wondering what he might find. This was the moment when the Yavuz might have been useful, but it was locked away in the safe. As he put his hand out the door swung softly open before him. The interior was dark, cut only by the faint glow of reflected light filtering up through the windows from the hotel's exterior.

The image of Nadir Sulayman lying on the floor of his office with his tongue hanging out was still fresh enough to instil caution. He stepped aside, close to the wall, aware that a silhouette in a doorway makes a perfect target.

Immediately he noted the faint smell in the air. A perfume that was both strange and yet familiar. It stopped him in his tracks. He pushed the bathroom door open. It was empty. He moved further inside, towards the main room. The doors to the balcony were open. A soft breeze stirred the curtains and the sound of the traffic in the street below could be heard.

Marty Shaw was sitting in the armchair in the corner of the room. His head was tilted back and he wasn't wearing his hat. The pink shirt had two small holes in it, on the left-hand side, just above the heart. On the floor next to him was a pillow with burn marks on it, and next to that, the Yavuz.

The wardrobe door was slightly ajar. Makana slid it back. The safe was open. The money was gone. Makana stepped back to take another look at Marty Shaw. Two shots from close up. The noise muffled by the pillow. There was less blood than you might expect, but the heart would have stopped pumping instantly.

What was Shaw doing here? Haluk had only mentioned a woman, which meant that Shaw had managed to enter the hotel without raising suspicions. Makana stepped out onto the balcony. To get over from the next room entailed a simple hop over a

173

railing. A child could have forced the French windows. The distant sound of approaching sirens broke into his thoughts. Whoever had planted this problem in his room was probably not leaving anything to chance. There wasn't much point in waiting around here for the police to arrive. The chances of explaining the situation to Inspector Serkan, or worse, his sidekick Sergeant Berat, were slim at best.

Makana took one more look around the room. As he turned to leave he noticed the bedside table. The photograph he'd left standing there was gone. Through the open door he could hear the sound of the lift jerking into motion, grinding its way slowly up through the building. He walked quickly to the top of the stairs, only to hear voices coming up from below. Moving back along the corridor, Makana knew he was trapped.

'We meet again.'

Makana turned to see the woman from the elevator. Aysun. She was straightening the hem of her dress.

'Perhaps you have reconsidered.'

'Some other time, I'm afraid,' said Makana. He made to move on and then stopped. 'You don't know if there is a back way out of here.'

Aysun examined him with a cool gaze for a moment.

'There's always another way.' She led the way through an unmarked door to a service corridor. She smiled over her shoulder. 'I use this from time to time. Sometimes one must be discreet, don't you find?'

'More often than I'd care to admit,' said Makana.

Chapter Twenty-two

Istanbul Day Five

T he Koça Mustafa was an unassuming little place that stayed open all night and didn't seem to mind who came and went through its battered doors. In the early hours of the morning it was inhabited by a selection of the city's nocturnal creatures. They swam through the bank of blue smoke that enveloped the place, faces looming in and out of focus as if in a recurring dream. On the wall above the bar a picture of the Grand Vizier, after whom the place was named, sat alongside one of Atatürk in a manner that made the latter look like an upstart. There were other contenders occupying lopsided frames up on the wall, along with Turkish flags, Galatasaray shirts and photographs clipped from magazines of football players who had long since faded from the public imagination.

Through the layer of smoke the air hummed electric in the white neon glow. The stark light cast a garish mood over the interior. Many of them looked like regulars; taxi drivers who yelled to one another in a familiar way. They drank coffee and raki and watched the television with the sound turned down. A radio behind the counter played a grinding series of what Makana assumed were popular classics. The gurgling voices and swirling strings cast their own spell over proceedings. It was a long way from the Blue Ozan where he had met Kara Deniz.

Makana sat alone in the corner drinking tea. Nobody paid him much attention, and he was too caught up in his own thoughts to care much about the occasional curious glance. The situation was spinning rapidly out of his control. He had hoped Marty Shaw might provide another way out of the labyrinth he seemed to have walked into. His doubts about Winslow, coupled with the loss of Nadir Sulayman, left him in a vulnerable position. Having a dead British agent in his hotel room was not the way Makana had expected this little venture to go.

He turned his mind to the new element introduced by the 'Bosnians' he had met earlier in the evening. The voices he had heard in the long room as he was making his escape had not been speaking Arabic, but Hebrew. And that confirmed another serious complication.

As it started to get light he joined the crowds making their way to work. The streets were busy but oddly quiet, as if people were wary of disturbing the early morning tranquillity. Sunlight filtered between the grey buildings. Makana had begun to question everything, no longer sure of the ground on which he was standing. What did he actually know about Marcus Winslow? Accents could be faked, as could passports and identity cards. He had no real idea who he was working for.

Makana spotted Fateema Brown as she was approaching the gates of the British Consulate just before nine o'clock. He fell in beside her and walked in silence until she realised she had a companion. She ignored him at first, shifting her course to take her away from him. The guards outside the consulate were already within sight. There was a small gathering of staff around the entrance, preparing to go through the barriers and into the guardroom, already shrugging off their coats in preparation for the obligatory security scan. When finally she turned to look at him she stopped in her tracks.

'Keep walking,' said Makana. 'We need to talk.'

From the look on her face Fateema Brown's first impulse was to scream for help or break into a run, or perhaps both. The guards would surely come to her aid if she managed to attract their attention.

'All I'm asking for is five minutes,' he said softly. 'That's all.'

Makana knew he was taking a risk. He wondered how long he would have if she raised the alarm instead of talking to him. At this hour of the morning most people on the streets were still half asleep, or perhaps preoccupied with what lay ahead of them, what they had to do today, letting go of their private lives in order to step into their roles as professionals.

'I'm not going to hurt you,' he said, gesturing towards a side-street off to the left. 'Five minutes, that's all.' He could see her struggling. She was conventional by nature, not comfortable breaking the rules. When she finally made a move towards the sidestreet it surprised him.

The alleyway was a row of shuttered shopfronts. A few shopkeepers were starting to open up, looking for keys, wrestling with padlocks. Makana led the way past all of these.

'What do you want from me?' Fateema Brown's voice cracked as she spoke.

'I don't mean you any harm.'

They had reached a small square. Makana indicated a small place on a corner. It had two entrances, one on each side, and was empty save for a grey-haired man sweeping the floor.

'I'll be missed if I don't turn up for work,' she said, sitting on a stool at the bar and clutching her briefcase against her chest.

'Marty Shaw,' Makana began. She didn't let him get further.

'Did you kill him?' she asked, looking him in the eye. It struck him that she wasn't actually as scared as she pretended to be.

'He was in my room at the hotel when I got there.'

'The police are looking for you. Our people are looking for you.'

She took a deep breath, as if trying to decide whether to trust him. 'I can't do anything for you. You must contact the consulate during working hours.'

'I don't think that's really an option right now.'

Fateema Brown hesitated. 'He told me that he thought you were working for Winslow. Are you?'

'Winslow asked me to help him to locate someone.'

'Ayman Nizari.'

Over her shoulder, Makana watched the man put aside the broom. As he approached, Makana ordered coffee for both of them. He didn't bother asking how she wanted hers, he suspected they weren't going to be there long enough to drink it.

'You're the intelligence agent who spoke to Ayman Nizari when he called the consulate asking for help.' Makana paused before pressing on. 'Shaw wasn't available.'

Fateema Brown took a deep breath and looked down at her hands.

'Shaw was away. He has, had, a mistress in Beirut.'

'And when he's away you run the intelligence side of things?'

From her accent Makana guessed that she was British, or at least she had grown up there, perhaps with Turkish parents. There was something self-conscious about her manner. The awkwardness of trying to belong, but knowing that she didn't quite fit. Despite her clothes, the headscarf, she was more Western than Eastern.

'This is your first posting?'

'I was in Ankara for a year, but yes, this is the most responsibility I've had,' she said. 'Not that it's any of your business.'

'I'm just trying to work out how all of the pieces fit together.'

The fact that it was her first posting explained why she was so unsure of herself. She still had to prove, to herself as well perhaps, that she wasn't just some fancy dress the British were putting on to impress their Turkish hosts. The coffee arrived and she spooned sugar carefully into the little cup. 'Shaw took over when Winslow was suspended,' she began.

'Marty Shaw was a good man. He had to tread carefully. Winslow has a reputation. You don't go up against a man like that unless you know what you are doing.'

'How did Winslow find out about Nizari, if he was suspended?'

'Nizari insisted on it.' Fateema Brown shook her head. 'Winslow was the only person he would negotiate with.'

'Did they know each other?'

'Not as far as we could tell.' She frowned and sipped her coffee. 'Winslow was supposed to coordinate everything with Marty. He never did. The first we knew that the operation was actually going ahead was when you came into the picture.'

'Winslow told me that he didn't trust anyone, that there was a risk of a leak.'

'Well, he would have to explain why you were on your own, I suppose.'

Makana lit a cigarette. His picture of Winslow was beginning to grow slightly clearer, although he still wasn't sure exactly what he was up to. Did he really just want Nizari, or was there some other target in sight?

'Okay, what about Abu Hilal?'

'He's the real mystery man.' Fateema gave a shake of the head. 'I mean, the man is literally a ghost.'

'Why does Winslow want him so badly?'

She looked directly at him. 'Winslow was responsible for the attack in Yemen when they tried to take out Abu Hilal. The information was flawed.'

This tied in with what Shaw had said about Winslow wanting to bring in Abu Hilal single-handedly.

'Winslow is old school, he probably thinks he has to restore his honour or something. Hilal's family was killed in the attack.' She stirred her coffee. 'Do you know who killed Shaw?'

It was Makana's turn to shake his head. 'He was dead before I got to my room.'

'What was he doing there?'

'I don't know what he was doing there. Either he was waiting for me, or …'

'Or?'

'Or he was checking up on me. In either case, someone else was there. Perhaps he surprised them, or the other way around. Whoever it was killed him and left him in my room to pin it on me.' He didn't mention the woman Haluk had told him about. Or the fact that this might have been the same woman he had glimpsed in Nadir Sulayman's office. Some protective instinct made him keep that information to himself. But protective of whom: of himself, or of the woman who might or might not have been his daughter? Could she be the one who had killed Shaw? Makana recalled the blurred shadow he had seen reflected in Nadir Sulayman's window. He didn't like where his thoughts were leading him.

'Now Shaw is dead. After Nadir Sulayman was killed, he was my ticket out of here. I'm stuck.' Makana looked at her. 'I can't trust Winslow. I don't know what he wants, or what he plans for me.'

Fateema Brown shifted awkwardly. 'I understand your position, really I do, but I can't help you. Officially, the British government is not involved.' She drummed on the bar counter with her fingertips.

'We can't risk getting involved at this stage. You're wanted by the police on suspicion of two counts of murder. Just being seen with you compromises both my personal integrity and that of the British government.'

Makana shifted in his chair and winced as he felt pain shooting up his back. 'There's something else,' he said, quickly sketching out the events of the previous evening.

'You think they were Israeli agents?'

'They lost Nizari. They want him back more than anything.'

She reached for a paper napkin from a dispenser on the counter.

'Do you think you can find Nizari?'

'I think I'm close.'

She produced a pen from her bag. 'You need to stay away from the Israelis. You bring Nizari to us and maybe there's a chance we can help you. But you must break all ties with Winslow.' Her gaze fixed on him. 'I can't help you unless you make it clear whose side you're on. We can't afford to take any chances when it comes to Winslow.' She was holding out the paper napkin. 'Call me in twenty-four hours. I'll see what I can do.'

Makana looked at the telephone number and wondered where he'd be in twenty-four hours.

Chapter Twenty-three

Nikos Godunov, or Boris, as he was otherwise known, operated out of a string of garages spread across the city. Kara Deniz led Makana down to the waterfront and on a ferry across to Kardaköy. It might be unwise to be seen openly with her so soon after his warning from Inspector Serkan, but Makana didn't feel he had much choice. He would get nowhere by hiding and he had no time to waste.

His conversation with Fateema Brown had confirmed to him that he was on his own. With Shaw dead she was not going to go out of her way to help him. On the contrary, if it came to a choice between loyalty to her government and helping an outsider, it was clear which way she was going to jump. As for Winslow, it bothered Makana that the Englishman had assumed he could use him as a pawn in achieving his own complex aims. He wasn't entirely sure why he was determined to see it through, but finding Nizari was no longer simply about helping the Iraqi scientist to safety. It was personal. Now he saw Nizari as the first step on a path that led the way back into the maze of his own life. The reason he needed to find Nizari was not for Winslow or for anyone else, but for himself.

Which brought him back to why he was here with Kara Deniz. Right now, his most immediate concern was getting out of this city without being caught. With or without Nizari, he needed a backdoor exit, one that no one else, not even Winslow, had a key to. At best, there was a leak somewhere in Winslow's little network. At worst, Winslow himself was playing a double game.

Makana, expecting a run-down garage that reeked of diesel, was mildly surprised to find himself being led along an avenue of fashionable boutiques and cafés to a brightly lit showroom stocked with shiny BMWs. Nikos Godunov dressed like a disco king from the 1970s, complete with flared trousers and a crushed velvet jacket. The only thing out of place was his hair, which was shorn to bristles. He snapped a silver lighter into flame and waggled his ringed fingers at a tall blonde in a microdress so tight it looked as though it might rip if she sneezed. She sat inside a glass-walled office, tapping her fingernails on a mobile phone. Although it was still early afternoon, she was pouring what looked like neat vodka into a tiny glass that she tipped down her throat with alarming regularity. The sound of music escaped through the closed door.

'So, what's this all about?' Boris puffed smoke from a slim cigar. He was speaking English for Makana's benefit. It lent the conversation an air of theatricality.

'You heard the news about Nadir?'

'Of course.' Boris gave the grunt of a man who has trouble expressing his emotions.

'You were friends, I understand,' said Makana. Boris surveyed him closely, as if searching for something he might have missed.

'Business partners,' Boris confirmed, glancing back at the office. The blonde was now dancing with her eyes closed, every move challenging the dress to stay in one piece.

'He was strangled, with one of those plastic things, you know?' Kara Deniz mimed.

'Interesting,' Boris grunted again. Makana wondered how much of this was for his benefit.

'This is the man who found him,' Kara explained. Boris looked at Makana with renewed interest.

'You called the police?'

'No,' said Makana. 'I was hit on the head before I could do anything.'

Boris frowned. 'You saw the man who killed him?'

'I saw someone.'

'Someone?' A crash came from the office. The blonde had disappeared from sight, apparently having fallen over. 'Excuse me.'

'Are you sure about this?' Makana asked Kara as Boris marched away.

'He's your best bet, believe me.'

They watched Boris as he entered the office and hauled the girl to her feet. She rubbed her head as he sat her on a chair and yelled at her, some of it audible through the glass walls and closed door. The girl rubbed her elbow and tossed her hair back defiantly.

'Sorry,' Boris apologised when he returned. 'She thinks she knows how to drink. She doesn't.' Impatient now, he snapped his fingers. 'What was Nadir doing for you?'

'He was arranging transport,' Kara said. 'Overland to Sofia.'

'What is it, you don't like to fly?' Boris grinned, tugging at the cuffs of his jacket.

'Not this time.'

'Okay.' He looked from Makana to Kara and back again. 'How many people?'

'Myself and one more.'

'Normally, anyone comes to me with this kind of proposition, I don't know him from Adam, I show him the door. If he's lucky.' Boris looked pained. 'But since you come to me with a friend, and because Nadir was my partner, then I do this for you. We can talk about money later.'

'A price was agreed.'

'Yes, but Nadir is no longer available.' Boris smiled like a man who holds all the best cards. The girl appeared unsteadily in the doorway behind him, clinging to the doorframe.

'Boriiiss!' she called, staggering and nearly falling again. Boris swore under his breath. 'I have to take care of this.' He held out his hand. 'We have a deal, then?'

'We have a deal.'

'Good, I make the arrangements and then we can talk.'

The two men shook hands. Boris kissed Kara on the cheek and laughed.

'Now this is a woman who can drink! If only there were more like her.' He rolled his eyes and marched off in the direction of his office.

'Do you trust him?' Makana asked when they were on the deck of the ferry again. The noise and clamour of the Asian side of the city was already fading, disappearing beneath their wake.

183

'Boris cares about money. As long as you pay him he is loyal.'

'He doesn't seem like Nadir's type somehow. They must have made an odd couple as business partners.'

Kara turned her back to the railings and cupped a hand to light a cigarette. 'Years ago Nadir would never have had anything to do with someone like Boris, but he changed.'

'After he came out of prison?'

'Contacts on the inside.' She exhaled smoke as the deck shuddered beneath them, the engines churning the water. 'Prison changes people. You find parts of you that you never knew existed.'

'Is that what happened to you?'

'I wrote an article and was accused of supporting the Kurdish militants. You know the old saying, one man's freedom fighter is another man's terrorist. They gave me three years, suspended. I served six months. It was enough to make me hate them.'

Makana's mind was elsewhere. He studied the water below and recalled staring down from the bridge and seeing his car sinking slowly out of sight. How was he to make sense of the fact that this city seemed to be pulling him back into his former life?

'Nadir may have been killed for what he was doing for me.'

'This person you are taking out of the country, who is it?'

'I'm not sure it's a good idea for you to know.'

'Hah,' she laughed. 'That's another way of saying you don't trust me.'

'Two people are already dead.'

'Two?'

'It's a long story.' Makana pointed into the distance. 'Are those the Princes Islands?'

'Yes, that's Heybeliada.' She turned to look out. They fell silent for a time, the engine grinding far below, the sea churning off the bow.

'When Nadir came out of prison he would have had a grudge against the government.'

'Everyone with half a brain has a grudge against the government.' She narrowed her eyes. 'What's your point?'

'Something like that might drive a person to form strange alliances.'

'You're talking in riddles.'

'Could Nadir have been working for the Israelis?'

That brought a laugh like a cough. 'That's insane,' she said, as she tossed her cigarette butt down into the water.

Insane sounded about right, as a description of Makana's present state of mind.

Chapter Twenty-four

They parted company on the quayside and Makana walked in a slow circle up and down the winding streets, going through his usual routine, perhaps a little more carefully than usual, until he arrived back at the ferry port where he had started.

It was now just gone midday and the terminal was fairly quiet. He bought a ticket and made his way back through the turnstiles and onto the upper deck of the island ferry. Almost before he got there he felt the vessel judder beneath him as the engines started up and they began to slide away from the quay. Seagulls swirled around them, screeching at their own hysteria.

Makana imagined himself on a voyage to unknown parts, far away from anywhere. The idea held a certain appeal, and for a time he lost himself in it. The truth was he didn't much like travelling by water. His memories of learning to swim in the river as a child were over-shadowed by fear. The sense of what was concealed, of what lay beneath the surface, the darkness that lurked there. His father had been a good swimmer, driving himself out into the water with strong, firm strokes, his black hair alive, as he slid through the water as slick as a fish. When he came to teach his son to swim he had little patience. To the boy, the river's calm surface was deceptive. There were dangerous eddies and undercurrents. His father would hear nothing of it. 'Don't be afraid. Keep going. Just trust in yourself.' But the boy was afraid. He preferred dry land, where he could see what was coming. Maybe that was what made him uneasy about this city: he felt as though he was skimming over a surface with no idea of what lay below.

He took himself round the ferry, walking at the leisurely pace of a man who is in no hurry to get anywhere. He circled the upper deck, pausing to study the receding coastline, the hulking shadows of the narrow strait with its rocky sides, and over them the arc of steel and concrete that was the Galata Bridge, so high and long it looked almost like a natural feature. How could anything so big have been constructed by man? But this was the city of Justinian the Great, of Theodosius and Constantine. The walls spoke of the passage of peoples traversing the globe from east to west. It was hard not to be intimidated by that kind of history.

The ferry was half empty. There were two stops before they reached Heybeliada and the journey took just over ninety minutes. Before they reached it Makana descended to the lower deck and walked between the rows of fixed plastic seats. He chose a spot close to the rear where he could observe the other passengers as they came and went. For the most part these were locals, carrying bags and boxes, sacks and small children. The men smoked while the women chattered and handed out food to the young ones. There were also some tourists, foreign and local alike, who concerned themselves with posing by the railings for photographs of themselves and the view. No one stood out and no one looked familiar, but that didn't mean anything. He didn't really know who he was looking out for. It was like feeling your way in the dark, not knowing what shapes are going to materialise out of the shadows, which ones pose a threat and which don't.

Makana joined the file of passengers as they threaded their way down the gangway to the quay. He spent some time on the water-front, making his way slowly along the row of cafés and restaurants, stopping here and there, for coffee and a smoke. The people who had arrived with him dispersed in different directions, families settling themselves around tables, the adults calling for refreshments while the children ran wild around them. Some couples climbed into horse-drawn carriages and clopped away hopefully in search of a romantic setting. Painted wooden houses rose up the hillside, some blue, others a tan shade of varnish.

Everywhere he went, Makana asked if the name Aksoy meant something. He was looking for an old friend, he explained. He thought the family had a place here. It was on his third try that at last he found someone who knew.

A woman in black, her greying hair tied back, called across the room to the man washing dishes behind the counter. He was an older man with a bushy white moustache, who spoke no English, and Makana assumed he was her father. Yes, of course he knew the Aksoy family. They had owned a house on the island since he was a boy. They had been coming here for generations. Which one did he know?

'Hatice Aksoy, a professor at the university.'

The woman in black nodded and translated, but the old man shook his head.

'She's not around any more. She passed away.'

'Well, I should like to pay my respects to the family,' Makana said.

They gave him directions and he was soon walking up the road that curved along the coast. He had been assured it was no more than ten minutes away, but this proved optimistic. It took him the best part of twenty before he came to a halt before a large wooden house set on a corner. It was painted a light blue and had two floors. A path led up to a front porch that extended around the side of the house. Makana followed it round to the rear where the sea was visible beyond a row of pines. At the edge of the garden, where the trees began, stood a small pavilion for spending the summer evenings watching the sun go down.

'*Effendim?*'

He turned to find a woman in her thirties standing in the doorway. She held a small child in his arms.

'Excuse me, I was looking for the house of Professor Aksoy. I was told she lived here.'

'My mother?' The young woman's English was good. She looked him over suspiciously. 'My mother passed away five years ago.'

'I'm sorry to hear that,' began Makana. He stopped. 'Look, this is a little difficult. I'm actually trying to find an old friend of your mother's.' Her eyes flickered over his shoulder in the direction of the pavilion in the trees.

'Are you a friend of his?'

'He's expecting me,' said Makana. 'I've come to take him home.'

The child in her arms was restless, and she jogged the little boy up and down a few times before he settled again. She seemed to be trying to make up her mind.

'He just appeared out of nowhere. He was in a bad state. He refused to see a doctor.'

Makana looked back at the trees. Through the windows of the pavilion he could make out a figure moving about.

The woman seemed to make up her mind.

'I've been worried about what to do,' she said, stepping down from the veranda and leading the way along the path. 'My husband is not happy to have a strange man in the house.'

'I understand.'

'He said he was a friend of my mother and he needed help. I couldn't turn him away.'

'Of course not.'

She studied Makana carefully. 'He's in some kind of trouble, isn't he?'

'That's why I'm here.'

The woman nodded. 'I didn't know who to call. I didn't know what to do.'

'It's all right. Let me speak to him. Hopefully we can resolve this quickly.'

The pavilion was elegant and simple. An octagonal roof protected a single room with windows on every side. A small porch contained a low table, a rocking chair and a bench. The air was perfumed with the faint trace of resin. Through the trees he could see the sea, shiny and flat, and in the distance cargo ships that slid across the glassy surface like wooden clogs across a slippery floor. Tankers lined up, patiently waiting their turn to enter the Bosporus Strait that would feed them north and deliver them to the Black Sea. Their lights were like electric echoes of the first stars to emerge in the sky.

Ayman Nizari stepped onto the porch looking more dishevelled than the last time Makana had seen him.

'What are you doing here?' Like a cornered animal's, his eyes darted back and forth between the woman and Makana.

'I came to help you,' said Makana, trying to sound reassuring.

189

'I don't need your help,' snapped Nizari.

Makana glanced at the woman, who shifted awkwardly. Nizari turned on her.

'Did she tell you I was here?'

'Nobody told me.' Makana circled the room casually. He picked up a book and set it down. 'They didn't have to tell me.' He glanced up at Nizari. 'Others will be coming. If I could find you, so could they.'

'What about my money?'

'We can discuss that later.'

'I told you, I want my money.' Nizari was growing frantic. 'Did you tell them? Did you tell Winslow?'

Makana tried offering a cigarette, which Nizari gratefully took. 'You can't stay here for ever,' he said after a moment. 'You're putting these people in danger.'

'I'm not leaving until I get my money.'

'Then you're going to be here for a long time.'

Nizari shifted his weight and then, passing a hand over his face, he sighed and sank down into the rocking chair.

Makana smiled at the woman, who looked worried. He peered inside the interior. There was a smell of mould in the air that competed with the general unwashed odour coming from Nizari. A heap of crumpled clothes tumbled from a half-empty bookshelf in one corner. An old turntable and a handful of battered LPs hinted at summer evenings and spirited parties. The whole pavilion seemed to speak of other times. Ayman Nizari was an incongruous addition to somebody else's memories.

'You shouldn't worry too much about the money,' said Makana softly. 'The main thing is to get you to Cairo. Winslow is there. That's what you want, isn't it?'

Nizari wrung his fingers. 'I want it to be clear that I've done nothing wrong.'

'Nobody is saying you did anything wrong,' Makana assured him. This wasn't the moment to be reminding Nizari that trying to sell your skills to a known terrorist can make you a lot of enemies.

'How do I know I can trust you?'

'You don't have much choice, I'm afraid,' said Makana. He turned to address the woman, who looked as though she was two steps away from calling the police. 'You wouldn't happen to know when the next ferry is?'

Visibly relieved, she looked at her watch. 'In about forty minutes. You have plenty of time to make it back to town.'

'Okay.' Makana turned back to Nizari. 'Here's what we'll do. For the moment it's probably best for you to stay here. If that's all right,' he said, consulting the woman.

'For how long?'

'One night, two at the most.'

'I thought you were going to get me to somewhere safe.' Nizari's hand trembled as he puffed quickly on the cigarette.

'I am, but I need to make arrangements, and right now this is as safe a place as any. Less chance of being seen.'

'Are we in danger?' asked the woman.

'Not if you do as I say. You've told nobody that he is here?' Makana waited for her to nod. 'Good, then let's keep it that way. He should remain here, and not go out, any more than can be helped. I will be back as soon as possible.'

The young woman looked as if she were trapped in a nightmare, with no idea of how she had got here.

A horn sounded and Makana looked at his watch. 'I have to go.'

'You can't just leave me here,' Nizari whined. Already his voice was grating on Makana's nerves.

'Stay here and be ready to move quickly. We won't have much time.'

He thanked the woman and then he stepped down from the shadows and walked away across the slope without looking back.

By the time he reached town people were gathering along the quayside in anticipation of the ferry. Makana circled through the crowd looking for familiar faces. His last words to Nizari echoed in his head. Time was running out.

Chapter Twenty-five

The dockside was crawling with police. Makana threaded his way through the crowds, skirting from one group to another – construction workers, tourists, a party of Spanish students shepherded by a pair of nervous teachers. Clearing the terminal building, he edged towards the shelter of the nearest streets.

Koçak was waiting as agreed.

'Amin Bey, everything is all right?' he asked as he opened the door for Makana to climb into the taxi. They moved off slowly, chugging up the steep incline between pedestrians, leaving a plume of black exhaust in their wake.

'Before we go anywhere, I need to make a phone call.'

There wasn't time to find another place, so he told Koçak how to find the Mukarrameh call shop and asked him to wait around the next corner for him. An anxious Marcus Winslow was waiting for his call. He answered on the first ring.

'Where have you been? I've been worried.'

'You heard about Marty Shaw, then?'

'Of course. What was he doing in your room?'

'I can't say,' said Makana. 'My best guess is that he was searching it, and someone surprised him.'

'That's all there is to it?' Winslow sounded sceptical.

'What are you asking?'

'I mean, I'm wondering what he was doing in your room. Did you have any contact with him at the consulate?'

'He took an interest in me when I was collecting my passport.'

'What does that mean, he took an interest?'

'He asked what I was doing in Istanbul.'

'And what did you tell him?'

'I stuck to my story.' Makana looked out at the interior. Over the top of the high counter a pair of bloodshot eyes swivelled to observe him. It probably wasn't a good idea coming back here, but he was in a hurry. He knew he needed to put Winslow's mind at ease. 'What are you getting at?'

'If Shaw was leaking information, that might explain things. Otherwise …'

'Otherwise, what?'

'Nothing. I'm just trying to understand why Shaw was in your room.'

'Does it really matter? Right now, the main thing is getting Nizari out of here, don't you think?'

'You're right, of course.' Winslow sounded weary. 'You can't stay there. You'll be on every wanted list in the country now. If they had any doubts about your involvement in Sulayman's death, I'd say you'd pretty much put those to rest now. That makes your situation untenable.'

'I can't argue with that,' said Makana. The man behind the counter was speaking into a phone in a low voice, his hand cupped over the receiver.

'You can forget about the airport. Even without Nizari you'll be detained.'

'So what do I do?'

'Leave it with me. I'll find an alternative route.' Winslow sighed. 'You need to remain calm and sit tight. We'll get you out of there, I promise. Are you anywhere near finding our man?'

'I'm working on something.'

'That sounds like progress. Just make sure you're careful. You'll need somewhere else to stay.'

'I've taken care of that,' said Makana. 'Look, about Shaw, do you think it could have been the Israelis?'

'At this point, to be honest, anything is possible.' The more Makana needed from him, the more vague Winslow became. Makana wondered what that meant.

'I want you to carry on checking in, every twelve hours. And call me if there are any more developments, and I mean, call me immediately. Is that clear?'

The man behind the counter resumed his silent observation of his only client. Makana listened for sirens.

'One last question. The Israelis.'

'Again?' Winslow sounded annoyed. 'This is beginning to sound like an obsession. All right, what about them?'

'I'm having trouble working out which side we're on.'

'I don't even know what that means,' said Winslow.

'I mean, are you working with them?'

There was a long silence. So long that Makana wondered if the line had been lost.

'I thought I explained this to you; they're our allies.'

'What does that actually mean?'

'It means that we share everything with them … in theory.'

'In practice?'

'In practice we are competing species in the same evolutionary pond.'

'Which means what exactly?'

'It means we don't turn our backs on them. Is all this your way of telling me you've had a run-in with them?'

'I'm not sure. It's possible.'

Winslow gave a tut of annoyance. 'There are times when I really wonder what it is you're trying to say.'

Makana could have said the same thing. Nobody seemed to be able to speak plainly, least of all Winslow.

'I have a feeling I may have run into them.'

'Are you sure?'

'They were masquerading as Bosnian jihadis.'

'Nice touch,' muttered Winslow. 'I'm sorry. I was hoping to keep this simple. I want you to focus on coming through this in one piece. Keep out of harm's way, and as for our friends in Tel Aviv, steer clear of them at all costs. As for Marty Shaw, I'll get onto our liaison in the MIT and see if we can't come in on the investigation.'

'Can you do that?' Makana wondered if Winslow was just making this up to reassure him, or if the Englishman really thought he could influence an investigation by Turkish intelligence.

'If we tell him he's a person of interest to us, it might take some of the pressure off you.'

'Why can't you tell them he's one of yours?'

'Because we don't do that kind of thing. Ever.'

It was becoming more and more clear to Makana that he was an expendable part in Winslow's grand scheme. Had Winslow ever really trusted him? Somehow he doubted it. He wondered whether Winslow had doubts about Makana's innocence when it came to Shaw's death, or whether he knew more about that than he was letting on. Winslow had come to him because he needed to use an outside agent, someone who wasn't connected: once his status changed, Makana would no longer be of use to the British.

He dropped some notes on the counter and left the call shop quickly, half expecting to find the place surrounded when he came out into the street. A light rain had started. Turning a corner he doubled back right and left. He bought a newspaper and stood under the awning pretending to read it while watching the entrance to the call shop. No police cars appeared. When he was satisfied he was not being followed, he made his way back to where Koçak was waiting.

'All is good, Amin Bey?'

'*Tamam*, Koçak,' said Makana, using one of the few words of Turkish he had managed to pick up. 'Everything is good.'

'*Tamam, tamam!*' Koçak responded enthusiastically.

'I need to ask you a favour, Koçak.'

'I am at your service, Amin Bey.'

'Wait till you hear what it is.'

Koçak lived with his wife Ayçe and three children, the youngest of whom was five, the eldest thirteen. The entire family had assembled on a small sofa in the narrow living room of their apartment to greet Makana. Koçak introduced each one with the solemnity of a caliph presenting his court. Makana slept in the spare room, which Koçak assured him was the honoured place where his wife's mother slept when she visited from Anatolia. Makana envisaged a large woman, whose bulk had worn the trough in the mattress into which he rolled and from which he seemed to spend the night fighting his way out of. Appropriately, he dreamed of being buried alive.

When he woke it was light and the house was quiet. Koçak was in the kitchen, his usual unshaven self, smoking a cigarette and listening to the radio.

'Amin Bey, *alhamdoulilah*, I hope you have slept well.'

'Very well, thank you. It's very good of you to help me like this.'

'My wife is worried.' Koçak shook his head fretfully as he prepared coffee. 'She thinks it is strange that a man such as yourself is not staying in a fine hotel. I told her, Amin Bey is different. He wants to see how real Turkish people live.'

'And she was satisfied with that?'

'Ah …' Some more head-wagging. 'I tell her you are a Muslim and she must be a good host and not ask too many questions.'

'I don't mean to cause any problems for you and your family,' said Makana. 'But I'm in a bit of trouble. In a couple of days it will be over, I hope, and I'll be out of your way.'

'Amin Bey, just tell me what you need from Koçak.'

'Well, first of all I need to find a place I was taken to a few days ago.'

Makana explained the problem. He had not seen where he was taken, although he had the idea that it was in the neighbourhood of Eyüp. He also described his escape through the houses before he abruptly found himself on a dual carriageway.

'So from house to road – big, small?' Koçak held his hands apart in the air. He was sketching a rough map with a crayon on the back of a child's school notebook. Makana thought about how far he had run.

'Maybe two hundred metres in a straight line?'

Koçak grinned and tapped the crayon on the notebook.

'Amin Bey, I think Koçak can find this place. No problem.' Beaming, he set a cup of coffee and a plate of simit on the table. 'You should eat something.'

Despite his enthusiasm, it proved a little more complicated than Koçak thought it would be.

They started where Makana had been picked up outside the bazaar. He knew the direction his abductors had taken and so they followed the road along the waterfront. He closed his eyes as Koçak drove, recalling the sounds he had heard, feeling the car stopping and starting as they moved uphill away from the sea, the sound of the seagulls dying away in their wake.

196

That was the easy part. After that it became more complicated. They took several wrong turns, having to back out of narrow alleyways that proved to be blocked. Eventually, there came a moment, when they were locked solid with people moving past them on both sides, that it became obvious they had to proceed on foot. Koçak, although reluctant to leave his beloved vehicle unattended, nevertheless conceded it was necessary.

'What could you see?'

Makana turned to look down at the Golden Horn. What could he see?

'The Topkapi Palace?' Yes. The Blue Mosque, yes. Further to the left. Higher up. They turned and walked up more streets. Makana tried to concentrate on the sounds again. Men hurried by bearing sacks. Quieter. The sound of a muezzin struck him as significant. How far away had it been?

By the end of the morning Koçak was sitting on the kerb looking exhausted, his optimism having given way to despair. They collapsed into rickety wooden chairs outside a corner café and ordered tea.

'Amin Bey, please, tell me why this is so important to you.'

Makana offered his cigarettes and lit one for himself. 'I came here to help a man whose life is in danger. I need to get him out of Istanbul.'

'Mr Amin Bey. I believe you are a good man, so I will help you, but please, we must find another way.'

So Koçak led the way up towards the big road that ran behind Eyüp. They stood on an overpass and Makana tried to fix the place where he had caught a taxi. From there they worked their way back down through the narrow streets.

At some point Makana noticed an old woman emerging from a narrow gap between two buildings and suddenly realised there was a way through. Calling to Koçak, and getting a weary wave in return, Makana slipped through the gap and climbed a steep ramp to find himself miraculously delivered to a familiar corner. He turned slowly in a circle and realised that he was standing opposite the spot where the van had been parked. To his left the road began to wind down, and the house he was looking for was thirty metres away to his right.

Now that he had found it everything seemed to fall into place. It had all looked different in the dark. Walking up, he examined the house more carefully. It was big. The part he had been in was the front section, but the outer wall, cracked and shedding plaster, stretched all along the side road to the next street. A painted sign that he could not read stretched along the wall. A loose web of wires dangled overhead, connecting the house to telephone and power networks. The door had once been painted green, and flecks of paint still clung to the wood, reminders of a splendour long departed. Koçak had joined him now. He looked up at the house and frowned.

'Is an old school,' he said, pointing to the sign.

Together they walked round to the other side. At the rear of the building there was a small door leading into a basement which was held shut by no more than a rusty bolt.

'Wait for me here. Keep an eye out.'

'For what, Amin Bey?'

'Anything or anyone who doesn't look right.'

Koçak nodded, although it wasn't clear he completely understood Makana's meaning.

The basement was dark. A long corridor brought him to a wide set of steps that opened onto the inner yard where he had been. There was a tree in the middle of the yard and washing hung on a line on the roof opposite. Grey bed sheets flapped gently in the wind, dusty and ragged from hanging for far too long. Makana stood for a time and just listened. He could hear pigeons cooing somewhere inside, the sound of wings flapping. He made his way carefully around the courtyard, peering in through open doorways and windows at a kitchen, then a communal washroom and toilets. All of it was fairly run down. He saw cracked tiles and broken taps. No one had cared for this place in a long time.

Most of the other side of the yard was taken up by what might once have been an old schoolroom. Here he saw signs of change. The door and windows had been repaired. A new lock on the door was reinforced by two shiny new bolts secured by hefty padlocks, one high and one low. The windows were not shuttered but the glass was grimy and sheets of newspaper had been taped over the inside to hide the interior. Both tape and newspaper looked new.

198

Through a gap he could see almost the full length of the room. The interior looked as if someone was doing repairs. He could make out a tarpaulin draped over something in one corner, and the room appeared to be partitioned by sheets of clear plastic, although there wasn't enough light to make out what was behind them.

Outside, Makana found that Koçak was making friends with the neighbours: two elderly women dressed in black, grey hairs sprouting from chins and underneath their headscarves.

'Amin Bey, please.' Koçak waved him over with all the panache of a professional guide. He was smiling and flirting with the two ladies, who seemed to view him as perfect son-in-law material.

'They tell me that you are not the only person to take an interest in this house.'

'Who has been using it?'

Koçak turned back to continue his introductions. The women nodded as they gave Makana a wary appraisal. Their expressions suggested some scepticism.

'I tell them you are an inspector of police,' Koçak grinned cheerfully.

'I'm not with the police.'

Koçak held up a hand to stay all objections. 'Amin Bey, I am telling the ladies what I think. That way nobody can say that Koçak was lying.' He closed his argument with a smile before turning back to address his subjects.

'They say government is very bad for closing this school. Everybody not happy. Where can children go for learning?' The ladies continued their summary. 'Then, one month ago, suddenly very busy. People coming and going. Everyone is happy. They think maybe the school is going to open again.' Makana tried to follow the nodding and smiling. Koçak clearly had talents that went above and beyond his abilities as a taxi driver. 'But school is not open. People come at night.'

'What kind of people?'

'Men and women. They come at night and they leave at night. Then nothing. During the day nobody, except one woman.'

Makana stiffened. 'A woman alone?'

More consultation. Makana fought his impatience.

'Yes,' Koçak announced after what felt like an interminable delay. 'This woman, she come alone. Not with the others.'

'Can they describe her?'

More back and forth ensued, this time with some amusement. The women were covering their mouths and giggling like schoolgirls.

'What are they saying?' Makana asked.

'Dark, they say.'

'I thought they said she came during the day.'

'Yes, yes,' Koçak explained with the patience of one who is used to dealing with those slower-witted than himself. 'It was not the day that is dark, but the woman.'

'The woman is dark?'

Koçak smiled. 'They say she is like you.'

'Like me?' Makana echoed, his heart beating faster.

Koçak elaborated. 'A young woman dressed in trousers and a coat.' He broke off to listen to more of their comments. Everyone seemed to be having a good time, except Makana. He looked into Koçak's laughing face.

'They say she not only looked the same as you, she behaved like you, asking a lot of questions. Funny, eh?'

Makana was deep in thought as they drove back down towards the centre of town. He noticed that Koçak was paying a lot of attention to the rearview mirror.

'What is it?' Makana asked.

'I don't know, Amin Bey. Maybe I am catching your sickness, but I think that Mercedes is following us.'

Makana craned his neck to look back just as the silver Mercedes accelerated and cut in front of them. Koçak stamped on the brakes. Two men were already out of the other car and coming towards them. Both wore suits and both looked familiar to Makana in the way that one's countrymen always look familiar.

'I have a bad feeling about this,' he said. Then his door was wrenched open.

'You need to come with us,' said the man.

Chapter Twenty-six

There were four men in the Mercedes. Makana was sand-wiched between two of them in the back seat. The car smelt of air freshener and plastic. The driver spoke to the man next to him, but it was impossible to make out the words. The vehicle took off, screeching down one narrow lane after another, bumping over the intersections with little concern for people or livestock. Makana placed his hands on the backs of the seats in front of him to brace himself. Neither of the men beside him objected. He could have thrown himself at the driver, or tried to reach the handbrake and create a diversion, but apart from possibly causing himself damage, he couldn't see the advantage of such a move just yet.

The man to his right was around forty years old. He remained tight-lipped and silent, staring out of the window, his face expressionless. The man to his left was younger. They were doing a job and they were clearly not interested in engaging with him. They were the messengers and Makana was the package they were charged with delivering.

They drove for about ten minutes. Once they reached the main road they slowed to a reasonable pace, slotting into the traffic, moving cautiously, as if trying not to draw any attention. When they came to a halt the men got out on either side and invited him to step out. They each took hold of an arm.

'Don't make this difficult on yourself,' the one to his right whis-pered. Makana knew by now that they were neither Mossad nor the MIT. This was worse than that.

He was led forward, through a row of parked cars and along a pavement beside an old stone building. He had seen this place before. Koçak had driven past it on one of their tours. The Yerebatan Seray or Sunken Palace: the old Basilica Cistern. Built by the Byzantine emperor Justinian, it had once been a reservoir that held the city's water. The two men led Makana through the entrance. They seemed to have been expected, as they were ushered through the door without fuss. Someone had gone to some trouble to stage this visit, but to what purpose Makana could not say.

The underground palace was a vast subterranean cavern ten metres deep supported by hundreds of massive stone pillars arranged in rows to support the structure. They descended the steps to a wooden walkway that led deeper into the darkness. It wasn't long before they had left the tourists behind. They passed a huge carved pedestal of the head of Medusa lying on her side. In the shallow water on either side of the walkway Makana could make out the twinkle of orange carp swimming in the eerie green light.

They came to a halt at an intersection in the boardwalk. One of the men placed a hand on his shoulder to restrain him. They stood in silence as a couple in their sixties wandered by, laden with cameras and rucksacks like elderly children lost in an enchanted forest.

Off to the right, down a side path, a figure stepped from behind a pillar. Makana squinted, unsure of what he was seeing. The two handlers let go of him and stepped back. He moved along the walkway. With each step he felt as though he were moving deeper into his own past.

The years had not been kind. Mek Nimr's face was grizzled and swollen.

'I thought you'd feel more comfortable in a public place,' he grunted as Makana drew near.

'That was thoughtful of you.' Makana stayed just out of reach, not trusting his own anger. He could feel his fists clenching so hard that his knuckles hurt. Mek Nimr had changed, but not so that he was unrecognisable under the fleshy layer. Now he carried himself with the bearing of an important man, the kind who made people jump to his commands. He wore a suit that hid some of the weight he'd put on over the years, but although his skinny frame had filled out, his face still had the same rigid lines that lent it a wooden squareness. He'd never been an attractive man to look at, but now it was as if the bitterness he carried within him had seeped out to permeate his skin. On either cheek he bore a wide cross: tribal scars that had been cut into his skin when he passed into manhood. It was a practice almost forgotten nowadays, and on Mek Nimr it added a sense of age, lending him the air of a primordial beast that had outlived its natural term of life.

'You look surprised,' Mek Nimr said. The smile was reptilian in its coldness. 'Surely you must have suspected ...'

'There's a difference between suspecting something and knowing,' said Makana. 'I was hoping I was wrong.'

'The world has moved on,' said Mek Nimr, waving a hand magnanimously. 'We are now collaborating with British intelligence.' He smiled. 'I find that particularly amusing.'

'I'm sure you do. Collaborating how exactly?'

'I shall come to that.' Mek Nimr had been planning this for a long time, Makana realised. This was his moment, and he was going to savour it. 'I wonder how that makes you feel.'

'Why should it make me feel anything?' asked Makana.

'You with your moral code, your sense of right and wrong.'

'I never assumed the British represented good.'

'Really?' Mek Nimr's face was a picture of mock surprise. 'Yet you looked down on us, on your own people, for trying to restore our country's cultural integrity.'

'Is that what you call it, imposing Islam as the solution to all the country's problems? It didn't work out too well, did it?'

'And yet here we are, with you on the losing side of history, and me on the winning side.'

'You really believe there are winners and losers?' Makana was wondering just how deep the water was on either side of the walkway, and how long it would take to drown someone before the guards managed to shoot him.

'You have a choice. You can work for me, or you can die.'

Makana shook his head. 'You should have killed me all those years ago, when you had a chance.'

'And miss the pleasure of watching you suffer for all this time?'

'You didn't need to kill them,' said Makana slowly. 'You could have just killed me.'

'Ah, but I wasn't the one who brought your family into the picture. You did that all by yourself. You could have left them out of it. You could have fled the country alone, but to you that would have been defeat.' Mek Nimr smiled slyly. 'It was your pride that killed them.'

A packet of Benson and Hedges and a matching gold lighter appeared out of his pocket. There was an expensive Rolex on his wrist. All the trappings of a man determined to show he has come up in the world. Makana wondered just how lucrative it was to be head of what was now known as the Directorate for Intelligence and Counterterrorism. They kept changing the name in an effort to keep up with the times. No doubt it bought you privileged access to government contracts. The last decade had seen the economy boom thanks to the revenue from oil exports. The reserves weren't going to last for ever, but those in power had made sure that they saw the benefits before they got around to thinking about the rest of the country.

'I get it,' Makana shrugged. 'You're an important man these days. Why should that change anything? As far as I can see, you're the same small-minded subordinate seeking approval.'

Mek Nimr snorted as he had expected something of the kind. The world might have changed, but underneath it all, he was still the same.

'You were always too hasty to pass judgement,' said Mek Nimr. 'Have you not asked yourself why you are here?'

Above him swallows, or perhaps bats, flew through the shadows, circling the carved pillars of this stone forest.

'I don't answer to you,' Makana said.

Mek Nimr threw his arms out magnanimously, but there was no warmth in his smile.

'There's no need to be like that. We're on the same side now. Where do you think Winslow got his information about Ayman Nizari?' He squinted at Makana through the smoke.

'That still doesn't change who I work for.'

'You're a stubborn man, you always have been. That's why you could never accept that a man from my background could rise above you. Your pride again.' Mek Nimr blew out his distaste in a thin stream of smoke.

Makana glanced back towards the minders, who stood at the end of the path deflecting anyone thinking of walking in their direction. How long would it take them to register? They would hear a splash and then they would come running. Two to three minutes to cause death by drowning. Mek Nimr seemed to read his mind and took a step backwards.

'There are things you never saw in me.' Mek Nimr tossed his head impatiently, like a horse preparing to bolt. 'I am thorough. I am methodical. You leave everything to chance.' He leaned back, getting into his stride. 'That was what really surprised me; how anyone could take you seriously as an investigator, when you leave everything to chance. You're a man without a system, and look where it has brought you.'

'Why did I provoke such anger in you, such hatred? I've never understood that.'

'My father was a servant who waited on the tables of the rich,' Mek Nimr said slowly. 'My mother sold vegetables in the market.'

'So what?' Makana demanded. 'My father was a teacher. He wasn't rich.'

'He was a national poet. A folk hero. He gave lectures at the university. He was someone.'

'You were jealous of my father?' It seemed an absurd idea.

Mek Nimr brushed the air with his hand. 'You had that look. The look that said you could do whatever you set your mind to. An arrogance, an assumption of superiority, as though you had something that set you apart. Maybe it didn't come from your father, or your background. Maybe it was just you, just the way you see the world.' He dropped his cigarette to the floor and ground it out with his heel before straightening his jacket. 'Anger? Hatred? Maybe once upon time, but not any more. I'm a wealthy man now. I look at you and I feel pity.' He shook his head. 'I see a man who has nothing. No dignity, no money, no family.' Mek Nimr thrust his hands into his pocket and rocked on his heels. 'It can't have been easy for you, all these years, knowing you had caused their deaths.'

205

Makana felt the hammering of his heart against his ribcage. The dark air seemed to press down.

'She's here, isn't she?'

'You know the answer. You've always known it.' Mek Nimr lit another cigarette with his fancy lighter. 'Do you think you mean anything to her, after all these years?'

'She's my daughter.'

Mek Nimr shook his head. 'Not any longer.' He leaned closer. 'I brought her up. I taught her right from wrong.' He stabbed a thumb to his chest. 'I am right, and you are wrong.'

'You sabotaged the car. You cut through the steering rods. That's why the car went off the bridge.'

'You can believe that if you want to,' Mek Nimr shrugged. 'It makes no difference.'

'She's still my daughter.'

'Not any more. I'm the only father she knows. She wants nothing to do with you.'

'I'd like to hear her say that.'

'Why, don't you believe me?' Mek Nimr asked. 'You abandoned her. You walked away when you could have saved her life, and perhaps even her mother.'

Mek Nimr had changed. He was no longer the figure Makana had carried around with him all these years. He seemed to have grown in stature, bigger, more powerful than ever. When he glanced off to the right Makana turned his head to follow his line of sight.

She was standing there beside the Medusa. Silent, dark and still. The light from beneath the water outlined her silhouette.

'Admit defeat,' said Mek Nimr softly. 'It will make it easier to face your death when it comes.'

Makana watched him walk slowly up to his men and beyond. He made a move to follow, but the guards remained in place, barring his exit from the walkway. They straightened up, hands held in front of them defensively. He watched Mek Nimr approach the woman and then together, the two of them carried on towards the exit. Neither looked back.

206

Chapter Twenty-seven

Makana's mind was a blank when he finally made it up to the surface. He was walking in a daze, numbed by what he had just seen. Mek Nimr had triumphed. Finally, after all these years, his moment had come. He'd brought Makana his daughter, back from the dead, only to take her away again.

'Amin Bey? Is everything all right?' It was Koçak. Makana was glad to see him.

'You followed us.'

'Yes, I follow you. I say, this is not good for Amin Bey.'

'Thank you, Koçak. I'm fine. I just need a few moments.'

'You look like you need some *çay*.'

'Maybe you're right.'

So Makana allowed himself to be led to the taxi and Koçak drove them back to the place they had drunk tea on their first excursion. They stood by the railings where the breeze was strong and the sea seemed to heave with distress.

After all these years he had finally found his daughter, only to learn that she was no longer his. He didn't know which of the two facts was the harder to accept. He felt elated by the knowledge that she was alive, and yet crushed. He meant nothing to her.

'The world is not easy, Amin Bey,' Koçak offered. 'That is why we all need Allah to guide us.'

Makana wasn't convinced Allah was involved in this particular instance. If he was then things were a lot worse than he imagined.

When they had finished their tea, Koçak drove Makana to the white mosque at Ortaköy. Makana peeled off five hundred dollars from the money he had left. Koçak refused at first.

'It's too much, Amin Bey.'

'No,' said Makana. 'It's not enough.' Koçak finally accepted the money. He got out of the car to kiss him on both cheeks.

'If you ever need me again, you know where to find me.'

Makana watched him drive away, realising that he had just said goodbye to perhaps the only person in this city that he really trusted.

It was now late afternoon and an air of calm hung over the quayside. Tourists and locals wandered by in search of somewhere to sit and have a bite to eat before dinner. The air was filled with the gentle hum of conversation over which the distant traffic and the seagulls' ceaseless crying added a discordant tone. The ivory-white mosque had a slender beauty to it that distinguished it from the more flamboyant Blue Mosque of Sultan Ahmet, or the more audacious Fatih Camii. It projected no ambitions or declarations of victory but seemed satisfied to provide an elegant presence. Its position, tucked beneath the looming arch of the Bosporus Bridge, lent it a touch of fragility.

It was fair to assume that Boris had no particular interest in mosques. Mooring his yacht alongside it was probably more a matter of creating a photo-opportunity than out of necessity. Still, even in this it failed. The contrast only underlined the vulgar decadence of the vessel. Today there was no sign of the female companion who had been with Boris in the car showroom.

Makana and Kara Deniz were shown up onto the aft deck, where they found the man himself reclining on a sofa juggling phones. He wore an officer's cap and a bright green shirt decorated with red and yellow parrots, open to the waist to reveal a hoard of pirate treasure: medals, gold necklaces and silver coins. A pair of sunglasses added the finishing touch to the image of a modern-day freebooter. An indefinable industrial dance beat throbbed from speakers built into the teakwood panelling. Boris fluttered a handful of ringed fingers at the heavily laden table to one side.

'Help yourselves, please, don't be shy. We don't stand on formality here.'

Kara Deniz glanced at Makana and shrugged before going over to the bar to open a bottle of beer. Makana looked back at the quayside and the crowds moving past.

'I know what you're thinking.' Boris pointed a finger adorned with a large silver skull. 'Too exposed, right? Believe me when I tell you this is the best place to have a quiet chat. Not even the most sensitive microphones of Russian FSB can pick up anything above all of this.' It was plain what he meant. Between the sea, the chatter of the birds, the heavy traffic running over the bridge along with ferry horns, tourist babble, even the flap of the canvas awning above their heads, it would be hard to pick out any conversation. Boris indicated the bench opposite him. 'Nadir's big mistake. He never knew what he was dealing with. Me, I don't like to take chances.'

Boris got up to mix himself a drink in a blue glass the size of a small fishbowl. Ice cubes shaped like dolphins bobbed cheerfully on the surface. He propped his sunglasses on the top of his head to reveal small sharp eyes that darted between them.

'I understand you've had a bit of trouble.'

'A few complications,' conceded Makana. 'How much do you know of what Nadir was doing for me?'

'Only that you need a car and drivers as we discussed.' The dolphins chased one another around his glass as Boris swirled it. 'Sure you don't want one?'

'I'm fine, thank you.' Makana looked over at Kara Deniz, who was sipping her beer, trying to hold her hair back from blowing in her face.

'What you have to understand about Nadir is that when he came out of prison, he had lost his belief in politics. All he cared about was the money. He didn't care where it came from.' Boris glanced in Kara's direction. 'You may not want to hear that, but it's true.'

'Do you need to know who the passengers are?' Makana asked.

'Yourself and one other. I don't need to know more. I provide the cars, clean, untraceable number plates – we need two. Also drivers who are reliable and don't talk.' Boris tilted his chin up. It looked like something he had picked up from a gangster film. 'Last time we talked, you had a problem locating your passenger.'

'That's been resolved.'

'You found him?' Boris glanced away, dropping his sunglasses back into place. 'So that's no longer a problem.'

'You found him?' echoed Kara. Makana looked over at her before turning back to Boris.

'How soon can you arrange the transport?'

'A day or two. Normally, I would say sooner, but considering the situation it is best to be cautious.' Boris popped a fistful of peanuts into his mouth and chewed thoughtfully. 'How about you, how are you doing?'

'I'm fine, but much as I love your city I don't plan to stay here any longer than I have to.'

'Wise man. Me, if I was in your shoes, I would already be gone.' Boris flashed a brief smile. 'Some would say you outstayed your welcome.'

'I don't have much choice,' said Makana.

'You still want to find out who killed Nadir.' Boris shrugged. 'I understand. When you find out, you just tell me.' He stabbed a thumb to his chest. 'I'll take care of it. Free of charge.'

'You've heard nothing?'

'No.' Boris took a long swig from his glass. The dolphins shuffled around. He wiped his mouth with the back of his hand. 'But I'll get them.'

'He thinks the Israelis are involved.' Kara Deniz had switched from beer to vodka, which seemed to be something of a tradition around Boris. She downed one shot quickly before pouring herself another, the icy liquid in the bottle moving sluggishly, thick and slow. The alcohol gave her a mean, hard look. Boris laughed.

'What makes you say something like that?'

'This and that.'

'The Mossad here?' Boris cackled. 'They would never come here. It would be a scandal.'

'That's what I told him,' Kara Deniz said defiantly.

Boris patted Makana on the shoulder. 'Look, take my advice. You're new to this town. The Israelis cannot operate here. If they were discovered it would be a national outrage.'

'I thought Turkey was Israel's strongest trade partner in the region?'

'Don't you believe it.' Kara Deniz answered. The vodka seemed to have aged her ten years in as many minutes. 'Sure, Erdoğan went to Tel Aviv last year. I was with him. I watched him at the Holocaust Memorial. Like an obedient puppy. He said all the right things. He always says the right things. He wants the world to see him as progressive, but also as a strong man in the region. So, on the surface it looks like they're close friends, but since the Americans strolled into Iraq things have gone sour. It's a civil war over there. Shia against Sunni. The Iranians accuse the Israelis of bombing the Askari mosque.'

Boris grinned. 'Listen to her! Press the right buttons and she goes off like a rocket. Imagine what she's like in bed.' He walked over to put a hand on Kara's neck, but she shrugged him off and poured herself another drink. 'Easy with that stuff, *balim*.'

'Don't *balim* me, I can drink you under the table any day of the week.'

Makana was in no doubt that she was right, but he wondered what was making her hit the vodka so hard. She turned her flinty grey eyes on him.

'Nadir was a dyed-in-the-wool Marxist. He supported the Palestinians. He'd never work with the Israelis.'

'People change,' Boris offered, in a spirit of reconciliation. He added something else in Turkish before turning to Makana again. 'We are set now. What was your arrangement with Nadir?'

'We were to meet close to here.' Makana gestured at the open area in front of the mosque.

Boris nodded his approval. 'It's a good spot. Access from the sea as well as the road. Maybe we can use it.'

'Okay, then what?'

Boris scratched one of the red parrots in his armpit. 'A short drive up the coast. We change vehicles for safety's sake, then across the border to Belgrade. Once out of the city it's just a matter of speed. We give you a fast car.'

'We haven't discussed money.'

'Forget it,' Boris waved a dismissive hand. 'This one's for free. I'm not going to make a profit out of a friend's death.'

Makana glanced over at Kara, who was staring sullenly out at the water. Boris walked over to the table to fix himself another drink. 'You sure you won't join me?'

'No, thank you. I'm fine.'

'Where you come from it's not impolite to refuse another man's hospitality?'

'Under the circumstances, I think I need to keep a clear head.' Makana smiled apologetically. 'Tell me more about Nadir.'

'Nadir?' Boris held up the bottle of vodka to examine how much was left. He splashed it liberally over a handful of fresh dolphins scooped from a bucket before drowning them in pink soda. 'Nadir was a changed man when he came out of prison. It does that to you. Nobody is the same.' He spoke like he knew what he was talking about. 'For me it happened when I was still young, just a kid. I got over it. Nadir was already grown up. He had established himself, he had a reputation. That can crush you. Everything you thought you knew about yourself is destroyed. After that, all he cared about was money, looking after his family.'

'Maybe that was his motivation,' said Makana.

'To work with the Israelis, you mean?' Boris shook his head. 'I don't think so.'

'He was a businessman, maybe they made him an offer he couldn't refuse.'

'We're all businessmen.' Boris glanced at Kara, who was silent. He wore the sleek, satisfied grin of a man who has all the answers. 'In business it is all about the terms of agreement. If they are acceptable, then everyone goes home happy. If not, somebody usually dies. But Nadir was not like this. He still had principles, ideals. That's why he was so bad at business.'

As a philosopher, Boris belonged in the category of those who will believe anything that pops into their heads for as long as it coincides with what they want to do. Makana knew the type. They slip and slide over the surface of the world with the minimum of friction.

'The question is who stood to profit from killing him,' Makana said.

'Perhaps it wasn't profit,' Boris suggested. 'He was tortured, you say. Then someone wanted information. After that they were just covering their tracks.' He shrugged as if it was all too obvious.

The sound of a car horn brought their attention to the quay-side where a large silver BMW had pulled up. Boris waved as four women descended from the vehicle. All were clad in bikinis covered by loosely tied wraps. Their arrival brought a touch of a carnival feel with it. Their colourful clothes matched Boris's parrots. They tottered up the gangway on high heels and even higher laughter, clutching sunglasses and handbags.

'So now the party begins,' declared Boris with a wink.

'Maybe it's time to go,' muttered Kara. Makana was in agreement. They waited for the women to come aboard. Makana recognised the statuesque blonde who had been at the showroom earlier. She had brought some friends along.

'Anoushka!'

'Boris, darling!' she cried as she threw her arms around his neck. He gave her a squeeze and a pat on the behind before turning to greet her friends, all of whom got the same treatment.

'Text me when you're ready to go. I'll give you a time. We know the place. No phone calls.' Boris laughed and patted Makana on the shoulder. 'Don't worry, my friend, you're in safe hands!'

Chapter Twenty-eight

Once on the dock, Kara walked quickly ahead of Makana, either still incensed by Boris or fuelled by the vodka – it wasn't clear. Makana let her go. Eventually, the anger burned away and she slowed to allow him to catch up. They stopped at a waterside terrace and ordered coffee. Kara pushed the hair out of her face.

'I get the feeling there is something between you and Boris,' said Makana after a time.

'Once upon a time. Long ago.' She dismissed him with a wave. 'I was young and impressionable. He was reckless. A hoodlum, running with a gang. What is it about dangerous men?'

'You're asking the wrong person.'

They both fell silent as the coffee arrived.

'I got tired of his mood swings. He would get drunk and beat me up.' Kara tossed her hair back. It was obviously a sore point. 'In the end I managed to summon the courage to leave him.'

'But you remain friends.'

'Of a sort. He has useful contacts for me. This is a small town. You have to choose your enemies carefully.'

'And Nadir wasn't so careful?'

'Nadir was too trusting. Always helping people.' Kara hung her head to one side, looking up at him. 'Boris always has his own best interests at heart. You have to be careful with someone like that.'

'That sounds like a warning.'

She pushed her coffee aside. 'I need a proper drink.' She waved a hand at the waitress. Over her shoulder Makana noticed a couple of young tourists sitting behind them, a few tables away. When he looked at them they grew very interested in the guidebook they were consulting.

'This man you're trying to help, how important is he?'

'In the wrong hands he could be very dangerous.'

'If you want my opinion,' said Kara, 'you're out of your depth.'

'It's possible.'

The waitress brought over a small bottle of Yeni Raki and a bowl of ice.

'You should forget this whole thing and just leave,' said Kara as she poured herself a drink.

'I'm not sure how easy that is now.'

'You trust the people you're working for?'

Makana wondered if he had ever truly trusted Marcus Winslow. He thought he had taken the job on as a kind of favour to his old chief. Now he wasn't even sure who he was working for.

'I wish I could answer that.'

Kara gave a snort of laughter as she refilled her glass. 'That's not a good position to be in.' Drinking seemed to do something to her eyes, making them somehow sadder and more desperate.

'You and Nadir, was it personal?'

'He had a wife and three children.' Kara stared at the sea. 'He would never have left them. He'd lost too much already.'

Which wasn't an answer, but perhaps it told Makana what he needed to know. He glanced back in the direction of the tourist couple. The woman had disappeared.

'Nadir was terrified of going back to prison.'

'You said he gave up all of his ideological beliefs.'

'All he cared about was providing for his family.' She was silent for a moment, studying him. 'Somehow you don't really seem the type.'

'What type is that?'

'The type to be involved in subterfuge. You have an honest face, but you're what, Egyptian intelligence? Syrian?'

'What makes you think that?'

'All this talk about Israel.'

'I'm here to help someone, as a favour to an old friend.'

'Come on,' Kara scoffed. 'You can do better than that.'

'I'm sorry to disappoint you.'

'Nobody would believe you. You're a wanted man. The Englishman who was murdered in the Pera Palas hotel. Did you kill him?'

'No.'

'So, who did it?'

'Maybe it was the *karakoncolos*?'

Kara smiled, a lopsided, endearing smile. 'You know about that. People are saying the *karakoncolos* killed those people they keep fishing out of the sea. There's some metaphor there about societies that refuse to face the facts.'

'Maybe you should write about that.' Makana glanced back at the table by the wall. The woman still had not returned. The man had now put down the guidebook. His glass of beer was empty and he swapped it for the other one, which was still untouched. A man with a thirst.

The table was by the corner of the building, which meant that Makana could look straight through from one side to the other. Thin curtains covered the glass on both windows so that he could make out only the shadow of someone standing on the far side.

'We should go.'

'Why?' Kara glanced over her shoulder. Through the flimsy drapes Makana saw the shadow move, a person stepping back. He dropped some money on the table and got to his feet.

'I'm a little uneasy about staying anywhere for too long these days,' he explained.

They walked quickly, past a fire-eater and a stall selling candy floss. A police car prowled along the seafront, but the two officers inside were too busy talking to one another to notice them.

'It's probably safer for you to go on ahead. You don't want to be caught with me.'

She laughed. 'What is that, some kind of Arab macho bullshit?'

'I'm a wanted man, remember?'

'I'll take my chances. I've been around some pretty tough characters.'

He probably couldn't argue with that, he decided.

They jogged over the wide road and cut up along a path that curved steeply into town. Kara moved off quickly down a sidestreet and Makana had to hurry to keep up. She seemed determined to lose any potential tails, and practised too. They turned left and right, walking in circles around whole blocks, dropping into shops, even going into a café and leaving through a rear exit. They wound up heading down a steep, winding valley of daunting buildings, all in varying states of decay.

'I get this impression this isn't the first time you've done this.'

'I'm protective about my privacy.'

They turned another corner and almost at once went up a couple of steps and in through the narrow entrance of an ashen, crumbling building. Plaster dust crunched under their feet. She shut the door behind him, and motioned for quiet. They paused, and listened. No footsteps came. As they stood there Makana could feel Kara Deniz's gaze in the low light filtering in from outside. After a moment she nodded to herself and then moved on.

He followed her along a hallway to a rear staircase that rose steeply into darkness. The stairs creaked as they climbed, and there was a strong smell of old varnish and paint. The second-floor landing was partly blocked by a stack of large framed canvases that rested against the wall. They were covered by a dirty tarpaulin daubed with paint. Kara Deniz leaned down to reach underneath for a key before squeezing by to unlock the door of her flat.

It wasn't so much a flat as an artist's atelier. A row of high windows made up most of one side. There was a sleeping area in one corner occupied by an unmade bed surrounded by piles of books, newspapers and magazines. To the left was a kitchenette, illuminated by a low light over the counter that revealed bottles along with glasses, plates and polystyrene takeaway boxes. Domesticity clearly ranked low among Kara Deniz's priorities.

The centre of the room was a kind of living area. A chequered sofa with the stuffing escaping through the seams took up central stage. The sofa faced a small television set that stood on an uneven tower of books. Around this stood an easel, and a rough bench covered in tubes of oil paint, brushes, cans of thinner. Coasting through, picking up and then tossing aside a heap of post that had been lying on the floor, Kara picked up a remote control and snapped on the television to flip through the channels looking for news. Images of President Bush beaming on the White House lawn. A plume of smoke rising over Basra. The world went on.

'Before you ask, it's not mine. I'm not an artist. All this' – hands on her hips, she surveyed the chaos that took up more than half her living space – 'it's all his. The stuff in the hall. He was supposed to clear all this shit out a week ago. Artists! What a waste of time and space.' She turned on her heels and headed past the bed where a door led to a bathroom. 'Make yourself at home. I'm going to take a shower.'

Makana sat on the sofa and, encouraged by the overflowing ashtrays on every surface, smoked two cigarettes before Kara Deniz emerged wrapped in a cloud of steam and a skimpy towel. By then Makana's feet were beginning to itch. He would have left, except that it wasn't too smart an idea to go roaming the streets. He wasn't keen about calling on Koçak again either – he'd done enough already, and Makana didn't want to bring trouble on him and his family for trying to help.

'Are you hungry?'

'No, thank you. I'm fine.' Makana replied.

'I don't blame you,' she laughed. 'The state of this place would put anyone off.'

The television was now showing images of flashing lights, somewhere that was recognisable as Istanbul. An excited commentator was narrating the action as an ambulance crew carried a body on a stretcher out of an alleyway. Makana recognised the waterfront scene from three nights ago. He thought he could make out the figure of Inspector Serkan standing in the background talking to someone.

'They never get tired of running those clips, over and over.'

She flipped off the television and tossed down the remote as she perched herself next to him on the arm of the sofa holding a piece of pizza and a bottle of beer which she offered him. He shook his head.

'You don't eat, you don't drink,' she said, licking her fingers thoughtfully. 'What else don't you do?' Leaning over, she drew close and he pulled away. 'Okay,' she laughed. 'That solves that issue.' She was already on her feet again. Crossing to the window, she rested her head against the glass. 'You're the kind that always has someone waiting for them.' She took another swig of her beer. 'Me, I just get involved with the crazy ones. Psychopaths and artists!' She snorted in disgust. Then she turned and crossed to the shelves of clothes.

'You never told me,' Makana began.

'Never told you what?'

Makana looked away as she dropped the towel and began to dress, quite unselfconsciously.

'Why you didn't follow up on the story of that ambulance crash.'

'There was nothing to follow,' she said over her shoulder.

'The woman who was killed. Her name was Nadia Razvan. She was a waitress at the Cherry Beach club.'

'I don't know what that is.'

'It's the place Nizari was snatched from in Spain.'

'Nizari is your mysterious passenger?'

Makana nodded. 'The first time we met Boris, you told him I was heading for Sofia.' He waited. She pulled a sweatshirt over her head as she came towards him. 'I never mentioned where I was going.'

'You must have done. Maybe you don't remember.'

'I would have remembered something like that.'

She folded her arms. 'What are you trying to say?'

'I was wondering if maybe Nadir had told you.'

'You think maybe he was a little too talkative, and maybe that got him killed?' She was pulling on a pair of jeans.

'I'm just asking a question.'

She shook her head. 'Nadir was careful about that sort of thing.'

'You're saying he trusted you.'

'Of course.' Her eyes narrowed. 'You're not accusing me of betraying him, I hope.'

Makana smiled. 'Somebody betrayed him.'

'Fuck you!' she said, turned away again. 'Nadir was a friend. More than a friend.'

'You were thrown in prison. You hated your own government. What better way to get back at them than working for the Israelis?'

Kara Deniz marched over to him and looked him straight in the eye.

'I would never betray a friend, no matter how much I hated the government. Is that clear?'

Makana nodded.

'Okay, good.' She was moving around the room, gathering up money and cigarettes. 'I'm going out to meet some friends. You can stay here. Help yourself to anything. If you leave, just put the key back where it was.' She was already by the door, pulling on her leather jacket. She paused to look back at him. 'Maybe you have issues trusting people, or maybe it's something to do with me being a woman, but not everyone who tries to help you is after something. Try to get some rest. It sounds like you need it.'

She was right. Makana felt suddenly exhausted. He emptied the ashtray and made himself some tea before settling himself on the battered sofa, which he discovered was lumpy but not uncomfortable. He looked at his watch. Still a few hours to go. The day was drawing to a close. A gloomy light filtered in from the street below as he closed his eyes and tried to assess his position. Right now the best thing for him to do would be to get out of this city as fast as he could, with Nizari if possible. But that would leave something unresolved, something that had preoccupied him for so long it had become a part of him. To leave here now would tear still wider the wound he had carried with him for fifteen years. He wasn't even sure that the woman he had seen with Mek Nimr was Nasra. All he knew was that if he didn't find out one way or the other he would never be able to live with himself.

Chapter Twenty-nine

Istanbul Day Six

It was late now, and the ferry port was crowded with drunken revellers, which made things easier for Makana. At the entrance policemen surveyed the crowds, but at this time of night there was too much for them to see, too many people to watch. He slipped by among a large group of tourists without drawing their attention.

Once free of the harbour, the demons seemed to leave the passengers, as if the sea brought its own sense of calm, mortality, even a touch of poetry to proceedings, and people slumped into a state of exhaustion. Most of them disembarked on the Asian side of the city, before the ferry plunged back out into the dark sea, heading across the water on the second leg of its triangular course, delivering the last stragglers to their homes on the islands like mariners who had spent lifetimes toiling the seven seas.

An air of reverence hung over Heybeliada as Makana made his way up the coastal path to the house. A lone white owl swooped ahead of him up the road, wings outstretched like a vision of ghostly hope, before being swallowed by darkness. Following the road as it curved away from the bay and up into the trees, Makana remembered the story of the exiled princes from whom the islands got their names. He imagined that being exiled here might not be so bad. The hustle and bustle of Istanbul already felt distant, another country, almost another universe.

As he walked, he was accompanied by the gentle creak of the pines overhead. The air was perfumed with the faint trace of resin. He saw only one other person, the driver of a horse-drawn carriage that trotted by him on its way back to town. The man lifted a hand in greeting and Makana stood and waited for the carriage to disappear around the bend before moving on.

There was a chilly edge to the breeze, and he pulled his jacket tighter and hunched his shoulders. This time he didn't bother going up to the main house but pushed open the gate, closed it quietly behind him, then stepped off the drive and cut across to the path that led over the grassy lawn to where the land fell away. The lights were on in the main house and the sound of a piano trickled across the lawn behind him. The elegant outline of the wooden pavilion was silhouetted against the rising moon. Through the trees he could see the sea, shiny and hard, with the flat outlines of distant cargo ships moored to the glassy surface. Makana moved into the deep shadows under the trees.

In the pavilion, Ayman Nizari was snoring peacefully to himself. The room reeked of aniseed and raw spirit and it seemed pretty safe to assume that he had drunk himself into a stupor. Hardly surprising, thought Makana, that someone willing to sell chemical weapons that could strip the lining from a man's lungs might have trouble sleeping, but who was he to point fingers.

Makana settled himself into the old rocking chair on the porch and watched the finger of moonlight reach out of the sea towards him. It reminded him of nights he had spent on the awama, and for a time he was lost in reverie, and then he was asleep.

He opened his eyes to see Professor Aksoy's daughter staring up at him from the bottom of the porch steps, holding a tray of breakfast things.

'Good morning.'

'You have come for him,' she said as she came up the steps. 'Are you sure it's safe?'

'I think it's time,' said Makana.

She set the tray down on the table and poured him a cup of coffee from a small pot.

'To tell the truth, I am relieved,' she said, lowering her voice. 'I think it could be dangerous for us. I have a small child.'

'I understand,' said Makana, sipping his coffee.

'The truth is, I don't think my mother even liked him,' she whispered.

222

'No,' said Makana. He wasn't sure there was anything very like-able about Nizari. 'They wrote a paper together.'

'Yes, but my mother said it was the worst decision she ever made. It almost destroyed her reputation.' She glanced through the window at the cot where Nizari was sleeping. 'He falsified his results, and two years later he was creating nerve agents to gas the Kurds. He is not a good man.'

Makana took a deep breath. 'I know.'

'Do what you have to do,' she said firmly. 'But please get him away from me and my family.'

'I will.'

He watched her walk back up towards the main house. Through the screen door he could see a man looking out at them, the child held in his arms. Nizari jumped when Makana shook him awake.

'What are you doing here?' He sounded confused.

'Get dressed,' said Makana. 'It's time to go.'

By eight thirty they were on the quayside watching the ferry coming into the harbour. They had ridden down from the house in a carriage Professor Aksoy's daughter had summoned. She seemed to want to do everything she could to get Nizari out of her house. As they clip-clopped down the hill, Makana imagined himself in a nineteenth-century Russian novel.

On the quayside he concerned himself with observing their fellow passengers, but he saw nothing suspicious and the journey was uneventful. He texted Boris just before they disembarked in Beyazit. He noticed a police van parked close by and two officers randomly checking passengers as they made their way into town. Grabbing Nizari by the elbow, he steered him along the waterfront until there was a chance to slip into a sidestreet.

'Where are we going?'

'It's not far.' Makana wondered what he would do if Kara was not home and the key was not in its place. He decided there was nothing to do but wait and see.

It took them half an hour to walk from the ferry to the grey, crumbling entrance. An old woman was fighting with an umbrella, and as they waited impatiently for her to emerge, Makana was aware that every moment spent in the street increased the risk of them being spotted. When she realised it wasn't raining the woman laughed at herself and went on her way. Makana hustled Nizari inside.

There was no need of a key because the door stood open. Makana motioned for Nizari to stay behind him. The flat was empty and there was no sign of Kara. When he'd left last night he had locked the door and placed the key under the tarpaulin in the hall. Perhaps the boyfriend had come back for his things, although Makana couldn't see that anything had been moved. The bench covered in paint and brushes looked unchanged from the last time he had looked at it. The most likely explanation was that Kara had come and gone, forgetting to lock the door in her haste. No doubt this was normal for her. Makana felt a certain respect, perhaps even a touch of envy, for her bohemian lifestyle, although it would never have suited him.

'What is this place?' Nizari stared sullenly at the pile of dirty dishes in the sink where a cockroach was scuttling out of sight.

'It's just somewhere to rest for a few hours. I need to make arrangements.' Even as he spoke, Makana tried to decide how much of a risk staying here entailed. 'I need you to wait here for me.'

'Where are you going?' Nizari seemed jumpy.

'I have to make some calls. You'll be safe here. Close the door. The woman who lives here might return, but she's a friend. Oh, and there's an artist.' Makana jerked his head in the direction of the easel. 'He might come to pick up his things.'

'How long will you be?' Nizari looked stricken, the panic returning.

'Half an hour, maybe a little longer.' Makana saw the fear in the other man's eyes and for a moment considered taking him along, but it was far too risky and he felt no obligation to try and make Nizari feel more comfortable. At this point, he didn't feel much sympathy for the Iraqi. If he was going to sweat out every minute of being alone here, then so be it. Leaving him on his own was certainly safer than taking him along. Apart from anything, he would slow Makana down. To take him along seemed an unnecessary risk.

It was only when he stepped out into the hall that he realised he had no choice. Coming up the stairs you wouldn't notice. It was

224

only now, as he stood in the doorway, that he realised that Kara Deniz would not be coming back any time soon. She already was back.

The body had been slid into the space between the large frames and the wall. The tarpaulin almost covered the gap, but someone had been careless. The worn tip of a boot could just be seen in the corner. Makana pulled the canvas aside and heard a sharp intake of breath from behind him.

'Who is that?'

'We have to go.' Makana let the canvas drop back into place.

'Is that the woman who lives here. Is she dead?'

The man's face was frozen in fear. He was backing away. Makana grabbed his shoulder.

'Wait,' he said, holding up a hand for silence. He could hear voices. Somebody was coming up the stairs. He held a finger to his lips and then pointed upwards towards the roof. Nizari's eyes were wide with what he had seen. He was about to panic, backing into the apartment. Makana grabbed his arm, pulled the flat door shut as quietly as he could and then propelled him up the stairs. Nizari stumbled and went down on one knee with a whimper. Makana hauled him to his feet and pushed him up ahead of him – they had no time for niceties. It wasn't easy. The Iraq was heavy and awkward. They hurried up two flights of stairs as quietly as they could before Makana motioned Nizari to stop. He listened. There was murmuring from below. Two men speaking in low voices. Makana wasn't sure of the language, but it didn't sound like Turkish. They were already inside the apartment and seemed to be searching it.

'Move!'

Nizari climbed with the slow, clumsy pace of an elderly dog. He wheezed and groaned up three more flights before they reached the top. A door creaked open onto a flat roof. Makana ushered Nizari through then ducked back to listen. The voices were growing more urgent. Perhaps they had heard something. Outside a light rain had started to fall. Makana circled the parapet looking for a way down. There was a long drop to the next roof.

'Climb over,' he ordered.

Nizari laughed. 'You're crazy!'

'Those men are not going to hesitate. They killed the girl and they will kill us both.'

'You don't know that.'

'Suit yourself. I'm not staying here to find out.' Makana straddled the low wall.

'I can't do that! I'm not a monkey.'

'All you have to do is hang down and drop,' said Makana, preparing to swing himself over.

'You can't leave me here!'

'You don't give me much choice. I'm not waiting for those Israelis to catch up with us. They'll kill me as soon as they're finished with you.'

'They're Israelis?' Nizari's face would, under other circumstances, have been almost comic.

'I could hear them on the stairs.' Which was true, although he'd been unable to tell if they were speaking Hebrew. It did the trick in any case.

'Okay, just give me a moment.' Nizari approached the parapet and leaned over. He gasped and drew back. 'I can't.'

'We're wasting time.'

Nizari finally summoned the courage. He swung one leg up onto the wall. 'Now what?'

'Swing the other leg over and let yourself down as far as you can go.'

'I can't!' he protested.

'Yes, you can. Give me your hand.'

Makana lowered the whimpering scientist until he was far enough down to drop onto the next roof without hurting himself. He jumped down after him and together they ran across the roof and clambered over to the next building with greater ease. Here a door led into the building. Makana managed to force the lock and peered inside a gloomy stairwell. It would have to do. He looked back. Still no sign of the two men. Perhaps they had been lucky.

Chapter Thirty

The stairs led down into a noisy street. They were in an area that Makana did not immediately recognise: narrow, busy streets that were crowded with cars, people and scooters that beeped as they squeezed past them. They moved deeper, glancing back to make sure they were not being followed, avoiding the temptation to descend further into the city. That would lead them towards wider streets, avenues and boulevards that would bring them back to the centre of town. What they needed now was obscurity: somewhere to hide. They found it, eventually, in a large, unremarkable basement filled with smoke. Men played chess and cards, sipped tea and slapped down dominoes and cards. They were all ages, middle-aged men with paunches buttressing their chequered shirts, younger types in tracksuits, the sides of their heads shaved bare. They all looked like regulars. Still, nobody paid much attention to Makana and Nizari when they entered. They found a table by the wall. Makana caught the eye of a waiter and pointed at the tea on the next table and waggled two fingers.

Nizari was unhappy.

'What are we doing here?'

'We're drinking tea like everyone else. Can you play chess?'

'Chess?'

'It's better that we just look like we're passing the time. We want to avoid attention, so try to sit quietly.'

Makana spotted a telephone in an alcove in the rear, next to the door that led to the washrooms. He wandered over and took note of the number, retrieving a chess set from a shelf beside the bar on his way back. He sat down and started setting out the pieces.

'This is crazy,' Nizari whispered. 'That woman was dead.'

'Consider yourself lucky not to be back there with her.'

'You're supposed to be helping me, protecting me!'

'No,' Makana corrected him. 'I was asked to get you out of the country, and that's what I'm trying to do. But if you make it hard for me I'm ready to leave you behind. Is that clear?'

Nizari stared at Makana with a look that could only have been described as disgust. Makana was beyond caring about hurting his feelings.

'You asked for me, and here I am, but don't push me.'

'I need a cigarette,' said Nizari.

Makana produced his packet of Samsun, which Ayman turned up his nose at. 'I can't smoke those things, can't you get some Marlboros?'

Makana wasn't inclined to run errands, but he had noticed a place across the street that sold telephone cards and cigarettes. It would give him a chance to take a look around without dragging the other man with him.

'Stay here,' he said. 'And I mean it, don't move from this table.'

He walked a block either way and decided there was nothing unusual or threatening, no familiar faces and nobody paying too much attention to him. At the shop he bought a packet of Marlboros and another international telephone card.

When he came back into the café he noticed a table of men by the door looking him over. Nodding a greeting, he returned to the table, where the tea had arrived. Nizari seized the cigarettes and tore off the cellophane wrapping. Makana took out the mobile phone Nadir Sulayman had given him and texted Boris asking him to call and giving him the number of the telephone in the café.

'I need you to sit here while I make a phone call.'

'Where?'

Makana nodded in the direction of the telephone on the wall. 'I'll be right here. Just smoke your cigarette and try to relax. Order something to eat.'

'I just want to go home.'

Wherever home was. Makana had the sense that Nizari was unravelling. If he didn't get him out soon, there was a chance there wouldn't be much to salvage. And when he got through to him, Marcus Winslow was of the same opinion.

'You'll have to sit tight,' the Englishman said. 'Things are proving a little more complicated than I had anticipated.'

'So what do you want me to do?'

'Improvise. Find a place that's safe and stay there until I can organise something. This thing with Marty Shaw has kicked up a lot of dust. People are asking questions.'

'Is there a problem?'

'Nothing you need to worry about,' said Winslow curtly.

Somehow, this came as no surprise. Makana had been wondering what kind of an excuse Winslow would come up with. Right now, he was playing for time. He needed to keep the Englishman preoccupied. He surveyed the room, the doorway, people coming and going. 'There's another problem.' Makana told him about Kara Deniz.

'You think our friends from Tel Aviv killed her?'

'I'm pretty sure of it.'

'Tell me again who she was.'

'She was a journalist.' The image of Kara's lifeless body resurfaced in his mind. Everything had gone so quickly, there had hardly been time to process what had happened. It made him angry that someone, somewhere, had decided she was a liability that needed to be removed. 'She had a history of political activism. She didn't deserve to die.' As a eulogy, it didn't amount to much. 'She was a loose end.'

'What does that mean?' Winslow sounded exasperated.

'It means that I think she's the reason Nadir Sulayman was killed. She was an informant for the Israelis.'

'You think that's why they killed her?'

'She investigated the ambulance crash and then buried the story. I think she's been helping to cover up any sign of their operation. They may be more closely involved than we thought.' Makana's gaze was drawn to the table by the door. The group of young men there appeared to be dominated by an older man with a clipped pencil moustache and a receding hairline. 'Unfortunately, they're not the only ones.'

'What does that mean?'

'I met an old friend, someone I really didn't expect to run into. Mek Nimr.'

'I was afraid of that.'

'He tells me you are working together.'

Winslow gave a tut of impatience. 'He means in broad terms. The British government. They are useful allies. You know all this. The war on terror makes for strange bedfellows.'

'Why is he here, Winslow? Just tell me that. What is Mek Nimr doing here?'

'I wish I knew.' Winslow was silent for a moment. 'Look, this doesn't change anything. I'll make some calls. Can you ring me back?'

'Things are a little chaotic right now. I'm not sure I can promise that.'

'Did you get our man?'

Across the room Makana could see Nizari smoking one cigarette after the next.

'I'm working on it.'

'You're working on it?' Winslow echoed in disbelief. 'We're out of time and you've outstayed your welcome in Istanbul.'

'Believe me, I'm more than ready to leave,' said Makana.

'Just find Nizari and I'll get you out of there.'

'I need to know,' Makana said. 'If we lose contact and I somehow make it to Sofia, will you be there for me?'

'Listen to me, Makana. Don't try anything by yourself. Do as I tell you. Find somewhere safe and wait for me to get you out. Look' – Winslow sounded like a man struggling to keep his head above water – 'I'm sorry things have turned out this way. It happens. The main thing is to keep your objective in sight.'

Talking to Winslow was like trying to read smoke signals. Makana still had no idea how far he could trust him. His instincts told him the only person he could rely on right now was himself. He rang off and made another call to Cairo, this time to Munir Abaza. The lawyer was surprised to hear from him. Even more so when he explained where he was calling from.

'I may be in a bit of trouble.'

'What kind of trouble?'

'The kind that requires a lawyer with a lot of influence.'

'How serious is it?'

'Two murder charges, possibly three.'

'You don't need a lawyer,' laughed Abaza. 'You need a genie in a bottle.'

'How hard would it be to get me extradited?'

'To begin with, you're not an Egyptian citizen. I suppose you qualify as a permanent resident, and of course a brother from our closest neighbour. I take it you're not in custody yet?'

'Not yet, but I have a feeling it's just a matter of time.'

'I must say, when you ask for the return of a favour you don't hold back.'

'I'm not there yet, this is just a precaution.'

'I'm not making any promises, but I can make some calls.'

'I suppose I can't ask for more than that.'

'No,' said Munir Abaza, 'I suppose you can't.'

Makana watched as one of the men from the table by the door went over to ask Nizari for a light. It wasn't a good sign. Someone was taking an interest in them. They might have to start moving sooner than planned. He hung up and was halfway across the room when the phone behind him rang. He turned in time to see the waiter make to pick it up. Makana intercepted him and smiled as he took the receiver from him.

'Who is this?' Boris snapped. There was music in the background. Not music exactly, more like some kind of underwater whale sounds. 'Why are you contacting me like this?'

'Our plans have changed,' explained Makana. 'We need to move quickly.'

'How quickly?'

'Tonight.'

'That's impossible.'

'They got to Kara.'

'Got to her how?'

'She's dead.'

'Okay,' said Boris. There was a long silence. 'We can do this, but I need a few hours to set it up.' Makana heard Boris speaking

231

to someone in the room behind him. The whale sounds cut out. 'I don't like the way this is going. Who would kill Kara?'

'I have an idea,' said Makana. 'But if I'm right, these are not people you want to mess with.'

'That's for me to decide,' said Boris. 'She was a friend. I'm losing a lot of friends these days.'

'These are professionals, Boris.'

'And what do you think I am, a fucking amateur?' Boris fell silent for a moment. 'The car will be at the place we agreed. No names. Midnight.'

Makana ended the call and rejoined Nizari, who jumped as he sat down.

'What's happening? You can't just leave me alone like that!'

Makana held up a hand to silence him. 'It's being arranged for tonight.' Reaching for the cigarettes and lighter on the table, he lit one for himself. He was reminded of the fact that there were a lot of unanswered questions he would have liked to have put to Nizari. For now they would have to wait, but he realised that he didn't trust the other man, not for a second. He nodded across the room:

'Who's your friend?'

'He just wanted a light.' Nizari was dismissive. His hands shook as he tried to light a cigarette for himself.

'Maybe you should eat something,' said Makana. 'We might not get another chance.'

Nizari took quick puffs, the way a man underwater might suck air from a straw.

'What about my money? Why do I get the feeling you're not telling me everything?'

'I might ask the same thing,' replied Makana. He looked up as a figure stepped up to their table. It was the man with the receding hairline and the thin moustache pencilled in over his upper lip. He pulled up a chair without asking. He wore a tweed jacket with worn cuffs and a polo-neck sweater covered in what appeared to be cat's hairs. Over his shoulder Makana could see the other men around the table by the door. Every set of eyes was on them, as were most others in the place. Their visitor seemed to command a lot of attention. He began in Turkish, but since he must have heard the two of them talking Makana assumed this was for show. He was getting the feeling they had stepped onto somebody's home turf. This was their place of business, their office.

'Tourists?' asked the man, switching into English.

'Not exactly,' said Makana. 'Just passing through.'

'Ah … where from?'

'Egypt …'

The man nodded. He spoke English well. 'I find it shameful that we cannot speak the language of the prophet together.'

The choice of words surprised Makana. He wouldn't have taken the newcomer for a religious man, but you could never tell.

'It's a shame I speak no Turkish.'

'Atatürk, father of our republic, took our language from us.' The man was smiling in an odd way, like a used-car salesman trying to prove he has a conscience. 'We face to the west now and not to the east.'

'You should see what they did to my country,' Nizari chipped in. 'We were one of the most advanced countries in the Middle East, now we are back in the Stone Age.'

Makana gave him a hard glare, hoping it would stop him talking so much. If the reference to Iraq confused the newcomer, he did not show it.

'You have my sympathy.' The man gave a slight bow. 'My name is Batuman. Everybody here knows me. I am at your service. What brings you to our great city?'

Makana glanced at Nizari, who looked as though he was about to say something and then thought better of it.

'There seems to be some misunderstanding,' Makana began. 'We only came in here to rest for a moment. We will soon be on our way.'

'Oh, please, do not take offence. I have not explained myself. I am a man of business. I pride myself on being able to spot an opportunity.'

'Opportunity?' Makana frowned.

The man lifted a hand. A man in a tracksuit and jeans who was standing nearby stepped up and handed him a newspaper. Batuman unfolded it and laid it on the table. Makana studied the photograph. It wasn't a particularly good likeness of him, taken, he assumed, from a security camera in the Pera Palas lobby. Still, it wasn't hard to see who it was.

'Opportunity,' said Batuman with a flourish.

'You want to take me to the police?'

'You misunderstand.' A bemused frown creased his face. 'We do not cooperate with the police. They sometimes cooperate with us, but not the other way around.'

'I'm not clear what you have in mind.'

'You are in need of friends.' The man beamed, like a true entrepreneur. 'We all need friends.'

Chapter Thirty-one

M akana was fifty metres away from the Sultana Harem Hotel when he spotted them. Approaching from the narrow alleyway opposite the entrance – one of the reasons he had chosen the hotel as his alternative accommodation – he was almost at the end of it when he spotted a familiar bulky figure. There were two men, both silhouetted by the green haze of a neon sign. He recognised the unmistakable shape of Sergeant Berat. The big man was trying to keep the contents of his döner kebab from escaping the paper in which it was wrapped. He licked his fingers while he talked to a man in a fake leather jacket. Makana recognised him too. He had been seated at a table outside the Iskander Grillroom a couple of days ago. He was eating roasted melon seeds and spitting the husks on the pavement.

His new companions signalled and led him away to the right. They turned again and again until they came to another spot where they had an unobstructed view of the hotel entrance. Makana handed over his key and explained that the money was taped underneath the dresser. One of them went ahead and the other stayed with him. Neither of them was out of his early twenties. The one who stayed had a missing front tooth and a bent ear. He lit a cigarette and leaned his back against the wall.

The second one, the one whose head was shaved at the sides, was in and out in ten minutes. He walked straight past the policemen and straight out again, turning left off the main street. Missing Tooth nodded and they all moved off. They met the boy with the shaved head by a stall selling tea and simit rings. The envelope was folded into a newspaper and Makana opened it to check the money was all there. His two minders rolled their eyes, as if they would stoop to such a thing. As they turned to go a shadow detached itself from the wall.

'You must really love this city,' smiled Inspector Serkan. 'I get the feeling you might never leave.'

'This is a surprise, Inspector.' Makana signalled to his two minders to stay back.

'And not a good one by the look of it.' Serkan ran his eye over Makana's companions.

'Well, there have been a few setbacks.'

'A somewhat optimistic way of looking at things.' The inspector stepped forward into the light. 'Considering the fact you are a wanted man.'

'Sergeant Berat?' Makana looked over his shoulder.

'Sergeant Berat has his own methods,' Serkan shrugged. 'I try to allow him to develop in his own style.'

'Are you here to arrest me?'

'Unfortunately, the case is being taken out of our hands. The death of a British Consulate official has resulted in the case being declared a matter of national security. The MIT has stepped in.'

'Turkish intelligence services?'

Serkan nodded. 'Mr Shaw turns out to be an intriguing character, one about whom almost no information is available. The Consulate have requested that we hand all our information to a team of British investigators who are on their way to Istanbul as we speak. They have closed all the doors and we have nothing. He remains a blank. So, I ask myself, what is such a man doing dead in the hotel room of Mr Amin Bey?'

'I'm not what you think I am,' said Makana.

Inspector Serkan arched his eyebrows. 'And what is it that I think you are exactly?'

'Some kind of intelligence operative. I didn't kill either of those men and I'm not here to do any harm.'

'But you're not going to tell me what you are doing in Istanbul ... apart from this agricultural machinery nonsense.'

'If you're off the case, why are you here?'

'I am of the old school. I don't like it when MIT are involved because it messes up everything. Then it is no longer about bringing the facts to light but, on the contrary, to conceal as much as possible.' The inspector gave a heavy sigh. 'I'm here to give you a chance to tell me what you know.'

Makana took another look up and down the street. No sign of any other policemen, but he doubted Serkan would be on his own.

'You're suggesting we could help each other.'

'Nobody likes murder, Amin Bey. As I said, it's bad for business. I have to give you credit. A second hotel room. We checked everywhere. You made a good choice. The Sultana Harem is run by what you might call a dysfunctional family. They never talk to one another and they leave things in the hands of their newly arrived relatives who are more used to tending goats than running hotels.'

'But still, you managed to find it. I'm impressed.'

The inspector gave a small bow. 'We searched the room, and found the money. So we knew you would have to return.' Serkan offered his cigarettes and lit one for each of them. 'I had a disagreement with Sergeant Berat. I told him that it was a mistake to put guards outside the front door. Amin Bey was too smart to walk straight into a hotel with police officers outside.' He gave a philosophical wave. 'Anyone with two brain cells to rub together would have spotted Sergeant Berat and his goons. I asked myself, if I wanted to retrieve something valuable from the room, how would I do it?' Serkan looked past Makana. 'Where did you find your companions, by the way?'

'Our paths crossed at a useful moment.'

Serkan made a clucking sound like an impatient hen. 'You know, right now you don't have too many people on your side. I'm offering you a chance to come clean. I can help you. I can get you out of the country.'

'Don't you think MIT might object?'

'We're on the same side. That doesn't mean we have to agree on everything.'

Makana was reminded of the conflict he had had with Mek Nimr. It was so long ago it felt like another lifetime.

'How do I know I can trust you?'

'What I'm trying to tell you is that you have no choice.' Serkan smiled as though it was obvious. 'If they get hold of you, you could disappear from the face of the earth. They can do that. They don't respect laws. And I don't need to remind you that there are others interested in you.' The inspector tilted his head to one side. 'We need one another.'

'I wish I could help you,' said Makana. 'There's nothing more I'd like to do than to get this over with, and to leave.'

'What's stopping you?'

'I don't know,' said Makana. 'Maybe, like you, I'm old-fashioned. Once I start something I believe in seeing it through to the finish.'

'The last time we talked, I asked you about Kara Deniz. Now she is dead. Do you know anything about that?'

'I know that you would be better off leaving that to your friends in MIT.'

'Okay,' nodded Serkan. 'That's something.'

'I can't say any more.'

'You understand that just by standing here talking to you I am incriminating myself? Associating with a suspected felon.'

'I appreciate that. Kara Deniz was mixed up in something much bigger than she realised.' Makana recognised the inadequacy of his words. Kara's death seemed pointless. Someone was tidying up loose ends. He suspected that she had betrayed Nadir Sulayman, and in that sense she had caused his death. He would have confided in her, as an old friend, perhaps one-time lover, what he was doing for Winslow, and she had passed on the information to her contacts in the Mossad. The bout of heavy drinking was brought on by the fact that she knew she had caused her old friend's death. The Israelis wouldn't have told her what they were going to do. She might have calculated that they would talk to him, put a tail on him, but nothing more than that. In the end it didn't matter which side you were on. They were all as bad as one another. All that mattered was protecting those you cared about.

'I've been in this business a long time,' began Serkan. 'But you know the truth? It's often my instinct that guides me, so in that sense I am no better than a superstitious grandmother reading people's fates in the bottom of their coffee cups.' The inspector gave one of his characteristic shrugs. 'Istanbul, as you know, lies on the faultline between East and West. We are accessible to both and so we find ourselves at times the victim of our own greatness. I don't know if I express myself. You know, my English …' Serkan tailed off into a moment's silence. 'There are forces working in this city which are beyond my humble capacities.'

'Marty Shaw was working for British intelligence.'

'Ah, and you, with your British passport, are you working for them also?'

'Right now I'm not sure who I'm working for,' said Makana. He was concerned that Batuman would be growing impatient and about what Nizari might be thinking. Everything had taken longer than planned, and even before this he had been as jumpy as a cat. Still, he had no choice.

'I pride myself on being a modern man, a man of science and logic. Observation, analysis, deduction. These are the tools of detection. But there are times when that is not enough and I am outvoted by those brute forces. I can't protect you for long.'

'I appreciate that.'

'Then take my offer, tell me what you know. If not, who knows, the next murder I am called to might be yours.'

'That's a consideration.'

'More than a consideration.' Serkan moved closer. 'Here we are talking like colleagues, but we are on opposite sides of the law. Make no mistake, Amin Bey. I cannot protect you without your cooperation. If our paths meet again, I will not hesitate to arrest you.' He handed Makana a card. 'Call if you change your mind, but don't wait too long, for your own sake.'

Inspector Serkan started to walk away. Makana watched him turn the corner, half expecting a horde of policemen to come chasing towards him, but there was nothing. He waited for a time and then turned towards the two young men, who were standing close to the wall, as silent and still as stone.

Together they walked quickly in the direction of the taxi rank in Cihangir and the first available vehicle. It was as the two others were climbing in that Makana glanced over the top of the car and saw something that made his heart stop in mid-beat.

She stood like a frozen frame in the middle of a moving picture. Around her people walked, yet his eyes saw only her. Suddenly everything was clear. All his doubts were gone. He knew also that he had to follow her.

'I'll catch up with you,' he said to the others, closing the door on their protests. He didn't wait to see the look of surprise on their faces; he was already crossing the street. The wisdom of this, of walking openly through the streets when his face was plastered across the newspapers, echoed dimly in the back of his mind, but he dismissed it. Right now, nothing else mattered so much.

With every step he grew more convinced that his instinct was right. It was her. He kept his distance as she moved along the avenue at a steady pace. Not fast, not slow. Confident.

Out of her line of sight, he had a chance to study her more carefully. She was, without doubt, the same woman in the scarf at the Blue Mosque, the same he had seen in the bazaar, and later in the Sunken Palace. She was not a ghost, not Muna, but the one person he had never dared to imagine he would meet. For almost fifteen years he had believed her dead. Yet here she was. Now he could see the resemblance to Muna, but also the distinctions. Her walk was different. She was a little taller, and he sensed, stronger. Dressed in black trousers and a three-quarter-length coat, her hair was loosely covered by a scarf. She seemed to move through the world less as a person than as a shadow.

The afternoon was fading as evening fell over the city. The sky was a deep indigo streaked with crimson banners. Sparks flew overhead as a red tram rumbled by and neon signs flickered like signals from distant corners of the universe. In greens and blues the names of dead emperors and caliphs brought the street to light in a ghostly electric echo of former glory.

The question ran through his head now over and over like the beat of a refrain, like the chant of a sufi seeking transcendence. Who was she? Could she really be his daughter, or was she Mek Nimr's agent? He wasn't sure he wanted an answer. In a way it better like this, not really knowing, but still believing in the existence of possibility. That his daughter could be alive somewhere still held out hope. Now, following this woman, he felt as though perhaps, in some entirely irrational way, she were the real reason he had come to this city.

Now that she was so close, he feared that one false move would scare her away. Instead, he moved with her, binding his cadence to hers, slowing when she slowed, speeding up when she did. At times she seemed to have a purpose, a destination, an appointment. At others she appeared to be in no particular hurry, almost as if she were killing time, allowing him to see her.

At the back of his mind was the possibility that this was too easy, that he might be walking into a trap. Still, even if he had known with certainty that this was the case, he doubted he could have stopped himself. She stopped to study a window display and he turned to look the other way. When he turned back she had disappeared. Hurrying forward, he guessed she had branched off onto a sidestreet. At the corner he caught a glimpse of her disappearing across a lighted square filled with market stalls. By the time he'd reached the other side she was already moving down a steep winding street lined with high buildings.

The noise of the main road, the vendors announcing their wares, the hubbub of tourists, all soon fell away behind them. The street was so narrow that little light entered, the high walls forming a dark gully through which she walked, trailing him behind her. In the fading light Makana could just about make out her silhouette. Keeping close to the wall, he walked as quietly as he could, careful to keep his distance. He wondered where she was going. The street angled downwards and to the right. A group of Spanish tourists, clearly lost, stood on a corner loudly consulting a map. He slowed, allowing her to gain some ground, afraid the tourists would cause her to look over her shoulder.

At the next corner he thought he had lost her again. He moved up and down, left and right, convinced she must have spotted him or heard his footsteps behind her. Cats huddled in doorways, lifting their heads to watch him go by. Out of the corner of his eye a slight hint of movement spun him round in time to spot a shadow flitting through an archway to his right.

He counted five uneven steps that brought him into an enclosed yard. Grass poked through uneven flagstones. A row of broken windows glinted in the moonlight. The enclosed space was eerily silent. He waited until he could make out the sound of footsteps on stone somewhere to his left.

An open doorway brought him to a staircase that threaded its way upwards, losing itself in darkness. It felt exposed, as if the staircase was open to the sky. He could make out shapes moving through the air above, pigeons flapping lazily. Feathers and gritty droppings scraped under his shoes. There were no sounds or signs to indicate that anyone was living in the building. His hand touched railings coated with a thick layer of bird excrement. The air was heavy with an acid ammonia stench. Makana climbed slowly, cautiously, in the dark.

When he reached the first floor he stopped. There was water dripping somewhere and the sound of movement drew him through a wide doorway into a hall lined with cracked windows and missing panes. An old factory, he concluded, the air still heavy with the smell of machine oil. Pigeons fluttered between the rafters high above. Along one side a row of textile looms stood idle like a giant set of mechanical teeth. His eyes began to adjust. Light entered the room through broken skylights in the roof. The floor was damp from the rain. He could make out a scuffling sound from somewhere off to his right, quite distinct from the footsteps he'd been following.

He moved deeper into the gloom. There was somebody there. He could feel it. Moving over, past the first row of looms he stopped. In the poor light he sensed rather than actually saw the figure. It was standing between the machines and the wall. Not quite still, but shuffling on the spot, as if preparing to make a run for it. Something felt wrong. Makana edged forward, taking careful steps as if creeping up on an animal that might dart away at any moment. A part of him wanted to believe the impossible, that it was her.

'Nasra?'

Just speaking her name aloud added an air of the surreal to the situation. As soon as he spoke he knew it wasn't her. It was impossible. This was someone else.

The figure stood with its back to him. He took another step forward. They were standing deep in shadow, facing the wall. He reached out a hand. The warning signal came too late, too slowly. A lazy, hazy semaphore from the other side of his brain, clicking away

242

in his head. The shape of her was wrong. The height was different from the woman he had been following. Even as he started to withdraw his hand she spun round and his confusion was complete. Not Nasra. Not his daughter, but a face disfigured by acid. A face he had seen before.

She gave a slight cackle as she threw herself forward, spinning past him. She was strong and fast, or else he was simply too slow, his mind confused. A burning sensation on his thigh told him he'd been slashed by something sharp. A distraction. Before he realised what was happening the noose was over his neck and pulled tight. His mind flashed to the plastic tie he had glimpsed on the rabbit sticking out from one of her plastic bags even as the sharp edge cut into his windpipe. He was jerked backwards. Caught off balance, he threw out a hand and managed to connect with the wall. The thin band dug in harder, cutting off his breath and the supply of blood to his brain. He knew that he would pass out in a matter of seconds. He thrashed about desperately, but she was on his back, all her weight pulling down on the nylon band, drawing it tighter. He felt his face and neck bulging. Her legs were wrapped tightly around his waist. She seemed barely human, rather a mad, sinewy creature whose strength came from some inner fury.

Makana threw himself backward and was rewarded with a cry of pain as she crashed into the corner of a machine. Her legs weakened their grip slightly. The zip tie was still locked in place. He saw spots before his eyes as he dropped to one knee and twisted forward. The weight lifted from his back as she slid over his shoulder, crashing to the floor in front of him and sliding away. Makana staggered backwards, wrenching at the plastic strip locked around his neck. The narrow band had dug itself into the flesh so tightly and deeply that he couldn't get a purchase on it.

He saw her pick herself up, jabbering to herself. It was too late. He was choking, the fight draining from him as he sank down on both knees and started to lose consciousness. Somewhere far off he heard the cackling receding, footsteps padding away as the woman skittered off, laughing or weeping to herself. He clawed frantically at the band dug into his neck but was still unable to get a purchase.

He felt his strength ebbing. If he passed out he knew he would be dead. He collapsed onto his back in a pool of dirty water that stank of old oil and rust.

He felt himself slipping into a dreamlike state. Perhaps devoting his life to another profession might have been a better way of spending his time on this earth. A less complicated life. Something connected to the earth, to nature. Farming, or herding animals perhaps. The lack of oxygen was taking his mind down a long, meandering path back to his childhood and the day his father had taken him to the river to teach him to swim. Trust yourself to overcome your fear.

It felt as though he had spent his life trying to prove himself. Maybe it was time to admit defeat. Things had a habit of always becoming more complicated. The darkness before him was expanding, drawing him softly in, forcing everything else outwards until there was only one receding spot of light before him. He tried to focus on this, knowing that when he could no longer do so, he would be dead.

Somewhere far off on the periphery of his vision he heard a metallic snick. A shadow bent over him. He was too weak to struggle any longer. Light gleamed on the blade as it drew near. He braced himself, sensing that it would be over quickly, feeling the steel sharp against his skin, the prick of the cut, and then miraculously the pressure was released and his lungs were filling with air. He rolled over and lay there, coughing and gasping. Eventually, he managed to lever himself up onto one elbow. His clothes were damp and the smell of oil was making him feel sick. The crazy woman's rancid smell was all over him. He felt like vomiting, but at least he could breathe. When he looked up he realised she was standing over him.

'How … ?' he rasped.

'You know who I am?' She stepped back and waited a moment.

Makana struggled to sit up. He rested his back against the machine and rubbed his neck. A wet trickle ran down his collar. He put his hand to it and saw blood. He watched her wiping the blade clean, tucking it somewhere inside her coat with a neat, practised movement. In the dim light he could barely make out her features.

'You saved my life.' His voice was a hoarse croak.

She didn't reply. Her eyes were in shadow, but he could feel her watching him.

'This is strange,' he said.

He watched as she moved back towards the window, pacing slowly, moving in and out of shadow. Behind her shards of splintered glass glinted in the moonlight.

'I can't tell you how many times I imagined this moment,' he said. 'But I never pictured it like this.'

'Neither did I,' she said. Her voice was cold but he no longer had any doubts. It couldn't be anyone else.

'What did Mek Nimr tell you about me?'

She stopped pacing.

'He told me you were a traitor and a mercenary who sold his services to the highest bidder.'

'And you believed him?'

'What was I supposed to believe?'

'I never stopped looking for you.' The words sounded wrong, insufficient. There was a long silence. 'For years I thought you had died along with your mother—' Makana broke off, a part of him still unable to believe they were having this conversation.

'Why are you telling me this?'

'Because it's important,' he began. 'It's important to me.' None of his words seemed right. 'I think you should know.'

'I know all I need to know,' she said.

'You saved my life,' he said. 'You didn't have to do that.'

'What was I supposed to do?' Nasra gave a shrug. It was a gesture that made her look unsure of herself, and young. 'Between you and her, you've managed to double the police presence in the city in a matter of days.'

'You knew she was here,' Makana said, feeling his head begin to clear. 'You led me to her.'

There was silence from the shadow that was Nasra.

'You thought she would get rid of me.' Makana's throat hurt so badly he had to stop talking for a moment. The figure by the window stood motionless. 'Why did you change your mind?'

'Does it matter?'

'It matters to me.'

She remained where she was, one eye on the yard and the other on him.

A part of him didn't want to speak, wanted to hold back the thousand and one questions that had been amassing in his mind for over a decade. A part of him wanted to just sit here and let her presence sink in. He leaned his head back against the metal behind him and closed his eyes.

'Mek Nimr must have great confidence to bring you along on a mission like this,' he said finally.

She came towards him then, moving with the slow, well balanced strides of a gymnast, and squatted down in front of him. He had to admire her control of the situation. She had been well trained.

'I'm not interested in you,' she said. 'So let's be clear about that. I'm here to do a job, that's all. It has nothing to do with you personally.' The look of pity in her eyes hurt him more than he thought it would. He longed for a cigarette, but wondered if his throat could take it, or his heart. Which was the more vulnerable at this time?

'To take a single life without justification is to kill all humanity,' he said.

She gave a short laugh. 'You think you have the right to quote the Quran to me?'

Makana felt as though he was feeling his way in the dark, speaking his thoughts aloud as he worked things out.

'We should talk.'

'There's nothing to talk about.' She turned to the window for a second, then swung back and pointed a finger at him. 'You stay here. Wait five minutes before you leave.'

'Wait,' he said.

'What for?' She paused to look at him.

'There must be things you want to know?'

In the poor light he could not make out her eyes, just the shadows that seemed to dissolve her. She looked so familiar and yet he felt he knew nothing about her.

'You turned your back on us, on everything, your faith, culture, country.' She gave a hollow rattle of a laugh. 'After that, leaving behind your wife and child must have been easy.'

246

'It's never easy,' he said. His questions suddenly seemed irrelevant. It all felt unreal, just trying to take in the fact that she was his daughter. Not dead, at all, but standing there right in front of him. That she clearly hated him made it all the more absurd.

'There isn't a day when I don't wish I had jumped after you,' he said. 'If I could, I would have tried to save you both.'

'But you didn't, did you?' she said. She stared at him. 'Five minutes. Don't try to follow me.'

Makana sat on the floor rubbing his neck as the sound of her footsteps sank into the fabric of silence. After a time he decided he deserved a cigarette. He sat on the floor for a long time, easing the acrid smoke down his throat.

Chapter Thirty-two

C oming out of the building, Makana looked at his watch. He needed to get back to Nizari, but before he could do that he needed to be sure that he wasn't being followed. He walked one way and then doubled back the way he'd come. The air was cold and damp as he moved through the evening crowds on Istiklal. He tried to focus on losing a possible tail, but his thoughts kept straying to Nasra. Somewhere in the back of his mind there was a possibility that he could not completely dismiss: that all of this could be part of an elaborate charade constructed by Mek Nimr.

Was that possible? He had trouble believing that even Mek Nimr could be devious enough to find someone to pretend to be Nasra, just to inflict more pain on him. Makana had been convinced that it was really her. Now he felt his doubts returning. He would put nothing beyond Mek Nimr's twisted mind. If he left this city without finding the answer to that question, he knew he would spend the rest of his life wondering. But if he didn't get out of this town quickly, and take Ayman Nizari with him, then he might not have that much longer to reflect on anything.

Mek Nimr's religious faith was no more than a channel for the dark forces within him. Makana knew that he would never be able to stop blaming Mek Nimr for the death of his wife and daughter. He had no evidence that anyone had tampered with the steering on his car. He would never be able to prove it, but he knew. He knew.

Back then Mek Nimr had been a rising star in the People's Defence Forces. His head dizzy with power, he had found his own personal reasons to settle on Makana as an adversary. He had resented working under Makana's command. The resentment, as

Makana now knew, went deep. He envied the fact that Makana was a leading light in the Criminal Investigations Department, praised by the department head, Chief Haroun, and clearly destined for great things. It wasn't just professional rivalry: Mek Nimr found fault with Makana's entire moral outlook.

More important, he was part of the old guard. Makana was associated with the intelligentsia that had ruled the country since independence, thanks to his father. A schoolteacher and respected poet, Makana's father had been a focal point in the national imagination. In the popular uprising of October 1964, it was his father's words that had been on the lips of the students and protesters who took to the streets demanding change. Even in retirement he had been wheeled out time and time again as a figurehead, the old boy enjoying every moment of attention. Makana had had his own issues with his father, who thought Makana was squandering his talents chasing petty criminals rather than building up the nation. Such distinctions were irrelevant to Mek Nimr. Makana was a worthy trophy, a head to mount on his wall, and a useful tool, a stepping stone in his own rise to power.

In a strange kind of way, Makana understood his former adjutant. Even now, after all that Mek Nimr had achieved, rising through the ranks to become head of the Directorate for Insurgency and Counterterrorism, Makana remained the one person in the world from whom he seemed to need recognition. Was that why he had been brought all this way here? So that Mek Nimr had a witness to his hour of triumph, in the moment of Makana's own downfall?

When Makana had first begun to hear the rumours that Nasra might have survived the fall into the river, he had come across a strange variation in the telling. It was too dangerous for him to return home, and his inquiries had been frustrated by logistics and the matter of who he could trust. But of all the stories that had come his way, the most twisted of all was the curious tale that she had not only survived the crash but had been taken by a high-ranking official into his own household. This version held that Nasra had been kept for years as a domestic servant, working in the kitchen, cleaning and waiting on the master and his family. Despite all his efforts, Makana had never been able to confirm it, but the story had pervaded his imagination, as if the seed, once planted, was nurtured by his frustration and anger. If that story had any substance to it, then that high-ranking official was none other than Mek Nimr himself.

The thought burned deep into Makana's mind. As a form of revenge it could hardly be bettered. It was perfect. To have the daughter of your sworn enemy waiting on you hand and foot. Every time he saw her hard at work, scrubbing floors, hanging out washing, bearing a serving tray, Mek Nimr would have been reminded of his triumph. And now he had turned her into his own agent, a trained jihadi officer, loyal to him and him alone. Having witnessed her contempt for him first hand, it seemed to Makana that Mek Nimr had finally won.

Nizari was slumped over the table, but at least he was still there. He leapt up as Makana sat down.

'Where have you been?' he whined. His eyes had the haunted look of a dog that expects a beating. He was ready to make for the door, but sank down with a sigh of despair. Batuman himself was beaming like a showman, arms thrown wide. He had freshened up, shaved, changed into a silk shirt. Now he snapped his fingers and one of his boys rushed off to fetch tea for them all.

'I can't drink any more tea,' Nizari groaned. 'I'm tired. I just want to sleep.'

'You can sleep later,' said Makana.

The tea arrived along with a plate of baklava. Makana realised he was hungry. He drank thirstily and chewed one of the sticky pastries. As he did so he became aware that Batuman was watching him closely.

'Two of my men will go with you tonight.' He waited for Makana's nod before continuing. 'That way, if there is any trouble they will bring you safely back here.'

'I hope that won't be necessary.' Makana slid the folded newspaper across the table. Batuman lifted it cautiously and saw the two thousand dollars Makana had placed there. He nodded approvingly.

'That is generous of you.'

'You have been kind with your hospitality,' said Makana courteously. His phone beeped to notify a message. He fished it out of his jacket and clicked through to see the words: Midnight. Beşiktaş Vapur Ferry. The caller identity was hidden. He knew who it was from, but he wondered why Boris was telling him something he already knew. He deleted the message and then switched off the telephone and removed the battery.

'I am curious,' Batuman said. 'Did you really kill all those people, like it said in the paper?'

'You're interested in a reward on our heads perhaps?'

'You misunderstand.' Batuman laughed off the suggestion. 'You have nothing to fear. Here you are among friends.'

'It's nothing personal,' said Makana, reaching for his cigarettes.

'It is a matter of professional curiosity, nothing more.' Batuman leaned forward to light Makana's cigarette, his eyes glinting in the flame. 'One becomes accustomed to sizing up a man, judging his strengths, what threat he might present. You understand?'

'I think so,' said Makana.

'Maybe we should go,' said Nizari, the flutter in his voice giving him away.

'You will be going, very soon,' Batuman said, without taking his eyes off Makana. 'I pride myself on being able to judge a man, but I look at you and I don't know what I see.'

'What do you need to know?'

Makana wondered if he was making a mistake. Right now he didn't have many people on his side. He didn't need to make an enemy of Batuman. Over his shoulder he saw the two young men leaning on a table, cracking their knuckles. The choice of the table by the door now made perfect sense. They controlled who came in, and who was allowed to leave.

'You mistrust me,' said Batuman.

'I'm not sure what it is you expect from me,' said Makana.

Batuman held up his hands in a gesture of peace. 'We are humble people, just doing our best to make a living; we try to help our local community, to provide the protection they need. Perhaps you'd like to make a contribution.'

'I thought I just did.'

'Yes, and very generous it was too.' Batuman smiled. 'But these are difficult times and, frankly, helping a man wanted for murder

251

can bring a lot of trouble down upon us.' He had the smooth delivery of a showman who had honed his performance over the years.

Makana had expected something of the sort. He produced a second envelope which contained less money than the first. Batuman's face broke into a broad smile. To him it must have seemed as easy as taking baklava from a baby.

Makana held onto the envelope for a moment longer. 'There is something I want in return.'

'Anything.' Batuman grinned. It felt like paying the wolf to guard the sheep, but at this point Makana didn't see that he had much choice.

Midnight found Nizari and Makana sitting in the back seat of a battered Renault that squeaked every time either of them shifted his weight. In the front seat sat the two young thugs from the café. Batuman had sent them along for insurance. The rain was coming down thick and hard now, hammering at the sea like a thousand demons trying to get into a locked room. Through the windscreen the lights of the Beşiktaş terminal were barely visible. A ferry was toiling on the rough water, trying to dock. There were a surprising number of people around, considering the weather and the late hour.

'We'd better get out,' said Makana.

'In this weather?' Nizari seemed to be under the impression that he had a choice. Makana was going to be glad to see the back of the man. There was something about him that left a bad taste. Underneath all that whining and fussing was a cold self-seeker prepared to concoct the chemicals that would cause their victims painful convulsions while they died. It took a certain kind of person to do something like that.

'They're not going to show themselves until we do.' Makana checked his watch and cracked open the door. 'Let's go.'

Once you were out in it the rain wasn't that bad. Makana turned up the collar of his jacket and led the way towards the ferry terminal. They were halfway there when a set of headlights flashed to their right. The car Boris had sent was a yellow taxi. It was in slightly better condition than Koçak's, though not much.

'We're not going all the way in this, are we?' Nizari asked as soon as they were inside. The two men in the front seat were older, heavier versions of the two they had just left in Batuman's car. Neither one gave any indication that he understood the question.

They moved off. The car rolled through the slick streets, along the coast road, travelling north, out of town. Makana glanced back but saw nothing but the blur of lights on wet glass. If anyone was following them it would be almost impossible to tell in this weather. They drove slowly. The two men in front occasionally spoke to one another in low tones. Nizari stared out of the window in silence. Makana wondered what they would find when they got to Sofia. A part of him still hoped that Winslow would keep his end of the bargain and arrange transport. His more cautious side told him he could expect nothing from the Englishman. But with the money he had left he could buy a ticket to Cairo, and as for Nizari, well, he would deliver him to the British Embassy and let them sort out the mess.

As an afterthought he reached for his mobile phone and called Inspector Serkan. This was probably the last chance he would have.

'Where are you?'

'I'm afraid I can't tell you that,' said Makana.

'I could trace the call.'

'There won't be time for that. I called to give you some help.'

'I'm listening.'

'The killer you are looking for, the one they are calling the *karakoncolos*?'

'What about him?'

Makana rubbed the side of his neck. It had taken him a moment to place her, and even then he couldn't quite believe that his attacker was the same deranged woman he had seen outside the telephone booth he had used.

'He is a she. An itinerant. I'm guessing she's a homeless woman with mental problems and a history of abuse.'

'Interesting,' said Serkan. 'Can you tell me how you came across this information?'

'You need to look for someone like that. She frequents the centre of town and usually has a collection of plastic bags with her. She's not that hard to find.' He described the location of the phone booth where he had seen her. 'She's probably not even aware people are looking for her.'

'I shall certainly look into it. And how shall I thank you?'

'I don't think you need to worry about that. Our paths are not going to cross again.'

'I see, and you can't tell me where you are?'

'I'm sorry,' said Makana. 'I have to go.'

He ended the call and sat for a moment wondering at the wisdom of what he had just done. Then he wound down the window and tossed the phone out into the darkness.

'What was that about?' asked Nizari.

'Nothing that need concern you.'

As they drove, the radio provided a muted backdrop of soft horns and strings while the drumming rhythm of the rain played them out of the city. The darkness ahead was broken only by the blinding flash of headlights coming from the occasional lorry that rushed by in the opposite direction and battered them with its tail-wind. They drove for about an hour, winding along narrow roads, leaving the city behind. The rain grew heavier. The wipers swept back and forth over the windscreen, pushing the wave of water from side to side. It was almost impossible to see where they were headed. Alongside them to the right the rain glittered darkly off the cold wet tongue of the Bosporus.

'Where are we going?' Makana leaned forward to ask. The faces of the two men were impassive in the low glow coming from the dashboard.

'We change car,' said the driver tersely.

'And where exactly is that supposed to happen?' Makana squinted ahead, trying to see through the silvery curtain of water. When neither man answered he sat back.

'I don't like this,' whispered Nizari. Neither did Makana, but as he saw it they had little choice at this point.

They began to slow. To the left Makana could make out a few sparse lights, pinpricks that marked out a dark, forgotten hamlet. Beyond that he saw nothing, no lights, buildings, streets. They came to a turn-off, a dirt road that took them around to the bulge of a hill, and then to a dip that led into a stone quarry. The car rolled slowly down a shallow rise and came to a halt. The rain pattered on the roof. The driver and the other man started to get out of the car.

'Wait a minute,' said Makana, starting to open the door. 'Where are you going?'

'You be here,' said the driver. He smiled, pointing at the sky and turning up his collar. 'Is raining.' He pushed the door gently closed.

'Why don't you do something?' Nizari demanded, his voice quavering with nervous energy.

'What do you suggest?'

Makana watched through the rear window as the two men disappeared into the darkness. Now the silence was broken only by the sound of the wind whistling around the car and the urgent hammering of the rain on the roof.

'Oh god!' Nizari put both hands to his head. 'I've been such a fool.'

Makana turned to look at him.

'I should never have got into such a mess.' He rocked from side to side.

'Would you care to explain?' Makana tried to understand where this was leading.

'None of it should have happened.'

'What exactly are you trying to say?'

'I've been a fool. I'm not cut out for this. You understand? I'm a technician. I work with formulae, chemical reagents, elements. In the lab, everything does what it is supposed to do.'

'Unlike people, you mean?'

Nizari gave a quick jerk of the head that was meant to be a nod.

'My wife …'

'You're doing this for your wife. Is that what you are saying? She's ill.'

'She's dying.' Nizari whimpered.

'Why don't you start at the beginning? Tell me how you became involved in all this.'

'I don't know. I was tired. Tired of living in poverty. Tired of Khartoum. My wife was ill. I thought this was my chance, finally. I could make things better. Make them right.' Nizari stared at a fixed point in the darkness. He hardly seemed to notice Makana. 'They asked me to do it, and I agreed.'

'What did they ask you to do?'

'No, I can't, I can't.' Nizari shook his head from side to side. It was as if he was paralysed by the weight of it. Makana took a deep breath and forced himself to speak slowly, trying to draw the man out of himself.

'You went to Spain to meet this middleman, Santamaria.'

'That's it.'

'And he was to introduce you to the mysterious buyer, Abu Hilal.'

'Exactly.' The mournful eyes lifted briefly. 'Only Abu Hilal does not exist.'

Makana was silent for a moment. 'Go on,' he said, finally.

'We knew, they knew,' Nizari corrected himself. 'They knew the Israelis would jump at the chance to catch someone like that.'

'Who invented him?' Makana had a feeling he already knew the answer to that one, but he had to ask. Nizari didn't hear the question, or else his mind was elsewhere.

'They spent years setting up stories, building rumours.'

'To make the world believe Abu Hilal was a real person, a dangerous terrorist?'

'That's it.'

'Okay, so tell me why.'

'Why what?' Nizari blinked.

'Why go to all of this trouble?'

The other man hung his head and was silent for a moment. When he began to speak it was in a mumble that Makana could barely make out over the rain.

'A story will appear in the press revealing that the Mossad had been operating in Istanbul without permission. They knew of the existence of a lab producing nerve agents right in the middle of the city and they failed to inform the Turkish authorities.'

'Because they wanted to catch Abu Hilal themselves.'

In the darkened interior, Nizari gave a brief nod. 'They wanted all the glory.'

Makana reached for a cigarette. He wondered why he hadn't seen this coming. The whole thing had been a set-up. Right from the start. Not even Winslow knew what was really going on.

'When you asked for me to bring you in,' Makana asked slowly, 'it had nothing to do with my old chief, did it?'

Nizari's head sagged even lower. Makana passed over his cigarette and cracked a window open. It squeaked as he wound it down. Drops of rain spattered on him.

'I never met him.'

'And at some point you got cold feet.'

'I couldn't bear it any more. The whole thing. I couldn't sleep,' Nizari whimpered. 'There was an accident. A bus hit the vehicle we were in and I knew it was my chance to escape, so I ran.'

'Who was planning all of this?'

'You know who.' Nizari lifted his head. 'Mek Nimr talked me into it. He said the British would take care of me. That I would get a reward, they would give me asylum in England, my wife would get the treatment she needed.' Behind the spectacles, Nizari's eyes were darting left and right, and he was biting his lower lip so hard it looked like he was having a seizure. He ran a hand over his head, back and forth like he was polishing it. 'He's a dangerous, dangerous man. He can turn everything around in your head until you don't know what's up or down.'

'How does it end?' Makana felt his mind spinning, trying to think of a way out.

'A controlled explosion. A small amount of sarin released. There will be casualties locally. It will all be tied to an undercover Mossad operation that went wrong. That's how it will look, anyway. Turkey will be outraged and the finger will point at the Israelis.'

It had the kind of twisted logic that somehow fitted Mek Nimr. It seemed like a lot of trouble to go to for such trivial gains, but maybe that was the point, this was all an elaborate exercise in strategy. Maybe having a point was no longer relevant. It was all about staying in the game.

'The Dutchman, he's Mossad?'

'Yes, he's the leader. Elie something.'

'So, the Dutchman along with the two pretending to be Bosnians makes three. How many more?'

'Two, maybe three. I don't really know.'

'A couple, a man and a woman?'

257

'Yes, I think so.'

'And Kara Deniz was working for them?'

'I don't know,' said Nizari. 'I never met her.'

That made sense. Kara was just a minor player, an informant who had got herself mixed up in something bigger than she could handle. She'd led them to Nadir Sulayman, but it didn't really matter. They decided she was a loose end. They couldn't risk knowledge of Mossad involvement being made public. She was a journalist after all.

'They believe Abu Hilal is real, and that he's here, in Istanbul?'

Nizari began to giggle. Makana wondered for a moment if his mind had snapped. He was sniggering and snuffling, crying and wiping his nose on the back of his hand, all at the same time.

'What? What is it?' asked Makana.

'Don't you see?' Nizari let out a snort. Desperation seemed to have pushed him over the edge, or else he was the type of man who couldn't help laughing at the misfortunes of others.

'They think I'm Abu Hilal,' said Makana slowly. It was obvious when you said it out loud, logical even. 'Was that why Marty Shaw had to be killed?'

'Who?'

Makana waved his own question aside. Marty Shaw had figured it all out. He had been waiting in Makana's hotel room to let him know, perhaps even to get him out. Only someone was already on to him. Mossad, or Mek Nimr's people? The latter option left him with an uncomfortable feeling.

'So they were going to take care of you and your wife? Did they promise you a fat reward for setting up the sarin lab for them?'

'I gave them a detailed plan of what they had to do.'

'That was helpful of you,' said Makana. 'So this lab is actually functioning?'

'It has to look convincing. There will be people coming in from all over the world. The FBI and all kinds of agencies, experts with experience in these things. There are protocols, you understand, and …' Nizari stopped mid-sentence. 'What is that?'

Makana was wondering the same thing. A coughing sound some-where in the distant like a giant clearing his throat, followed by a steady rumble. He strained to see through the darkness.

'What is that?' Nizari repeated his question. He leaned over and fumbled with the light switch so that the interior light came on.

'Switch that off,' Makana ordered, momentarily blinded. He leaned forward to do it himself. Whatever it was, he could feel it now.

'I don't like sitting in the dark,' whined Nizari.

'Keep quiet.'

The noise was vibrating up through the wheels. Makana started to wind down the window further in an effort to see better. There was something out there, a lumbering shadow rising out of the ground, coming towards them. Then a row of huge white spotlights came on, blinding him. A truck and a big one came over the rise. A monster with wheels that were bigger than the car they were sitting in. And it was gaining speed as it came down the slope.

Makana moved then. Even as he did so he realised there was no time to get across Nizari and out of the car before it hit. Before he'd finished the thought he felt the impact and was thrown back to his side as the car seemed to bounce, lifting into the air. It crashed down and skidded along the ground. The left side had caved in, jamming the doors and throwing the two men together. The second impact was hard, and this time the lorry's crash bars stayed in contact, scraping the car sideways along the ground. The glaring headlights were so close you could feel the heat from them. The heavy roar of the diesel engine was deafening. Through the window on the other side he could see the sea gleaming darkly in the headlights below them.

'They're trying to kill us!' screamed Nizari.

Makana didn't respond. His mind was on other things, like how to get out of the vehicle before they hit the water. But it was already too late. The car was sliding away down the incline, away from the truck, gravity doing its job. They careered towards the edge of the hill and bumped straight over. It felt as if they were suspended in mid-air for minutes. It wasn't more than a few metres to the sea, but they hit the water with a such a jolt that Makana felt his head thrown back against the roof of the car with a jarring blow.

Cold water came rushing in. Hot metal hissed and clicked as engine parts cooled suddenly. The sea spurted up through gaps in the floor, pouring through the windows, the shattered windscreen. They would be dead in a matter of minutes. Nizari was screaming and kicking hysterically, as if he might be able to push the water away.

'Open the door,' Makana shouted, but Nizari was beyond responding to any kind of simple command. The problem was getting past him to reach the door. The front of the car lurched suddenly forward and down, the interior now flooded. The left-hand side was so badly crumpled that the door was jammed and impossible to open. They were pushed up against the roof as the remaining air was compressed into a pocket. Makana tilted his head back, water swilling into his mouth as he tried to gulp in the last of the air. There were creaking sounds all around as the frame of the vehicle bowed to the pressure. He struggled to hold onto Nizari. Then he heard, or rather felt, the rear window pop as the interior light went out, plunging them into darkness. The car was sinking more slowly than he would have imagined.

It felt fitting somehow. Dying like this connected him to that night all those years ago when he had watched the old Volkswagen Passat carrying Muna and Nasra topple off the bridge. How often had he told himself that he should have died with them? How many times had he replayed that scene in his mind, trying to imagine their last moments, trapped in the car, sinking into dark oblivion? Their faces came to him at night, their fear breathing into his face, their cries stifled by water as they cried silently in the drowning light. Now, finally, he would learn what it was like.

He recognised the irony. To die this way now, when for the first time he had been given a glimmer of hope in the darkness. When he had reason to believe his daughter was alive. To die now when at last he had something to lose.

It took seconds for these thoughts to pass through his mind. As they did so he realised that he was losing consciousness. He was drowning. When was death ever anything but untimely?

Hands were reaching for him. He thought, for one brief moment, that it was Muna. He allowed himself to drift into their embrace. Dark angels drawing him into the depths. This was how it should be. An arm wrapped itself around his neck, but to his surprise, instead of pulling him down deeper, it was trying to lift him up. Not down into darkness, but up towards light. A bright light that cut through the water like an all-seeing eye. Convinced that it was Death drawing him in, he struggled, but this arm was strong and persistent and he was too weak to fight.

Makana felt himself being hauled up and dumped onto a wooden platform at sea level. Someone rolled him on his side and he vomited a thin stream of acid bile.

Chapter Thirty-three

Istanbul Day Seven

Trying to open his eyes had never been this difficult. Once upon a time, he recalled, it had needed no effort at all. Now, he felt as though his every thought was being telegraphed from a great way off. He imagined the words jangling along a line in the air before him. Then came a thump and he felt the rising and falling of a heaving deck, the whine of an engine toiling against the waves. He could taste the sea on his lips. He was shivering with cold. His clothes were soaked through and stuck to his skin.

He was on the open rear deck of some kind of motor launch. He was hauled up and deposited in a large chair that swivelled from side to side. His arms were secured at the wrists to the frame, his feet bound together at the ankles. Hands tore at his jacket, ripping the seams. A knife cut through his shirt. Then a needle was stuck into his shoulder. There were two of them doing this, a man and a woman. It came back to him, as if from a lifetime ago. They were the couple at the quayside café where he had sat with Kara Deniz. And again before that: the night he had been mugged. Staggering into the lift at the Pera Palas hotel to find a smartly dressed couple. He in a cream suit and she in a long dress.

A movement from behind made him turn his head, as much as he was able to. Someone was coming down the steps from the bridge to his left. The Dutchman, Snowfleet or whatever his name was. He smiled as he came to stand in front of Makana, feet apart, balancing expertly in the swell.

'So, here we are again.'

'Mossad,' muttered Makana. He had trouble moving his lips. The cold perhaps, or whatever they had just injected him with. The Dutchman nodded.

'Well, that's dispensed with the introductions. We both know who we are. You've played a long game, Abu Hilal, but now we come to the end of the line.'

'You're wrong. I'm not ...'

The woman was tucking the syringe back into a small case. She and the man, both dressed in black, had stepped back to watch him with their arms folded. Makana wondered exactly what they had injected him with.

'It's a simple relaxant.' Snowfleet said, reading his mind. 'It takes the fight out of you.'

'You pulled us out of the water.' Makana's jaw was chattering uncontrollably.

'We don't want you dead just yet.'

His head felt fuzzy. It seemed to take a lifetime to process a thought, to move a word from the back of his mind to the tip of his tongue.

'The truth is I admire you.'

'Why?' It seemed the obvious question.

'It's important to empathise with one's adversaries.' The tall Dutchman seemed to be enjoying himself, as though he had waited a long time for this moment. 'The only way to defeat the enemy is to see into their minds.'

'The enemy?' It all seemed so absurd that Makana was having difficulty making sense of anything. He stared dully at the inky dark sea and the distant constellation of lights that was dry land floating just out of reach.

'Nizari?' Makana managed to get the word out, more or less complete.

'Ah, interesting question. Your Merlin, your magic-potion man.'

The man and woman had disappeared somewhere inside the boat. Makana tested his bonds, tensing to discover there was very little give. A strange sense of calm came over him. The boat's engine had stopped and they were drifting gently. Waiting for something, but what? The light, the moon? Some signal from far away?

263

Makana could hear voices. A telephone conversation. Whoever was on the other end was on speaker. He couldn't understand any of the words and he wondered if that was normal, or if the drug was taking effect. Far away a muezzin's steady call spiralled up into the night sky.

Makana wondered why Boris had betrayed them. Perhaps it wasn't just money. Boris was a businessman. He had weighed up the pros and cons and decided it was in his interest to hand them over, probably around the time he heard about Kara Deniz.

'That's a first, being saved by you.'

'Ah, do I hear a note of thanks?' The Dutchman was fiddling with an electronic device. A transmitter of some kind. 'Music to my ears. We are so often depicted as the epitome of evil, the man in the black hat, when really we are trying to save the world from a terrible threat.'

'Please,' Makana groaned. 'Spare me.'

'Of course, it is wasted on you. But nevertheless, we get tired of always being demonised.'

'What happened to your Bosnian friends?'

'They served their purpose.' The Dutchman clicked his tongue in disappointment. 'They were a temporary measure, a compromise. In my opinion a bad choice.'

'Where are they now?'

'Why should this concern you? As I said, they served their purpose,' the Dutchman shrugged.

So if he was still alive, Makana reasoned, it was for a reason. He wondered if Nizari was dead, and whether they had recovered his body or left him in the sea.

The other two returned. They brought with them the smell of coffee and tobacco which made Makana long for a cigarette. He looked back out at the water and wondered how far they were from the shore. Far enough to make no difference, he guessed. There was some conferring going on between them now. Everything sounded fuzzy in his head. Makana shook his head to try and clear it. Where was Mek Nimr and his team, where was Nasra? He realised that the others had fallen silent; some kind of decision had been settled between them. Makana braced himself.

'What have you done with Nizari?'

'All in good time.' The Dutchman was smoking a foul-smelling cheroot, blowing smoke at the stars. Makana felt his teeth chattering. He saw the glint of light on metal as the woman unzipped the pouch that was strapped to her waist and produced another syringe. The hypodermic needle winked in the deck lights. 'No need to be alarmed,' she laughed. 'Your time hasn't come yet.'

She drew near, avoiding his gaze. He felt the needle go into his arm. He tried to speak, to summon a shout, but as with everything in his life, or so it seemed, he was much too slow.

—

Chapter Thirty-four

T he first thing he noticed was the smell. A harsh acid reek that stung his nostrils and made his eyes water. There was a dull ache in his head and he was shivering. He couldn't move. He was still tied up, but the situation had changed. The chair was different, and the deck had stopped moving. When he opened his eyes he knew why.

It took him a moment to realise where he was. What had been a long, empty space was now filled with objects. The windows along one side were covered with newspaper. He remembered peering through them from the other side when he'd been here with Koçak. Now the faint orange glow of streetlights filtered through from outside, throwing long shadows here and there in skewed geometric patterns. A table ran along the wall underneath the windows. A long sheet of transparent plastic covered it. In the gloom he could make out objects underneath, the vague outline of bottles, jars, scientific instruments.

The chair he was seated in was an old one. His hands were taped to the rear of the frame and it creaked beneath him when he tried to shift his weight. This seemed like a good sign. If the chair was weak, perhaps he had a chance of getting free. On the other hand, what he saw when he turned his head to look round wasn't encouraging. In the corner behind him stood a row of oil drums. From the stencilled images painted on the sides he could guess what they contained. Highly inflammable, toxic, hazardous chemicals. He counted six barrels. Next to these a row of six tall gas cylinders stood like sentinels against the wall. An olive-green tarpaulin was bundled in the corner.

In front of him, part of the room appeared to have been turned into a makeshift chamber sealed off by a wall of heavy plastic sheeting. Through the opaque layer he could make out a bank of machines, what looked like a laboratory workstation, airtight chambers, measuring instruments. Thick tubes and rubber pipes connected them to a large tower in the corner that looked like an extractor or air filter.

What most surprised Makana was that none of this had been here when he had visited the place just a few days ago. He was pretty sure he was inside the long room he had seen from the yard of the house in Eyüp where he had been taken by the two 'Bosnians'. Now it was a lab, and there were no prizes for guessing what it was intended to be used for. The restricted area behind the curtain seemed to be for the containment of sarin gas, or whatever kind of nerve agent they were supposed to be making here. Somebody had worked very fast indeed, no doubt using Nizari's plans.

There was no sign of anyone else. He wondered where the Dutchman and the two others might be. He couldn't tell what time it was, although he had the feeling it would soon be light outside. He shifted around, not so much to free himself as to ease the pain in his shoulders and arms, which had been clamped in the same position for hours. But there was something encouraging about the way the chair creaked. He rocked back and forth, trying to work the joints of the chair loose without tipping over. If he went over he would be stranded like a turtle on its back. His arms shrieked in protest as he strained this way and that. The good news was that it felt as if something was coming loose.

He stopped his struggling for a moment as something caught his eye. Through the heavy plastic sheeting Makana thought he could make out a shape sprawled on the floor inside the sealed-off area. He couldn't be sure what it was. It could have been an old coat, or a person. But something told him it had to be Nizari. He tried calling his name a few times without getting a response.

With renewed energy he resumed his work on demolishing the chair, his hopes rising when he was rewarded with a loud cracking sound. The chair was coming apart. He rocked his weight onto the front legs and then back again, coming down as heavily as he could.

Once, twice, three times, bringing his full weight to bear. On the tenth try he broke one of the legs and found himself sprawled on the floor. Blood gushed from the point where a sharp splinter had embedded itself into the palm of his left hand, and made it hard to grip anything properly. He rolled over and managed to work his other hand free. It took another five minutes of struggling but finally Makana could strip off the duct tape and toss aside the wreckage of the chair.

Moving across the room, he looked over the drums and gas tanks. He gently rocked one of them to check that it was full. He peered under the tarpaulin to find the shaven-headed 'Bosnian' and his friend, a day or so dead by the look of them. The bodies were wrapped in plastic sheeting. Makana was more interested in what was next to them. It looked like an improvised incendiary device. Large cans of what appeared to be hairspray, probably to act as an accelerant, had been taped together along with an electronic detonator and a mobile phone. It didn't appear to be activated, but it was reason enough not to hang around here longer than was necessary.

He let the tarpaulin fall back into place and went over to examine the sealed-off chamber. Heavy-duty plastic sheeting was taped firmly at the top and bottom. A steady mechanical hum came from within, where a polished steel drum was turning and a fan was sucking air through a vent. The entrance was a sealed rectangle held in place with Velcro strips. Makana put out a hand.

'I wouldn't do that if I were you,' said a voice behind him.

He turned to find her there. She was holding a gun. Not pointing it exactly, but it was in her hand, her arm hanging by her side.

'You're bleeding.' She pointed with the barrel of the pistol. Makana looked down and saw the blood dripping from between his fingers. She reached into her pocket and produced a scarf which she threw over to him. He wrapped it roughly around his hand.

'You should clean it before it gets infected,' she said.

'I'll try to remember that.' The gun was a small Beretta. She was, he noted, left-handed, just like her mother. 'You know what's in there?' Makana nodded at the plastic chamber.

'It's a protective screen. If something escapes one of the incubators or vacuum chambers, then you have a problem. It's dangerous stuff. You can kill someone with a drop the size of a pinhead.'

'Nobody is actually making sarin here, right?' Makana looked around at their surroundings.

'I wouldn't be too sure about that, but' – she waved the barrel of the gun – 'if you're feeling lucky …'

It was hard to look at her and not think how much she reminded him of Muna. But there was something else as well. A hardness, an anger that would have been alien to her mother. It was that part of her that he didn't know, the part that told the story of the years between, of how she had gone from the little girl he had last glimpsed inside a car just before it went over the side of a bridge to the young woman who stood before him holding an automatic pistol. There was something there that he suspected he would never know. Her eyes gave nothing away. She was watching him as carefully as he was watching her.

Makana turned to the plastic screen.

'I need to know if he's dead.'

'You think he wouldn't leave you?'

Makana didn't need to be told. He knew enough about Nizari to be certain the Iraqi scientist would never risk his own neck for him. Still, it felt strange to be listening to her telling him what to do. She was right, of course. It didn't make much sense to take the risk, but he'd never been very good at taking advice.

'Well, I'm not him.'

He took a deep breath and tore the Velcro open. Then he stepped inside, sealing the plastic curtain behind him. Nothing happened. How long would it take before he started to feel the effects? Would he feel anything before it was already too late? He knew nothing about toxic nerve agents.

'We don't have much time,' he heard Nasra call. Makana glanced back towards her. He wasn't sure what she meant, nor indeed what her part in all of this was. Through the translucent plastic her outline seemed blurred, as if her very existence was in doubt. He could almost believe that she wasn't real, that she had somehow sprung from the well of his imagination. When he came back out she might have vanished. He wasn't sure which was the harder to live with – the memory of her, or with her existence in this new form.

'Is he still alive?'

Makana knelt beside Nizari and felt for a pulse. There was nothing. He leaned over him, trying to establish the cause of death, and found the thin red line around his neck where a plastic zip tie had cut into the skin. There was a reason they hadn't bothered to tie him up.

He rocked back on his haunches and looked around him. They had gone to a lot of trouble to make it all look convincing. When it was discovered it would be an embarrassment for the Turkish government. Tourism would be hit of course, but that was not the point. The Israeli plan was to expose a chemical weapons lab right in the heart of Turkey's greatest city. Erdoğan, would look like a gullible fool who allowed dangerous terrorists like Abu Hilal to operate right under his nose. To Israel it would be a victory in the propaganda war. They would gain a bargaining point. It all seemed so petty. Makana rose to his feet and came out of the plastic chamber.

'The Mossad team set all of this up.' She was silent, so he went on. 'You were watching them all the time. You let them do this.' Makana nodded at Nizari. 'You let them kill him.'

'He was a liability. It was only a matter of time before someone killed him.'

'Is that what Mek Nimr taught you to believe?'

She shifted her weight and glanced at her watch. Makana was trying to work out what was coming next.

'Where are they now? On their way back to Tel Aviv?'

'Not quite.'

'At the airport, then, to be picked up by Turkish intelligence?'

She tilted her head. He had to admit it was a neat plan. Turning the tables on the Israelis. If they were caught operating in this country without authorisation it would be a major international scandal for the Mossad. If they were tied to this laboratory it would be a victory for Turkey. He wondered why they hadn't killed him as they had Nizari. Was this some kind of gift to the Turks? Surely if he was alive there was a chance he could prove that he wasn't Abu Hilal? Makana thought of the incendiary device. There was something here that neither of them was seeing.

'Why did you come back?' he asked.

'I wanted to see for myself.'

'You wanted to make sure I was dead.'

She hesitated, shifting the gun from left hand to right before reaching into the pocket of her coat.

'This is yours,' she said, holding something out. He took it from her. It was the old photograph that had been sitting on the bedside table in the hotel. Worn from years of travelling with him in his wallet, a cracked and folded fragment of time. All the more precious for being the only reminder he had of them: the picture of Muna smiling, holding their baby daughter in her arms.

'You were in my room at the Pera Palas.' He looked up to see her shrug. 'You killed Marty Shaw?'

Nasra shook her head. 'When I got there it was all over.'

'The Dutchman?'

'I didn't see. Shaw went into the room. Someone was waiting there. I heard the shot. When I went in he was dead and the room was empty.'

'The balcony. They went over to the next room.'

She nodded. 'I followed, but they were gone. And I couldn't stay, the hotel staff were already suspicious of me.'

Makana handed the picture back. 'You should keep it.'

'It doesn't mean anything to me.'

'If that was true you wouldn't be here.'

She looked at him and for a second he thought he saw something in her eyes, doubt perhaps, the faint glint of another possibility. Then something caught his eye and he reached towards her neck. She didn't try to stop him. He pulled the gold chain until it came free to reveal the little crescent moon dangling on the end of it. A trinket Muna had bought and hung in their car. The sight of it made his throat suddenly dry.

'Why did you come to my room?'

'What?' She blinked.

'My room at the hotel. You came there for a reason,' he said. 'You wanted to talk.'

She met his gaze evenly and he thought for a moment that perhaps he had been wrong, but then she lowered her head in what was an almost imperceptible nod. When she looked up she was ready to speak. But whatever she might have been about to say was trapped there for ever.

'Well, this is very touching,' said a voice behind him.

Marcus Winslow certainly knew how to make an entrance. And he dressed well. The slightly rumpled elegance that had no doubt stood him well over the years. He even managed to make the gun in his right hand look like a fashion accessory. But there was no mistaking the intent in his eyes. However playful he might have wanted to appear, there was no doubt he was here on business.

'I knew that you two would find one another. It's almost inevitable when you think about it.'

'I had a feeling you might show up,' said Makana.

'Well, I hate to disappoint,' beamed Winslow.

'Do you really think this is going to get you reinstated?'

'Oh, I don't care about that. I've had my share of working within the constraints of government service.' Winslow pulled a face. 'It's so dull.'

'So what is this about, money?'

'We haven't known one another for long, but I have to say that I would be disappointed if I thought you really believed this was all motivated by greed.'

'Then what?'

'The game, old man. It's all that's left. To play on. To win.' Winslow cracked a smile. 'I used to think that these things would become less important in the fullness of time, but I was wrong. Getting older just makes you more determined to beat the odds. I thought I was dedicated as a young man, but that dashing fellow has nothing on the current version. Believe me, I'm more driven today than I ever was.'

'You know this man?' Nasra asked.

'He's British intelligence,' Makana replied, before switching back to English. 'Or perhaps I should say, ex-British intelligence. Isn't that correct?'

Winslow tugged at his ear with his free hand. He was wearing light cotton gloves. A nice touch, but then you would have expected nothing less.

'Not exactly. I'm still officially on the books.'

'But disgraced, now freelancing for the Israelis?'

'Keep guessing. No, a man has to make a living. You might say I've gone into the consultancy business. I lend my expertise to whoever needs my services.'

'I think the word you're looking for is mercenary.'

Winslow frowned. 'There's no need to be insulting.'

'Shaw was on to you,' said Makana. 'That's why you had to kill him.'

'Marty Shaw was an amateur. I blame the education system. Level playing fields and all that nonsense.' Winslow grimaced in distaste. 'Never more than an exercise in deception, and that is a subject I know a little about.' He stepped forward to take the Beretta from Nasra, offering a grin to Makana.

'How does it feel, to know that she hates you? I imagine that's must be hard to take. Not just you, of course, but everything you stand for.' He looked Nasra over. 'I find her rather magnificent myself. A warrior, a *jihadiya* of the first order. You should be proud of her.'

'You used me to get at Mek Nimr,' said Makana. Suddenly everything seemed clearer.

'Ah, now you are getting warmer.' Winslow smiled briefly. 'I knew that the chance to watch you suffer was something he would never be able to resist. After all these years, everything he has invested in your child. A man can devote his life to hatred. And what's the point of it all if he doesn't get to watch you suffer?'

'He'll think I set him up.'

'I honestly don't think that's your biggest problem right now.' Winslow said drily. 'Look on the bright side, at least you won't have to worry about that for long.'

'Is he that important to you?'

'It's nothing personal. He's been leading us around by the nose for years. Playing his own double game. Laughing behind his hand at us British *khawajas*. Fair enough. Colonial history and all that. We all have an inheritance to pay off. Truth be told, there has always been something of a question mark hanging over this Directorate for Counterterrorism of his.'

He smiled at Nasra. 'It's a common enough strategy. You set up a body to serve a cause. Human rights, for example. It makes you look good, even though the real purpose is simply to mask your activities. It's the perfect cover. We suspect them of funding hundreds of small operations around the world. Never directly, always in the background, channelling funds and logistical support. From Baghdad to Sydney by way of Mumbai and Massachusetts. Jihadism is the new industry.'

'So where is he now?'

'At this moment ...' Winslow glanced at his watch. 'On his way to a black site somewhere nobody will ever find him.'

'That can't be right,' said Nasra, taking a step forwards. The gun swung towards her. 'You betrayed us.'

'Guilty as charged, I'm afraid.' Winslow gave an apologetic shrug. 'Sorry. I dropped a word to our Israeli friends. He'll manage and it will be cleared up eventually, but he's going to have a rough ride.'

A black site effectively meant falling off the ends of the earth. There would be no official record of Mek Nimr having been picked up and flown to a detention camp for interrogation. Normally, there was no way back from such places, unless you believed in miracles. Makana ought to have cheered, but somehow he didn't feel like celebrating.

Makana reached for his cigarettes and found the packet empty. The condemned man denied his last request. Winslow took pity and tossed over his Benson & Hedges. Makana used his own lighter and, glancing at Nasra, he threw them back. Winslow caught them without taking his eyes off either of them. He lit one for himself while Makana spoke.

'Mek Nimr is the reason for your disgrace.'

'I gambled on him once too often. Mek Nimr has been passing us snippets of information over the years. Always reliable, except when he wasn't. Sometimes the cavalry charges in, or in this case the drone, only to find the target has fled. It didn't happen that often, but when it did, it tended to be significant. One instance in particular. An Al Qaeda operator believed to be the strategist behind the attack on the USS *Cole*. Mek Nimr claims to have a personal contact close to him. He gives us a time and a place. The missiles go in and we destroy a house full of women and children. Nineteen deaths. That can weigh heavily on a man's conscience.'

'Abu Hilal.'

'That's what I was led to believe and that's what I staked my reputation on.'

'He must have given you some good information?'

'Oh, he did, but he was smart that way, mixing up the good with the bad. And of course, the point is that it was a judgement call. At the end of the day, I trusted him, so it's on me.'

'So when he offered you a chance to get your hands on Abu Hilal, you couldn't resist.'

'It was too good a chance to pass up. Only this time I intended to take the initiative. I played along, the gullible Englishman trusting his native informant. Times change but the old tropes still last.'

'Only by now you had figured out that Abu Hilal didn't exist.'

'Exactly, only he does now.' Winslow wagged the gun at Makana. 'Two can play at that game.'

'Mek Nimr planned to use Nizari to lure the Israelis into his own trap, not realising that you were one step ahead of him.' Winslow said nothing. Makana went on. 'So you hand my body over as Abu Hilal and you are vindicated. British intelligence apologises and probably gives you a medal into the bargain.'

'The medal's not really the point, although I admit it would be nice.'

'You warned the Israelis they were walking into a trap, and in exchange you wanted the credit for the sting.'

'You are actually good at this,' Winslow conceded. 'Unfortunately it's a little late in the day for enlightenment.'

Makana gestured around them. 'Nobody's going to believe this little show of yours.'

'Well, that's where I'm afraid you're wrong.' Winslow stepped over towards the wall and swept the heaped tarpaulin aside to reveal the incendiary device. 'Crude, but as I'm sure you will agree, effective.'

'And Nizari?'

'A pawn in the game. Granted, a rather erratic pawn, but I shed no tears over a man like that.'

Makana was feeling like something of a pawn himself. He looked across at Nasra and wondered if she had any other weapons on her.

'We have a lot to learn from our friends in Tel Aviv. They are ahead of us because they are ruthless. They aren't held back by colonial guilt, or quaint ideas about ethical codes and moral responsibility. They just get the job done. They are like a big angry hound that can never say no to a fight.

'The truth is,' Winslow went on, 'We don't understand what goes on these days. That's our Achilles heel. We fell in love with the idea that technology would solve our information-gathering problems.' He smoked in silence for a moment. 'We lost the human factor. Partly it's because the world changed and we didn't. I mean racially, ethnically. We're still pulling in people from the same narrow band. When someone like me walks through the bazaar in Peshawar, or Baghdad or Cairo, they stand out a mile. We're the *khawaja*, the *gaijin*, the *mzungu*. James Bond was fine when the world was ruled from London. The spy game was all about class. They mingled in gentlemen's clubs. Not any more.'

'And you hate that because it makes you dependent on people like Mek Nimr,' Makana commented. People like us, he might have said.

'I get it, I really do. They don't hate us for what we stand for. What do we stand for anyway? They hate us because they want what we've got. It's as simple as that.' Winslow shrugged. 'And for bombing the shit out of their loved ones. The point is that nobody wins any more, not really. Not in the long term. Short-term gains perhaps, but nothing lasting. Nothing of value. Shakespeare understood that. We seem to have forgotten it.'

'Looks like you've played everyone to your advantage.'

'That's what I like about you,' said Winslow. 'Always so pragmatic. Never one to let your feelings get in the way. I suppose that's necessary for someone like you. Still, it's a shame our partnership has to end here.'

Makana nodded at Nasra. 'You can let her go. She's not a threat.'

'Everyone's a threat,' said Winslow, raising the gun. 'But I'll spare you the pain of watching her die.' He aimed the gun at Makana.

Where the knife came from Makana couldn't say. His best guess was a sheath concealed in the spine of her jacket. It caught Winslow just below his right collarbone, a handspan away from his throat, which she must have been going for. She probably would have hit it if she'd had the chance to stand and take proper aim. She didn't. She just threw it.

The shot meant for Makana went wide and he heard the bullet ring as it hit something metallic. With the knife still buried in him Winslow dropped to one knee and fired the gun again. Nasra collapsed. Winslow stood and ran bent double towards the door behind him. Makana knelt over Nasra. She had her hands to her stomach, blood seeping through her fingers.

'Go after him,' she hissed through clenched teeth. 'Stop him!'

'I can't leave you,' he said, taking off his jacket, thinking of how to stem the blood. She clutched his arm.

'Go!' she urged. 'Don't let him get away.'

By the time he came out into the yard Winslow was nowhere to be seen. How far could a wounded man get? Splashes of blood led in a wavering arc across the cracked cement. Makana tracked along it cautiously, pondering the wisdom of pursuing an armed man. A cornered Winslow would be all the more dangerous.

A pair of pigeons flapped noisily into the air and Makana looked up in time to see Winslow aiming at him from the roof. He threw himself left and felt the bullet hit the ground at his feet even as he heard the shot.

There was a simple stone staircase in the far corner leading to the flat roof that connected around the four sides of the yard. Makana ran up the stairs to see rows of washing lines strung between poles stretched out ahead of him. Beyond them, he glimpsed Winslow sinking down onto the parapet at the far end. Long strands of his thin hair blew back and forth in the breeze. He was bowed forwards, clutching at the knife embedded in his shoulder.

'I must be getting old. I used to be better at tying everything up neatly.' He gritted his teeth as he pulled the blade out and pressed a handkerchief to the wound to stem the flow of blood.

'It's over,' said Makana, edging closer. The automatic rested on the low wall next to the other man.

'You're forgetting something, aren't you?' Winslow reached into his pocket and held up a mobile phone. It took Makana a moment to realise what he was going to do. 'Look, you can't blame me for the girl. Self-defence. She shouldn't have thrown the knife. Nice shot, though, I have to admit.'

'There's nowhere for you to run.'

'There's plenty of places.' Winslow shook his head and raised the phone. 'No matter what happens to me, I can't let emotion stand in the way of a careful strategy. Sorry.'

'Wait!' Makana knew he was too late. He was always too late.

He saw the flash of the blast rushing through the schoolroom behind the papered-up windows before he heard the explosion, before it knocked him flat on his back. Then the windows blew outwards and glass and smoke erupted in a cloud, taking Nasra with it, back to that non-existence from which he had just started to believe she had escaped. His ears rang. The air was thick with concrete dust that clogged his nose and mouth, forcing him to close his eyes. He didn't want to open them again. Just to lie there and let it all wash over him. The world. Death. He didn't care what happened next. He opened his eyes and looked upwards, seeing the gently swirling scraps of paper floating in the air like butterflies. He had the sense that he was falling, far down inside the ground, as if the earth had opened up to swallow him.

Chapter Thirty-five

H e heard voices, as if from far away, speaking gibberish, sounds that he couldn't translate into words. It was all muffled by a blanket of cloud. Like the whispering of ghosts, spirits of the past come back to plague him with their unfulfilled dreams, their unlived lives. He wanted only for it to go away, to leave him here, floating in darkness, where there was nothing more to lose. A light shone into his eyes, hard and sharp, and then the sounds increased. He sensed the excitement around them as they set to the digging with renewed enthusiasm, then the darkness flooded back in and carried him away like a magic carpet.

In his dream they were all together again. A little family. He and Muna and Nasra. Only it wasn't Muna, he realised, but Jehan, which confused him at first, and then made perfect sense. They lived in a place he thought at first he'd never seen before. It was by the sea. The wind was blowing through the pines. The world was far away. He recognised it as Heybeliada, the Princes Island. It seemed fitting. An exile from all the dangers of the world. Nasra was about twelve years old. An age he had never known in her life. As they walked towards him the little girl began to rise up into the air. 'Stop her!' he heard Jehan call, again and again. But although he ran towards them the little girl continued to rise slowly upward. He jumped to try and catch her. Nasra herself didn't seem too concerned. She gazed down at them with a peaceful look on her face.

When he came to again he was lying in bed. For a moment he imagined he was dreaming, but then the smell of the sheets told him he wasn't home on the awama but in a hospital. Now the rest came back to him. His first thought was for Nasra. Was it possible she had survived? Everything told him it wasn't, but he would not rest until he knew.

He started to sit up and felt a sharp pain cutting into his side. When he tried to put his hand to it he discovered he was handcuffed to the frame of the bed, only it wasn't a bed, it was a stretcher. It wasn't a hospital either, but a windowless grey corridor. He heard the roar of jet engines, the sound of loudspeaker announcements in the distance. He was in an airport.

'My wife keeps telling me that we should get proper health insurance, as an investment for the future.'

Makana craned his neck to see Inspector Serkan standing behind him.

'She is right, of course, thinking ahead. One day we will be old and sick and then, when they give us a nice clean room with a magnificent view, we will be happy that we spent so many years paying for health insurance.' He shrugged as he turned to look at Makana. 'Me, I think it is better to live in the present than to prepare for some sad day in the future. Who knows, I could get hit by a meteorite falling from the sky when I walk out of here, or I could be one of those people who seem to live a charmed life, as if watched over by angels. I mean, of course, people like you.' He folded his arms as he came round to stand in front of him.

'You have important friends in high places, Mr Makana. That is your real name, right? I had a call from a lawyer in Cairo. Mr Munir Abaza. He has contacts in ministerial positions. One person pulls a string and … like magic' – Serkan circled his hand in the air – 'one thing leads to another and here you are, having passed through the best clinic in Istanbul.' He nodded at a male nurse standing at a distance.

'No doubt you are surprised to see me. I wanted to thank you.'

'To thank me?' Makana still felt dazed, his mind elsewhere.

'For your help with the murders. We picked up the woman you told me about. She had been keeping souvenirs from her victims, carrying them around in plastic bags.' The inspector twirled an unlit cigarette between his fingers. 'She was a sad case. A victim all her life after being abused and raped at a young age. She suffered a breakdown followed by years in a mental institution. She was released when they shut down the hospital.'

'It makes as much sense as anything I suppose,' said Makana. His throat was sore and the words were barely audible. 'Tell me about the explosion.'

'Ah, yes, of course.' Serkan nodded. 'It appears you have managed to embarrass our secret intelligence services to such an extent that nobody wants anything to do with you.' He produced a newspaper that was folded into his jacket pocket and dropped it on Makana's chest. The front page was dominated by a photograph of the schoolhouse in ruins. Men in overalls covered in dust, their faces covered by masks, were sifting through the rubble. 'The MIT are denying this had anything to do with foreign powers or mysterious Englishmen being murdered in one of the city's finest hotels. There are articles all over the press calling for more safety regulations to be implemented in the matter of household gas supplies.'

'They're calling it an accident?' Makana croaked.

'Oh yes. Questions are being asked in parliament as we speak. New legislation is being drawn up. So perhaps you have achieved something in your short stay in our country.'

'A domestic explosion?'

'These things happen.' Serkan shrugged as he retrieved the paper. 'Whatever else happened in that house is being kept from me. I was asked to accompany you to the airport, to see you out of the country. On condition that I do not ask too many questions.'

'What about survivors?'

'Apart from yourself?' Serkan frowned. 'None so far. How much do you remember?'

'Not much. I was on the roof when the bomb went off.'

'That explains it. You must have missed the force of the explosion. You suffered cuts and bruises. A couple of cracked ribs. As I said, you live a charmed life. I would very much like to know what you have been doing in Istanbul, but as I told you, I am not permitted to ask my questions. Frankly, I'm not sure I want to know.'

Makana struggled to sit up. 'I need to know if she was in there.'
'She?'
'My daughter. Did they find any women in the ruins?'

281

'No.' Serkan frowned. 'But it's slow work and in a case like this one has to proceed cautiously, for fear of provoking another explosion. Nobody knows what is underneath that rubble.'

'But no women have been found? You're sure?'

'So far only three men have been found.'

The two Bosnians and Nizari. Makana slumped back down on the cot. Despite his exhaustion he felt something like elation.

'Where does your daughter fit into this?' Serkan asked.

'It's a long story.'

'Well, if she was in the building it would seem she was very lucky.'

Two uniformed men were making their way down the corridor towards them, their boots ringing out loudly in the confined space. In the other direction an air-bridge led down towards the waiting aircraft. Inspector Serkan glanced at his watch.

'I'm afraid our time is coming to an end.'

'If you hear anything, you'll let me know?' said Makana. 'It's important.'

'I promise you.' Inspector Serkan patted Makana on the shoulder. 'Try to stay out of trouble, at least for a time.' He nodded at the two uniformed officers. 'They are here to escort you to the plane.'

'That's it, no questions? No charges?'

'My orders are to get you out of the country as quickly and as quietly as possible – before you cause any further embarrassment.' Inspector Serkan paused. He leaned forward to undo the handcuffs. One of the officers stepped forward, but Serkan raised a hand to stop him. 'It's okay,' he said. 'He's not going to make a run for it.' He reached out to help Makana to his feet. 'Can you stand?'

Makana tried, and found to his surprise that he actually could. He was wearing some kind of tracksuit. His own clothes would have been left in shreds. On his feet were a pair of white sports shoes of a kind that he would normally not have been seen dead in. Still, they were soft and cushioned his feet, which ached. Standing was not so bad.

'Do you think you can make it?'

'I think so.'

Serkan let go and stepped back. Not falling over felt like something of a miracle to Makana.

'Consider yourself a very fortunate man. If you'd been in the main building when the charges went off, you'd have been plastered across the neighbourhood. We would be lucky to be able to identify you. But maybe that was the plan. What do I know?' Serkan held out a hand. 'I'd like to think that under other circumstances we might have been friends.'

'Or colleagues,' said Makana as he shook the other man's hand. 'Thank you for everything.'

'Don't thank me, just make sure you never come back.'

'I'll do my best,' said Makana. He tried to take a tentative step forwards. His whole body seemed to scream in agony. His ankles and knees hurt. The two large policemen stood to one side, unsure what to do. Serkan held out an unopened packet of Samsun and a lighter with a picture of the city on the side.

'A souvenir.'

'Goodbye, Inspector.'

Makana tucked the present into his pocket, then he turned and hobbled down the incline towards the aircraft. Oddly enough, he found that he was smiling. There was only one thought running through his head: Nasra was alive. Somehow she had managed to get out of the building. He was sure of it. He could feel it, the way he'd believed for years that she had survived. The way he had never lost hope. Ahead of him, in the open hatch, he could see the flight attendants staring at him curiously, as if wondering who this strange passenger might be.

A Note on the Author

Parker Bilal is the author of the critically acclaimed Makana Investigations. *Dark Water* is the sixth novel in the series, the third of which, *The Ghost Runner*, was long-listed for the Theakstons Old Peculier Crime Novel of the Year Award. Born in London, he has lived at various times in the UK, Sudan, Cairo and Denmark. He currently lives in Amsterdam.

parkerbilal.com

A Note on the Type

The text of this book is set in Baskerville, a typeface named after John Baskerville of Birmingham (1706–1775). The original punches cut by him still survive. His widow sold them to Beaumarchais, from where they passed through several French foundries to Deberney & Peignot in Paris, before finding their way to Cambridge University Press.

Baskerville was the first of the 'transitional romans' between the softer and rounder calligraphic Old Face and the 'Modern' sharp-tooled Bodoni. It does not look very different to the Old Faces, but the thick and thin strokes are more crisply defined and the serifs on lower-case letters are closer to the horizontal with the stress nearer the vertical. The R in some sizes has the eighteenth-century curled tail, the lower case w has no middle serif and the lower case g has an open tail and a curled ear.